2018 YOUNG EXPLORER'S ADVENTURE GUIDE

DREAMING ROBOT PRESS

1 3 5 7 9 10 8 6 4 2

Publisher's Cataloging-in-Publication data

Names: Weaver, Sean, 1968- , editor. | Weaver, Corie, 1970-, editor.
Title: 2018 Young explorer's adventure guide / edited by Sean and Corie Weaver.
Description: Las Vegas, NM: Dreaming Robot Press, 2017.
Identifiers: ISBN 978-1-940924-25-0 (pbk.) | 978-1-940924-27-4 ebook | LCCN 2017909688
Subjects: LCSH Short stories. | Science Fiction. | Children's stories, American. | BISAC JUVENILE FICTION
/ Science Fiction | JUVENILE FICTION / Short Stories
Classification: LCC PZ7 .T9332 Tw 2017 | DCC [Fic]—dc23

Contents

Acknowledgements

Thanks to our families for putting up with all the madness, our authors for sharing our vision, and our friends for helping spread the word. We'd also ask for a round of applause for our editorial team of Amanda Coffin, Nicole Brugger-Dethmers, and Sue Currin.

We would also like to thank our beta-readers for their invaluable opinions: Kaia Baird, Warren Baird, Jamie Hull, Helen Jacobs, Dina Pfeffer, Meg Ward, and Chris Ward.

Lastly, we thank Jose Garcia for this year's cover illustration.

Together we're creating a better universe.

Permissions

Introduction
by Emily Lakdawalla

Emily Lakdawalla is a passionate advocate for the exploration of all of the worlds of our solar system. Through blogs, photos, videos, podcasts, print articles, Twitter, and any other medium she can put her hand to, Emily shares the adventure of space exploration with the world.

She joined The Planetary Society in 2001 to oversee a portion of the Society's Red Rover Goes to Mars project, an education and public outreach program on the Mars Exploration Rover mission funded by LEGO. She appears weekly on the Society's Planetary Radio podcast, answering listener questions or rounding up the latest space news from the blog.

I am a planetary geologist. I study geology on Mars, and Mercury, and Europa, and Pluto. That is a real job you can really have in 2018.

But it's not like being an Earth geologist. I've never whacked a Mars rock with my rock hammer, or picked up a Plutonian methane crystal and studied it with my hand lens. I've never felt the slow-motion, giant drops of a Titan methane rainstorm, or fallen into the fluffy snow on the surface of Enceladus. To explore space, planetary geologists make do with robots. Human engineers designed and built robots, sent them to land on Mars and Titan and comet Churyumov-Gerasimenko, places humans can't yet go.

To make those missions happen, somebody (actually, a lot of somebodies) had to imagine them first. Some people like to draw a line between creative arts and mathematical sciences, but that line doesn't exist. Spacecraft engineers are some of the most creative people I know. In fact, a lot of them go home from their day jobs creating spaceships and do hobbies like sewing, singing, painting, cooking, and theater. (A lot of them wish they could do those things, but they are parents and don't have time right now.)

Space exploration begins with curiosity – what's out there? Why are those other worlds so different from ours? And then it moves to the practical – how can I find out the answers to those questions? Can I do that with the technology I have? And then it gets creative – how do we design a machine that can survive the physical challenges, make the observations we need, and survive for years without any human intervention? And then it gets even more creative – what are all the possible ways our spacecraft could break? How do we design its hardware and software to prevent every imaginable disaster from happening?

And then finally we launch the spacecraft. Whenever we send robots to new worlds, we always discover that nature is even more creative than we were. There's always something new to find. That's wonderful, because then we get to ask new questions, and the cycle repeats itself. Curiosity, creativity, and wonder: that's what real space exploration is all about.

In this book, you'll get to enjoy twenty-four creative visions of life in a future where humans aren't limited to their own planet. Some of them are joyful: space pets! Hoverboards! Many of them feature adventure and danger. Many are dark: there is disease, piracy, corruption, slavery, civilization collapse.

Science fiction, both the hopeful and scary kinds, has always been vital to real space exploration. Science fiction writers remind us that when we go out into the universe, we don't just bring our technology, we also bring our humanity. Our creativity, curiosity, and optimism, but also our potential for prejudice, avarice, and violence.

What will the future be like? We don't know. The choices we make now will change the future. You, a kid reading this book, are likely to be a member of the first generation of people living in space. How can you make that future a good one, benefiting all of humankind?

We don't only need engineers and scientists, though they are important. We need political scientists and sociologists to warn us how people make bad decisions, artists and writers to envision the future, journalists and judges to keep everybody honest. We need maintainers – people who keep up the equipment, manage the data, care for the people, generally help everybody get what they need to do their jobs well. And we need all these opportunities to be open to every kind of person – people of every gender, any color, whatever age.

This book is full of the kinds of protagonists I know can make our future better. Black and brown kids. Clever and brave kids. Lonely kids and kids who love being alone. Kids who get into trouble but are guided by a moral compass. Do you see yourself in these pages? How? If you don't see yourself – well, you can write your own future, and make it happen. Good luck.

The Great Broccoli Wi-Fi Theft

by Nancy Kress

Nancy Kress is the author of thirty-three books, including twenty-six novels, four collections of short stories, and three books on writing. Her work has won six Nebulas, two Hugos, a Sturgeon, and the John W. Campbell Memorial Award. Most recent works are the Nebula-winning novella "Yesterday's Kin" and *The Best of Nancy Kress* and *Tomorrow's Kin*, the first novel of a trilogy based on "Yesterday's Kin" and extending its universe for several generations. Kress's work has been translated into Swedish, Danish, French, Italian, German, Spanish, Polish, Croatian, Chinese, Lithuanian, Romanian, Japanese, Korean, Hebrew, Russian, and Klingon, none of which she can read. In addition to writing, Kress often teaches at various venues around the country and abroad; in 2008 she was the Picador visiting lecturer at the University of Leipzig. Kress lives in Seattle with her husband, writer Jack Skillingstead, and Cosette, the world's most spoiled toy poodle.

Do you know what a *pas de chat* is? I didn't either, two months ago. But I know now and it's going to make me a hero. Really! Everybody will applaud for me so hard, their hands will sting—especially Mom! They'll give me a medal! It's going to be great!

I'm going to solve a mystery that nobody else can solve.

Just as soon as I figure out how.

My name is Nia. I'm ten. I live sometimes on the moon, at Alpha Base, and sometimes on Earth, in Illinois. I like both places, but Illinois has a big problem: GRAVITY. There's too much of it here. I wish they could just ship some of this gravity to the moon and even things out a little bit, but it doesn't work that way. On the moon there isn't enough gravity to keep human muscles strong unless you exercise a lot, and I got lazy. So now I'm back on Earth because my mom's job moved us here—again!—and my muscles aren't strong enough. Which is why I was in ballet class doing a *pas de chat*. It was not my idea.

"No, no," said Mademoiselle Janine, who was in charge of the class. "Nia, you must land lightly. Lightly! Ellen, show her the *pas de chat*."

Ellen smirked at me and raised her arms. *Pas de chat* means "step of the cat," which is a really stupid name because it doesn't look anything like a cat. I know—we *have* a cat. In the *pas de chat* you bend one leg, jump off the other leg, bend that one in the air, then land lightly. If you can find a cat that can do that, I'll give you a million dollars.

Ellen did the step. She landed lightly.

"Now you try, Nia," Mademoiselle said.

I landed like a baby elephant.

"Well..." said Mademoiselle. "These things take practice."

Did I mention that ballet class was definitely not my idea?

"I want to quit ballet," I said at dinner. "I'm no good at ballet."

Dad said, "You're probably better than you think." Dad is always on my side.

Mom said, "You might not be good at it, but you can't go on quitting things when they get hard." Mom is always on the side of doing hard things.

"But I stink at ballet," I said. I pushed my mashed potatoes around with my fork. "I'm not good at anything."

"That's not true," Dad said. "You're good at a lot of things."

I said, "Name three!"

"Well...you're good at spelling."

"Nobody needs to spell good. Autocorrect fixes it."

Mom said, "Nobody needs to spell *well*. 'Well,' not 'good.'"

"See?" I said. "I'm not good at sentences, either! I'm not good at anything!"

"Yes, you are," Dad said. "You're good at training our pets."

That was true. We have a dog named Bandit, a robot-dog named Luna, and a cat named Pickles. I trained Bandit to fetch. I programmed Luna, which is the closest you can get to training a robot. I couldn't train Pickles to do anything, but... *cats*. They do what they want.

I said, "That's only two things."

Mom smiled. "You're good at getting into trouble."

Dad said warningly, "Angela..."

"I'm teasing! Nia, I just wanted to make you laugh!"

I wasn't laughing. Mom never understands!

But then she said, "Look, Nia, everybody has to practice and work hard in order to get good at something. Do you know how many times my broccoli has failed?"

Mom is a plant geneticist. That means she changes plants' genes to make them better. Right now she's changing broccoli, which in my opinion can't ever be made better no matter what you do to it. I hate broccoli. She was just making me feel worse.

She knew it, too, because she put her hand on mine and said, "Nia, honey, after dinner let me show you something."

I said, "As long as it's not broccoli."

It was broccoli. Mom sometimes brings samples home from her work to show us. She took a plastic box out of her briefcase and, sure enough, there was broccoli. Then she opened the box.

A horrible smell filled the room, something like rotten fish mixed with turds mixed with the icky water at the bottom of a vase when the person who is supposed to throw away dead flowers (me) didn't do it for too long. Like broccoli wasn't bad enough without smelling like a garbage dump!

Mom said, "This is my latest genetic tweak to try to increase broccoli's defenses against insects that eat the plant. It didn't work."

Dad said, "Put it back in the box, please!"

Mom said, "I'm making a point here, Wayne. This genetic change is obviously a failure. But I'll keep trying until I get it right. Do you see my point, Nia?"

"Yes! Put it back in the box!"

Mom did. The smell disappeared, but not completely. She said, "I'm going to just leave this sealed box on the coffee table where we all can see it, just to remind us that a failure only means we should work harder. And not only that—working on one idea sometimes sparks another, better idea. That's how creativity works. Nia, do you understand?"

I said, "I hear Bandit barking to go out."

Mom sighed.

I put on Bandit's leash and took him for a walk. He trotted along and sniffed everything and tried to chase a rabbit. I was thinking hard; maybe Mom was right. I could think of a lot of times when she wasn't, but maybe this time she was.

So in my bedroom, I worked harder. I did three *pas de chats*. The first time, I crashed into the dresser. The second time, I fell over because my balance was off from trying to not crash into the dresser. The third time, I stepped on Pickle's tail, and she yowled and glared at me. Then she threw up on the rug.

"Mom! Pickles threw up again!"

Mom appeared in my doorway. "Well, let's clean it up. She doesn't look sick. Probably she was just eating grass again."

"Why do cats do that?"

"I don't know," Mom said. "Get the rug cleaning stuff while I pick this up. Ugh."

Later, lying in bed, I thought about all my friends who were really, really good at something. Wayne was good at basketball. Kezia was good at computers. Alice was good at thinking up cool games. Ellen was good at the *pas de chat*, but that didn't count because we didn't like each other, and anyway the *pas de chat* was still a dumb dance step. Did those cool hip-hop dancers on TV do *pas de chats*? They did not.

Dad didn't even say a third thing he thought I was good at.

In the morning, everybody was late going to school and work. I had a bad day. Dividing fractions didn't make sense—a fraction is already divided! That's what makes it a fraction! Cafeteria lunch was stuff I don't like. In gym, we were supposed to climb a rope hung from the ceiling, and I couldn't. I just hung on the end, and Ellen laughed. In science, the teacher reminded us that next week we had to hand in our idea for the science fair. I didn't have an idea.

Kezia invited me to come over after school and see something cool, but I told her I was tired. I would only be bad company.

"You really should come," Kezia said. She looked at me anxiously. Kezia gets nervous if she thinks you're upset with her. I didn't want that, so I said, "Okay, I'll come. Thanks." Even though I didn't want to.

However, what Kezia showed me really was pretty cool.

"Stand in the doorway, Nia," she said. "Now walk across the room to my bed...there it is!"

"There what is?" I didn't see anything except Kezia's collection of purple stuffed animals. She likes purple.

"Not on my bed," Kezia said, "on my laptop screen. Look."

Her laptop screen had a bunch of squiggly lines that made a weird shape. I said, "So?"

"That's you. That's the pattern of how you walk. My Dad

helped me write a program that uses the wi-fi in our house to identify people. When you walk through a room, you walk right through the radio waves that go from the router to the computer. You kind of mess them up a very little bit, like wading through water messes up real waves at the beach. That interruption makes a pattern in my dad's program, and then whenever the program makes that same pattern, I know it was you that was here."

"No way!"

"Way," Kezia said. She was smiling.

"You walk through the room. Let me see your pattern."

She did. Her pattern on the laptop screen was different from mine.

I said, "I bet I can fool it if I walk a different way."

"Let's try. I need a lot of different data because this is going to be my project for the science fair. Walk a different way."

So I ran across her room. The pattern still said it was me. I walked very s-l-o-w-l-y. Still me. I put my hands on my head and sort of wriggled across the room. Still me. I jumped, then skipped, then walked on my hands, which made an upside-down pattern of me. Then I did a *pas de chat*, because if anything could confuse the program, it would be my ballet steps. But it still recognized me.

Next we got Kezia's little brother, Joey, to do different walks across the room. Kezia had to give him a quarter to do it. No matter what he did, the pattern was always Joey. Kezia's mother's pattern was always Mrs. Delaney. The FedEx guy rang the doorbell and delivered a package, and I wanted him to come in and make a pattern, but Mrs. Delaney said no.

"Kezia, how does the program *know*?"

Dad says it measures all sorts of information and puts it together."

"But if you wanted to know who walked around in your house, why not just have a surveillance camera?"

Kezia thought hard. "Maybe a burglar or somebody would shoot out a surveillance camera. I saw that on TV once. Or maybe people wouldn't buy cameras. Our house doesn't have one—does yours?"

"No."

"But everybody has wi-fi."

"Yeah. It's cool, Keez. And a good science fair project."

"What's yours?"

I was going to show some moonrocks from when I lived on Alpha Base, but all of a sudden that didn't seem like such a great idea. Moonrocks don't do anything. They just lie there, being rocky.

I tried to look like a person who had so many good science fair ideas that she couldn't pick just one. "I'm still choosing."

She said, "Well, I'm sure it'll be really good."

I wasn't.

When I got home for dinner, Mom said, "What did you do with the broccoli?"

"The what?"

"The genetically altered broccoli sample from last night. Look." She pointed.

In the living room, the plastic case lay on its side. The lid was on the floor. The broccoli was gone.

"Nia," Mom said, "I know you don't like broccoli, but that sample was the property of the lab, and you had no right to destroy it to make whatever point you were making. Did you put it down the garbage disposal?"

"No. I didn't take it."

Mom looked at me for a long time. Then she said, "I believe you."

I was getting excited. "Did you ask Dad if he threw it out?"

"Yes. He didn't touch it."

"Did anybody else come over after I went to bed last night?"

"No," Mom said. "Why do you look so happy?"

"Because that means we had a burglar!"

Now Mom looked confused. "Nia, do you feel all right? Why are you happy that we had a—no, that's ridiculous. Nobody would steal a smelly piece of broccoli."

"Yes, they would! I saw it on TV—these bad guys stole a formula from a scientific lab and sold it to another company! It was called industry spinach."

"Industrial espionage," Mom said. "And we were not burglarized. Nothing else is missing."

Of course not. If the bad guys took any electronics or jewelry or anything, Mom would call the police. But she wasn't going to call the police about stolen broccoli. They would laugh at her. But I wasn't laughing, because I knew what was really going on.

"Okay," I said. "Can I help with dinner?"

Mom looked startled. "Well, sure. Thank you."

During dessert, I said casually, "I thought of a science fair project."

"Great!" Dad said. "What is it?"

"It's about genetically altered food. Mom, could you bring home other samples of the broccoli experiments?"

Mom said, "Yes, I'd be glad to." She looked really happy. I felt a little guilty, but not much.

"And I want to show you something. Kezia gave me a copy of the program she and her dad are doing for the science fair. It's cool."

I got Dad, and then Mom, to walk around the living room to get their patterns into the laptop. I even got them to do *pas de chats*. "It's part of the project," I said, even though that wasn't exactly true. Dad looked pretty funny leaping into the air. But Mom surprised me. Her *pas de chat* was perfect.

"I did ballet as a child," she said. "The training comes back to you."

It wasn't until I was already in bed that I realized something important: Mom was so pleased I was interested in science because she did science. She signed me up for ballet because she did ballet. Mom wanted me to be her.

I could get mad about that, but I didn't, because I was going to do something nobody else did. I was going to catch burglars. And I was going to be really good at it.

Only it didn't exactly happen like that.

We learned a new step in ballet class: the arabesque. This is sort of like your arms reach forward and your leg reaches back, and it's just as dumb as the *pas de chat*. If you're reaching forward for something, why stick your leg out the back? It makes no *sense*.

"It makes no sense," I said to Mademoiselle, who frowned. Ellen giggled. The smallest girl in class, Elaine, got all wide-eyed because I was talking back. I stuck out my lower lip.

Mademoiselle said, "Its sense is beauty. The arabesque is beautiful."

"No, it's not."

"It will be when you learn it properly. Now, fifth position... arm out...reach your chin along the line of your extended arm... Elaine, straight back, with no arch. Nia, no weight on the back right leg, or when you lift the leg, you will fall over. Now lift!"

I fell over.

"Ow! Ow!" I said, even though nothing hurt. "I think my leg is broken!"

"Your leg is not broken," Mademoiselle said. "Again, everyone."

Nobody ever listens to me.

That night I said to Mom, "I want to quit ballet."

But Mom didn't listen to me either. "No, Nia. The doctor said this was the best way to strengthen your muscles."

"But—"

"If you practice more, you'll get good at ballet. Meanwhile, I brought home another broccoli sample from the lab, like you asked."

"Great! Is this one another failure?"

"Yes. It didn't stop the insects from eating it at all." Mom took another plastic box from her purse. "Can you use this for your science fair project?"

"Yes!"

Mom stared hard at me. "What exactly is your science fair project?"

"It's a secret. I want to surprise you." I took the plastic box from Mom. Tonight, I was sure, the industrial espionage thieves would steal this one, too. And I would be the one to identify them and be a hero!

In bed, I set my alarm for midnight. It was hard to wake up then, but I did. I put my open laptop in a corner of the living room, all ready to catch the walked-through radio waves and prove that someone who wasn't me or Mom or Dad broke into our house and stole the broccoli. I did an arabesque in front of the program to make sure it was working, and this time I didn't fall over, only wobbled a lot. I could see myself in the mirror over the fireplace. The arabesque might have worked my muscles, but it wasn't beautiful.

I put the broccoli sample on the coffee table, with the lid off the box so the thief could be sure he was stealing the right thing and not, say, my lunch for tomorrow. Then I went back to bed.

In the morning, the broccoli was still there.

Okay, so the industrial thieves skipped a night. They'd be back soon. Every night I put out broccoli samples. Every night they were still there in the morning. What was wrong with these industrial espionage thieves? How come they were so bad at their jobs?

Meantime, ballet got worse and worse. I couldn't do the steps. I didn't want to do the steps. I didn't do the steps. Mademoiselle called my mother.

"Nia," Mom said, "Tomorrow we're going up to Chicago on the train."

"Really?" I liked Chicago. "Can we go to the museum with the cool dinosaurs?"

"We're going to go to the ballet. Maybe if you see one danced, it will inspire you. We're going to see *Giselle*."

"No! That's just a waste of a good Chicago trip!"

Mom looked tired. "Can you just reserve judgment until you actually see the ballet?"

I reserved judgment. I saw the ballet. All I can say is, it was worse than class. Giselle is this girl in a village who dances around a lot and meets a prince hunting in the forest. They fall in love. It turns out that the prince is going to marry somebody else, and Giselle is so upset that she goes crazy and dances herself to death. *What*? If I ever liked a boy and he lied to me like that, I wouldn't go crazy, I'd get mad! Then Giselle dies from a broken heart and becomes a ghost. I don't know what happens after that because I fell asleep.

On the train on the way home, Mom said, "Okay, Nia. Okay. You can quit ballet."

"Really?"

"Really. Just answer me one thing, and answer truthfully. Was Mademoiselle right? Did Giselle create beauty?"

"Yeah," I said, because it was true. The ballet was beautiful. But beauty was just one more thing I wasn't good at.

When we got home, the latest broccoli sample from Mom's lab was gone.

But there was no pattern of any wi-fi interruption on my laptop.

◄🚀►

"I know what happened," I said to Kezia. "The thief was really clever. They crawled along the floor, reached up maybe two fingers to get the broccoli, and crawled away. I found little bits of broccoli all the way on a path to the door. But the burglars were never high enough for the laptop to see them, so it couldn't make a pattern of how they moved."

Kezia shivered. "What are you going to do? You should call the police and tell them."

"No! This is my project. I'm going to put the next sample that Mom brings home on top of a big stack of books so the thieves have to get high enough for the wi-fi to interrupt their radio waves. Tonight."

"Do you have another broccoli?"

"Yes. And the thieves will know it's there because it smells even worse than the first one. Mom says it does better at keeping away insects, but not enough better."

Kezia said. "I wouldn't buy broccoli that smelled bad."

"Mom is working on that." Not that it would help. I wouldn't buy broccoli even if it smelled like chocolate. Even dumb Giselle wouldn't buy this broccoli, which smelled like a dead mouse.

At midnight, I held my nose and put the broccoli sample on top of a huge stack of Dad's books. One of them fell off. I was going to put it back when I saw the title: *Animal Diseases*. The book was full of pictures of skeletons and worms and a lot of other things we didn't have at Alpha Colony on the moon, where we didn't have any animals, either. I was curious.

It turned out that the book was *full* of interesting stuff. Did you know that mice can catch a disease that makes them lose all fear of cats? They'll just walk up to a big cat and grin at it. Did you know that cats can get the flu? Or that vets find all sorts of weird things in the stomachs of dogs that they do operations on? One Labrador retriever ate sixteen pairs of socks!

I got so interested that I took the book to our big blue chair and started reading, using a little flashlight so too much light wouldn't wake Mom. Only it was so late that I fell asleep and didn't wake up until the thief came for the broccoli.

CRASH!

MORE CRASH!

SCREAM! (That was me.)

YOWL!

Yowl? The industrial espionage thief yowled? I swung the flashlight around just in time to see the whole huge tower of books fall on Pickles, who had the broccoli in her mouth.

"Pickles!" I leaped off the chair and dashed over to my cat. She hissed and scratched me. Was she hurt? Did the books break her bones?

Dad and Mom and Bandit rushed into the living room. Mom and Dad shouted, "What happened?" Bandit barked. Pickles yowled. The only reason Luna didn't add to the noise was that she was turned off. Sometimes a robot dog is a really good thing.

"Nia, what have you done now?" Mom said.

"Pickles is hurt!" She was trying to limp away, still with the broccoli in her mouth. When Dad tried to pick her up, she almost bit him.

I burst into tears. "I hurt Pickles! And there was no thief! I'm not good at anything!"

The vet was grumpy about getting out of bed in the middle of the night, but he met us at his office. Mom, Dad, and I drove there, all of us still in our bathrobes and Pickles quiet now, munching the broccoli. Mom kept staring at the cat like she couldn't believe it. I couldn't, either. Who likes broccoli?

The vet said Pickles was fine, just cut and bruised from the books falling on her, and that we all overreacted and should have more sense. We went home and I fell into bed and slept and slept. Mom didn't even make me go to school the next day.

And that was the day I found out what I was good at.

I was the only one Pickles would let put medicine on her cut paw. Then she curled up on me while I sat in bed reading the dinosaur book. In the afternoon, Mom came home from the lab.

"Nia, I have some exciting news."

"What?" This better not involve another muscle-strengthening class like ballet.

"I spent the morning testing the two broccoli samples that Pickles stole. Both of them, you remember, smelled really bad."

Of course I remembered; nobody could forget that smell.

"But," Mom continued, "they didn't smell bad to a cat. We had a lab meeting this morning, and we think that with a little tweaking, we can adapt those broccoli samples to create a pet food that really appeals to animals and contains the vegetable matter they need, so they don't go on eating grass and throwing up. One of our biologists said that dogs and cats eat grass because they need folic acid, and broccoli has lots of folic acid. A new pet-food formula could be good for animals and profitable for the lab. And we wouldn't have discovered it without you."

I said, "Do I get any of the money?"

Mom smiled. "No. You didn't create the broccoli."

"Well, I have some news, too. I'm good at taking care of animals. I'm going to be a vet when I grow up, probably a vet for dinosaurs."

Mom's face changed. "Nia—"

"Just kidding. I know there aren't any more dinosaurs. But I'm still going to be a vet." I stroked Pickles, who purred. And who knows—maybe there were a few small dinosaurs left someplace, deep in caves or at the bottom of dark lakes or something. Even scientists don't know everything. Look at Mom—she didn't know why Pickles ate grass until some biologist told her. But if there weren't any more dinosaurs, I'd be a vet for dogs and cats and goats and chickens. Chickens get a weird disease that makes them pull out all their feathers.

Mom said, "Being a vet is a wonderful ambition, honey."

"And I'm going to do weight lifting."

"Weight lifting?"

"Yes," I said. "It will get my muscles just as strong as ballet. Stronger."

"Well... I'll look into it."

I knew that was all I was going to get right now. Instead of arguing, I opened my laptop and showed Mom a wi-fi-interruption pattern. She said, "What's that?"

"That's the pattern that Pickles made in the wi-fi radio waves when she jumped onto the books, scrambled in the air, yowled, and fell with her legs all stuck out funny."

Mom squinted at the pattern. It made a perfect *pas de chat*.

I said, "Isn't it beautiful?"

The Sting of the Irukandji
by Kristy Evangelista

Kristy Evangelista lives in Australia, a country that loves its giant things. She grew up down the road from an enormous banana and drove past a mighty prawn on the way to visit her grandparents, who lived near an oversized pineapple. With her very first author paycheck, Kristy bought a large rusty pear for her backyard. She is very fond of it, even though the pear barely reaches her chin and cannot exactly be called gigantic. "The Sting of the Irukandji" is Kristy's first foray into the world of middle-grade fiction. She chose to write about a giant space jellyfish in order to honour her Australian heritage and also because giant things are just really cool.

My name is Kishi, and I live in a jellyfish.

Not a real jellyfish of course; they only grow up to two metres wide. I am a regular-sized ten-year-old girl. I need way more room than that.

I'm talking about a space jellyfish: an Irukandji Class A mining ship.

Irukandjis are wicked. In the old Earth oceans, they were teeny-tiny little sea creatures, but in the space mining world, they are giants. Their tentacles are strong enough to crush even the biggest asteroids. When I was little, I used to be scared of the creaking and groaning that shook the ship when we were in the middle of a mine. But then Dad told me that it was the sound of success, and now it doesn't bother me.

I've lived in the Iruki with just my two fathers and my little sister for as long as I can remember. We've been happy as we travel through the galaxy, feasting on the stars, and then visiting a planet or space station to sell our goods. We never visit the same place twice; Dad says that the universe is too big for that.

We would have stayed happy if my cousin Andro hadn't arrived. Stupid Andro, turning up his long face at everything. Stupid Andro, with his heavy bones and expensive netgear.

It was his fault we were attacked by space pirates.

I didn't realise how stupid Andro was at first. In fact, when my fathers first told me he was coming, I was excited at the thought of spending time with someone my own age. Abby is a dear, but she is only eighteen months old, and her favourite game is peekaboo.

I'd never had any problem making friends whenever we visit a space port; I'd go straight to a spiderball court, find a bunch of kids, and ask if I can join in. I didn't think Andro would be any different.

On the day that Andro arrived, Papa, Abby and I waited for him in the mud room. If you picture the dome shape that is the body of a jellyfish, the living quarters and flight deck are located at the bottom of the dome, right near the tentacles. In fact, the longest jellyfish tentacle ends right in the mud room, which is a large room filled with space suits.

We use that tentacle as a sort of travelling tube to get in and out at a space port. It's fast and fluid and fun. Way better than any of the rides on a theme park planet.

The travel hatch opened, and Dad helped a heavyset, slightly dazed boy out. I marched right on over to him, gave him my best smile and said, "Welcome, Cousin Andro! I'm Kishi. We have our own spiderball room, want to play sometime?"

Andro didn't smile back. He didn't even look at me, "No, thank you," he said, "I don't enjoy zero G-ball." And then he vomited right onto my new spiderball shoes.

It took a lot of scrubbing to get all the vomit out.

"Are you sure we're cousins?" I asked Papa as I helped him get dinner ready. "He doesn't look anything like us."

It's super dangerous to have an open flame on a space ship, so when we make dinner, we put everything in plastic pouches and cook them really slowly in hot water. It's a method of cooking called suvee, and it's been around since the Earth ages.

While we worked, Papa kept an eye on a black and white hologram of Abby; she was napping in her room.

"Andro has the same black hair and eyes as you," Papa pointed out as he pulled the chicken out of the suvee machine.

"But he's so... wide." Andro has a thick neck and serious muscles, which is weird, because as far as I can tell, all he does all day is sit in his room and play virtual reality games.

"That's from living on a planet with heavy gravity." Papa explained.

"And his skin is brown!" We were all deep-space white.

"That's from living on a planet with a sun," Papa said. "You know, a sun? Those giant flaming balls we fly past sometimes?" He pulled the suvee'ed chicken out of the bag; the chicken was cooked but still as pale and pasty as I was.

"Ohhhhh right," I said, "he's been chargrilled." I ducked as Papa swatted me.

"What's this about, Kishi?" he asked. "Is it because he doesn't play spiderball? Why don't you try something he likes instead? You might find you like it, too." He poked at the chicken with a fork. It looked juicy. "This is ready. Can you call everyone in for dinner?"

Andro was strapped into his VR goggles and gloves. I wrinkled my nose when I saw the state of his room; it was like a mining site, with debris piled up on every surface. As I entered, he punched something in the air, and laughed.

I didn't know he could do that. Laugh, I mean.

"Hey, Cuz," I said. "Papa's got dinner ready in the mess." Andro took off his goggles. By the time he did, his smile had turned back into a flat line. "Thank you, Kishi," he said formally.

I remembered Papa's advice. "Maybe we could play that game together sometime?"

Andro paused. "I'm sorry," he said. "I'm not meant to share my netgear."

I shrugged, like no big deal—even though it felt like a very big deal—and went to find Dad.

The flight deck isn't too far from Andro's room. Inside is a large table in the shape of a semicircle, which sits flush against the viewport. A 3D colour holographic appeared in the air above it; right then it was charting the course to the nearest asteroid belt. Dad was sitting on a chair looking at it.

"How long is Andro staying again?" I asked as I jumped into the second seat. Directly in front of me was a joystick and a console that looked a bit like a round chess board.

Dad was nobody's fool; he narrowed his eyes and looked at me closely. "You guys aren't getting along, huh?"

"He doesn't play spiderball," I explained, "and he won't let me borrow his netgear."

"Well, we need to cut him a little slack," Dad said. "Andro is in a new place, with people he doesn't know well. And he's had a tough year."

I mulled that over for a parsec. "What happened?"

Dad leaned over and tweaked my ponytail. "You should ask him that sometime."

At dinner, I watched as Andro ate a tiny bite of chicken,

made a face like someone burped in his space suit, and then put the fork down. He didn't even try the vegetables. (I don't blame him for that, they were grey and slimy; less like beans and eggplant and more like the snails that ate the beans and eggplant.) I glanced at Papa to see if he'd noticed, but he was cutting up some food for Abby.

It's against the cousin honour code to tattle, I decided reluctantly.

"Excuse me, Uncle," Andro said, halfway through the meal. "Why can't I connect to GalaxyNet?"

"We're too far from any of the settled regions," Dad explained, "and unlike a space cruiser, we aren't set up with the right kind of comms gear. We have lots of games on board, though, and the latest version of Encyclopedia Galactica."

Andro's broad face dropped faster than his fork had.

"Don't you like your dinner, Andro, dear?" Papa asked in concern.

Papa's finally noticed! I thought, glad that I hadn't had to break the cousin honour code.

"I'm sorry, sir." Andro was always polite. It was one of the worst things about him. "But this isn't like the food back home. And my stomach is still unsettled from the travel tube."

"That's okay, honey," said Papa kindly, taking the plate away. "We'll sort something else out. Kishi, eat your vegetables."

"But he doesn't have to eat them!" I objected.

"He has a name, Kishi," said Papa sternly. "And Andro is our guest. Eat your vegetables." My nose scrunched as I looked at a snail-y bean. I gathered my courage and forced a spoonful into my mouth. The old Earthans used to eat snails, I thought as I chewed the grey mush. They were a delicacy. I swallowed and then watched in disbelief as Papa placed a bowl of ice cream in front of Andro.

"That's so unfair!" I said in outrage. But part of me wondered: What could be so bad that you get ice cream for dinner?

It took a few days, but eventually I found something that Andro and I both liked: chess. So I brought my board to his room and challenged him to a game.

I moved out my bishop and tried to work up the nerve to ask him about his life. I wasn't sure why it was so hard, it was just a simple question. Something, like Hey, I heard you've had a rough year... what happened?

I'll ask the next time I move my knight, I decided. Knights are brave.

"May I ask you a personal question, Kishi?" Andro asked.

"Fire away," I said, moving a pawn.

"Don't you ever get crazy in this place?"

"Sometimes. But then we visit a new spaceport, and we get to go out and see something new. Last month we went to a zoo. It was wicked. They had old Earth monkeys!"

Andro seemed unimpressed. I guess he saw animals all the time, being planet-born and all.

"Do you have any friends?" he asked. "I mean, you don't dock at the same place twice, you can't contact people on the net..."

I wasn't sure I liked the faintly superior tone in his voice. "Sure I have friends," I said. "I have Papa and Dad and Abby."

"They're not friends, they're family."

I shrugged and moved my queen to take one of his pieces.

"You know it's not normal, right? You and your family, living the way you do, never seeing anyone else, barely connected to the rest of the world. My dad says you're missing out."

We got to live on an Irukandji. We got to see the universe. We weren't the ones missing out on anything. "Your Dad doesn't know what he's talking about," I said angrily.

"You're just saying that because you don't know any better."

"I know plenty," I said and took his queen.

Andro's thick neck went bright red. He took a deep breath. "Congratulations," he said, but his voice had lost its cool superiority. "You're going to win this game. So if you excuse me, I think I'll just call surrender and have an early night. I'm not feeling very well."

I was taken aback. "You don't want to finish the game? But we've barely started."

Andro shook his head. His chin wobbled, and he stared at the board.

"It doesn't matter who wins," I said. "You only get better playing against someone who is better than you."

Andro didn't say anything else; he just turned away and faced the wall until I left.

I have chores, just like anyone. Sometimes, after we've been carrying a lot of water, we get space barnacles growing on the inside of the cargo hold. They aren't actually living creatures but minerals that come from the water.

The surface of the Iruki is a special kind of membrane. It's slightly wobbly, even on the inside. If we're carrying helium, I strap on my space suit and jump to the barnacles like I'm on a giant bouncy castle. If we're carrying water, I put on my diving suit and swim through the water like a mermaid.

Well, okay, like an over-dressed mermaid with strange fashion sense.

It can take some scrubbing to get rid of the barnacles when I find them, but I don't mind. I'm very strong.

Other times, a piece of space rock will pierce a hole in the membrane, and I have to walk around the outside of the space ship to patch it up. I use my spiderball shoes; they're sticky on the bottom, which stops you flying into outer space, but not so sticky that you can't unstick them as you step.

When I get to the hole, I unclip the giant bottle of Fill-Gap from my back and squirt it inside. It comes out like a puffy white foam and dries really quickly into a strong flexible plug. Once I stuck my feet in by mistake; I was there for hours. Dad and Papa only noticed I was missing when I didn't turn up for dinner. They laughed and laughed about it, and the next day Papa served some kind of meringue dessert with a little figure in the middle. Then they laughed some more.

My favourite, favourite job is helping Dad mine an asteroid. And a few days after Andro arrived, we found a good one.

Just like always, the computer detected it first. It let out a cheery wimp womp that could be heard throughout the living quarters. I rushed straight to the flight deck. Dad was already in his chair, looking over the asteroid stats on the hologram. It was a big rock, about the same size as the Iruki.

There are a hundred different tentacles on the Irukandji ships, and they all do different things. The big frilly ones heat. There are some jagged ones that saw. And a bunch of long hollow ones suck up the water and helium like giant straws.

To use a particular tentacle, you select the matching piece from the chessboard and place it into a slot in the console.

Dad picked up the drill tentacle; there was helium trapped in the centre of this 'roid. Helium is hard to catch and super rare, which means it's really valuable.

I watched as Dad's large, capable hands moved the joystick. He had the finesse of a surgeon, drilling just far enough that he reached the helium and not an inch farther.

"Care to help me with the water, Kish?" Dad asked, and I grinned at him. Not many parents would let their kid mine a 'roid with them.

Mining water is easiest if you have two people working together, one to extract and melt the ice, the other to suck up the water onto the Iruki before it refreezes or floats away.

"I've just heated some H2O," Dad said. "Get that ball of water before it gets too far away!"

I switched out my drill for a sucker tentacle and swung the

joystick towards the wobbly ball of liquid. "Got it, Dad!"

"And another! This one's floating to starboard."

"Aye aye, Captain!"

We were having so much fun that it took me some time to notice Andro standing in the passageway, watching us with interest.

"May I have a go?" he asked.

"I'm sorry," I said, copying his formal politeness. "These are the only controls. And you're not supposed to share gear."

His face turned hard, and he stomped out of the flight deck.

"That wasn't very nice Kishi," Dad said.

Does anyone like apologising? I know I don't, but I don't know if that's normal or not.

Before Andro, I never used to wonder if I was normal. I just assumed that I was.

I found Andro in the mess. He was looking through the glass of the freezer, looking slightly green. Planet-boy had a weak stomach.

"I'm sorry," I said.

"Did your Dad make you apologise?" Andro asked.

"Maybe," I said.

"Well, you don't have to. And you don't have to try to be my friend. We both know that we actually have nothing in common, and we don't really like each other. So do us both a favour—stop pretending like you do and leave me alone."

Spiderball is a fantastic game. When I'm old enough, I'm going to go pro.

It's played in zero gravity. You can play it in any kind of large room, but the pros use a special shaped court, one with fourteen sides, like one of those special dice from Dungeons and Dragons, if you've ever played that.

There is one hoop, right in the centre of the court, and two balls. You get points every time one of your team members gets a ball through the hoop.

Have you ever tried moving around in zero gravity? It's not that easy. You have to push yourself off a wall, and you can't change direction until you reach something else with enough resistance. You can bounce off the walls, and sometimes another player, but it's a big court, so if that's all you use, it's a verrrrry slow game.

That's where the spiderball gloves come in. They shoot out a web; you can use them to swing in an arc from one side of the court to another, releasing and retracting them once you're done. You can also use them to fix ropes in different positions across the middle of the court. Once they're established, you can swing on them to change directions or even use them as a catapult to change direction mid court.

Wicked, huh? So you can understand my outrage and betrayal when Dad told me that I couldn't play anymore. Because of stupid Andro.

Usually we keep the Iruki gravity at Earth norm. Dad says that it is the best for our bodies; humans haven't changed all that much since old Earth, and if we live in 1G, we have fewer health problems.

All humans except for Andro, anyway. Even after a week on the Iruki, he's pale and shaky and prone to spewing his guts out. So Dad pushed the gravity up to 1.5G, which is the same as Andro's home planet. But that means that the spiderball room is now a P5G room. Point five gravity. Way too high to play ball.

Not being able to play made me MAD. Hopping, spitting, flaming, boiling mad. Whenever Papa sees me like this, he says, "Careful Kishi! We're not allowed an open flame on a spaceship!"

So I've been trying to suppress it. I'm ten now. A mature ten. And I'm going to be a gracious host. I'm going to show Andro that even if you live on a mining ship, that doesn't mean you don't have class.

I peeked my head around Andro's door. He does look a bit better with 1.5G. He's looking at a photo; it's a picture of him with his arms around a little girl, maybe four or five years old. She is chubby and built solidly like Andro but with bouncy golden curls.

"Who's that?" I asked. "She's cute."

Andro whipped his head around. "Nobody," he spat.

I was taken aback by his rudeness. It was very un-Andro. Then my own temper rose. I'd lost spiderball because of him, but he was acting like I was the jerk. "If she's nobody, why do you have a picture of her?"

Andro's face went red. He took something out of his pocket, and before I even had time to see what it was, he used it to set fire to the photo. The picture flamed brightly, like an orange butterfly, its fiery wings reaching up to the ceiling. "See?" He said, "It's nothing. Now get out!"

I shrieked, grabbed a blanket from the bed and stomped on the butterfly until it was nothing but ash. Then I ran out to the passageway. The red fire extinguisher is always kept there for emergencies, right next to the blue Fill-Gap.

I grabbed the fire extinguisher and squirted the ash, just to make sure it was safe. "Are you STUPID?" I screamed at him. "You can't have an open flame on an Iruki!! When Papa and Dad find out about this, you'll be getting out, out of the whole darn ship!"

I was wrong. Papa swept the ashes away like they were no big deal.

When I'm feeling really upset, I like to sit on one of the comfortable chairs on the flight deck. There's nothing like the gentle thrum of an Iruki as it flies through the stars. When we have a cargo of helium stored in the bulbous head, the ship glows violet, and the tentacles trail purple lines in our wake as we glide through the deep night of space.

Dad knows this, of course. Not long after the fire, he came into the flight deck. He didn't say anything, just sat down in the chair next to me.

We watched the stars for a while in silence. I could see a space cruiser in the distance behind us; this is a common space lane. At first it was just a green blip in the sky, but it quickly got closer and bigger. When it was pea-sized I could tell that it was a Whale Class cruiser.

Andro should be on that, I thought bitterly, he'd have access to the net and food that is cooked in the oven. And other kids who are 'normal.'

"It's not fair," I said, at last. "He doesn't have to eat his vegetables or do any chores; he's spoilt. He almost set fire to the whole ship. And he's crazy polite and a guest, so I'm always the one in trouble."

"I get that," Dad said quietly. "I get that it's hard having to accommodate someone new in our space. And I'll have a talk with Papa and see if we can't change things to make it easier for you. But there's something I want you to think about, Kishi. Fair doesn't mean treating people exactly the same. It means treating people with consideration of their different circumstances."

"What?" I asked, confused.

"Think about this: if Papa were in a wheelchair, would you expect him to climb a set of stairs?"

"Of course not!" I said.

"Why not?" Dad stood up to leave. "The rest of us don't need a ramp. If fairness means equality, shouldn't we treat him exactly the same as the rest of us?"

I was still thinking about Dad's words a few hours later when the pirates found us.

Earth Irukandjis are barely a few centimetres wide. Don't let that fool you, though—they are probably the most dangerous jellyfish of all. They are so toxic that their sting can kill a grown man.

Unfortunately, the people who designed our Irukandji didn't include a stinger, so when the pirates came, we were defenceless.

The emergency alarm is a panicked A-whee-ooo, A-whee-ooo; its shrill shriek squirms unpleasantly under your skin, like maggots made of fear.

I didn't panic when it went off, though, because I knew what to do: we drill for this all the time. I got quickly into my space suit, then went into Abby's room to help her.

Papa was already there. "Go help Dad," he said. He pulled me into a quick bear hug before pushing me out the door.

I ran down the corridor towards the flight deck. Dad was there already, of course, frowning at the holodeck. He zoomed in until we had good look at the incoming vessel. It had an impenetrable shell, and the blunt turtle head was just starting to creep out. "It's a War Turtle," Dad said. "You know what that means."

I did know. "Space pirates." Scum of the 'verse, scourge of the seven galaxies. That turtle would open its jaws and use them to lock onto the Iruki, creating a bridge between the two ships. But... "Why would they attack?" I asked. Our valuables are helium and water, and their ship isn't designed to hold them. "What do we have that they want?" A shiver tickled my spine. "Not... the Iruki itself?" Not our home...

Dad looked behind me; Andro had appeared at the doorway. His tanned skin turned a sickly mustard yellow as he looked at the holo. Stupid planet-boy wasn't in his space suit; he'd die if the hull were breached.

"They don't want the ship, Kishi," Dad said. "They want him."

PlanetBoy? "What? Why?"

"There's no time to explain now. Help Andro get into his space suit," Dad said. "Then you two go and hide." He looked at me meaningfully. "C16, Kishi. Just use close comms."

"Got it," I said, dragging Andro to the mud room. I might not know what was going on, but I knew Dad's serious voice when I heard it. I knew that he was trusting me to keep Andro safe.

Andro was slow on his feet and clumsy, but I managed to help him into a suit. I was just in time—almost as soon as we clicked our helmets on, a ripping, shrieking sound tore through the ship. My ears popped, and a wind dragged at my feet. I felt zero gravity kick in.

The pirates had blasted the living quarters.

Fighting the turbulence, I typed C16 into the travel door, counted to twenty, and pushed Andro inside. Then I pulled myself in after him.

The travel tube isn't just for transport to space docks. You can also use it to get to other parts of the ship.

My stomach did a somersault as I dropped through the tentacle feet first. I kept my arms folded on my chest. The air whooshed me along at incredible speeds and then got slowly denser as I reached C16.

The travel door was open at the other end, and so I shot out into a cloud of purple—the largest helium hold in the jellyfish. I tumbled and spun out of control until I hit the bouncy membrane on the far wall. Then I flailed some more until I hit the other side of the hold. This time I managed to hit the wall feet first; my sticky spiderball shoes meant I stayed there.

I pushed myself over to Andro, my breathing loud and shaky in the space suit. He was sitting slumped by the travel door.

I twisted as I floated towards him and landed feet first on the wall near his head. He started in surprise.

I put my hands on my hips and glared down at him. "What the heck is going on? Why do they want you?"

Probably every boy's parents tell him he's a prince at some point. But most don't have the creds to back it up. Andro's parents do: they're king and queen of a whole world.

As we bobbed around in the purple haze of helium, Andro finally shared his story.

Over the last year, a plague swept through his planet. When Andro's little sister fell sick, his parents decided to send him away to keep him safe.

"You should have told me earlier," I said, slightly cross. "I thought you were being mean when you wouldn't share your netgear."

"I was being mean," Andro said miserably, "although maybe not about that. About the chess and the photo of my sister. Everything here is so strange, and every time something goes wrong I just want to cry or punch something... I'm a prince. I'm not supposed to lose control."

"Will your sister be okay?" I asked, thinking of the small blonde girl in the photo.

"She's really bad," he said. "When I logged onto the net yesterday, she was critical."

"I'm really sorry," I said, awkwardly patting him on the back of his space suit. I tried to pat him, anyway; with my big puffy glove, it was more of a soft thump. "Wait a parsec—how did you log onto the net?"

"You remember that whale cruiser that passed us?"

I nodded.

"I jumped onto its comms. I think... I think maybe that's how the pirates found us."

"This is your fault?"

"I was trying to find out how my sister was!" he said. "I thought it was a secure comm."

"Yeah, well, now they have my sister," I said. "And my parents."

A thought occurred to me. If the pirates wanted Andro so badly, maybe... maybe I could somehow trade him for my family.

⋅)●

We sat a while in silence, wondering what was going on. I kept sneaking glances at Andro, wondering if maybe I should pretend to leave and call the pirates.

It was only fair, I thought. It was his princely worth that had attracted the pirates, his comms that had given them our location. But I could hear Dad's voice in my head. Is that really fair, Kishi? Consider his circumstances.

Dad was right; when Andro sent that comm, he was just worried about his sister. It wouldn't be fair to turn him in.

All of a sudden, I slapped Andro on the helmet. "You idiot!" I said to him. "We can use the baby monitor to find out what's going on!"

I pressed a button on my space suit, and a black and white holograph appeared. It was Abby, sitting on Papa's knee. They were hiding in the pantry. Abby was crying, and Papa was whispering to her, trying to get her to shush.

Where's Dad? I wondered uneasily.

The pantry door was kicked open with a crash. Abby screamed.

A giant stepped into the range of the holo monitor. She pointed a blaster at Papa and grinned shark-like at Abby. "Coupla strags 'ere, Brady. No prince, tho'."

Brady? I bit my lip. Brady Stambaugh was known across the galaxies for his determination. He achieved everything that he set his mind to.

He was also known for his ruthlessness. Papa drew Abby closer to him.

A boy – Brady —entered the holo. He was around my age and had light blonde hair and blue smiling eyes. Brady smiled, squatting down so that he was closer to Abby's height. He didn't look like a ruthless pirate. He looked nice. Like someone I'd play Spiderball with.

"Hey, little one." The boy's smile tightened and became sharp at the edges. Not so nice after all. "Won't you fetch a good price at the slave market?"

I glared daggers at the hologram. No she WON'T, I thought fiercely, clapping down on the image.

"We can't just stay here," I said. Andro nodded; he looked as horrified as I felt. "Can you jump onto the turtle's comms, like you did the cruiser? If we can send a message to your parents, they could send us some Class A military ships. Then they'd blow the pirates to space-dust."

Andro's fingers started to move; he was already using his VR gloves within his suit. Even in the puffy outer gloves, his fingers moved faster than I'd ever seen. "Done," he said in no time at all.

"You, sir, are a net master," I said, feeling very glad that I had not turned him in.

But Andro wasn't finished being awesome. His eyes flicked from side to side as he read something I couldn't see. "How do you feel," he asked slowly, "about sneaking onto their ship and disabling their hyperdrive?"

I thought about little Abby in a slave market. "I feel very good about that."

"The pirate ship—it was a War Turtle, wasn't it?"

"Yes."

"Do you know which class?"

"No. Does it matter?"

Andro made a flicking gesture, and the plans for two War Turtles appeared on my suit visor.

"Look, this is Class A and B," he said. "Their hyperdrives are in a completely different part of the ship." Andro was right; in Class A, it was in the lower, flatter part of the shell, and in Class B, it was in the turtle's, er, bottom.

"I guess the only way to know is to actually board the turtle," I said.

The cargo hatch wasn't designed to be opened unless the travel tube was in place. And the travel tube wasn't in place; I had programmed it to detach from C16, and I wasn't going to draw attention to our location by calling it back. To get through we needed a lot of muscle.

It was a good thing Andro grew up in 1.5G.

"Do you have a crown?" I asked as he heaved against the transit hatch. I couldn't imagine Andro in a crown.

"No," he said. He grunted slightly, and the hatch moved an inch. "My father does, though."

I tacked a spiderball web to the door. "Do you have servants?"

"Yes."

No wonder he can't keep his room tidy. "How about enemies? How many of those do you have?"

"Are we counting space pirates?"

"No," I decided.

"Then one."

"Is that all?" I asked, disappointed.

Andro turned the cargo hatch another click. "But she's one really good enemy. She's an expert 'roid miner, and spiderballer. She's wicked good at chess, and she knows her way around a jellyfish."

A glow warmed the pit of my stomach, and I gave him a friendly shove.

Andro turned to look at me. "Are you ready?" he asked, and I saluted. He turned the hatch one last time, and then we were blown out into the empty vastness of space.

Andro and I floated together, tiny babies in the vast womb of the universe. The only thing stopping us from drifting into the darkness was a single strand of spiderball web, the umbilical cord that kept us attached to the Iruki.

I was worried about Andro—all this zero-G stuff was starting to get to him. He looked like he might vomit. I hoped he wouldn't; vomit is a nightmare in a space suit.

A second later, Brady's's warm honey voice purred into our helmets, and I had a lot more to worry about.

"Prince Andro." Brady was broadcasting on all frequencies. "I was expecting a proper welcome from you, my lord. At the very least you could have met me at the transit door. Don't you know it is rude to neglect your guests?" He waited a moment to see if Andro would respond, but Planet Boy's lips remained-clamped tightly shut. "No matter. I can live with your bad manners, my prince." Hee paused, and his voice turned into a claw, ready to strike. "But I'm afraid your host family cannot."

Fear trickled into my heart.

I couldn't see Brady, but I could hear his cruel smile. "You have one minute to respond before I shoot the grey one."

Papa.

With a shaking hand, I turned on the baby monitor. A holo of Abby appeared above my forearm; she was clutching Papa's legs.

And then the giant woman pointed a gun at Papa's head. I swallowed, and Andro actually swore. "Wait," he said through his mike.

But Brady didn't seem to hear him. He kept counting. "Forty seconds..."

"Brady! I said wait!" Andro looked at me in panic. "Why can't he hear me?"

"It's your radio!" I realised, "it's still on close comms."

"Twenty seconds."

Andro fumbled with the buttons on his glove, trying to increase the range of his comms. Abby started to cry.

"Fix it!" I bellowed.

"I'm trying ..."

"Close your eyes, Abby, sweetheart," said Papa.

"Ten, nine, eight..."

"STOP!" Andro shouted. "I mean, please stop, sir, I'm here. I'm outside the ship, near C16. That's one of the cargo holds."

There was a tense moment, and then the giant smiled. "Wait there, your highness. We'll send someone to you."

I slumped in relief as she removed the gun from Papa's head, and I watched him hug Abby. Now that the moment of panic had passed, I realised that they weren't on the Iruki anymore. They were on the War Turtle. Its deck looked a lot like the deck of the Iruki, though. I took in every detail that I could see, and an idea started to form.

"Well, it was a good plan," said Andro in defeat.

"It still is a good plan," I said. "They don't know about me yet."

"What are you going to do?"

"I'm going to take them out," I said. I quickly gave him a few instructions, then raised a hand, shot out a spiderball web to the jellyfish, and pulled myself away.

Spiderball is based on real zero-G equipment and real space manoeuvres. It was turned into a game by 'roid miners just like me, who were keen to pit their space skills against each other.

If the spiderball scouts could have seen me that night, they would have recruited me on the spot.

I ran down the outside of the jellyfish as fast as I could. The metallic taste of adrenalin added an extra burst of speed to my legs.

When I reached the bottom of the Iruki, I launched myself into the jungle of tentacles. I floated for a while, then lifted my arm and shot a spiderball web towards a tentacle, swinging myself around.

After a while I settled into a steady rhythm. Aim at at a

tentacle, shoot my web at it. Swing myself forward, release the web and aim again.

I needed to reach the flight deck before the pirates got Andro and took him back to their ship. If I wasn't quick, I would never see any of them again.

I flew from tentacle to tentacle, never missing a shot, never misjudging my release. I was a spider, a squirrel, an eagle. I swooped towards the flight deck and landed next to it in a triumphant crouch.

As I stared at the flight deck hatch, my triumph faded.

I didn't have Andro's muscles. How would I get inside?

The air in my space suit was starting to taste like stale fear. I made a small sobbing sound deep in my throat as I twisted the handle to the flight deck. I took a deep breath, anchored my spiderball shoes more firmly on the outside of the ship, and heaved. The hatch did not budge.

My adrenalin was spent. I couldn't get in this way.

Think, I said to myself. Why can't you get in?

The flight deck hatch was only for emergencies. It wasn't designed for everyday use, so it didn't have an airlock. That meant I was fighting the pressure inside of the ship. Even Andro and his 1.5G guns would have had trouble getting through this door.

So... I needed to find a door with an airlock.

I ran toward the hatch in the mud room; lucky for me it wasn't far away. I peeked inside the nearby port window. I was fairly sure that the pirates had left, but I didn't want to take any chances.

The airlock was clear, and so was the room beyond. I tugged at the handle and almost cried when it opened.

I got through the airlock as quickly as I could and sprinted through the living quarters and onto the flight deck. At the entranceway, I slipped and skidded on something wet. Something red. Blood.

Dad's chair was tipped over; I picked it up and sat down in it, trying to ignore the stickiness on the seat. My heart bashed against my ribs, like a wild bird trying to escape its cage.

I wanted to cry. I wanted to puke. But most of all I wanted to know that my Dad was okay.

I set up the baby monitor by the chessboard and tapped it to turn it on.

Abby was sitting on Brady's lap in the flight deck. As I watched, the giant lady pirate entered the holo and pushed Andro onto the deck. He immediately kneeled in front of Brady, as if he were the royal, sitting on a throne of gold.

I'd made it in time. I picked up the drill tentacle and placed it in the console.

Brady lifted Abby off his lap and walked over to Andro. The young pirate grabbed Andro roughly by the hair and yanked his face up so he could inspect it. After a moment he smiled his raptor smile. "Jo-Lee," he said to someone off the holo, "start the hyperdrive. We have our cargo."

"May I ask you a question, Captain Brady?" Andro asked politely.

"You can ask, my prince. I may not answer."

"It's about your ship. I was impressed by its power."

Brady smiled smugly. "Yes, it made short work of that pathetic sea jelly, didn't it?

Pathetic? My blood boiled at his words.

"Is it a Turtle Class A?"

"Yesit is. You have a good eye."

Turtle Class A. I moved the joystick and drove the drill tentacle right the soft underbelly of the pirate ship.

Not so pathetic now.

꧁

The deck of the War Turtle bucked under foot, taking everyone by surprise.

Well, almost everyone; Andro was waiting for it.

While the pirates were stumbling in confusion, he pushed himself off the ground and ran to the right of the flight deck. There was an emergency can of Fill-Gap there, right where we keep ours. Andro sprayed it onto the giant lady pirate, still scrambling on the deck. It covered her in fluffy white foam.She went for a knife and tried to stand, but her leg caught in the Fill-Gap, and she fell. The knife clattered harmlessly away.

I cheered.

Brady growled and launched himself at Andro. He was stopped short by Papa, whohad the giant's knife in his hand and looked like he was ready to use it.

Back in the Iruki, I laughed and spun around in my flight chair. A ding drew my attention to the radar—a royal warship had appeared. It was a Sea Star Class A. Andro's friends, I assumed.

I opened comms to the War Turtle. "Now that you have been skewered by an unknown but very awesome enemy," I said, "where is my dad?"

It took us a long time to find Dad. The pirates had stabbed him and dumped him into a cupboard. They hadn't bothered to bandage his wounds or anything, and by the time we found him, he was really bad.

The navy had a medic. She did the best she could but said that he had lost a lot of blood and needed a hospital.

The Sea Star took us straight to Andro's planet. It turns out that Andro really is our cousin, and that makes Dad very important. They spared no expense to make him better, so I guess there is some use to being royal after all.

"It'll be ok," said Andro, "We have the best doctors in the galaxy." They'd saved his sister, so I hoped he was right. "You must stay at my place until he gets better," Andro insisted. "We have plenty of room."

⋖〗⊳

Andro's castle is HUGE, with white towers and turrets just like the rooks on my chessboard. Andro says that it is their smallest castle, but sometimes I got lost looking for the bathroom. It's nice, I guess, but way too big for a regular-sized ten-year-old girl.

The doctors wouldn't let us see Dad. They told us that he had been stabbed in the kidneys, and he might not wake up. I started to cry when they said that, but Papa gave me a hug and whispered that Dad was strong and not to worry.

Each day we attended the royal court for lunch (or nuncheon, as they call it). I got to eat all kinds of fresh fruit, grilled meat, and vegetables that are crisp instead of slimy. But I was so worried about Dad that I barely ate anything.

The king and queen are even more polite than Andro. "How do you like court, Kishi?" the queen asked one day.

"It's okay," I said. "The spiderball court is better, though." Everybody laughed, which was embarrassing, because I wasn't trying to be funny.

Andro tried to distract me with visits to the zoo and aquarium; he said they have actual Earth jellyfish there, and turtles, and monkeys, too. It sounded really great, but it didn't seem right to go without Dad. And besides, living in 1.5G all the time was exhausting. By mid-afternoon I really needed a nap.

It was while I was napping that everything changed. I woke to find that Papa was carrying me somewhere. I was still bleary-eyed with sleep, but I knew something big was happening; Papa hadn't carried me like that since I was just a littly.

"Is it Dad?" I asked in a small voice.

"Yes, Kishi, honey," Papa said. Except his voice wasn't sad, it was happy. "He's going to be okay. He's awake and asking for you." We stopped in front of a large white door, and he put me down. "You can't hug him, okay, sweetie?" Papa said, and I nodded. "But you can hold his hand."

"Like a hand hug?"

"Exactly, hon."

"Isn't Abby coming?"

"I think it's a bit early to bring her just yet. Don't be scared—everything inside is to make Dad better."

Inside the room, Dad was propped up on a tall hospital bed. Tubes ran from his nose and his stomach to a machine near his bed. The machine made rhythmic grinding sounds, which freaked me out.

"Hey, Kish," Dad said. He was so skinny, and his eyes were sunken. "Papa tells me you saved the day. I'm so proud of you."

I leaned against the bed, trying to get as close as I could without bumping any of his tubes. "The king fixed the Iruki for us," I told him. "It was only a little banged up by the pirates. We're ready to go as soon as you're better."

"I'm really sorry, sweetie," said Papa, rubbing my back, "but that might not be for a really long time. Maybe not ever. Dad has to stay near the hospital."

My face crumpled. My beloved Iruki. My home. "But we can't stay on one planet!" My voice wobbled. "The universe is too big for that. That's what you always say."

"I'm sorry, Kish," Dad reached out a trembling hand. His grip, which had been so strong and steady on the joystick, was now weak and flimsy. Abby could probably beat him in a wrestling match. "I know... I know it's not fair."

Fair.

I wiped my tears away. "It wouldn't be fair if we left you behind." I thrust my chin up sternly. "We have to consider the circumstances."

Dad squeezed my hand, and I squeezed it tightly back, the biggest hand hug ever.

Polaris in the Dark

by Jameyanne Fuller

Jameyanne Fuller is a law student by day, writer by night. Sometimes she sleeps. She was a finalist in the 2014 and 2015 Dell Award, and her short fiction has appeared in *Abyss and Apex* and *Cast of Wonders*. In the rare moments when she isn't studying or writing, Jameyanne can be found reading, playing the clarinet, or plotting world domination with her superheroine seeing-eye dog, Mopsy. She blogs at www.jameyannefuller.com and tweets @JameyanneFuller. She is currently planning a novel about Amèlie and Zoe's adventures as space pirates for good.

The Grand Three-Ring Railroad slowed as it coiled into Saturnalia's airlock. Amèlie crouched under the galley counter. In the main compartment, music and chatter burbled, dice rattled, and Jupiter's tail thumped the wall.

Amèlie felt for the barrel of Earthen olive oil. She found the tap with one hand and pulled the empty bottles from behind the barrel with the other. She'd been repairing and programming other passengers' tech for months, trading for synthetic olive oil. Master couldn't tell the difference, and real Earthen olive oil was valuable. Valuable enough to pay for the surgery.

Now oil slid, silent as silk, into the empty bottle. Her wristband buzzed when it was full. She sealed it, stowed it in her pack, and filled the next.

She was sealing the sixth bottle when Jupiter woofed. Master was coming. Amèlie shoved the bottle into her pack and stuffed it behind the barrel, out of sight, she hoped.

"Move it, Jupiter," Master snapped. Jupiter's paws scrabbled at the floor. A thump. Amèlie winced.

She held her right wrist up to the oven. "Thirty seconds remain on timer," the wristband said. "Twenty-seven seconds."

Amèlie opened a cabinet above her head and felt along the row of canisters as her wristband read the labels. She took down sugar, cinnamon, cardamom, and ginger. The galley door slid open. Jupiter darted in and hid behind her legs. He wasn't a real dog, but he was Amèlie's only friend.

"What's taking so long?" Master hissed. "We're hungry."

"Almost done," Amèlie whispered. The timer pinged and the tray of sizzling scallion cakes slid from the oven onto the counter. Amèlie focused on measuring out the spices. She was quivering. It was ten times worse when she couldn't see the slap coming.

She turned on the cake duster and stood statue-still as it ground and blended the spices, then sifted them over the cakes. "They should have been ready ten minutes ago." Master slapped her face, hard enough to send her spinning to the floor. Jupiter barked, but Master had already grabbed the tray and stomped out.

Amèlie sat up, holding her cheek. "Jupiter?" He crawled to her. She ran her hands over his sides, feeling for breaks in his delicate silicon ribs. This time he was fine.

The train sped up. The airlock had pressurized. They were descending into Saturnalia Station. Amèlie seized her pack and stuffed her clothes and tools around the half dozen bottles of olive oil. She brushed her hand one last time over her inventions, the duster, the talking measuring cup, the all-purpose kitchen sensor. It gave her a pang to leave them, but she couldn't carry anything else. So she slung her pack onto her shoulders and slipped into the corridor, Jupiter at her heels.

Amèlie put six train cars between them and Master before joining the line at a door. She could see artificial daylight through a window, but nothing else. The light shimmered with bright flashes of color and shifting shadows. Amèlie squinched her eyes shut.

She'd always known she could go blind. There was a cure, but Master wouldn't pay for expensive eye surgery. In the last months, the darkness had crept into the corners of her eyes. And just two mornings ago, she had woken to find the center of her vision obscured by a shifting curtain of glittering darkness, a film she could barely see through. Knowing she would go blind was very different from actually going blind. She did not want to be trapped in the dark.

Amèlie pulled out her sunglasses and swapped them for her regular glasses. She hated sunglasses—the dark tint and lack of magnification cut back her already bad vision—but they made the darkness less distracting.

Jupiter leaned his head against her thigh, and she scratched his soft, half-pointy, half-floppy ears. He was meant to be a cross between a Labrador and German shepherd, with huge feet, a small head, and an erect tail. Master had wanted a guard dog. Unfortunately for Master, Amèlie had programmed Jupiter, and while Jupiter's bite still came with fifty thousand volts of electricity, he was loyal only to Amèlie.

Escape the train, Amèlie told herself. *Find a doctor. Get cured. Get off the rings. Easy as pie.*

There was a bump as the train lowered onto the tracks. The door hissed open, and Amèlie and Jupiter jumped down onto the platform.

Amèlie followed the crowd along the platform. Someone ahead wore a helpfully visible scarlet jacket, and she followed it into the terminal.

Sounds echoed brightly all around Amèlie. Shoes clicked. Wheels rumbled. A train whistle blew—not the Grand Three-

Ring, which would stay in Saturnalia for days. People chatted. Vendors shouted about food and news chips. Amèlie smelled fried food, metal, bleach, and the tang of body odor mixed with perfume and hair spray.

As she walked, the sensors on Amèlie's belt and wristbands detected obstacles, and the wristbands vibrated in different places around her wrists, guiding her around them. She gripped the straps of her bag so her wristbands were in a good position to read the signs.

"McDonalds at two o'clock. Saturn's first McDonalds! Solar flare fries and rocket fuel soda for forty-nine centisolars. Top Tech at nine o'clock. All the chips you can dream of. Restrooms at twelve thirty." Amèlie flicked her left thumb across her right wristband to target the bathroom.

Inside, she set her bag on the counter, listening for sounds of anyone else. She ought to do this in a stall, but the bathroom seemed empty, and the idea of cutting out her ID chip next to a toilet made her skin crawl.

Amèlie removed her left wristband then swabbed her wrist with an alcohol wipe and cleaned the paring knife from the galley. She rested her hand palm up on the counter and laid the knife across her wrist. She could feel the small ID chip under the blade. She pressed down. The tip pierced her skin.

"Not like that!" a girl cried. "You'll chop your hand off!"

Amèlie whirled, heart hammering. The bathroom wasn't empty after all.

The girl was a head shorter than her. She had puffy, dark hair—brown or black, Amèlie wasn't sure—and her skin was several shades darker than Amèlie's warm brown. Amèlie guessed she was a year or two younger than her, ten or eleven. She held a bright pink board under her arm. Jupiter growled.

"Unless you're *trying* to chop your hand off," the girl said.

Amèlie gaped.

"Didn't think so. Here." She took the knife, ran the water,

and held Amèlie's wrist over the sink. Then she positioned the knife along the side of Amèlie's wrist, to the left of the veins. "I'm Zoe," she said. Then she cut. Amèlie yelped but held still. "Don't worry," Zoe said. "I've done this three times, and I only ended up in the hospital once." She was doing something that pinched. "What's your name?"

"Am—" She stopped. Even without an ID to track her, she had to be careful. She remembered stories her father had told her, about slaves in the American south centuries ago, following the north star to freedom. "I'm Polaris."

"That's an Earthling star, right? Are you an Earthling?"

"Stars don't belong to just one planet, you know. But yes, I'm Earthen."

"Wow! How'd you get all the way out here? Why are you running away? Here you go!" There was a tugging sensation on Amèlie's wrist, and Zoe set the chip and knife on the counter. She held Amèlie's wrist under the water. "You're ID-free, Polaris."

With her free hand, Amèlie pulled the first aid kit from her backpack. Zoe took it and cleaned and bandaged the wound.

"Thanks." Amèlie decided to answer Zoe's questions. "I need an eye doctor. If they specialize in retinas, that's even better."

Zoe laughed. "My dad's a retina doctor."

"Really?" Could it be this simple? "That's luckier than light-speed! Would you take me to see him? It's important."

"Sure." Zoe didn't sound sure. "But why cut out your ID?"

"It's... complicated." That was stupid. "It's—I'm not coming back to the train."

"You were on the Three-Ring?" Zoe sounded impressed. "Daddy says it's all drinking and drugs and parties, and they just go round and round Saturn."

"That's pretty much it." Amèlie fastened her wristband over the bandage.

"So where will you go?"

"I don't know."

"If I take you to see my father, can I come with you?"

"Um..."

The door opened. Amèlie saw a neon vest. The knife and Amèlie's bloody ID chip were still on the edge of the sink. "Don't move," the woman in the vest said, steps echoing as she strode forward. Jupiter leaped between them, snarling.

Amèlie grabbed her backpack. Zoe seized her hand.

"Stop!"

Zoe towed Amèlie towards the back of the bathroom. Amèlie made out a glowing red splotch. Zoe forced open a door.

"Jupiter, come!" Amèlie screamed. She heard him scramble after them. The moment he was outside, Zoe slammed the door, and they ran.

It wasn't cold out, but it was snowing, and the pavement was slick beneath their feet. Zoe led her around a corner and pulled her behind something hulking and stinking—a dumpster. Amèlie rubbed her eyes.

"What's wrong with your eyes?"

"Well, I'm seeing pink snow."

Zoe laughed. "It is pink, silly."

Amèlie put her sunglasses back on. "I thought the colonies copied Earth. On Earth, snow's white."

"This is Saturnalia. White snow's boring. Mmmm. Pomegranate lemonade."

Amèlie opened her mouth, letting the fat flakes settle on her tongue. They were sweet and sour at the same time.

"So why do you need an eye doctor?"

Amèlie bit her lip. Zoe was a stranger. But she couldn't expect Zoe to help without any explanation. "I have—it's called retinitis pigmentosa. There's a cure, but my parents couldn't afford it and then— Anyway, I'm—I'm going blind. I've never been able to see well, but now it's happening so quickly and—" She was speaking faster and faster, her voice rising. She stopped. "I don't want to be in the dark," she whispered. "I like seeing, even if it's only a little. I like colors." Jupiter thrust his head under her arm.

Zoe was silent for a moment. Amèlie waited. "Why run away?" Zoe finally asked. "Why cut out your ID?"

It wasn't the pity Amèlie had expected. It startled the truth from her. "Master wouldn't pay for a doctor."

"Master?"

"I'm—I was indentured." As Amèlie understood it, most people in the solar system disapproved of indentures, but skyrocketing debt after the transition from credit cards to ID chips a century ago had made it necessary.

Zoe stood. "Can you carry your dog? It'll be faster if we use my hoverboard. Put these on your shoes." Zoe gave her two rubber and metal contraptions. Amèlie fumbled with them for a moment before understanding the shape: metal soles, probably magnetic, with rubber straps that fit around her toe and heel. She put them on and lifted Jupiter into her arms. Then she got on the hoverboard behind Zoe. It hummed. She tried to shift her feet but couldn't. The magnets on her shoes held her in place.

The hoverboard lifted. Amèlie tightened her grip on Jupiter and seized Zoe's shirt with one hand as they zoomed forward and swerved around a corner into a brighter, louder street. Everything was a blur of pink snow and bright lights. They sped up. Zoe whooped as they swooped under a brightly flashing sign even Amèlie could see. They rose rapidly then dropped as something massive flew at them. Amèlie shrieked. Her stomach shot up and wrapped around her ears.

Zoe was laughing. Jupiter was barking furiously in Amèlie's arms. Snow whipped her cheeks, and the warm air blew back her braids. And Amèlie laughed, too. A weight disappeared from her shoulders. She was free. Zoe did a loop-the-loop, and

Amèlie laughed and screamed at the same time. She was free!

They zipped around another corner at breakneck speed. A fountain splashed below them. Zoe dove towards the sound.

"Don't you dare!" Amèlie screamed.

Zoe pulled the hoverboard up and they soared over the fountain.

Finally they slowed. Shadows of high walls rose on both sides. It was quieter. They took a few more turns, descending until the hoverboard's wheels touched ground and they glided to a stop. Amèlie staggered off the board, a smile stretching her cheeks. Her feet tingled. She set Jupiter down, and he cowered against her legs, whimpering. Amèlie pulled the magnets from her shoes and gave them to Zoe.

"Come on. It's upstairs."

Amèlie tapped her left wristband four times quickly so it would guide her to follow Zoe. She walked forward, and when her wristband vibrated, she turned, found the first step, and began climbing. Jupiter scampered behind her.

"We're all the way at the top," Zoe said. "But Daddy won't let me land on the roof, and the fire escape's for emergencies only." Her voice became mocking.

"Isn't there an elevator?" Amèlie asked as they climbed the third flight of stairs.

"Only in buildings with more than ten floors, unless you can't walk. It's for energy conservation and public health."

"How tall is your building?"

"Nine floors."

"You know, I can't climb stairs because I'm blind." Amèlie was so out-of-breath her sarcasm was lost.

"You're doing fine."

"Yeah, but you'd be surprised what people believe."

"Now you tell me."

They had breath only for climbing after that. Amèlie's thigh muscles screamed with every step. Finally, they reached the top.

"Here we are." Zoe's voice was suddenly gloomy.

"You're sure your father won't mind...?"

"Mind? He'll be thrilled."

There was a beep, then hydraulics hissed. "Welcome home, Zoe," said a bright, automated female voice.

Amèlie and Jupiter followed Zoe inside. Their footsteps echoed off the wood floor.

Someone came down a set of stairs towards them. "Another one, Zoe?" a man asked. He sounded exhausted and exasperated.

"Daddy, this is Polaris. She has retinitis pigmentosa. She needs help, and I know you've always wanted to see someone whose retinal deterioration has progressed." She sounded too formal, nothing like the girl Amèlie met in the station.

"Really? Excellent. Let's take a look and see what we can do." Zoe's father crossed the room and placed a big hand on Amèlie's shoulder, ushering her forward. Amèlie stumbled over her own feet.

"I'm Dr. Song," Zoe's father said. "What's the best way for me to help you?"

"I can just follow you," Amèlie said. "My wristbands will vibrate to guide me." She held up her right arm to show him.

"Incredible. Come right this way. I apologize for what I said earlier. Ever since my wife died, Zoe has been bringing home... strays."

Amèlie was suddenly conscious of the fraying cuffs of her faded jeans and her too-small, patched jacket. And Zoe still stood behind her, alone. "Jupiter," she murmured, "stay with Zoe." Jupiter whined. "Stay."

"Tell me," Dr. Song continued, "where did you purchase those wristbands? How do they work?" He moved ahead, and Amèlie followed.

"I designed them myself."

"Incredible. We're coming up on some stairs. Have you invented anything else?"

Amèlie's cheeks burned. "Some talking kitchen tools. I made a universal chip that reads screens and controls, too. I have other ideas, but I could never—" She shut up.

"Tell me, how much vision do you have?"

"I can see light and shadows and colors in the center of my vision," Amèlie said. "Or I could three days ago." At the top of the stairs they turned left.

"You're young for it to be so advanced," he said. "You're eleven? Twelve? And, forgive me, your accent... Are you Earthen?"

"I'm twelve, and yes. I'm from Paris. My mother was French; my father was American. I came to Saturn's rings when I was nine."

"With your parents?" Amèlie imagined his eyebrows rising. She pictured him with bushy eyebrows. "But if they could afford the trip from Earth—"

Amèlie interrupted. "They couldn't afford the surgery. I was on a government waiting list before...." Before Mamman had died in that accident, and her father had gambled everything. Before he'd gambled her.

"Here we are," Zoe's father said, ignoring her trailing silence. He took her elbow and steered her into his office. Wood became tile beneath her feet. He led her to the exam chair. Amèlie set down her bag and sat. A beep—sensors taking her measurements—and the chair rose to the perfect height for the doctor to examine her.

"There's an ID scanner in the armrest to send me your medical records."

"I, uh..." She had no ID now. Could he see the bandage under her wristband? She usually assumed people could see everything—it was safer—but he'd asked her to scan her ID, so maybe he couldn't. She tucked her hand under her thigh. "They aren't on my ID. The doctor my parents got didn't have the tech to upload records to IDs."

"I see," he said slowly. Amèlie winced. "Tell me, when were you diagnosed?"

"I was five. I couldn't see the screens in the front of the classroom."

"And when did your vision start deteriorating?"

"A few months ago. It was just in the corners of my eyes. First the outside corners went dark, then the inside corners. I lost my vision in my left eye faster than my right. It's totally dark now except the center. I can still see some out of the inside corner of my right eye. And the rest of the edges of my vision on the right side are more gray and shifty than black. Except now it's like there's a dark, sort of shimmery screen over everything."

"Hmmm. When you have RP, the cells in your retinas die. That's probably what's happening here. But it's so fast. I wonder if your space travel..." He trailed off then said, "I want to do a complete examination of your eyes, Polaris, so we know exactly what we're dealing with."

He tested Amèlie's vision. How many fingers was he holding up? Could she identify the colors of lights he held before her eyes? Could she tell what was in the picture on his tablet? Read the text on the chart on the wall? On the card a foot from her face? On the card pressed against her nose?

Next, he gave her numbing drops and checked her eye pressure. Amèlie watched the blue light at the tip of his machine press against each of her eyes.

He held a cold, wet, buzzing device against her closed eyelids to take an ultrasound. He couldn't do more advanced scans here at home, he said, but he would take her into the hospital for further tests before they tried anything major.

Then he tilted the chair back, slid plastic rings into her eye sockets to hold her lids open, poured water into her eyes, and stuck a small camera into the water. Amèlie could see the camera's shadow, and she fought not to jerk or cry out. A whimper escaped her.

"You're doing great, Polaris," Dr. Song said.

Finally, it was over. Amèlie had a pounding headache and felt sick to her stomach. She hugged herself, trembling, and waited as Dr. Song read the scans.

"Incredible," he murmured. "Just incredible." Amèlie squirmed. She felt like she was under a microscope. She hated it. "I've never seen anything like this. Polaris, could I incorporate these scans into my research?"

"Sure, but... can we fix it?"

"Of course." He drummed his fingers against something hard—his desk or his tablet. "We have two options. A retinal transplant is cheaper, but less reliable. Your body could reject the transplant, and then you'd be totally blind. Or there's the stem cell surgery. We would harvest some of your own stem cells and inject them into your eyes." Amèlie nearly gagged. "Your stem cells would create new, undamaged cells to build up your rods and cones and restore your vision. But..."

"But...?"

"There isn't any research on the surgery's effectiveness against advanced RP since its early years. Today everyone has surgery as soon as they're diagnosed. And the surgery has developed significantly, so the original research on advanced RP patients isn't valid."

"I don't understand. I thought the surgery was a cure."

"Normally it is a cure, but for such an advanced case, there are still risks. The deterioration in your retinas could be so advanced the stem cells might have no effect. Your body could reject the new retinal cells. Your brain could have developed such that even if we restore your sight, you won't recognize what you see. And we cannot quantify the possibility of success with any certainty."

"So, the surgery might not work, and I could lose all my

vision? But if we don't do it, I'll still lose all my vision?"

"Exactly."

She wanted to try. She didn't want to be in the dark. But she couldn't shake the feeling he cared more about the science of her eyes than fixing them.

"There's also the matter of payment. Without an ID..."

"I have six bottles of real Earthen olive oil. You can have them all." Her voice climbed in desperation. He could report her. They'd send her back to Master.

"I'm afraid even that won't cover the cost. But, if you want, you could work as my research assistant to pay for the surgery. We could document your results over the next few years. And I could give you a good education and scope for your inventing talents."

"So I would work for you," Amèlie said, voice small and flat, "to pay for the surgery." She remembered laughing as she and Zoe swooped through the city on Zoe's hoverboard, flying free at last. She hadn't escaped Master to become someone else's servant. But to have some vision back—any vision back. To not be trapped in the dark. Wouldn't that be worth it?

"What do you think?"

A war raged in her head. In her heart. "I—I don't know." She rubbed her eyes. "I just—I don't know."

"It's a big decision. Think it over. We can talk about it later."

"So," Zoe said, "are you gonna do it?"

"Don't know." They were on the floor of Zoe's room, wrestling with Jupiter for a ball. "It's complicated." Amèlie got the ball away from Jupiter and tossed it in Zoe's direction. Jupiter woofed as he lunged for it, and Zoe giggled. "My parents couldn't afford the surgery," Amèlie said. "Mamman worked three jobs. She saved everything. She'd almost saved enough. But my father tried to win the rest by gambling. Only he lost, and he kept losing. He gambled all Mamman's savings, and he lost *everything*. And then—then there was a hovercab accident,

and Mamman was dead. My father's gambling only got worse
after that. He gambled everything we had. And then he indentured *me* to pay his debts. He said he'd get the money back and
come for me. Of course he didn't. He just kept gambling, and
now he's working off his debts in some asteroid mine. Master
brought me to the Rings, and ever since I've been trapped on
that train, cooking and cleaning and going blind. My father
calls, on my birthday. Sometimes."

Zoe was silent for a moment. "He could still come for you."

"He won't," Amèlie said dully. "His whole life is gambling,
like he can't stop."

"So that's why you ran away," Zoe said.

"Master wouldn't let me see a doctor, and I know my
rights." Amèlie sighed. Jupiter nudged her knee with the ball.
Amèlie took it and tossed it from hand to hand. "If I took
your father's offer, it would be *my* choice, not anyone else's,
but... My vision going is scary, but I've been adjusting all my
life, and the surgery might not work. I could be a slave for
years for nothing." Amèlie leaned against Jupiter. "It might
not be so bad here. He said he'll teach me and let me invent
things."

"And you'd get to stay with me, Polaris," Zoe said.

"It's Amèlie," she said. "My name is Amèlie."

"Amèlie," Zoe said. "That's pretty."

"So why do *you* keep running away?" Amèlie thought she
knew the answer.

"It's stupid," Zoe said. "When Mama died, Daddy buried
himself in his research. He forgot about me. I thought, maybe
he'd remember if I'm gone, but he didn't. The first time I cut
out my ID, when I wound up in the hospital, all he said was
that I interrupted his research. I don't get what's so important.
It's not like Mama died because her retina detached. So then I
thought, maybe I should just go for myself, make my own life. If
he doesn't need me... I know it's stupid."

"It's not stupid," Amèlie said. "I get it." If she stayed, she and Zoe could be friends. Zoe wouldn't be so alone. But Zoe's father would probably spend more time with Amèlie, and Zoe would be more alone than ever. The more she thought about it, the more confusing everything became. She wanted to get her vision back. She wanted to be friends with Zoe. She wanted to be free. Why couldn't she have all of it?

Downstairs, a bell rang. Zoe and Amèlie went out onto the landing in time to hear Zoe's father say, "Can I help you?"

"I'm looking for Dr. Song," Master said. A shudder ripped through Amèlie. She couldn't breathe.

"Amèlie, what's wrong?" Zoe whispered.

Amèlie flung herself back into Zoe's room and snatched up her bag. Zoe followed her. "I have to go," Amèlie said wildly. "I'm not going back with him. I won't. Jupiter, come. You said there's a fire escape? How did he even find me?"

"I bet he's checking all the eye doctors in the city," Zoe said.

It was too much to hope Zoe's father wouldn't tell Master she was there. "You can come if you want, but I have to go *now*."

"I'm coming." Zoe was already rummaging through her drawers and throwing things onto her bed. "Hold out your hands," she said. Amèlie did, and a backpack flopped into her arms. "Can you pack the stuff on the bed? I'll grab my hoverboard. We can go to the port and take my father's ship."

"What's its range?" Amèlie asked, feeling around on the bed. She found rumpled clothes, a plastic box of media chips, and a stuffed sphere with felt bands that after a moment she recognized as a snuggly Saturn. She stuffed it all into Zoe's bag.

"It can get us to Ganymede or Triton, and we can trade for a long-range ship. Or we could go somewhere else on the rings and find a different doctor."

Amèlie bit her lip. She didn't know what she wanted to do. All she wanted right now was to get away before Master could take her back.

Zoe pushed the shoe magnets into Amèlie's hands. "Put these on. We're going to go downstairs to the living room. There's a balcony where we can take off."

Amèlie fitted the magnets over her shoes then lifted her bag onto her shoulders. "Jupiter, come but be quiet," she said.

They crept onto the dark landing. Voices climbed the stairs.

"Can you hear better than everybody else because you can't see?" Zoe whispered.

"Not if you're talking to me," Amèlie hissed.

"I'm looking for a girl," Master was saying. "Little thing. Twelve-years-old. Dark skin. Black hair, usually in braids. She's almost blind, and she ran away. We're trying to find her before she gets hurt."

"A blind girl?" Zoe's father said. Amèlie crossed her fingers, hoping against hope he would say she wasn't there. But no. "As it happens my daughter brought a blind girl home from the station this afternoon." He raised his voice. "Zoe-bear, can you and Polaris come down here?"

"Coming," Zoe called back. To Amèlie, she whispered, "Run. Down the stairs take a left. Go." They pounded down the stairs, wheeled around a corner, and dashed down a hall, the metal soles of their shoes clacking against the floor. Amèlie's heart pounded in her throat.

"Zoe? What are you doing?"

"Nothing, Daddy. We're coming." They reached the end of the hall.

There was a beep, and the same bright voice that had greeted them at the door said, "I'm sorry, Zoe, your father has not granted you permission to enter the living room at this time."

"Zoe!"

"Your parents lock the living room?" Amèlie whispered.

"Since Mama died. But I know the override code."

A click. Several beeps.

Sweat slithered down Amèlie's spine.

"Permission granted," the computer said. The door slid open.

Footsteps pounded on the stairs.

Zoe seized Amèlie's wrist and yanked her through the door. Jupiter bounded after them. Zoe slammed the door, and her fingers thumped against a screen.

A moment later, the computer said, "I'm sorry, Dr. Song, Zoe has not granted you permission."

Amèlie and Zoe tore across the room.

"Look out!" Zoe cried.

Amèlie's shins struck something. She toppled forward. Something shattered. Glass cut her hands and knees, shredding her jeans.

The door slid open. Zoe wasn't the only one with the code. Amèlie made out two shadows in the doorway.

One shadow crossed to Amèlie, and hands pulled her to her feet. "Polaris, are you all right?" It was Zoe's father.

Amèlie pulled free and stumbled back, tears spilling down her cheeks. She wrapped her arms around herself, holding her bleeding hands against her ribs.

"Zoe, my bag," Zoe's father said. "Now." Zoe ran from the room.

Amèlie could not look at the other shadow, still in the doorway. Terror slunk up her back and coiled around her neck. It was a feeling she'd had ever since her father handed her off to Master. She hadn't realized she was always so scared until she wasn't. Being free, even for just these few hours, she hadn't been afraid. She had felt strong. And now it was gone.

Amèlie took another step back, but Zoe's father caught her shoulder and ushered her into a chair. "Let me help you," he said, not unkindly. He pulled Amèlie's hand away from her side. "There's glass in these cuts. We need to get it out." When Zoe returned, he set to work plucking out the glass and cleaning and bandaging her cuts. Amèlie waited.

Zoe's father had tended her hands and was inspecting her knees when Master finally spoke. "I was going to get you the surgery, Amèlie."

Amèlie decided she liked feeling strong, like being free. Liked it more than seeing. "You could have fooled me," she spat. "When I asked, you said no."

"I've reconsidered. I'll pay for the surgery. We'll add it onto your indenture."

"I'm not going back with you!" Amèlie leapt to her feet. Her knees throbbed. "You can't make me!"

"Polaris—Amèlie?—sit, please." Zoe's father pushed Amèlie back down. "Mr. Rolent, I'll buy her indenture, if you're willing. I said she could work as my research assistant to pay for the surgery. Before I knew the situation, of course. I'd give her a good education and cultivate her inventing talent, and she'd have a friend in my daughter."

Master considered. "I admit I could have done a better job caring for the girl. I did promise her father I would look after her. But I never wanted to be a parent. I accept your offer, Dr. Song."

And so it was decided. Zoe's father finished tending Amèlie's knees, and he and Master discussed the price of her indenture. She would get the surgery, and she would work off the rest of her father's debts and now her own as Dr. Song's assistant. It wouldn't be so bad. She wouldn't be trapped on the train. She and Zoe could be friends. She could learn to invent new things. And if the surgery worked, she would see again.

But if the surgery didn't work, she would be in the dark, suddenly and permanently. Did she really want to risk everything on a surgery that would cost her years and might not work? Was it really worth it?

If she was honest, it wasn't about her vision anymore. It was about her freedom.

"What do you want to do, Amèlie?" Zoe's father asked. "Pay off the surgery by working for Mr. Rolent or for me?"

Amèlie breathed in, out. Stood. Reached back for the chair and guided herself behind it, placing the chair between her and Master. "What if I don't want the surgery?"

"But that's what this little rebellion was all about, wasn't it?" Amèlie heard the sneer in Master's voice.

"It might not work," Amèlie said. "What if I don't want to do it?"

"Then you work for me for the rest of your indenture," Master snarled.

"Or you work for me," Zoe's father said, "I'll still buy your indenture. But really, while there are risks, I'm confident it will be successful, even if we can't restore *all* your vision. And if you don't go through with the surgery, you *will* go blind."

"So, what do you choose?" Master asked.

"Zoe?" Amèlie asked.

"Yep," Zoe said beside her.

Amèlie found Zoe's elbow. "I won't work for anyone anymore," she said.

Zoe moved. There was a thunk and a skidding sound—wheels on wood—as she stepped on the end of her hoverboard, flipping it up into her hand.

"No!" Master yelled.

Zoe spun, Amèlie clinging to her arm, and they raced for the balcony. She felt the air change as they made it outside. Then someone grabbed her bag, yanking her back.

"You're not getting away again!" Master shouted.

Amèlie kicked back and twisted from his hold. "Jupiter! Zap!"

Jupiter snarled. A thump. Master screamed. Amèlie saw the blue-white flash as fifty thousand volts of electricity shot from Jupiter's teeth into Master. He hit the ground so hard the balcony shook.

"Jupiter!" Amèlie held out her arms, and he vaulted into them. He rubbed his head against her cheek. Then Amèlie found the hoverboard with her toe and stepped on. The board hummed to life and her feet stuck fast. And then they were flying.

After a few moments, Zoe said, "That was incredible."

Amèlie didn't feel incredible. "They could still come after us."

"They won't. Trust me. They won't." Zoe's voice broke. It occurred to Amèlie that Zoe *wanted* her father to come after them. She hadn't removed her ID.

They turned sharply, rose through the air then dropped again.

"Where do you want to go?" Zoe asked. "We can do anything we want. We could be space pirates. For good, of course."

Amèlie laughed, but she remembered real sunlight on honey-colored stone and rolling green hills. Real, sweet wind blowing back her hair. Real snow on her tongue. She remembered feeling safe and strong and brave and free. "Earth," she said. "I want to go home. I want to see it, one more time, before—before I can't anymore."

"I'm sorry," Zoe said, "about... the surgery."

"It's all right." Amèlie was surprised to realize she meant it. It was all right. "I've been losing vision for years. I'll figure it out. I'll miss it, but I'd rather be free."

In the twilight outside the bright city center, Amèlie could ignore her encroaching darkness. She looked up at the purplish sky. Bright spots winked and flashed across her vision. She imagined they were stars. She focused on one shimmering dot, and pretended it was Polaris, the north star. The star that led slaves to freedom centuries ago. The star that burned still, through the darkness, guiding Amèlie home.

Dance Like You're Alone in Your Environmental Pod

by Eric Del Carlo

Eric Del Carlo's short fiction has appeared in *Analog*, *Asimov's*, and is upcoming in *Year's Best Adventure and Military SF Volume 3*. He cowrote with his father Victor Del Carlo the urban fantasy novel, *The Golden Gate Is Empty*. His latest solo book is the YA title *The Vampire Years* from Elder Signs Press.

"Asoka! Outside, I hear a... breather."

Asoka clicked back angrily over the com, "You don't know how to be funny, Chloe. Don't try."

But of course Chloe wouldn't let it go. "Air is going in and out of its *lungs*. Oh! It's scratching at the hatch now..."

Such scares had been effective when they were both twelve and back in the Big Cave. But now they were two years older, with their own pods, out reclaiming the Earth. Although "reclaim" was a bad term according to every Lighthouse Asoka had ever known. The larger world wasn't theirs to conquer or command. Instead, they were supposed to "cooperate" with it.

Fine. Asoka could do that. Even with Chloe being so immature.

Then Chloe said the thing she must have been saving up. "It... it wants my pod. Asoka, I think the breather outside used to *live* in this pod!"

It put a chill into her, despite everything she did to prevent it. The scare was too precise. They were, after all, cruising about in pods built by the breathers. Of course, the environmental seals had decayed, and all the unnecessary air-scrubbing equipment had been removed, but the pods still functioned as durable transports.

Asoka loved hers, a love burgeoning yet intense. The longer you had a pod, the more it became yours. So the olders said, and they proved it with how they decorated the insides with all sorts of fun junk they found. Javor's pod had bones and crystals epoxied to the walls. Tirunesh's was strung with beads of melted metal and metaplastic. Cort's, ivy—the new, tough, gummy ivies that had evolved these past centuries. They were crawling all over the interior, still alive, still growing. You could hardly move around inside Cort's pod.

Asoka's was barren but for the bag of travel supplies she'd unpacked into it. The mobile living unit still had more of its previous occupant's personality imprinted on it than her own. Which was why Chloe's comment was twitching her so badly.

"Shut up, Chloe," she clicked at the communications grille. But she heard, to her chagrin, how quivery her tongue sounded flicking against her teeth. Like a frightened child's.

"It wants its pod back! No! It's getting inside—"

She dropped her fist on the button to kill the com, even though they were supposed to stay in touch on this cruise as much as possible, since they were out of range of the Big Cave. They had both more than qualified on pod operations, had absorbed years of wisdom and practical knowledge from the Lighthouses, and their exploration area was a tame one. But none of that meant she had to put up with such teasing.

She and Chloe had always been friends. And rivals. And adversaries. And friends again.

Asoka kicked at the floor plate. She was supposed to cooperate with the whole world? She couldn't even cooperate with her best friend.

A Lighthouse would expect better of her. But a Lighthouse, those patient mentoring presences in the Big Cave, would also tell her to forgive herself, so long as she tried harder next time. She would. But next time could wait a little while.

She concentrated on her movement controls. The saucer-shaped vehicle handled well, its gimbal-mounted treads keeping her level. She would remain safe in here. The pod could take hard terrain, but this was an easy sector. It was also picked over. She wouldn't be finding any treasures out here, nothing to start personalizing her interior.

That idea touched her with a soft thrill. What would she make of her pod? She looked from her screens around the circular enclosure. Bare sloping walls, struts, wedges of the interior set aside for sanitation, food prep, sleeping. She could live in here, which was the point of this first real exercise away from home. Maybe this was a soft sector, but it was still subject to exploration. She was supposed to cruise about, observing, investigating—and cooperating.

The blank walls suddenly seemed too empty, and she winced, returning her attention to the exterior screens. She clicked out a quiet curse. Did she know enough about herself to begin decorating the inside of her pod? What artifacts or debris would she find that might seem suitable to express her personality? So far all she'd shown was that Chloe could still scare her with ridiculous stories.

The ground around her was flat and stony. The sky was mucus, soft and oozing. She saw no features anywhere, nothing to report. The interesting stuff was farther out. It was where Cort's ivies grew, where the olders took their pods into breather ruins.

She both longed to travel that far and dreaded it. Humans were ready to explore the Earth once again, so said the conical mobile Lighthouses that had been Asoka's caretakers and educators. But, the gentle machines cautioned, the Earth might not be ready for *them*. Humans had despoiled the world once. They needed to proceed carefully, conscientiously, making sure they worked within the planet's natural balances, not against them.

Of course, Asoka preferred to think that the breathers had spoiled everything, not humans. Not her people.

She had a good feel for the pod's operations, and that touch was only getting better with practical application. She forgot about Chloe and ranged about the exploratory sector. Some part of her truly realized for the first time that this was what pod life would be like. Sitting for hours at the controls—dogged observation, no excitement, no heroics.

It must be why, in part, you uniquely ornamented your pod. It was why you returned from a cruise strutting like a champion, bragging of sights seen, of distances covered. The instances of useful observation and meaningful accomplishment must be very rare.

This was a heavy, dull revelation, but Asoka wasn't demoralized by it. Rather, she decided it was another step toward maturity. She had been trusted with a pod. Now she could be trusted with the truth of life inside a pod.

She cruised until the mucosal twilight hemorrhaged into night, then she brought her pod to a halt.

Asoka reactivated the com while she made and ate her dinner. Chloe wasn't sulky; she didn't even mention being cut off earlier. Instead, she gabbled about plans for her own pod's interior decor, wild concepts. The best, Asoka thought, was to paint the inside like the ancient night sky, seething with icy pinpricks of starlight and a moon at some phase or other.

The Lighthouses promised that such a sky still existed, above the methanogenic murk. Asoka believed them, though it wasn't a matter of belief. Lighthouses discouraged faith. They presented facts, with supporting evidence.

They had many, many records of the world before the Great Belch and the Last Gasp. The machines knew of the breathers and the wreckage they'd left behind. Asoka's people were lucky the breathers' pods had survived so well in the Big Cave. It allowed this first generation of viable humans to roam the Earth freely.

Well...not *freely*. Cautiously. Prudently. Asoka understood how precious this second chance was for the humans.

She and Chloe talked over the com until Chloe started yawning. Despite the monotony of the day—Chloe's cruising had been no more adventurous than hers—they'd both been worn out, as if from excitement.

"Remember to keep your feet tucked in," Chloe clicked just before signing off.

It annoyed Asoka. Her friend couldn't resist one last bad joke. When they were just girls, the scary story had gone like this: you'd first feel a breather's breath on your feet as it snuck up on your dorm bed. But somehow covering your feet would keep a breather away. Children's stuff. The Lighthouses tried to stop such tales from circulating, but apparently you couldn't completely control kids.

Still, it was enough to make Asoka twitchy again. She told herself she wasn't tired yet and retrieved her entertainment device. It was programmed with lots of things from the archives. She liked old art. So did many other people. Some of the olders—those who had lived as long as twenty-five years (twenty-five!)—had started to try to make their own art, as well as developing the technical skills they were all trained in.

Asoka thought Chloe might be an artist one day, as evinced by her idea to paint the inside of her pod like the night sky. Asoka didn't have any artistic leanings; at least she didn't think she did. But she did have an ear for music. Old music. The kind with breather singing in it.

It rang suddenly in her pod as she chose a file. It was a wild jumping sound. She hadn't yet played music in here, and the acoustics were great, seeming to double the intensity of the noise. The audible energy seized her. Nerve endings popped. Her flesh prickled deliciously.

Then the vocals hit. The words. Breather words.

Everyone had seen footage of breathers in the old world. Everyone knew how they had talked. People said it looked like they were constantly vomiting, the way they moved their mouths and heaved sound out of themselves. She understood that revulsion. Those creatures had sucked in air and spewed it out, every moment of every day of their lives. They'd had *lungs*, organ sacks convulsing inside them that forced this sucking.

Of course, the atmosphere before the Great Belch had been a lot different than the muck now. Still, it was air—*air*—that the singer on this recording was using to make these lively sounds. She or he was shaping the outgoing air with his or her lips and tongue, funneling it into specific forms. The individual noises were distinct. It wasn't the cacophony most people imagined. This was language as precise as the tongue flicks and teeth chatters of humans.

But to her it was even more. The singing was what drove this frantic, blaring, old world music. The passionate lyrics took the song up to a whole new level, where the rhythms and words merged into a beatific splendor.

Asoka understood the words. She knew breather speech, even though the Lighthouses taught nothing beyond the basics of the old language. She had sought out further teachings, doing it in secret, aware that people would find deep interest in anything to do with the breathers... unseemly. But she had been captivated by breather music from the first time she'd heard it. She had wanted to understand the strange air sounds that went with the jangling crashing melodies.

In her pod the raucous music got her body moving. She was on her feet. Her arms started to swing. She stepped one way, then back the other. She spun in a circle. She gyrated her bony hips.

And she moved her mouth. She was as leery of the weird alien breathers as anybody. Even knowing what she did, it seemed impossible that any living thing should need to inhale and exhale in order to stay alive. What a cumbersome, evolutionarily perilous necessity that was.

Nonetheless, she "sang" along with the memorized song. She made no sound, but her lips contorted in that ancient way, in perfect time to the long-dead vocalist on the recording. Some of the words were quite strange, but most were universal, about joy and fear, love and loss. They touched her. She danced wildly, giving herself unselfconsciously to the music. This was what she would do with her environmental pod, she realized. Maybe the decor didn't matter so much. Maybe it was what she *did* in her private space, where she could express herself uninhibitedly, that counted.

A half hour later she had sufficiently tired herself. Anything Chloe had said earlier was more or less forgotten. She went to her bunk to sleep her first night away from the Big Cave. Outside, the wind was rising, the Earth's own pernicious exhalations, so full of the unlocked methane that had killed off all the breathers in the Last Gasp long ago.

She thought a bad dream awoke her, something about a breather's breath on her exposed feet, even though she'd dutifully tucked her toes under her cover. But no trace of a dream lingered in her head. Then, in those first gummy-eyed seconds, she guessed it must be the wind rousing her. Not just wind, though. Gusts. Very strong. Rocking the pod.

But that wasn't it, either. What had pried her up out of her heavy sleep was the knocking. On the metaplastic skin of the pod. Knocking from *outside.*

Asoka jolted up from the bunk. She suddenly felt very vulnerable. The pod wasn't hermetically sealed. It no longer mattered if the atmosphere got inside. But she had locked the hatch like she was supposed to, and she should be safe in here from any brute environmental effects, such as this storm that had apparently come up.

There was still life on the Earth. Sturdy strains of flora, swarms of bacteria, certain sea life, some insects and grubs. And humans, like Asoka. But explorations outside the Big Cave hadn't as yet turned up anything of size, anything mammalian, anything big enough to have knuckles. Knuckles like those belonging to the frightening life form her mind's eye conjured. Knuckles on the hand knocking on the outside of the pod. Which could only be the hand of a... a...

"Breather."

She clicked the word aloud and immediately cringed, though surely the clack of her teeth couldn't be heard from outside, over the howling wind lashing grit on the exterior. Maybe that was it! Maybe the wind was strong enough to pick up stones, and they were being pounded against the pod—

No. Too rhythmic. Too deliberate. Even a loose part on the pod's exterior wouldn't hammer so steadily in the chaotic winds. There was intent in the knocking, even a humanlike urgency. She strained her ears. It seemed to be coming from the other side of the hatch, like someone begging to be let in. A chill of fear tingled her skin.

She remembered her exterior screens and hurried to check them, but the outside views were useless, just a frenzy of blowing sand, without definition.

A gust struck, and the pod rocked, a harsher jolt than any yet. Utensils from dinner clattered to the floor plating. She herself had to grab an overhead brace to keep from stumbling. Lights glowed inside her pod, which no longer felt safe at all. Something groaned underfoot, as if the gimbals were struggling to keep the vehicle level.

There were protocols for emergencies, she frantically reminded herself. She had been trained. She lunged for the com.

"Chloe. *Chloe.*" Again she flinched, fearful of giving herself away to whoever or whatever was outside. Chloe's would be the only pod within communication range.

After a long delay, Chloe responded. Her tongue flicked tiredly, and her teeth clicked with displeasure. "It's so late, Asoka—"

"I'm in trouble!" Suddenly she couldn't get the words out. The storm. The straining gimbal. Everything bunched up in her mind. Without warning she heard herself saying, "There's a breather knocking on my hatch!"

Another delay. Chloe came back on, testily, "You can't even come up with something original? Go to sleep, Asoka." She cut the link.

Asoka saw the horrible mistake she'd made. Chloe didn't respond again, despite Asoka's desperate hails. Another brutal slap of wind jarred the floor out from under her, and she fell. The sound of overstressed metaplastic rose to a shriek, and there came a further drastic jolting. Abruptly the pod canted at an alarming angle, and she found herself tumbling toward the hatch.

The storm must be very localized, some remote mental part of her concluded. Or else Chloe would know something was really wrong. In the centuries since the Great Belch resulting from the catastrophic loss of the planet's permafrost, the climate had gradually stabilized. But meteorologic episodes of this level of violence still occurred.

Just above her head as she lay in a tangle on the floor, the knocking sounded loudly. She looked up wide-eyed at the dogged hatch. She felt the panic in that pounding. Then she heard the words. She heard the *voice.*

"Let me in, please! If you know any mercy, open this door!"

Not clicks and flicks, these. They were vocalizations, backed by lung power. Breather speech.

"For hell's sake, take me in or I'll die out here!"

It was, simply, too much like a scary story. An authentic breather, a creature of the old world, was out there asking for admittance. It was beyond belief. Nightmares were never supposed to turn real.

But Asoka recognized, from listening to the ancient songs in the archives, the anguish in the creature's voice. He or she was terrified, fearing for her or his life. Could Asoka just leave the breather outside?

Another concentrated gust knocked the pod. Sand scoured the exterior. It sounded strong enough to flail flesh from bones.

"Help! Please! H—" Exhaustion in the voice now, despair.

She knew how they sang. She knew their jubilations and sorrows. She had shared in the old music.

Her hand shook as she raised it over her head. She grasped the wheel and pulled. It stuck, stubbornly, but she put up her other hand and yanked until it spun. The hatch came unlocked. She scampered halfway up the new slope of her floor. Her hand-sized entertainment unit had fallen and fetched up against the base of a strut next to her. Distantly she hoped it hadn't broken.

With a clang the hatch opened. A shapeless form huddled there, a frenzied darkness in motion behind it. Wind yowled into the pod, clattering grit everywhere.

The creature hung a moment then dropped down to the canted floor. With hands, it heaved the hatch shut and turned the locking wheel. The wind fell back to its duller roar.

With eyes so wide they stung in her sockets, Asoka stayed absolutely still and beheld her visitor.

The amorphous thing straightened, and as it did, its outer skin shrugged, drably colored, billowy. But not a skin at all, Asoka quickly saw. It was a tattered cloak, woven from what looked to be natural fibers, unlike the synthetic clothing she and the other humans wore. The Big Cave was well-stocked with materials, including a self-sustaining plankton farm, which the Lighthouses taught everyone to tend.

Hands pushed back a hood, and a face peered out. Eyes swept the pod's interior, then, bringing a fresh chill to her, zeroed in on her where she huddled on the inclined floor plates.

"Thank you for letting me in," said the breather in breather language, heaving the words out of itself. *Him*self, Asoka amended. Plainly this was a male.

She winced involuntarily at the sounds. They were so aggressive, impacting her eardrums heavily. It was one thing to listen to ancient singers; it was something else to be in the same room with a living being making actual old world vocalizations, pushing air out of lungs. To be in the same room with a... breather.

Every spooky story she'd heard as a child regarding these creatures crowded at once into her brain. It made for a paralytic fear. What intensified her terror, of course, was that there weren't supposed to *be* any breathers, not anymore, not since the Last Gasp, when the adulteration of the Earth's atmosphere had reached its final, lethal levels. Even the breathers who had founded the Big Cave hadn't survived that. They'd had to build the Lighthouses to carry on the work with the genetic vats, where slowly, over centuries, the first viable generation of humans was produced. Asoka's generation. Humans unencumbered with the need to suck and expel air.

Hers was the new natural species. Feasible. Functional.

This creature, this person, this *man* simply could not exist. He was a fancy, an impossibility. Yet...

He shrugged again, and the whole cloak fell away, revealing a body garbed in skimpier garments, ones leaving bare arms and legs. How smooth his skin was, Asoka noted. How dry. Not moistly porous like hers. Still, he was so like her in so many ways. He had eyes and limbs and joints, so very human, looking like breathers did in archival footage.

Only the chest appeared different. Far broader than his build would account for. His upper torso swelled like a bellows with every inhalation and compressed visibly with each exhale. It was a fascinating, lurid process to watch.

They had been staring at one another for some time. Asoka cast her mind back over the past few moments. He had thanked her for letting him in.

"You're welcome," she clicked back.

Her words didn't register, she saw immediately. He frowned at the sounds, shook his head. "I'm sorry. We don't understand your language yet."

Asoka started. *We?* The implications of that word seized her, but she shoved aside her curiosity for the moment. She sat up on the floor but didn't yet stand. The storm continued to perilously rock the pod.

He was still recovering from being out in it. His hair was in wild disarray, and he had abrasions on those places where the wind must have gotten sand under his cloak. He wore a belt, and on it hung something in a case, she noticed for the first time. An implement. A... knife? Yes. He was armed, then.

He smiled at her. "I don't suppose you understand me?" He made a strange ratcheting sound in his throat. A laugh, Asoka realized with wonder.

Holding his gaze with her own, she nodded back at him.

He frowned once more. "Is that a nod?" he asked incredulously.

She nodded again.

His face clouded in thought. After a time he asked, "Can you tell me how many three is?"

She raised her hand, extended three fingers. His eyes went as wide as hers had been when he first entered the pod. "That's incredible!" His shout was thunderous. He saw her recoil. "I'm sorry. It's just... You can... Incredible. How did you learn?"

She felt an odd surge of pride, like when the Lighthouses

commended a lesson she had adroitly completed. She considered a moment, then reached out for her entertainment device. She restarted a song from earlier, glad to see the unit wasn't damaged. When the vocals came, she mouthed along with them, syncing up her lip movements perfectly.

He watched, transfixed, then shook his head again, but it didn't seem to be a negating gesture this time. She shut off the recording. "That is amazing. We never would've imagined... My name is Essex, by the way."

"Asoka," she clicked automatically. Then, thinking carefully how to make the shapes, she mouthed her name in breather language, mostly just to see if she could do it.

Essex peered closely at her lips. He was old enough to have hair on his face. He was as old as the oldest older she knew, maybe even a few years beyond. "A..." He frowned. "Asoka? That's your name?"

It startled a smile out of her. Her name, rendered in breather speech! As Essex would say, *incredible.*

"You've got a nice smile, Asoka."

Warmth drove the last chill of fear from her. She didn't think she had to be afraid of this man, even though he was so strange and carried a knife. She realized she had a thousand questions she wanted to ask him.

The pod jerked sharply again. She wondered how severe the damage to it would be. She was trained in repair, but this might be beyond her.

"I never would have disturbed you in here if I hadn't got caught in this blow," Essex said solemnly.

She mouthed, *You're welcome here.*

He read her lip's movements carefully. He looked contrite. "We're not supposed to even let you see us."

We? she asked, her intense curiosity resurging.

He let out air in a way that seemed to indicate exasperation. It was a sigh, Asoka realized. She had already decided that when he spoke it didn't look like vomiting. This breather and his speech weren't repulsive.

Essex sat, his back to the wall below the hatch. He looked resigned. "We know about you. About the sanctuary in the caverns. We've passed the stories down through the years. We didn't know if you would ever come out, or what you would be like when you did. Then you emerged and started scouting, in these—" He gestured.

Pods.

"Pods. Okay. We've watched you. You have a lot more equipment that works. We've got some radio gear, which lets us monitor you. We're still working on your language."

Keep trying, she mouthed then clicked a little smugly, "You'll pick it up."

His laugh sounded harsher this time. "I get it. You know my language so I can learn yours. Then again, we've been watching you for the past decade without you knowing. We move with stealth. We blend in with our surroundings. We know all this terrain."

They were cooperating with the world, Asoka perceived. Following the precepts of the Lighthouses without ever having heard them. Again, she was touched with awe.

But when he struck his knee with his fist, she jumped. "And now I've ruined the operation!"

How? She found she didn't like to see him upset.

"I blundered. I let you know we exist. All because I came too close and couldn't get to cover when this damn sand devil sprang. We wanted to approach your people one day, but only when the time was right. When we were sure about you."

Asoka struggled to absorb it. These were crazy conditions in which to learn something of such immense magnitude. The pod juddered, and then seemed to tip a little farther, though that might just be her own sense of disorientation. The groaning rose again from beneath the floor-plates. Maybe one of the treads was set to snap off.

Essex was worriedly looking around. She waved a hand to draw attention then mouthed, *Why so cautious about us?*

His eyes narrowed as he worked out her silent words. He gazed gravely. "Because we don't know if you're still human. I mean...you don't breathe. Do you?"

Asoka's mouth fell open in shock, a gesture unfamiliar to her but which felt appropriate to the situation. Essex's words were ludicrous. Outrageous! Not human? Her people? They were the only true humans on the Earth. They could travel freely. They didn't need hermetically sealed environments to keep them alive, like the breathers of old who had sucked up the final breathable bits of air before the Last Gasp shut the atmospheric cycle down forever.

But... Essex was here, alive, *breathing.* How was it possible?

My people, she mouthed distinctly, *are human. We want only to explore, to cooperate.*

The groan from below became a new shrieking, more frantic than before, and something gave with a fatal tear and a thud. The pod tilted now at a demented angle, and Asoka rolled helplessly toward the hatch again.

But Essex was there to catch her this time. His strong arms snared her, and his solid body cushioned her. The winds outside churned with even greater madness. Surely the pod was going to be torn apart.

Essex continued to hold her. She put arms around his neck, feeling his dry skin, and held him in return. It was oddly comforting, she discovered to her surprise, to feel and hear the steady draw and expulsion of air from the lungs inside his massive chest as they tried to ride out the storm.

The "sand devil" moved off and must have brushed the area where Chloe had brought her pod to a rest because she reactivated the com, clicking worriedly. Plainly, though, she wasn't experiencing the brunt of the storm, which had indeed severely damaged a gimbal-mounted tread on Asoka's pod. Asoka was immobile. It was still night. She would look at it closely in the morning, to see if it could be repaired.

She tried to tell Chloe something of her visitor, but her friend's infuriated disbelief made her give up rather quickly. Chloe would just have to meet him tomorrow. If he stayed, that was.

He was staying long enough to talk more, at least. Asoka shared some of her food with him, which he handled curiously. He was used to hunting and foraging, he said. *Hunting what?* she wanted to know. With a knowing look, he said that the small new animals of the world had been avoiding these mobile pods as well.

It made her think that despite all their cautious explorations, her people really knew very little about this current incarnation of the Earth.

How did your people survive? she asked. It was the crucial question, above all others. It would be the answer they would most want back at the Big Cave.

Essex' rugged face turned suspicious, but she just asked him again, insistently. He said, "Somebody survived. Somebody was able to breathe the sludge and not die from it. And if one somebody could, then a tiny fraction of the whole population could do it, too. Those people held out, hung on. They met up. They bred. There was only one critical trait to select for—better lungs, adaptive respiratory systems. So that's who survived, generation after generation."

The simplicity stunned Asoka. There had been no grand second experiment outside the Big Cave, at least none that Essex's people—and they were many enough to be a *people*, he said—were aware of. His kind—barrel-chested, every one—had endured by brute genetic will. They were given poison to breathe and they breathed it, and they survived.

There remained a language barrier, in spite of how well they were communicating. He couldn't quite sound out "anaerobic respiration" when she tried to explain how humans—how *her people*, she amended—respired without lungs, how the vats had given them the ability to absorb oxygen through the moist dermis. For her part, she didn't know what he meant when he said their two kinds needed to avoid an "Eloi and Morlock" situation.

His people had a culture, albeit a movable one steeped in secrecy and oral tradition. Her people were still essentially rooted in the Big Cave, despite how far they had ranged, isolated in their environmental pods.

Essex was uncertain if he should be the one to push their two kinds together. If he left now, it was unlikely Asoka would ever be able to convince anyone of his visit, much less that he'd brought of many others like him, inhabiting the landscape just out of sight. Hers would become another fable for the Lighthouses to discourage.

They sat near each other in the tilted pod. She put a hand to his arm. She felt empathy for this creature—for this person. The same as she had connected with the ancient breather songs she so liked to dance to and mouth along with.

Essex looked down wistfully at her hand where it touched him. "Asoka—" he started.

No, she said. And then she spoke it for him, her name, as she had always known it. She clicked it, with tongue flick and teeth clack. She mouthed for him to repeat it as she'd said it.

He laughed but quieted when he saw her expression. They weren't so different that he couldn't recognize an upset girl.

He tried it. Flick. Clack. Clumsy tongue, teeth with no finesse. But he persisted at her insistence, and on the sixth attempt he said her name passably well in the beautiful breathless language of her people. She smiled warmly.

"Okay, Asoka. I'll stay until your friend arrives in the morning. Then... We'll see what happens."

Fluffy Pets are Best
by Holly Schofield

Holly Schofield is the author of more than fifty short stories. Her works have appeared or will soon appear in *Lightspeed, Clockwork Canada, Tesseracts,* the Aurora-winning *Second Contacts, Cast of Wonders, Escape Pod, Brave New Girls, Analog,* and many other publications throughout the world. She travels through time at the rate of one second per second, oscillating between the alternate realities of city and country life. For more of her work, visit hollyschofield.wordpress.com.

Lissa angrily pushed the hand vacuum along the narrow shelf, sending her 3D-printed plastic animals tumbling onto the floor.

She'd woken up feeling great, looking forward to being one day closer to getting a pet. Before she'd opened her eyes, she'd hugged herself under her microfiber blanket, thinking about how it would be. Mom had promised that Kavi, the geneticist on the big spaceship that orbited overhead, would take a lab rat from the stasis chamber and unfreeze it for her as soon as they got back. Lissa could already imagine stroking its velvety ears and feeding it bits of soy-cheese.

The week until they were back up on the big spaceship would go quickly, too. Since her birthday two weeks ago, she was finally old enough to help her mom with the biological research on this not-very-explored planet. Today they were going to go on a long hike to the next valley to collect samples. It was going to be super fun.

But things had rapidly become un-fun. Lissa had thrown off her blanket and looked over at her mom in the other bunk, only a meter away in the tiny bedroom of their temporary habitat on Skag3's surface.

"Morning, Mom."

"Hmm." Mom was frowning and reading her tablet, exactly as she had been last night when Lissa had gone to sleep.

"Didn't you sleep?" Lissa asked, rubbing her eyes and sitting up. Lissa had dreamed about a baby pet rabbit snuggling up against her. She could still remember how it smelled of carrots and how soft its creamy white fur had been.

"A bit," Mom said, "and good morning. I'm afraid I have some bad news, though, kiddo. Kavi just messaged me that there are no more lab rats in the inventory. I'm sorry."

"Noooo!" That was so stinky! She was finally old enough and responsible enough for a pet and now there wasn't *anything* furry for millions of light years.

"I'll get you a rat or something after we get back to Earth. I promise," said Mom. "It's only six months away. And, for now, Kavi said she has a slushrock set aside for you."

Lissa pushed her face into her pillow, trying not to cry. Six months was forever. And slushrocks were tiny dull gray molluscs from Alpha Centauri used in Kavi's ethical research like the rats were. You could pat a slushrock's gritty little head with a fingertip and feed it stinky little food pellets. But that was about all.

Mom rubbed Lissa's shoulder. "But at least we have today's adventure. Come on, kiddo, let's get some breakfast." She zipped up her coverall and left the tiny bedroom.

Why did everything have to be so stinky? This hike to the valley better be fun. Lissa fished around on the floor for yesterday's coveralls. She was halfway dressed when Mom called out,

"Oh, darn it, Lissa. Why didn't you..." Her voice trailed off.

"Mom?" Lissa hopped out into the narrow hallway, holding her second sock.

In the main room, Mom was stuffing sample cases into her large backpack. Her lips were tight. "You'll be staying here." She snapped shut the pack's electrostatic latches.

"Mom! How come?" Lissa hopped farther into the room. "You *said* I'm old enough and responsible enough now to come with you on all the trips."

"And what else did I say?" Mom shot a glance at the pile of bent wires, hand tools, and electronic components that Lissa had left on the worktable. Then she frowned at the mess of crumbs and empty food wrappers on the small fold-out shelf where they ate their meals. Then she frowned at Lissa.

"I *will* clean up! I will! The whole hab! After we get back from the valley." Keeping the habitat tidy was one of Lissa's duties this trip so Mom would have more time to carry out the research project. Lissa was supposed to have done her chores last night, but she'd been working on building a cage for the rat instead.

"Responsible people don't procrastinate. Responsible people just do what they're supposed to without being asked a hundred times." Mom slung the backpack over her shoulders.

Lissa said desperately, "You didn't tidy up the water filter! You're just as bad!" The dismantled filter equipment took up most of the floor. They depended on the filtering system for all the water they used—for drinking, cooking, washing—and Mom had been doing routine maintenance on it last night.

"Nice try, honey. I will, tonight. There wasn't time yesterday. As it was, I worked on reports until long after you were in bed and for an hour before you woke up." Mom massaged her neck and sighed. "I could have used your help collecting samples today, sweetie. This project is bigger than I'd anticipated. It's too bad you can't come with me." She sounded disappointed now, rather than angry. "But you can't. Not this time. And I'm re-thinking whether the slushrock is a good idea or not. Maybe by next birthday, you'll show enough responsibility to have a pet."

After an extra big hug, Mom had left through the airlock and headed into the sparkling forest. Lissa had watched out the window until she was out of sight.

So now Lissa was stuck in the hab while Mom was exploring a new place, out of radio contact. Through the hab's window, white sunlight shone enticingly, practically begging her to come outside. "It's not *fair!*" she told an orange plastic snake before placing all her toys back on the shelf and patting the head of her favorite one: a furry, purple Irish wolfhound. Mom was scrupulously fair about most things, like splitting a dessert packet into exact halves, but other things, more important things, she just *didn't* understand.

The small galley where they prepared their meals needed cleaning next. Lissa sighed. Being grumpy was silly. She need-ed to change her mood. But how? Pretending everything was not so stinky sometimes worked. She forced herself to whistle a happy tune while she put food wrappers in the recycler. Next, she scrubbed at a spot of tomatoey food paste on the wall—how had that gotten there?—and sighed again. Whistling wasn't working. Maybe she should try singing, instead. *"Far away from Earth, we'll make a new berth,"* she sang loudly, mak-ing up the words.

Six repetitions of her little song didn't help. She was still grouchy. In the main room, her empty backpack slouched against the wall next to the spare sample cases, the ones she should have been filling today. Singing even more loudly, she vacuumed in a wide circle around the water filter parts spread on the floor, careful to avoid sucking up a nut or a computer chip. Last night, Mom had explained each component in the water filter as she'd dismantled it, and Lissa had been fascinat-ed. Someday Mom might consider Lissa skilled enough to tinker with it. But—Lissa stuck out her tongue—only if she proved herself "responsible."

Next, she tucked away the extra plastiwire and electronic bits left over from building the rat cage. She admired her construction job as she centred the cage itself on the now-tidy worktable. It was a large, almost-perfect cube, and she'd added some electrostatic latches for extra security. It would have made a fine, big home for a sleek-furred rat. Another sigh and she turned to survey the whole room.

There! The hab itself was finally clean. Just one more chore left: the airlock.

Mom's strict protocol was to first make sure the outer door was closed. Only after that were you supposed to open the inner door. Since Skag3's air was similar to Earth's, they didn't have to use the airlock as it was intended to be used: to avoid breathing any of a planet's air. But Skag3 wasn't entirely what Mom called "benign" either. There were still sharp things, poisonous things, and stuff they hadn't explored. But all that was true of places on Earth and other habitable planets, too. Lissa had learned to be careful the last three weeks, watching where she stepped and what was around her.

The lights on the airlock panel were all green, but Lissa dutifully looked through the window into the small room and made a visual check. Sure enough, Mom had closed the outer door when she'd left.

Lissa cranked open the handle and stepped inside. The floor was dirty with tracked-in mud and leaf litter. The side bench was strewn with gloves and coveralls. *"Far away from Earth, I'm bored and, um...need some mirth,"* she sang as she straightened up the scattered equipment. Gloves went *here,* and helmets got hung up *there.* The last item, Mom's spare coveralls, went on the overhead shelf. Lissa folded them and managed to put them on the shelf standing on her tippy toes. They promptly fell off onto the dirty floor. She picked them up again, folding them even flatter. The coveralls were not as heavy as a space-suit, of course, but still cumbersome. Mom said they made her feel clumsy, but Lissa kind of liked tromping around outside like a big-footed, marauding dinosaur. The nearby marshes and swamps were so pretty—full of emerald greens and caramel browns. In fact, since singing wasn't working to change her mood, a short jaunt outside was probably just what she needed to make herself happy.

Should she? Lissa slowly lifted her helmet off the hook. Why not? She'd earned some fresh air after her morning spent cleaning. The airlock floor was still dirty, but she could clean that when she got back.

Without Mom's help, the helmet was hard to fasten. And guilt made it heavier, too. She tucked her coverall cuffs into the big, heavy boots. She really *was* supposed to get Mom's permission to go outside. But it wasn't dangerous here, not much anyway.

She stepped outside, responsibly closing the outer door behind her.

The sunlight was whiter than Earth's, giving everything sharp shadows and crisp colors. Mom had invented long, complicated plant and animal names that she was hoping would become official. Lissa had made up simpler names for them, like "sparkle tree." It was fun to squint through the helmet visor and picture the sparkle trees as if they were a glittering maple forest back in Canada.

Even the bugs and worms here were kind of pretty. Dull red questionworms littered the path with their curvy punctuation-mark shapes. She observed them like Mom would, pretending she was a grown-up scientist. She sniffed hard, trying to use all her senses: the worms probably had a smell to them, but she couldn't tell through the helmet filters. They probably felt rubbery, too, but she wouldn't find out. Taking off her gloves would be irresponsible.

She began to skip. Being outside *had* improved her mood. All she needed now was a golden retriever puppy bounding ahead of her through the puddles, its silky fur coat gleaming in the sun. Or a brown and white hamster in her pocket so she could stroke it as she walked. She jumped over puddles from last night's rain and sang, *"I need a pet, need a pet, need a pet, don't get wet."* She headed down the path to where she and Mom had collected samples last week. That way, she wouldn't get lost.

The next puddle was even bigger. Lissa took a big running jump but didn't make it. Splat! Big clods of muck flew everywhere, including the legs of her coverall. She brushed at the sticky clumps with her heavy glove. A kitten must be the best pet since it cleaned its own fur. And it would lie on your lap and purr all day long. She sang louder, *"I need purring in my life, I don't need, um...any strife."*

The path led into the dense forest. Since her trip there with Mom last week, sparkle trees were already extending new branches across the path. Lissa pushed them aside, sending a shower of translucent golden leaves pattering down on her helmet and shoulders.

Bright blue birds that she'd nicknamed "sidle birds" shifted sideways along tree branches and complained noisily among themselves as she passed. They wouldn't make very good pets because they didn't have any fur you could cuddle. After a while, the sidle birds scattered, and she was alone again. She stopped singing and walked faster. It was longer to the clearing than she had remembered.

The trail grew narrower. She ducked under a pink and glossy spider web. The spider, as big as her hand, sported broad pink and gray stripes on its round tummy. It waved a couple of legs at her as she scooted beneath it, and she bravely waved back. There was no danger of being bitten. Mom had explained that to her several times. The difference between silicon and carbon made Skag3 a fairly safe planet. Silicon-based lifeforms weren't interested in carbon-based lifeforms like her. *"I'm made of carbon, and nothing's gonna harm me,"* she sang, even though that didn't quite rhyme.

Finally, she reached the clearing. A large sparkle tree had blown down in a storm, and Mom had smiled when she'd found it during one of their survey trips. Lissa hadn't been so happy—the tree had looked so sad and droopy—but the research project needed lots of kinds of samples if there was ever going to be a colony here. Lissa had helped Mom carry container after container filled with the sparkle leaves, the ones that had grown high up in the branches, back to the hab. When Lissa grew up, she might want to be an exobotanist like Mom.

Although—she paused and watched a sidle bird dance along the ground with some nesting material in its turquoise beak—being a spaceship designer like Dad would be cool, too. He was back on Earth, helping to build more ships for people to live in so they could travel to new homes.

After the tree had tipped over, its roots stuck up from the base of the trunk like pointy fingers and left a big hole in the ground. Lissa could remember how dark the hole had looked several days ago, beneath the leaves glittering in the noonday sun. Mom had said she thought the loam might be rich with all kinds of beetles and seeds and eggs and things that had been waiting for daylight to bring them to life.

Now the leaves still sparkled with the morning rain, but the pit had a bright green patch in the deepest, shadiest part. Did Skag3 grass grow that quickly? And were those pink flowers under the fringed bit at the edge? Lissa stepped over a fallen branch, then grabbed one of the large, exposed roots to help keep her balance. She lowered one foot down into the hole. A humming sort of noise came through her helmet. It didn't sound like any bird she'd heard before. The grassy bit was still in the shadows. Could *the grass* be humming? That didn't make sense. She put her other foot down in the squishy muck and squatted for a closer look.

In the shade of the thick roots, the grass looked like a piece of lime-green carpet the size of her bed pillow.

Maybe it was a fungus or a moss? Cool! Mom wouldn't know it was here. Maybe Lissa should collect a sample. But then she would have to tell Mom that she'd come out here without permission.

How did it fit into the ecosystem? It would be cool to study it. She nudged the fringe of it with one of her big boots. The carpet-thing rippled, then surged forward a centimeter, scrabbling at the toe of her boot.

Lissa squeaked and stumbled backwards, up and out of the pit. The fallen branch caught her heel and she tripped back onto her butt. The thick coverall protected her bottom, but she lay there a minute anyway. She remembered what Mom always said: in an emergency, don't panic; stop and think before you act.

She craned her head toward her feet. The carpet had caught up and was almost at her boots. Mom's advice was so wrong. Time to get out of there! She scrambled to her feet. The carpet raised its fringe a little bit, as if it were sniffing at her or something. Lissa turned and ran.

Getting back to the hab took forever. Clods of mud flew off her boots as she splashed through puddles. She slammed the outer door of the airlock shut and tore off her boots, helmet, and gloves in record time. Then she dived into the hab, banging the inner door shut behind her.

That had been scary! She plopped down on the sofa and waited for her heart to stop pounding. "You're okay, you're okay, you're okay." It wasn't a song, but it helped a bit. She hugged herself, and that also helped. Except her hands had gotten muddy taking off her boots, and now her arms were all grubby, too. Yuck! This mud was different than the mud just outside the hab and on the trails. This mud smelled like mint and oranges and looked like stiff chocolate pudding. She managed to rub most of it off herself with a microfiber towel, but the sofa and floor had gotten muddy, too, and some had even spattered onto the dismantled water filter pieces.

What now? Maybe she should radio Mom and ask her to come back? No, Mom was in a valley behind a tall hill that blocked radio signals. And she wouldn't be home until after sunset. Maybe she should hike to the valley so she could tell Mom about the nasty carpet thing in the grove? That made sense. Telling Mom was what a responsible person would do.

And a responsible person would clean up the mess they'd made. After ten minutes of vacuuming the sofa, the tiny vac canister was full. She carefully checked that the outer airlock door was shut and entered through the inner door. As she turned to close it, she noticed she'd left a trail of muddy footprints right across the main room and into the airlock. Her socks were *that* dirty.

More cleaning! It never ended! *No fair!* She jerked open the outer door. One flick of her wrist and the dirt sailed out of the canister onto the path. She closed the outer door, and something made a humming noise right at her feet. The carpet-thing! It was in the airlock with her!

She scooted into the hab and slammed the inner door shut. Peeking through the window, she watched for long minutes as it explored the airlock floor and then stopped next to one of her muck-covered boots. It must have followed her home and been lingering outside the door.

She was trapped. She couldn't leave to tell Mom. And, worse, when Mom reached home, she'd head right into the airlock, unaware that the carpet was going to attack her or eat her or do whatever it wanted to do.

She kept watching, pressed against the door. The carpet pulled itself up onto a boot heel and flipped up its fringe, exposing a tiny row of white things, teeth or something. That sound came from the carpet again, a vibrating tone like a bee or a hummingbird. In less than a minute, the carpet had shifted its attention to the boot's ankle, twisting itself sideways and settling down there. The heel of the boot was now clean and shiny, but there were thin, parallel gouges right across it.

She didn't want her boots eaten! Maybe if she had a stick, she could lift her boots out of the airlock without touching the carpet. She looked around the hab. The only stick-like object was her orange plastic snake. She grabbed it and cranked the inner door open partway. The other boot was closest. She stuck out her arm and leaned through the gap. The toy snake wasn't quite long enough to hook inside the boot. She leaned in a tiny bit more.

The carpet reared up and sort of sniffed all around, rippling its fringe. The humming stopped. It glided toward her and into the door opening. She closed the door quickly, squishing it in the middle. It squeaked! Was she hurting it? She opened the door a crack, and tried to push it back into the airlock by poking it gently with the toy snake. It squeaked again and then oozed forward, right toward her toes.

She backed away, stepping over the water filter pieces, until she was up against the worktable. Tears welled up. Don't panic! Think!

First, she'd better rescue the water filter. It was the only one they had. Without it, they'd have to leave the planet and go back to the big ship, spoiling Mom's research project. Maybe she could put the pieces in the steel galley cupboards? The carpet didn't look like it could eat through metal. She carefully dragged bits toward her with the plastic snake. Then she edged along the window to the galley and put her armful on the empty top shelf and closed the cupboard door.

The carpet was still investigating the main room. Its fringe nudged against the sofa, then the worktable legs, then turned toward her. It did that sniffing thing again and surged at her.

Lissa danced out of the way and sat up on the worktable, shifting the rat cage to one side. Hey! Maybe she could capture the carpet in the cage?

She put the cage on the floor and swung the door open with her toes. The carpet sniffed at it and rippled, then turned away, heading for the galley.

What could she use as bait? Think! It liked mud from the pit, that much was clear. Lissa stripped off one of her dirty socks and placed it in the cage.

The carpet paused. Then it flowed backwards, fringe rippling. It entered the cage and flowed right on top of the sock. Lissa slammed the cage door shut and triggered the latches. "Got you!"

Now to observe it the way Mom would. Under the fringe, dozens of little flat teeth lined up in neat rows. Lissa ran to get a multi-tool and turned on the magnifying lens. What she had thought were pink flowers were a row of tiny eyes along the upper edge. They all swivelled at once as if they were watching her. She leaned closer. The carpet hunched up and tried to back away, but it was almost as large as the cage. Her face must look huge. It must be so scared.

"Don't be afraid, you're behind a barricade," she sang gently. It rippled and seemed to settle down on her sock again, so she kept singing.

Its bright green furry topside looked soft and pretty, catching the sun streaming through the windows. It was actually kind of cute. She wished Mom were here so they could study it together and admire its cuteness.

But if Mom were here, she'd say cuteness was not a scientific observation.

In fact, if Mom were here, she'd probably say Lissa was being irresponsible somehow. Lissa looked around the room. Oops, the inner airlock door was still open. Better close that, and then, like a responsible scientist, begin to study the carpet.

She entered her observations into her tablet as she went along. After the carpet had cleaned off her sock with no harm done, there was no more dirt to give it. The hab was so clean that Lissa finally had to go back to the airlock to scoop up bits of mud.

After an hour, the sofa was strewn with bits of mud, forks and spoons, her plastic animals, and the rest of her toys. The room smelled like mint, oranges, and her own sweat.

She studied her results. The carpet liked mud of any sort, but sand swept up from the airlock floor and washed in the galley sink didn't interest it. And it definitely liked the mud from the pit the best.

When the carpet nibbled off the mud, its teeth left tiny grooves on some materials, like her plastic boots. Other materials, like the heavy wire of the cage door, were too hard for it to mark.

It hadn't eaten her sock or the microfiber towel. Nor the glass tube she pushed through the bars, even though glass had silicon in it. Maybe it couldn't digest quartz because that was in glass, too, Lissa remembered from her schoolwork. So their hab windows were safe, and so were their furniture, dishes, and clothing. Only some softer plastics were at risk of being ruined by the carpet's tiny teeth.

Lissa smiled down at the furry creature. It didn't actually seem any more harmful than most pets.

She was still taking notes when she heard the outer airlock door open. As soon as Mom came through the inner door, Lissa ran and hugged her. "Mom, guess what! I found—"

Mom held up a hand. "Why is the airlock so dirty, and what is in that cage? What happened?" Mom suddenly pulled her close and hugged her. Then she held her at arm's length and frowned. "Are you all right?"

Words spilled out of Lissa, about how she had broken the rules and gone outside, about how the carpet had followed her home, about how she'd bravely captured it. "I acted responsibly, Mom. Well, mostly. And my latches work!"

She danced in place while Mom checked the integrity of the electrostatic latches using her own multi-tool. "Well done, Lissa. Nice and tight. You were wrong to leave the hab—and we'll talk about that later—but I'm so glad you kept your head and didn't panic."

"I've been watching it all afternoon. It only wants the organics and stuff in the dirt. Sometimes its teeth scrape on things a bit, that's all."

"You can't be sure—"

"See?" Lissa made a small ball from the remaining clump of sweet-smelling mud and put it on her fingertip. She held it through the bars. The carpet rippled closer and smelled her finger. It reared up and Mom gasped. Lissa didn't flinch, and the carpet lifted its fringe and delicately picked off the clump of mud with its teeth. It settled down happily to eat it, humming, and Lissa proudly held up her unharmed finger. "It won't eat clean stuff, just dirty stuff. And it wants the local dirt, not human dirt. It's safe as long as we're clean!"

Mom was still frowning but not so hard. "It's true, we don't have enough silicon in our bodies to be of interest to any of the lifeforms here."

"I named it Cuddles. It's so cool! I think it likes me!" Lissa bounced up and down.

"It does seem very cool, indeed." Mom peered through the bars.

The carpet rippled, all its eyes swivelled to look at Mom, and it began to hum.

Mom gave a hint of smile, the first in days.

Lissa bit her lip. Now was the time to ask. The carpet could be a good companion and a loyal pet. Already she could picture the fluffy thing on her lap, stroking it while it hummed. But was that fair to a wild creature? Wouldn't Cuddles miss its natural environment? Even though it was now chewing contentedly on the mud ball, it might hate being cooped up in a cage on a spaceship.

The trouble was, they just didn't know enough.

"Well, Lissa, what do you want to do with it?" Mom sat back on her heels and raised her eyebrows.

Lissa screwed up her face. "The responsible thing to do is... put it back in the tree pit." She held her breath. Maybe Mom would disagree and would want Lissa to keep it.

Mom slowly nodded. "Excellent, kiddo. You're showing real maturity by saying that. We've barely begun to study Skag3's ecology. These carpet animals could be quite common, and the loss of one might not change the dynamics of the forest's micro-ecosystem. Or it could be relatively rare and important. We'll tag it and release it and study it for the remaining time we're here and then make a decision about capturing it for further study. You've shown yourself to be careful enough that you can help with all that." Mom ruffled Lissa's hair. "Oh, and I've reconsidered. I was a bit harsh this morning. You can have a pet after all."

"A slushrock?" At least it was something. Maybe she could train it to ooze through a maze or something, after the carpet study was done. She hugged Mom in thanks.

Mom smiled down at her. "Better. I left in such a bad mood this morning that I forgot to tell you how nicely I thought your cage had turned out. In fact, I was so impressed that I sent Kavi a photo of it during my lunch break today. And she was so impressed that she did another search for a pet for you in the stasis chamber. She found something that was mislabeled and in the wrong compartment. She's waking it up from stasis now, and you'll have it when we get back next month."

"A rat?" Lissa started bouncing again. She hadn't thought that Mom had even noticed the cage at all this morning.

Mom laughed and Lissa realized how much she'd missed the sound. "A kitten, kiddo."

"A kitten! A soft, furry kitten!" Lissa did a little dance, nearly upending the worktable. "Maybe Kavi can send me a photo of it waking up! Can I message her right now?"

Mom leaned past her and picked up the hand vac. "Sure." Her eyes twinkled. "Just as soon as you finish cleaning. The airlock is a mess."

For once, Lissa didn't mind the cleaning chore. A kitten! She grabbed the vac and headed for the airlock and sang, *"I'm getting more responsible, we've got a carpet to study, and I'm getting a fluffy kitten,"* even though that didn't rhyme at all.

Moth Girl

by Abigail Putnam

Abigail Putnam lives in Tidewater Virginia. She is an MFA student at Arcadia University, and she has fiction out with Maudlin House and Alban Lake Publishing. She also owes an outrageous amount in library fines and doesn't know how to whistle.

I always take my lunch hour in the library. There is something soothing about dotting white pages with Cheeto-covered fingers, dropping bits of chewed nail between the covers, smearing yourself into the creases. I like to think of the next student flipping through the pages to find these small markings. They would say, "Who was this reader careless enough to leave bits of herself where anyone could see?"

The moth girl, I would answer. The one who has ten days left to live.

Despite being covered in a fine dusting of silky brown hairs and born last week to skeptical and nervous parents, school life has been uneventful. It's simple really—don't answer questions, not from teachers, or bratty, pin-straight-hair co-eds, or demeaning lunch ladies. And always have a snack ready. Snacks come in handy for the not answering of demeaning lunch ladies.

There is a "No Food or Drink" sign with faded letters on the door to the library. In fact, the letters are so faded that the sign is more of a light suggestion, really. It's not like anyone would care enough to enforce it. Certainly not the librarian, a Miss Pence, who spends her days locked in an eternal game of solitaire.

"Black ten on the red jack," I say as I pass her. She doesn't blink at the sound, let alone the crinkle of the potato chip bag that I tear open before traveling farther into the dark of the stacks.

It was the second day.

Between the shelves at the back of the library there is a foot-wide gap just large enough to slip through. Behind it is a large oval window, long since faded to architectural anonymity. It was an excellent place to sit and rub creases into the corners of encyclopedias and stack candy wrappers.

I had just collected a pile of novels with faded jackets, the kind that still have their old catalog cards in the back, when Caleb Denver crawled through the gap. First to appear was his neat blond hair parted dramatically in the middle, and then the rest of him, skinny and pink.

"Mind if I eat my lunch here today?" he said.

I ran my finger over a name on one of the cards, Denise Edwards, imagined her as a large older sister with soft hands and a nice way of patting you on the back when you were sad about seeing a cat run over on the way home from school. I certainly didn't notice if he was out of breath, as if he had been running, or that his glasses were bent, as if someone had stepped on them.

"Your name is Isabel, right?"

Gerald Morse. It was a nice name, scrawled in bold letters that wanted to jump off the card. He would be the type of boy who went door-to-door offering to do chores for a little extra cash, too serious to play but might be persuaded to tell you his latest joke in between cutting lawns and painting garden sheds.

"My name is Caleb. It's nice to meet you," he said with his mouth full of tuna fish salad sandwich. It smelled homemade.

I didn't tell him that I already knew his name, that we were in the same class.

Caleb shuffled through the gap again on the third day. He shoved a book in my direction and pulled out a cheese sandwich, another homemade lunch. I picked up the book, *Notre-Dame de Paris*, and wedged a thumb between the brittle pages. It smelled stale. I added it to the top of the stack before pulling out an oatmeal cookie and ripping open its cellophane casing with my teeth.

"They have pizza today in the cafeteria, you know," he said.

I shrugged. "The lunch ladies don't like me."
He chewed this thought over with his sandwich.

The oatmeal cookie was the type with the white frosting between both halves, and when I bit down, the frosting stuck to my fingers. I stuffed the rest of the cookie into my mouth and then set to brushing the white stickiness onto *Notre-Dame de Paris*'s cover.

"Here," he tore the sandwich in half before I could stop him and held it out, "you're probably still hungry."

I was. But not for his lunch, prepared by a mother who met him in a hospital instead of by accident one week ago, a mother who was probably looking forward to seeing him grow up, go to a nice college, marry, have children of his own. My own mother couldn't even bring herself to explain to the neighbors that I wasn't a foster child and just staying a short while. I had taken to calling my mother and father by their first names to avoid slips of the tongue when anyone else was around.

Caleb waved the other half of the cheese sandwich. I stared at it, waited, and when he didn't budge, took it between two fingers. Caleb was smiling and returned to eating his half. It didn't seem to bother him when I placed it into my pocket without eating it.

"Then she asked me why I hadn't partnered up yet," he said on the fourth day, "and I mentioned something about how no one seemed to want to be my partner, and they all just started laughing. I didn't know what to do."

"I was there," I said without looking, or caring for that matter. We wandered farther into the shadows of the stacks, the smell of forests long dead. Caleb's words spilled out of him in a rush, and it was too difficult to keep up. I let him empty them into the stale air.

Six more days.

"You know what your problem is?" I said. "You answer too many questions."

He shook his head. "That's easy for you to say; you're so peculiar that no one bothers you with questions. Well, except the lunch ladies, of course. They really don't like you. I asked."

I nibbled on one of the green apples Caleb had retrieved from the cafeteria as we passed the mystery section. The books here were all paperbacks with bright covers and slanting titles that issued vague threats. I retrieved one at random, fingered the worn paper edge, switched it with another. They deserved to meet new books once in a while. We continued our walk.

"Red six on the black seven," Caleb said as we passed Miss Pence's desk. She hovered over the mouse button but otherwise showed no signs of having heard.

Perhaps she just didn't want to hear. Perhaps she didn't want to see two children smearing apple-sticky fingers over the Dewey decimal-labeled spines.

The hair covering my arms and legs and now portions of my face had been growing a little more each day. If Caleb noticed, he didn't say anything about it.

On the fifth day, Caleb had yet to make an appearance. This in and of itself was not unusual. He would stumble in fifteen minutes or so after the lunch break had started, having gotten distracted with a missing bit of homework or a forgotten notebook. I selected several tomes of something Greek and retreated to the gap.

I had gotten hold of Miss Pence's pen and began to under-
line random bits of text in red, circling a word, sometimes just
a letter. At least there would be something to remember me by.
Only five days left. I was so involved in the work that I almost
missed the commotion going on in the courtyard below.

The library was on the second floor of the building, but
I could just make out the three figures from the foggy glass.
That blond hair with striking part was not easy to forget. The
other two I had a vague notion might have been in our class.

One, the taller one, held Caleb's arms. The other stood in
front and looked to be saying something. It was hard to tell
what, but I thought perhaps it was not a nice conversation.

Quite suddenly, the one who had been speaking struck Caleb in the jaw, once, twice. The taller one had let go, and Caleb
tumbled to the ground. The two began to kick at him. Slowly,
he raised his head to look at the window. I held my breath. He
must have seen me. I stayed where I was, watching.

It was over as fast as it had begun. They were gone. Caleb
peeled himself off the ground. He moved with the stiffness of
an old man. I waited, but he did not come up to the library.

When the bell rang, I went down to the courtyard below the
window. There was no sign where the fight had been except for a
pair of shattered eyeglasses. I scooped them into my pocket with
the now stale cheese sandwich and went to class. He wasn't there,
either, but I recognized the figures of the two boys.

Caleb had been avoiding me all morning on the sixth day.
Not that I had tried to talk to him. He had a limp and a black
eye but otherwise appeared to be all right, and that was good
enough for me. At lunchtime, I cut a straight path to the library
without looking back to see if he would be coming or not.

There were only four days to go, after all. Not much time to
dwell on these issues. My appetite would no longer be satisfied
no matter what I ate. Snickers bars, bags of salted pretzels, oranges, apples, even a cheese sandwich would not have stopped

my stomach from making those terrible quakes that traveled from limb to limb. I spread myself out on the long reading tables, having to first move a few lamps.

My hair cushioned my head. It was so thick that I had a hard time seeing anything. Father had tried shaving it that morning, but it was back within the hour. Mother was having a hard time explaining it to the neighbors.

It was peaceful against the dry wood of the table, an occasional click from Miss Pence's mouse dropping one card onto another. I imagined them stacked high like a shelf of books, their colored pattern an unbreakable chain spiraling on towards infinity. Life was so easy to arrange, to catalogue, to topple with one shove. It would be such a relief to have no more questions to answer, no demeaning lunch ladies, no bothersome boys trying to share their homemade lunches from loving mothers. Just the silence of the stacks.

The doors to the library flew open. Even Miss Pence jumped in surprise. Caleb surged into the room, his face red from anger or running, I couldn't tell which. He stopped before the table I propped myself up on, and he tossed his school bag next to me with a thump. There were several moments of quiet as he struggled to gather the words he wanted to say.

"Why didn't you do anything? I know you saw. Why didn't you get help? Why didn't you say something?"

I sat up, letting the questions wash over me. He knew I didn't like to answer things. I wanted to be sure what he was asking.

"Because it wouldn't have mattered."

"It would have to me." He turned away, and I slid off the table to follow.

"They would have come again, and again, and again. There will always be boys like that in this world. And what will you do when I'm not there?"

Caleb shifted, hiding his face from me. After several minutes

of the library settling into the quiet, I realized it was because
he was crying. He did not want me to see.

I meant to leave him, retreat to the gap with a book, any book,
and let him collect himself. But the temptation was too strong.
I took a notebook from his school bag, turned his face to me
to catch his tears in its pages.

He was sad. The feeling hovered over me with a weight like
a hard-covered dictionary. Caleb did not cry long, but when he
had finished, I shut the notebook and held it to my chest. Now
his sadness was mine as well, and it would be recorded forever.
I could touch each puckered mark in the pages, feel the history
behind it.

I gathered what pieces were left of him and retreated beneath the table. We sat there for the rest of lunch, after the
bell had rung, after the late afternoon light had begun to creep
across the floorboards to intrude on the peace of watching dust
particles drift through the air.

"I'm sorry," he said.

"There's nothing to be sorry about," I said. But I knew that
wasn't true because now dying did not seem so simple.

The seventh day.

Caleb attempted pleasant chatter all through the morning. I
was very close to punching him. The lunch bell was a mercy as
I hurried to gather my things for the escape to the library. He
had mentioned staying behind to talk to the dance committee
about getting more involved, a quick way to making new friends.
I agreed it was a good idea.

It wasn't until I was trapped in the cool reserve of the library
that I began to question if it was such a good idea. The gap was
a cell of isolation today; the books closed in on themselves. Even
the occasional noise from Miss Pence's game of solitaire did
little to cheer the place.

I removed the cushions one by one from the threadbare green
couches near the magazine racks. If they were leant a certain

way, they created a sort of insolated cave that I crawled into. I peeled back the plastic on the tiny package of bread sticks and fake cheese. Together with the notebook of Caleb's tears, I felt the sadness of being alive and comforted myself with thoughts of my mother's and father's now complete avoidance. Besides the bags of store-bought snacks, I was now free of even the pretense of a family. It would all be over soon. Three more days.

At about half an hour into the lunch break, Caleb swung into the library and peered into the makeshift cave. It was not big enough for the both of us, but with some adjusting, we managed a tent that covered our heads.

"They didn't seem bothered by me at all," he said, going on and on about the nice girls on the committee and how much fun the dance was going to be. It was all rather tiresome. But Caleb's happy chatter made the fake cheese taste better and the stubborn library bearable.

"You really should think about coming with me. I'd make sure you never stopped dancing."

I shook my head. "You should find someone else to go to the dance with you." I did not add that I would not be around. Neither of us ever mentioned my imminent death, but the length of my hair was unmistakable.

"If you could, you would go with me." It wasn't exactly a question, but there was a strange light in his eye that shouldn't have been there.

"I won't be able to," I said.

"Why not? Who makes these rules? How do they know you'll die? What if it's not the end, and you just come back, but better? I mean, has it happened to anyone before?" His questions grew, he asked them all at once and in a great rush. There were too many of them. I covered my ears to drown them all out.

The truth was, I didn't know. I didn't have these answers, and I didn't want to think about what they meant. So, I waited. Waited for them to just go away. I did not uncover my ears, no matter how much he pleaded with me. I waited for the bell to ring, for Caleb to pick up his bag and leave.

On the eighth day, I didn't bother with class. Went straight to the library, removed all the books on the bottom of the deepest shelf, shoved myself into their place and then replaced them one by one to hide myself. Caleb did not come at lunchtime. I slept on and off, dreamt of thousands of lives that flew like birds, cooed, settled into the books, and roosted around me.

On the ninth day, I must have spent the night in the library. The morning light woke me from between the hardbacks on the bottom shelf. I was so very hungry, but there was nothing nearby to eat, so I set in on the books. I cracked them open like oysters, chewed the pages to pulp and then drank them down with the binding paste. The words sank into my skin, washed my brain with so much information, so many stories. I forgot my name, forgot the time, and fell back into a hazy sleep.

Sweet, musical voices roused me. I wiped sand from my eyes and peered up into Caleb's face. He had removed several books and was crouched to peer down at me.

"You've slept for most of the day," he said.

I could only nod, still hazy from dreams. Past him, the library was lit in the dull glow of late afternoon. There were white strips of paper and golden stars hung from the ceiling, and the tables and couches had been pushed to the side. A stereo piped something from the classical station. It was smooth and slow.

"I tried to get everyone to move the date of the dance up so you could go, too," he said, "but they couldn't. So, I gathered some of the decorations to bring the dance to you."
I realized where he had been yesterday and nodded.

"Thank you," I said. The words were simple, but I could think of nothing else to say.

"Would you like to dance?"
With an effort, I struggled out from the shelf only to collapse on the floor. I shook my head. It was too difficult to move.

Caleb didn't seem to mind. He lay beside me and we watched the light fade from the library.

It was dark when I insisted he leave. He wanted to make sure I was comfortable for when it happened, but I didn't want him to see. Wanted him to remember me in the library, in the bits and pieces of myself that I had hidden everywhere.

When he was gone, I pulled myself between the gap in the shelves with the last of my strength and set out the old half of the cheese sandwich, his broken glasses, and the notebook with his tears. They would guide my journey into the afterlife. I went to sleep hungry and exhausted, and formed a solid cocoon.

It was the tenth day.

There was nothing but hair, and darkness, and dreams.

Were those voices?

The books answered,

Yes.

Station Run

by Sherry D. Ramsey

Sherry D. Ramsey is a writer, editor, publisher, creativity addict and self-confessed Internet geek. Her books and stories range from middle grade to adult, and she loves dragons and magic as much as she loves spaceships and aliens. Sherry lives in Nova Scotia with her husband, children, and dogs, where she consumes far more coffee and chocolate than is likely good for her. You can visit her online at www.sherrydramsey.com and keep up with her much more pithy musings on Twitter @sdramsey.

Vonni flew into the apartment and tossed her school tablet into the catch-all with a clunk. The apartment door *snicked* shut behind her. "Mom, I'm home!"

"Careful with your tablet!" Her mother's voice came from the study, even though she couldn't possibly have seen Vonni from there. "How was your day? Do you have homework?"

"It was okay. I have to play an hour of Station Run and watch one edu-vid," Vonni answered as she leaned down to kiss her mother on the cheek. A tracery of blue lines shimmered in the air above her mom's tablet, displaying a developing formula. Outside the study viewport, a pulsing orange glow marked a trading ship's engine vents. It lumbered past, headed for Unity Station's docking ring. Beyond that, the velvety black of space wrapped around them, stars twinkling as if giant fingers had thrown a handful of glitter and let it fall.

Vonni's mother cocked her head with a half-smile. "I'll be surprised if you log out after one hour of Station Run."

Vonni smiled. "Me, too. I love learning about how the station works—and fighting the occasional imaginary monster, of course."

"Any idea yet what work you'd like to do?"

Vonni shrugged. "I'm doing a coding module, like the software that runs the station systems and Station Run. That's interesting. Maybe I'll do tech work in Saturn Sector someday."

Her mother squeezed Vonni's hand and turned back to her formula. "It's not as easy as the intro modules make it look— ask your father—but still lots of time to decide."

Vonni left her mother to her numbers, following the short, curving hallway to her room in their small apartment. Unknown to her parents or her teacher, at thirteen Vonni was already far above her grade level in Station Run game modules. She'd investigated dozens of jobs and explored almost every twisting digital corridor of Unity Station in-game. Now she kicked a pair of pants under the bed and pushed her sketchbook and pencils aside, clearing space on her floor. Guilt twinged in her stomach as she slipped into her VR helmet and gloves. She'd lied. Vonni had learned the coding module months ago and immersed herself in the programming—finding and fixing weaknesses in the software and making it run better. Now she used that knowledge to access higher and higher levels of Station Run.

Unity Station had eight sectors, named for the eight planets of the home system, Sol. Vonni had already played all the modules for Earth Sector (food management, hydroponics, recycling, and life support), Mercury Sector (refining and fabrication), and Saturn Sector (administration, security, and computer systems). Now she was working her way through Venus Sector, which housed the station's power, maintenance, and waste management hubs.

As the virtual world of Station Run sprang to life around her, she immediately forgot that she was actually in her bedroom. The VR version of Unity Station seemed as real as the corridors she'd just hurried down on her way home from school. The sounds of the station played in her ears; the dull hum of engines and life support rose and fell; footsteps echoed on metal decking; voices leaked through doors and around corners. The virtual Unity Station of Station Run unrolled before her eyes, the floorplan precise, every detail exact, even to the slowly moving ships outside the viewports. It even smelled right—food and cooking scents in Earth or Mars sectors, steel and oil in Mercury, chemicals and medicine in Uranus. Only the people populating the corridors were different. In Station Run you met only other virtual players—students, mostly—and the game's generated characters, who helped or challenged you as you undertook quests and tasks and learned everything about living and working and your possible future here.

An input box opened in front of her left eye. *Choose a Game Mode.* The choices were *Adventure, Education,* and *Exploration.* Vonni hovered a gloved virtual finger over *Adventure—just half an hour fighting imaginary monsters and solving puzzle quests all over the station.* No. Better finish her homework first. She clicked *Education.*

Her friends thought waste management boring, but Vonni was enjoying it. True, she'd run a self-written hack on the game code and bypassed the three introductory modules. But the job-shadowing modules were so much more interesting than the theory stuff. She'd learned more watching technicians run chemical extractions on unwanted pieces of clothing than a boring lecture on the importance of proper waste streams would have told her. She'd go back and catch up on the intro stuff later.

She tapped a *Teleport* option in the upper corner of the screen and selected Venus Sector. Her helmet went briefly black, and then the game's Venus Sector materialized around her. Another menu popped up inside her helmet. It listed the available modules and jobs she could investigate today. One caught her eye: *Endgame - The last step in reclamation.* That sounded interesting. What happened to stuff when everything reusable had been removed from an item, but there was still something left? Unfortunately, that module was greyed out on the menu. There were other modules she should run first.

Vonni sighed. She *knew* she should do them in order... but she could hack the system and get into this one. It wouldn't even be difficult, building on what she'd already written. And whoever wrote the Station Run software hadn't anticipated a student who wanted to learn *more* than necessary.

With her VR-gloved fingers flying in the air in front of her, Vonni called up a virtual keyboard, ran a script to open her backdoor into the software, and inserted a few new lines of code.

The menu reappeared, with *Endgame* now available. With only a slight pang of conscience, she clicked it, and the configuration of Venus Sector in her helmet changed. Two doors appeared that hadn't been there before. *Two?* She'd only expected one. But maybe another module had been unlocked, too. Vonni walked over to the doors, and as she approached, the word *Endgame* hovered over the door to the left. Nothing appeared on the right-hand door.

She hesitated. The *Endgame* module was the one she'd wanted, but... she looked at the unlabeled door. That was curious. Vonni opened it and peered inside. Beyond lay a dark corridor, steeped in a dank, unpleasant virtual smell. What was this place?

Glancing over her shoulder, she saw no other players in the vicinity. She shrugged. It was only a virtual world game anyway—not like anything bad could actually happen. She slipped through the door and let it close behind her.

Every part of Unity Station Vonni had ever visited, in real-time or virtually, had been clean and well-lit. This dim, narrow corridor, illuminated only by a thin line of light tubes running along the ceiling's center, didn't fit. The walls, an unfamiliar scratched, grey metal, also bore dirty smudges and stains. And, it smelled—a little like the composting module in Earth Sector, where food management turned organic leftovers into nutrients for the hydroponics and garden bays. But there was something else. Like when she'd been sick with a virus and spent four days throwing up and suffering other unpleasantness. Vonni wrinkled her nose. Even virtual, it wasn't nice.

She rounded a corner and almost bumped into another player.

They both stumbled back, and Vonni couldn't stifle a gasp. Another player should be a green dot on the VR heads-up map, but she realized now that the map grid inside her helmet had cut out back at the door.

"Hey, who're you?"

The other player was Vonni's height, with a thin face and large blue eyes. He stared at her from under a shock of almost pure-white hair. He stood with his hands on his hips, feet planted solidly on the decking. His voice sounded friendly, though.

"I'm Vonni," she blurted.

"Dart," he said. He stuck out a virtual hand for her to shake. "How come you're not on my grid?"

"Um, I don't know," she admitted. "My grid's gone down. Maybe the game's glitching. Is this Venus Sector?"

"Ha!" Dart barked a laugh. "Good one. Yeah, later we'll go over to Mars Sector and eat in a fancy restaurant."

Vonni didn't get the joke. She and her parents had eaten in Mars Sector lots of times, although not all the restaurants were "fancy."

"Okay," she said slowly. "What sector is it, then?"

The boy stared at her. He shook his head a little. "Um, Pluto? You sure the game's glitching, and not your brain?"

Vonni stared back. "There is no Pluto Sector. There's a sector named for each planet in Sol System, but Pluto got downgraded long ago. It's not a planet."

Now Dart looked her up and down, then walked around her in a slow circle. Vonni turned her head uneasily to watch him. "You're really not from Pluto Sector?" he asked, eyes narrowed.

She shook her head. "I live in Uranus Sector."

"Whooo." Dart puffed out a long breath. "Looking at you—yeah, I can believe it. You stick out like a supernova. But how did you *get* here? You shouldn't be able to access this part of Station Run, just like I can't get anywhere else but here."

Vonni's cheeks grew hot inside the VR helmet. She was glad her blush wouldn't show on her avatar. "I... I ran a code hack. To jump ahead in the lesson modules—"

"A hack?" Dart cut her off. "You're a coder?"

"Well, just learning—"

"Shh!" The boy interrupted again. His avatar grabbed her avatar's hand and he pulled her a few steps down an even dimmer side corridor. Several sections of the overhead light strips were dark.

"Hey!" she said, shaking free of his grip.

He put a finger to his lips. "Someone's coming," he whispered. "You might not be on their grid, but you don't want them to find you here." He started down the hallway and motioned her to follow.

Vonni gulped air. *This is all VR. I'm still in my bedroom, in our apartment.* No one in this weird place called Pluto Sector could hurt her.

And she really wanted to understand what was happening. She followed Dart down the shadowed, narrow hall.

"I've never met anyone from the main station before," Dart said over his shoulder. "What's it really like? Is it true there's room for some people to live *alone*?"

"Uhhh." Vonni thought about her mom's friend Mapreet, who had her own apartment—smaller than Vonni's, it was true—but she shared it only with a black and white cat named Sagan. "Yeah, I guess. Some people."

"Wow. You are not going to believe what I'm going to show—"

But before Dart could finish, Vonni's vision went totally black. The words *Program Reboot* appeared inside her helmet in red letters. She pulled it off and stared at it, standing alone in her bedroom. That had never happened before.

Station Run had crashed.

Station Run didn't come up with her parents at dinner. Vonni didn't want to confess about her hacking, and she was also worried. She didn't want trouble for herself, and definitely not for Dart. *Did her parents know about Pluto Sector? Was it only a secret from kids?* Until she found out more, she wasn't comfortable talking about it.

They had a normal dinner, and watched a tri-d, and she watched the edu-vid to finish her homework. Vonni didn't try to go back to Station Run that evening but read a book on her flexscreen instead. She found it difficult to concentrate.

"There's a mandatory software patch for Station Run," the teacher told the class next morning. "Please install it before you start your next modules."

That wasn't too unusual; station admin patched the game every so often. Kind of a strange coincidence that it would happen right now, though. The school day dragged through Earth history, English, and math, and Vonni practically flew home afterward to log in and run the patch. Then she went straight to waste management in Venus Sector, where she'd been yesterday, ran her own code hack, and waited for the extra door to appear.

It didn't. Even stranger, when she accessed yesterday's logs, they didn't show she'd even been in Venus Sector. No trace of accessing *Endgame*, or Dart, or anything. A chill ran down Vonni's spine. No one should be able to alter her logs.

She stood very still in the middle of her room, thinking, her head encased in the VR helmet and her gloved hands on her hips. *What to do?* She really wanted to talk to Dart again, to find out about Pluto Sector, to figure out what was going on. She argued with herself: *safer and wiser to forget the whole thing.*

But she'd never be able to do that.

Vonni breathed a deep sigh. If she'd done it once, maybe she could do it again. She called up her coding interface and began to write new code.

It took two days before she had the code handshaking properly with the game and was able to create an undetectable backdoor. Finally, though, she thought it would work. She finished her homework in record time that evening and ran her hack.

In response, a message appeared in glowing red inside her VR helmet. A cold sweat broke out across the back of Vonni's neck. She swallowed hard against a thick lump that formed in her stomach and tried to crawl up into her throat.

ACCESS DENIED.

Station Run had locked her out.

Vonni slept little that night. She was sure that at any moment her parents would knock on her bedroom door, demanding to know what she'd done. Finally, she fell into sleep, tossing through nightmares of being chased through the corridors of Unity Station by giant red letters with monstrous mouths.

In the morning, she didn't go to school.

Vonni never skipped school. She felt terrible about it. But worrying in the dark the night before, she'd realized what she had to do. She had to find the real Pluto Sector, get in, find Dart, and get him to explain things to her.

She said goodbye to her parents and left with her school tablet and lunch in a satchel, then made her way to Venus Sector. One good thing about Unity Station, she thought as she hurried through corridors crowded with people going about their days' business, was that people assumed if you were in a place, you were supposed to be there.

When she reached the area where, in the virtual world of Station Run, she'd found the doors for "Endgame" and the unmarked door, it held only three workers, wearing lab coats and seated at computer consoles. On her way there, Vonni had worked out a plan. "Good morning!" she said, with her biggest smile. She held up her school tablet. "I'm doing a project. Is it okay if I look around?"

A tall woman in a white lab coat smiled. "Of course. Let me know if you have any questions. I'm Charri."

"I'm... Leyla," Vonni stammered. Giving her real name would be a risk.

The woman smiled and turned back to her work at a computer console. Vonni wandered around the room, making nonsense notes on her tablet. The door Station Run had marked "Endgame" was there, but where the unmarked door to Pluto Sector had been, a bank of metal shelves stood firmly against the wall. Vonni felt the cold lump in her throat returning and swallowed it down. She'd hoped to quietly slip through that door when no one was looking, but was the door even there? She kept up her charade of note-taking while her mind raced for alternative ideas.

After a bit, Charri said to the others, "Break time!" She turned to Vonni with a smile. "Would you like to come with us, Leyla? We have tea, coffee, water... and usually cookies. My treat."

Vonni shook her head. "No, thanks. I think I'm about finished here anyway. I should be getting back."

"Come back anytime," the woman said, and the three of them left the room.

In a flash, Vonni was over at the shelves, studying them. She managed to squeeze in next to one and peer into the heavily shadowed space behind. The outline of a door traced the wall behind it. With effort, she wriggled her hands behind the shelf and slid it out a couple of inches. It swayed, top-heavy, but

Vonni steadied it and blew out a deep breath. With agonizing slowness, she tugged the shelf out inch by inch until she could slip behind it.

And the door was there! Two rusty-looking slide bolts kept it tightly shut, but Vonni managed to pull them open even though her fingers were slick with the sweat of fear. To her great relief, the door swung open away from her, into the corridor beyond, so she didn't have to move the shelf out any further. The smells of Pluto Sector greeted her as she slipped inside the shadowy corridor. She took a minute to wrestle the shelf back into place behind her before closing the door and leaning back against it. Her heart jumped, and she slowed her breathing, taking deep pulls of the malodorous air to calm herself. She was in. For real this time.

The same hallway with the ceiling light strip led her to the side corridor, just like the virtual version where Dart had taken her. She passed the spot where Station Run had crashed, then she rounded a corner to find a closed metal door. Vonni put a hand on the cool metal, and with a deep breath, she pushed it slowly open. A riot of sound met her ears as soon as the door opened, and she peered through the crack into a long, high-ceilinged room. Clanking, whirring machinery and bubbling vats filled the space, along with people shouting to be heard above the din. Metal catwalks vaulted high overhead, thin ladders stretching up to them. Heat poured through the opening to meet her, carrying scents of machine oil, chemicals, old cooking, and human sweat.

Overwhelmed, she let the door close again. It reminded her of the manufacturing bays of Mercury Sector, and some of the recycling domes of Earth Sector. But this was different. Dirtier, smellier. Like the people. Vonni shook her head. This didn't make sense. Where was she? And how would she ever find Dart without the program?

Think. Well, surely there couldn't be that many boys named

Dart? She could go into that room and ask someone if they knew him.

Vonni's heart kicked up a hop-skip-jump in her chest. She didn't want to draw attention to herself. He'd said she stuck out—everyone would know she didn't belong here. But she had to find him. Her first thought was to use her avatar controls to change her appearance, but then she remembered: *this is real.*

Putting thoughts of her mother's horror out of her head, Vonni lay down on the floor and rolled and wriggled around, scruffing up her clothes with dust and grime. With her fingers, she scraped her hair back into a messy ponytail and caught it with an elastic from her pocket. She wondered if she should rub some dirt on her face but couldn't go that far. This would have to do.

This time she fully opened the door and stepped inside. The cacophony in the huge room hit her like a physical thing. She wished she could adjust her VR controls, but once again she had to remind herself that this was real life.

Not far inside the door, a tall man in a grubby coverall stood at a computer station, tapping the keys with black-streaked fingers. Mustering her courage, Vonni approached him. "Excuse me?"

He turned and smiled at her. "What's up?"

"Ha—have you seen Dart?" she stammered. "I thought he might be around here."

The man turned his head and craned to see around the crowded room. "I think he's over at the grub station," he said. "That white hair of his is hard to miss."

Vonni had no idea what or where the "grub station" was, but the man pointed diagonally across the room.

"Thanks!" Vonni said breathlessly and walked away before the man could get curious. She pushed through the crowd, heading generally where the man had indicated. Just as in the rest of Unity Station, no one paid attention to her. They assumed she belonged.

Finally, she dodged around a short woman in a dusty black tunic and came face-to-face with Dart. His face and clothes were dirtier than his avatar had been, and his greasy hair looked like it hadn't seen a shower or a comb for several days. His face went as white as his hair as he recognized her, and then he grabbed her arm and hurried away from the crowd.

"How did you get here?" he hissed as they half-ran. "This is dangerous!"

Vonni shook off his hand. "I found the door," she hissed back. "Station Run locked me out, and I want to know what's going on!"

Dart ducked into a shadowy alcove behind a high stack of battered crates. He turned as she followed him. "Station Run locked you out?"

"Yeah. I tried to get back here virtually, with another hack, but I guess it didn't like that. So here I am." Vonni crossed her arms in defiance. "What is this place, anyway? And don't just say 'Pluto Sector'."

For a few seconds Dart stared at her, a mix of fear, disbelief, and admiration in his look. Then he grinned. "You come from the Upside. This," he said, spreading his arms wide, "is the Underground. Everything that no one else wants to do gets done here. Everything you can't find on the rest of the station, you can find it here."

Vonni's head spun as she thought about the room she'd just passed through, compared to the eight other sectors. "What can't you find on the rest of the station?"

"Stay here," Dart said and squeezed past her to disappear into the big room.

Vonni swallowed. *Was he going to tell on her?* But in a minute he was back with a long, grubby, green sweater and a sweat-stained hat. "Put these on. We'll take a walk."

Now that Vonni blended in better, they strolled up one side of the huge room, and Dart pointed to machines and people as they went. "Foods that are banned on the station for one reason or another. Medicines, too. Illegal software apps. Clothing and fabric that's traded outside Unity Station's agreements with other planets." His voice held a clear note of pride. They reached the other end of the bay and passed through a door into another, oddly lit one. It smelled earthy and moist. "Plants that go into some of those foods and medicines," he said, "or things that Unity admin doesn't want us to have."

"But why wouldn't they want us to have these things?" Vonni asked. "They must be bad for us."

Dart shrugged. "Maybe sometimes. My Grandma Tix says most often it's because Unity admin wants to negotiate all its own trade deals for better money, but it's the people who live here who really pay the price."

This didn't make a lot of sense to Vonni, so she asked about the other thing Dart had told her. "You said people here do things that no one else wants to do. What do you mean?"

Dart motioned to her to duck under a low-hanging, peeling, grey duct and then led her into another room. More new smells and sounds. Vonni's nose wrinkled and she squinted. This one smelled like a huge garbage dump. "This is where we break down the stuff that doesn't go into any of the other recycling streams," he said. "Some of it's chemical, but some things you just have to chop up really tiny or melt down so you can make it into other stuff. You ever wonder where a lot of the raw material for making things in Mercury Sector comes from?"

"A lot of it comes from Venus Sector. That's what I've just been learning about," Vonni declared. She felt a prickle of annoyance with this boy who seemed so sure of himself and all these confusing things.

"Sure. But the really icky stuff or the really dangerous stuff— that ends up here for us to deal with," Dart said.

Vonni frowned. "That doesn't seem right. Why don't people complain?"

Dart shrugged. "No one listens. And if you're born in Pluto Sector, you're going to live and die in Pluto Sector."

Vonni's eyes grew even wider. "You never leave this sector? Why? Unity Station's so big!"

He looked her over intently. "That's why I was so surprised to see you. I halfway didn't believe the rest of Unity Station even existed before you came here. But one look at you, and I knew it was all true. We don't leave because we're not allowed to leave."

They'd stopped next to a cluster of large metal drums. Rust spots speckled the outside and traced the edges, but the symbol stenciled on the side of each drum in yellow paint was clear: the three circles Vonni knew meant *biohazard*. She'd seen it in the medical sector, although she hadn't studied the full modules yet.

"I—I don't understand," Vonni said, bewildered.

"Come and meet Grandma Tix." Dart led her away from the drums and into a narrow corridor. Cables ran along both walls and snaked down to the floor; Vonni stepped carefully so she wouldn't trip. Finally, they reached a spot where the cables looped up over a service hatch. No screws held it in place, and Dart slid it aside easily. Creamy light poured out into the corridor, and Dart motioned her inside. Vonni took a breath and ducked through.

The room was no bigger than her bedroom. But it was packed, every square centimeter of space in use. A hot plate and dishes marked a cooking corner next to a couple of boxes piled with rags—*no*, Vonni thought, looking closer, *those are clothes*. A shelf on the right-hand wall held an assortment of gadgets and tools in such a mishmash that Vonni couldn't begin to sort them out. Lines strung across the ceiling held small containers stuffed with assorted cloth, metal bits, cords, and electronics. Next to the back wall lay two sleeping pallets. On one, a small ball of white fur snuggled into a flattened pillow. On the other, an elderly woman sat cross-legged with a tablet on her lap. Her hair, as white as Dart's, curled out from underneath a blue cloth cap. She looked up silently as Vonni entered.

Dart said, "Grandma, this is Vonni. She's from Uranus Sector."

Grandma Tix squinted up at Vonni, deepening the already vast network of wrinkles on her face. She pursed her lips then smacked them derisively. "Don't believe it," she said and looked back at her tablet.

"No, I really am," Vonni said, pulling off the big sweater. "Look, I tried to dirty up my clothes, but Dart says they're different from any here."

The elderly lady at least looked up at her again. "Humph. Could have stolen them."

"From where? Dart says no one from here ever goes out into the rest of Unity!"

The ball of white fluff uncurled itself and stretched, then padded over to wind around Dart's legs. He picked the kitten up and stroked its fur. "She says people in the rest of Unity Station don't even know we're here, Grandma."

"Pfft." Now the woman sounded angry. "They know, all right. They just don't care. Don't want to mess up their precious station with the likes of us. We're only good enough to do the dirty work."

Vonni squatted down in front of Grandma Tix so the older woman wouldn't have to look up at her. She shook her head. "I really think a lot of people don't know," she said slowly. "I don't think my parents or a lot of their friends would be okay with this. How long has it been like this?"

The corners of Grandma Tix's mouth pulled down as she thought. "My gran used to say she remembered being a kid and eating at Mars Sector, before Pluto Sector got closed off. I always thought it was just a dream, or she was making it up. But... if it happened in her time, that's pretty long ago."

Vonni thought about it... a grandmother's grandmother's childhood could be a long time in the past. Long enough for uncomfortable secrets to be buried and forgotten by many. Station admin must know... even her dad? Vonni shook her head. No, she couldn't believe that.

"Gran!"

The voice startled Vonni, and she almost toppled over. She looked back to see a little girl with a dirt-streaked face and bright blue eyes in the doorway. The girl returned Vonni's stare and her eyes widened. "Is that her?"

"Her, who?" Dart sounded annoyed.

"Station security is looking for an Upsider. Is that her?"

Grandma Tix came to life. She glanced at Dart and then back down to the tablet in her lap.

"Get her down to Lugo," she said. "I'll tell him you're coming."

"Who's Lugo?" Vonni asked as Dart snatched her hand and pulled her out of the room.

"He pretty much runs the Underground," he said, but didn't elaborate. They scurried down a narrow hallway smelling of machine oil and cleaning fluid. He opened a metal door and motioned her into the dark space inside. "Careful, it's a stairway."

Vonni stepped inside and stopped. Steep, narrow stairs, more like a ladder, led down into darkness. Dart pushed past her and started down.

"Isn't there some other way I could just sneak back into the Upside?" she asked as she followed, trusting her feet and hands more than her eyes in the shadowed stairwell.

"They know you're here. And they won't want you to tell anyone. I don't think that will be easy to fix."

Vonni thought the descent would never end, but they finally emerged into another corridor. The air was much cooler, and the smells different—the stomach-rumbling hot oil of a stir-fry, a hint of perfume, and an unfamiliar, spice-like scent. Dart threaded through a messy warren of shops and living spaces that had been built into the spaces between ducts and pipes, machinery and storage crates. Jagged sheets of metal became walls; draped blankets created rooftops. An entire society existed here, forgotten by the rest of the station. Vonni knew she'd never find her way out of here without help and felt fear clench in her stomach.

They reached an open storefront spilling light into the corridor, blue-white and flickering from a bank of computer screens inside. Men and women sat at most of them, eyes glued to the glowing letters. Sometimes they pushed a money chip into a slot in the computer and pulled it back out. Gambling.

At the back of the room, a tall, thin man lounged in a battered armchair that might have once been blue. Puffs of greyish stuffing had settled into drifts on the floor. Through a doorway behind him, Vonni saw men moving crates around a large space, unpacking some and packing others. The man spoke into a headset and tapped on a tablet in his lap, but he looked up when she and Dart stopped outside. He lifted a finger and beckoned them in.

Dart made a strange little bow to the man. "Lugo, this is the Upsider. Can you keep her safe?"

Lugo pursed his lips, studying Vonni with dark-shadowed eyes. Close-buzzed black hair covered his head, and two long, red scars ran down one side of his face from temple to jaw. "Why would I do that?"

"It would make security mad," Dart said with a grin, "and she can't go back to Upside now. Maybe she could work for you, she's good at coding—"

"What?" Vonni stared at Dart. "I'm *going* back home. That's not the kind of help I need."

Lugo lifted an eyebrow at her. "Well, the girl's got a voice. Tell me, then, what kind of help *do* you need?"

For half a heartbeat she panicked. If Lugo hid her, how long would security continue to search? And if Dart helped her get back Upside—what then? If they knew who she was and that she'd been here and learned their secret, there would surely be consequences. That wasn't the answer.

And how could she go back to her old life anyway, knowing about Dart and Grandma Tix and everyone else trapped and ignored in the Underground? She couldn't.

But if station admin was dealing with its own consequences...

Vonni's lips spread into a hesitant smile, which grew to a wide grin as the idea took shape. She knew exactly how to answer.

"I need a VR headset and a login," she said, pulling her tablet from her satchel. "Preferably one with an alias. And a way to connect this."

"What are you going to do?" Dart asked her.

She winked. "I'm going to hack Station Run once and for all."

Lugo put up his hands, looking startled. "Whoa, whoa. What's this about?"

"Vonni says most people on Unity don't know we're even down here and wouldn't agree with it," Dart explained. "I think she wants to open the software so everyone finds out."

"Exactly," Vonni agreed. "You'd be able to leave Pluto Sector. Go other places on the station."

Lugo's eyes darted to the customers seated at his gaming consoles. "We might see a lot more security down here," he said. "Bad for business."

Vonni thought she probably wouldn't approve of Lugo's business, but she had to convince him to help her. "Think bigger. Your business might improve," she suggested. "There are a lot more people on all of Unity than there are in the Underground. You'd have new customers. You might even be able to move your business—well, some of it—into the main station. Imagine if you operated in Mars Sector, too, instead of just down here?"

Lugo frowned, obviously thinking it over. Finally he stood up and crooked a finger at them. "This way."

He led them to a small office, and pointed to the computer console. "Log in as 'coyote'," he said and pointed to a scribbled string of letters and numbers. "This password. Can't be traced back here. But I don't imagine you have a lot of time," he added.

Vonni connected her tablet and logged in, not looking at him. "I'll be quick," she said and muttered under her breath, "I hope."

She put her fingers on the tablet, opened a backdoor, and began to write code.

Two hours later, every instance of Station Run on Unity Station rebooted. So did the administration systems. When they opened again, a vast section of virtual space had been added to one end of the station's virtual map layout. It appeared on every screen and in every VR headset grid, labelled, "Pluto Sector." Every person logged in to the system in any sector appeared as a green dot. Every hidden door leading from the rest of Unity to the Underground was marked by a red "X".

Chaos erupted in station admin. Curiosity erupted everywhere else.

This message appeared on every instance of the new map:

We can't be called Unity Station if anyone is left out. It's time to open the doors. ~ Vonni

On the Lam on Luna
by Morgan Bliss

Morgan Bliss spends the first part of her day as an assistant professor, the second part of her day as a doctoral student, and the late evening trying to piece together story fragments with whatever brain power she has left. She calls herself the "Industrious Hygienist" (no, it has nothing to do with teeth) and spent ten years as an industrial hygienist and safety professional. She maintains a blog at industrious-hygienist.blogspot.com with technical articles, manga, and sock puppet videos about occupational health and safety.

According to the Company, I died 22 days ago. They even sent my parents a {{ping}} to notify them. The message said: *{{PING: Eunji Nexi expired 0221 Earth Standard Time [EST]. We regret the loss of your daughter. Acknowledge receipt of message.}}* My father forwarded the {{ping}} to me, asking what kind of malarkey I was up to and warning me not to mess with my implant.

I can't help but grin at the memory for two reasons. First, I should not be able to remember anything—the implant controls and enhances my memory, recording everything I see. Second, I didn't do anything to the stupid implant. It failed. None of this is my fault.

After weaving through crowds of people and robots between work shifts, I arrive at Medical. I stand in front of the locked sliding door, fidgeting and waiting to be noticed. I am supposed to check in with Medical every shift to show them I'm not dead and let them check my biolinks. Since my biolinks are keyed to my identification card, and my ident card has been deactivated, I can't get access to any secured locations.

"Are you dense, Nexi? Scan your card!" A grouchy medical technician brushes past me, flashing her card at the reader. I try to sneak in behind her before the door closes, clutching the edge of the door with my fingers, but I am unsuccessful. It slams shut, and I barely move my fingers in time. I wave both arms above my head at the camera, hoping to catch the attention of a security guard.

Finally, one of the guards notices me, and the door whisks open. Magboots clanking over the threshold, I jog into Medical and report to the guard, who has a peculiar expression on her face. Normally, I would call up her records through my implant and see her name and Company status. I give her a cautious smile.

"You're the broken Nexi?" she asks, raising an eyebrow.

"Affirmative. I am Eunji Nexi, Building Epsilon."

"I'll walk you back to the exam room." She gets up from behind the desk and holds the door open for me.

I follow her past the detector units and through wide hallways that all look the same. With a completely maxed-out implant, I can't access maps or files. I shouldn't be able to access my memories. We arrive at an exam room, and the door whooshes open to reveal the same medical technician I've seen multiple times per day for the last fifteen days. I don't know his name.

"Eunji, you successfully navigated the transition from Epsilon to Luna Central." The medical technician speaks in an eerily monotone voice, which lets me know he is recording this session with his own implant. "Your teachers say you are handling the assignments well. And your supervisor is amazed at your productivity despite the, um, handicap you have experienced."

Reflexively, I reach for my robotic left arm and try not to get angry. I hate it when they talk of handicaps and productivity. I'm just as capable as anyone else. I'd be more productive if I could afford a better prosthetic. This one twitches and spazzes out at the worst times. Gritting my teeth, I take a deep breath and clench my fists at my sides.

"I apologize," he says quietly. "I meant, the, um, inconvenience of your implant failure. Not your arm." Opening the assessment chamber, he gestures to it. "If you please?"

At his request, I step inside the assessment chamber, shivering under my coveralls. Lights flash, weird buzzing noises surround my head, and icy cold mist sweeps over any exposed skin. I feel pressure building inside my skull as the Company tries to access my implant remotely to reactivate it—every access attempt feels like a...well, I don't have words to describe it. Sort of like they are scooping out the area behind my eyeballs. It's weird.

Assessment complete, I step back out of the chamber and hug myself with my arms, trying to get warm again. The medical technician reviews the results on his vidscreen, making quiet noises to himself. Everything looks green, except the flashing red "FAILURE" next to my implant's status.

"It's the most curious thing," the technician begins saying, brushing his short hair back with his hands.

"Am I free to go, sir?" I ask, trying to interrupt him. I don't have time for another of his ridiculous theoretical discussions— the one last shift was bad enough.

He turns from the screen to look at me with newly curious eyes. "What? Oh, yes, you're free to go. It's just...I almost wish we had more time to study you. There's no point in wishing now." He points to the bottom right-hand section of the screen, where a brand-new update is flashing.

I read it on the screen at the same time the {{ping}} arrives in the corner of my vision. *{{PING: Implant repair for Eunji Nexi scheduled for 1830 EST tomorrow, pending arrival of Dr.*

Yasilvous on Luna. Absence from work and academic requirements is approved.}} Feeling a thrill of terror course through me, I can't hide the fear in my eyes.

"Don't worry, Eunji," the technician says, clearing the screen. "You'll feel better tomorrow, once the biolinks are reestablished and you have access again. It will be just like it was before." Gently pushing my shoulder, he moves me toward the open exam room door, where the same security guard is waiting for me. "It will be just like it was before," he repeats hollowly.

I let the guard lead me through the hallways and back to the Medical entrance, lost in my thoughts. I don't want it to be like it was before. I'm just a Nexi. They didn't need to rush this re-pair—it's only been twenty-two days. There's nothing important about my memories.

Without paying attention, I somehow make it back to Building Epsilon, to my dorm where all the other kids in my age group are getting ready for bed. Pounding on the door for them to let me in, my legs feel wobbly, and my hands, even the robotic left one, are shaking. I am choking back tears, feeling them burn at the corner of my eyes.

Everyone else is already dressed in their nightwear, milling around. I get ready for bed as fast as I can, hoping to crawl under the thin, scratchy blanket and be left alone. But my best friend Riko calls out to me as I emerge from the com-munal bathroom. "It's your turn tonight, Eunji! Your turn to tell a story." Taking turns telling stories is a favorite in our dorm room before heading to bed. My stories have been very popular of late.

All nine of my dorm mates are already lined up on floor pillows, faces expectant. Last week I told them a story about a space dragon and his pet astronaut. This time, since it is my last night of mental freedom, I'll have to make it an especially good story.

"I want you to close your eyes and imagine a mouse." My dorm mates are confused. I pantomime the action, using my fingers to close my eyelids. I know at first, when you close your eyes, there is only blackness. It's pleasant, underrated even.

"Don't search for images. Don't force a memory recall. *Imagine* a mouse." I open my eyes and peruse their faces.

Some of the kids from Earth are here—their parents are probably at a shareholders' meeting or some required training for the Company. I see their eyes moving frantically even when closed. This should be a simple exercise, really, but I'm sure it is the first time in a long time that anyone has asked them to imagine anything. They probably had to dictionary the word.

"Can you see it? Can you see the mouse in your mind?" I query, walking around the room. Several heads nod. "Open your eyes," I command with a quiet voice.

One of the kids from Earth, voice quavering, asks me, "Eunji, what color is the mouse?"

"What color do you want it to be? Brown?" I suggest, walking over to where he sits on a floor cushion. I crouch down next to him. He is startled for a moment when he sees my robotic arm, then blushes and looks away. I'm used to the stares—when I lost my arm, it was weird for me at first, too.

"Um, a gray mouse? Mice are gray, right?" He won't look at me now. Riko {{pings}} me a quick personnel file—she knows I can't look them up. His name is Nasim, and his parents are both on a training regimen for a few weeks. It's his first time off-planet visiting Luna.

"It could be a magenta mouse, if you want, Nasim," I tease. With a quick smile, I stand back up and start pacing in front of the room. "Now close your eyes again, and I'll tell you the story of the singing mice." All nine of my roommates shut their eyes.

I begin, "There was once a scientist on Earth who was in the middle of some very interesting research on long-range communications, but she was transferred to Luna for an important project for the Company because of her brilliance. Once she finished the Company project, she longed to replicate and continue her research on Luna. She asked permission from the Company to bring her special mice to Luna, and they said yes, under certain conditions. The mice would never be allowed out of their cages, and they would be recorded at all times. The scientist said she would be happy to comply, and she and the special mice were soon given lab space in Building Omicron."

"How much lab space?" This question comes from a brown-haired boy named Nathan, whose parents, per the file Riko {{pings}} me, work in research and development. Lab space is a touchy topic for research kids.

"Just one room. Barely larger than a storage closet," I answer. He seems satisfied by this answer.

Since I still have their attention, I continue. "You may be wondering what was special about these mice. They were cloned from extinct mice that used to live in the cloud forests of the Amazon. These mice were modified so their songs could not be heard by humans. The scientist's singing mice were supposed to be used for long-range communications research."

"Supposed to?" Nathan asks. Deviating from established lab procedures is also a disruptive topic for research kids. "Why didn't she follow the approved protocols?"

I smile even though they can't see it. "This scientist realized, when she brought the mice to Luna, she had accidentally separated some mating pairs. She tried to get the mice to participate in her experiments, but they were too sad, just lying around, eyes closed, singing songs. Although the scientist could not hear the songs with her ears, the songs set any nearby instruments into a frenzy of activity."

"Why didn't she just cancel the experiment and order new mice?" Nasim asks.

"She didn't want her special mice to be killed just because

they weren't working for her experiment, so she devised a new experiment. When she contacted her old lab on Earth, some of the sad, separated mice immediately cheered up. In the background of the vidscreen, she could see the other mice, their mates on Earth, clawing at their cages, and it looked like they were singing, too. Watching her mice, she noticed their bright, open eyes and joyous behavior. It seemed like the mice knew their family's songs even though they were worlds away."

{{*PING: Dream Sequence Initializing.*}} We all feel the dream {{ping}} from the Company. It is almost impossible to ignore. All nine of my dorm mates open their eyes at the exact same time. They rise from the floor cushions at the same time, go to their bunks at the same time, and slide under Company-issued blankets at the same time. Only I remain standing, fighting the urge to follow orders. The Company {{pings}} me again, this time with a cautionary warning that disobedience is not part of my contract.

I sigh in resignation. I didn't finish the story, and the end is the most important part!

Tomorrow, when the Company fixes my implant, I may not be able to recall the rest of the story. I haven't recorded it anywhere. I don't want to record it. I want to remember it, word for word, image for image, feeling for feeling. For twenty-two days, I have been free. For twenty-two days, I have just been a person, not a Nexi.

Crawling into the narrow bunk, I wrap the light blanket around my body and ignore the dream {{ping}} one more time. The Company wants us to dream about engineering specifications for a new geologist robot, but I decline the request again. If I have to go back to being a Nexi tomorrow, I am going to dream my own pleasantly chaotic and unpredictable dreams.

⟨⟩

{{*PING: Stop Rest Period.*}} Soon after being {{pinged}} awake, the Company notifies all Nexi children to report for work detail at the Production Room during first shift. We are scheduled to attend school the following shift, which is the reverse of how our day usually goes. Nasim and Nathan and any other Earth kids are exempt from work requirements since their parents are shareholders in the Company.

After our pre-shift meal, I learn that one of the surveying crews has returned early with a huge haul of minerals from the Trojan asteroids. I also receive a {{ping}} from the Company that the returning survey crew needs to complete overdue safety training before they can receive payment. With no adult safety coordinator immediately available, and the urgency of the surveying crew's pay schedule in doubt, the Company deems me the most qualified of all available Nexi. The Company {{pings}} me to step in at Production Line 4 and serve as safety coordinator for the day. Pulling on my green coveralls, I verify all the needed training requirements on a handheld tablet and shove cold feet into a pair of magboots. The surveying team won't be expecting a 14-year-old girl, and they certainly won't be expecting an amputee with the cheapest robotic arm available.

Production Line 4 is just down the hall from the communal Nexi living quarters in Building Epsilon. I hate Production Line 4. It's a stupidly designed room, with careless adult workers and bad memories. The Company knows I hate Production Line 4.

The exhausted group of surveyors laughs when they see me. "What's this? Are they all out of grown-up safety people up here in the sticks?" the survey team supervisor jokes, holding out his ident badge for me to scan.

"You're back early, and I'm certified to document your training." I scan the other badges and retrieve their training records from the tablet. "Supervisor, you're due for twelve modules of training. Take your place at Station 1A. Engineer, you're due for eight modules of training, please sit at Station 1B. Senior Miner, you're due for seven modules of training and a qualification exam. You can be at Station 1C. Robotics Technician, you have eight modules of overdue training. Please go to Station 1D."

The four workers groan and shuffle toward the labeled screens and, I know from experience, chairs no one would believe could be so uncomfortable. Once they are seated and facing me, I begin to speak again. "I am Eunji Nexi, and this session is being recorded. Survey Team 452V, you may begin your required training."

Swirling around to face the workstations, all the workers place their hands on the screen, speak their names, and then groan again at all the training modules that pop up. The robotics technician, a tall, blonde woman named DeWitt, grins at me and gestures toward the empty chair in Station 1E. "Do you have to stay standing to record us, or can you join me?" she asks, swiping through the first module.

Interestingly, Station 1E is not actually a separate cubicle like the other stations, but a screen and ugly chair combination shoved into a corner of the oversized Station 1D cubicle. The Company installed it in case it was needed for peak training times but then refused to allow anyone to use it since it is partially obscured from the Production Line 4 cameras.

"I can join you," I answer and sit down next to her, attempting to get comfortable in the awful chair.

"These modules are super easy," DeWitt confides, continuing to swipe through the screens at a fast pace.

"You are required to complete all eight modules of this training within the allotted time frame," I remind her, hiding my own smile in case she is recording our interaction.

"Oh. Well, that's stupid. I don't need eight modules to learn about hazardous gases and equipment safeguarding. I handle all that stuff every day, and there's a bunch of ways to work around the procedure—I mean, to...ugh. I forgot you were recording." Her voice trails off.

I meet her eyes with a hesitant smile and whisper, "Are you? Recording, that is?"

"Colliding comets, no! I have rules and regs on closelink recall. No need to document this." DeWitt points to the screen, showing her perfect score so far on the pre-tests and post-tests for each module.

"Can you keep a secret?" A ridiculous question, I know. Nexi have no secrets. I don't even know why I ask her this.

"Sure. It's been a long time since anyone asked me to keep a secret. But I'll keep my eyes on the screen just in case." Turning her head, she gives the screen her entire visual focus. In that moment, even for a few seconds, I feel like a real person.

"I'm not recording, either." I keep my voice quiet so the other members of her team can't hear. "I can't record. Haven't been able to for twenty-three days."

"But you're a Nexi!" Her face remains composed, but her voice holds surprise as she stammers, "How do they—how are you—how have they let it go for so long? What happened?"

I chuckle a little. It is so dumb. "You know how the Company only started implanting kids fifteen years ago?" She nods, so I continue. "My generation—Nex59F—was one of the first to get the implants. They're supposed to last until we're old enough to go on projects. The Company was sure they'd calculated the storage capacity correctly for eighteen to twenty years of memories."

Our implants, for now anyway, record only images. Every time the Company's tried to expand it to include audio, it's been disastrous. People would have balance issues or noisy, painful interference and quickly overloaded memory cores. If audio were feasible, I'd have probably maxed out my implant when I was a child.

"How old are you?"

"I'm fourteen. And I filled up the storage twenty-three days ago. I haven't been able to record anything since then, and my biolinks stopped transmitting when the storage maxed out." I laugh, this time loudly enough to receive curious stares from her team members. "Eyes on the screen, please," I call out in my best stern tone. My attention back on DeWitt, I confide, "They thought I was dead for about a week."

"Really? I'm surprised they haven't fixed it yet."

Just then, what flashes through my mind is the general strangeness of this situation. The Company is fully aware that Survey Team 452V's training session is not being recorded, so I have no idea why they assigned me to this group. There are other safety coordinators available among the Nexi. Part of me thinks that this is some sort of test, or a punishment for ignoring the dream {{pings}} for the last few weeks. I play with the frayed corner of my coveralls sleeve.

"It's happening today," I whisper. "And I don't want it."

"What's it like? Being Nexi?" She glances at me for a second and then focuses on the screen in front of her.

I chew on my lower lip and slouch in the uncomfortable chair. "I didn't mind it before. I didn't know any better. But now?" Pulling my feet up onto the seat, I wrap my arms around my legs and trace the seams of my magboots. "We know everyone hates us. We know everyone hates being recorded all the time. We're used to not having any privacy. We're used to the Company analyzing every tera of data for anything they can use or sell."

"When did you get the implant?" DeWitt answers some of the questions on the screen with quick jabs of her fingers.

"I've had it since just after I was born. My entire life has been recorded. The Company has every piece of data about me since my parents first found out they were having me: biolinks, memories, you name it."

DeWitt spins in her chair to look at me, examining me from head to toe, from my closely cut black hair to my too-big magboots. "You really can't turn it off? The implant is always on?"

I nod and sit up straight, throwing my shoulders back.

Suddenly remembering there are still cameras in Production Line 4, I realize I am too close to DeWitt. I should attempt to keep up appearances. "Every memory. Everything I see. Every excitement and every fear. They keep and analyze everything."

Standing, I look toward my Nexi dorm mates in the production room working at the production lines. Two of them sort crates of minerals while one ferries the crates to quality control. The remaining four wear complex, oversized goggles next to the micronizer to identify the type of minerals and contaminants. Children are no longer allowed to work with the micronizers. A memory, not a file recall, flashes into my head, and I feel a cold sweat break across my forehead.

"Are you okay?" DeWitt pauses from her training to examine me again.

Taking a deep breath, I sit back down, using my right hand to feel the cheap synthskin applied to my robotic left hand and forearm. "I'm the last Nexi child to work on a micronizer. Five months ago, something went wrong with the lasers inside the machine, so I called my supervisor over. Instead of following procedure, he just paused the machine and opened the sheath. A technician up at Base 2 noticed that the machine was paused, so he turned the micronizer back on."

Clenching my robot fist, I continue, "My supervisor was sucked in and, well, micronized. I tried to grab him, but the conveyor was too strong. My arm was sucked in, too."

DeWitt shudders. "Micronized. Yuck, that's a horrible way to go."

"Yeah. Nothing left to reconstruct. And since I'm still growing, they won't fit me with a proper prosthetic. Just this ancient relic." Rolling up my sleeve, I show her the crude attachment mechanism and the rough surface underneath the synthskin.

She clicks her tongue in disapproval. "I haven't seen work this shoddy since my days at university. This thing is at least thirty years old," DeWitt comments as she moves the stiff joints of my robotic wrist and fingers. Her fingernails are painted a bright blue and green, with chips at the edge of the nails.

I point her back to the screen, where a question on a timer is awaiting her response. "The worst part about all of it is the dreams," I respond, tracking the progress of her teammates on their training.

"Do you have nightmares about it?"

"Nightmares? No. We don't, I mean, we can't...we don't really dream. The Company pushes us, well, {{pings}} us what they say are dreams, but they're just problems they want us to work out. Sometimes it's just other people's memories that they sort of mash up together to make it seem like we are dreaming. I saw myself in one a couple months ago."

This apparently gets her attention. DeWitt jerks her hands back from the screen and holds them to her stomach for a moment, breathing deeply, glaring at the screen. "You can't dream?"

I spin around in the chair to gather my thoughts, swinging my legs in the air. "I can. I have, for twenty-two nights. At first I thought I was going crazy. I'd try to find the images I saw in my mind or search the details of the dream to see what the Company was trying to tell me. I even started making up stories to tell my dorm mates before bed. Fairy tales, I guess you'd call them."

She seems intrigued, so I continue, "I started one about these singing mice, you see. They sing songs we can't hear because the frequency is too high for our ears, but you can play the songs back at a lower frequency to understand them. They close their eyes, sing to their distant families and remember them."

DeWitt grins. "Singing mice? That's adorable. What happens to them?"

{{PING: Report to Medical.}} I suddenly feel sick. Woozy, with my heart pounding in my chest. It's too early. The implant repair isn't supposed to happen until next shift. Gulping in air, I feel the fingers of my right hand trembling against my leg.

"I'm sorry, I have to leave," I say, trying to stand and hold my shuddering body upright.

"But what about the mice? I want to hear the end of the story," DeWitt jokes, but she quickly realizes that something is wrong. "Eunji, what's happening to you?"

I just shake my head, too quickly, and feel even more dizzy. "It's time. They just called me to Medical. I'm not...I don't...I don't know the end of the story. I haven't made it up yet. But now, now I'll never know it." The Company {{pings}} me again with the fastest route to Medical. "They'll be sending another safety coordinator to supervise in a few minutes. It was nice to meet you, DeWitt." I give her the bravest smile I can and walk out of Production Line 4.

Once in the corridor, I wander, ignoring the {{pings}} from the Company with every wrong turn and detour. My path weaves around fellow Nexi, shareholders, robot partners, crates of minerals, and security guards. I keep my gaze at the floor and walk as quickly as I dare, running when no one can see me. When I reach the edge of my approved sector, I feel a growing tension at the base of my skull. The implant begins to pulse, sending cascading waves of pain down my spine. Ignoring the pulses, I wait until a group of scientists opens the gate between sectors and follow them through.

No one questions me. It is unheard of for a Nexi to disobey orders. Once out of the public areas, I try to use my ident card to gain access to the sections of the base that only Nexi travel, but it doesn't work. Wedging my robotic fingers into a service door frame, I pull with all my might and shove the door open. Taking the service tunnels, I jog to the farthest point of the base that I can get to: Building Omicron. Why did I pick this building as my story's focus? Why did I pick singing mice? What is the end of the story?

Once inside Omicron, I force open the service tunnel access and emerge into the main corridor. The floors are dull with moondust, and I can only see faint robot tracks. This building is mostly used for storage now, so there shouldn't be anyone to record me.

Turning a corner inside Omicron, I smack into a security robot. Before it can scan me, I shove it aside, smashing it into the wall, and run down a nearby hallway, magboots clanking against the floor. I hear the robot squawking as it tries to put itself upright. They already know I am here. They always know where I am. Breathless, I duck into an open doorframe and run down another short hallway. Through the windows in each door, I can see weird, colorful items stacked haphazardly, gathering moondust.

I soon hear voices and loud footsteps echoing from the main corridor. Human security guards, most likely. I try every door panel in the hallway, but all flash a red lock screen. Trapped. I could cower. I could beg. But in the end, I just stand there, arms folded across my chest, my face set in defiance.

"Eunji Nexi, you are out of your sector," the female security guard speaks calmly, one hand on her weapon and another outstretched toward me.

"Disobedience is not part of your contract, Nexi." The male security guard grabs my right arm and wrenches it behind my back, placing a demobilizer on my robotic left arm so that it hangs limply at my side. "You were called to Medical. You will go to Medical," he says in the same emotionless, prescriptive voice.

I don't fight. I don't cry. I want to beg, and plead, and fight, to scream at them and run away. But it won't help anything. They are just doing their jobs, and I am not doing mine. Instead, I just look them both in the eyes, sure they are recording or live streaming this, and repeat, "I was trying to find the singing mice. I was trying to find singing mice." Let them think I am malfunctioning. Let the Company try to figure out what I mean. I'm not even sure what I mean.

The guards march me to the main corridor, where a rover waits, blowing accumulated moondust up the walls. Shoving me onto the rover, the male security guard clips my immobilized left arm to the handrail while the female guard navigates us through a labyrinth of tunnels. It seems no more than moments until we arrive at Medical.

When they sit me down at the exam table, I start to shake uncontrollably, and I hate it. For twenty-three days, there has been no record of me except what the Company can compile from others' recordings. For twenty-three days, I have lived my own dreams and felt my own feelings. I remember what I want to and forget the rest. All the Company records will show is that I malfunctioned, I disobeyed, and I fear them.

"We know this has been a difficult time for you, Eunji," my usual medical technician says with a false smile. "We'll be updating your memory cores to prevent this from happening again. You may lose a few recalls during this process." He places a sleep patch on my neck, and I watch him fiddle with his equipment until I fall unconscious.

"Will you tell us the mouse story?" Nasim begs me with a curious smile.

Yuko's eyes are bright with excitement as she urges, "Yes, will you finish it?"

I pause from reviewing my school work and gaze around the dorm room. My other dorm mates are watching our interaction with hopeful glances. Nathan {{pings}} me a funny picture of a mouse wearing an opera costume, while Takuya and Yuko post an animated magenta-colored mouse that snacks on sheet music. I forgot how easy it is to connect, how it feels to have everything available with a thought, what it's like to recall perfectly curated memories.

"What mouse story?" I tease them. "I don't remember any mouse story." But I do remember the mouse story. I thought

about it as I fell asleep during the update, and I told it to myself while my memory files expanded and rearranged. I know
the ending now.

"Eunji, you don't remember? The singing mice and the
love songs?" Riko seems so saddened by this idea that I can't
help but laugh.

I set down the tablet I've been working from and gesture
to the floor pillows. They seat themselves quickly and give me
their focused attention. Stretching my arms out, as if to expand my thoughts and mind beyond the confines of my own
body and its new memory cores, I wait until they are all expectantly listening. "I want you to close your eyes and imagine a
mouse," I begin.

"This mouse has whiskers and ears and a wonderfully long
tail, like any proper mouse should. This mouse sings songs we
can't hear with our ears, and it sings to its love, worlds away.
Now, you remember that this mouse was taken from its family
and kept in a small cage with a bunch of other special mice.
They were supposed to be used in an experiment. But the mouse
and its friends missed their families so much that they couldn't
do the tasks the scientist wanted them to do."

"We know that part!" Takuya exclaims with closed eyes.
"Tell us the rest!"

I grin to myself. The Company is going to hate this if they
find out. "This mouse, we'll call her Miyako, could hear the
songs of her love. She knew he was not there because she could
not see him or smell him or feel him. But she sang to him
anyway, and she knew he could hear her, too. The scientist,
when she replayed the recordings and lowered the frequency,
knew that she was witnessing something wonderful. When the
scientist heard Miyako's song and the response of Miyako's
love, she was heartbroken."

"Why?" Yuko wonders, clutching her hands to her chest.

"Because mice don't live forever, and the scientist didn't

think the Company would let her bring up more mice for her experiment. The scientist realized that her experiment was cruel, and that, in just recording but not really listening to the mouse songs, she was doing more harm than good. Even with only that one live stream from the Earth lab, Miyako and her fellow mice seemed happy."

Nasim opens his eyes for a second. "Happy?" His voice is disbelieving. "How?"

I consider my answer and the rest of the story. How can I explain it to them? How can I explain what it means to be Nexi, what it felt like to dream and imagine, and to feel like it was taken away? Most of them are younger than me, except Riko, and they don't yet understand what our role is in the Company. They don't realize how our lives are manipulated and recorded to protect the shareholders.

"Yes, happy. They played and worked and did the experiment that the scientist had lost interest in. But afterwards, when the work was done, the mice sang the sweetest songs to their families, cuddled together with their eyes closed. They remembered. And it was enough."

Nathan and Yuko's eyes snap open, viewing me with confusion. "And then what?" Nathan asks, squirming on his cushion. "Did they see their families? Did they find their love?"

I sit down in front of the floor cushions, cradling my robot arm, which still aches from the immobilizer. "Some people say that, if you listen carefully, you can still hear the singing mice in Building Omicron. But you must listen, and remember, and close your eyes. No recall. No recording. As long as it is just you and your imagination, they will come out and play."

{{PING: Dream Sequence Initializing.}} We all stand up, go to our beds, and tuck ourselves in. We send each other pictures of mice of all colors and sizes, singing, eating cheese pellets, running in exercise wheels. I imagine, just for a moment, that my friends understand, before the Company's dream sequence

of mathematical models for mineral deposits pushes itself into my thoughts. I imagine a little mouse standing atop a hill, and it is enough to lull me to sleep.

Nocturnal Noise

by L.G. Keltner

L.G. Keltner fell in love with reading and decided at the age of six she wanted to be a science fiction writer. She holds a bachelor's degree in writing from Drake University. L.G. lives in Iowa with her husband and three children. When not writing, she enjoys amateur astronomy and playing trivia games.

There's no sound in space. That's what the textbooks say. There's far too much sound on a space station.

I sat on a hard bench on the edge of the Pryvale Station food court, my slender fingers curled so tightly that my fingernails dug into my palms. The buzz of hundreds of people talking filled my head. The clattering of trays and silverware made me grind my teeth. Each sound competed for my attention, causing my head to ache.

I caught sight of a familiar tuft of shaggy blond hair off to my left side. My body tensed. *Don't let it be him*, I thought as I closed my eyes. If only ridding myself of the image would make him go away.

"Hey! *Ear*-ina! What are you doing here?"

I shuddered. *Of course it's him. Where else would Raffee Fletcher be?*

Raffee had a habit of appearing whenever I least felt like seeing him. It didn't help that I *never* felt like seeing him. I closed my eyes so I wouldn't have to look at his sneering face.

That didn't solve the problem of hearing him, though.

"*Ear*-ina! Should you even be here by yourself? Why aren't you with your mommy?"

I could have argued with him, reminded him for the thousandth time that my name is Arina and that his name-calling is childish. Unfortunately, experience had taught me how pointless that would be. Instead, with a small smirk, I reached behind the shell of my right ear and flicked the small silver switch hidden there. Silence washed over me, and the tension bled from my muscles. The noisy world faded into the background. The faint vibrations of the floor beneath my feet were the only sign that I wasn't alone.

I bet Raffee's getting mad now. He doesn't like it when people ignore him. I imagined what he must look like waving his arms and yelling, his face turning bright red as he grew angrier.

Minutes passed, and when I opened my eyes again, Raffee was gone. I stood and began the long walk back to my family's quarters, leaving my ears off so I could give my aching head a break. I don't care how well my modified ears work. None of that matters when my head hurts too much to make sense of it.

Adults passed me in the corridor, their mouths moving silently as they chatted with one another. Sometimes I liked to make crazy guesses about the hilarious things they might be saying, though I wasn't feeling up to it at the moment. None of them gave me more than a passing glance, and I liked it that way. I was twelve years old, after all. Other kids my age didn't need anyone older escorting them around the station during normal operational hours. (You can't really call it daytime when there's no sunlight.)

I made it all the way home. The dull gray door slid closed behind me as I made my way over to the computer panel in the kitchen. "Arina Grey, ID number 6143726. One dose of my medicine, please." I couldn't hear my own voice, but my mouth had formed those words so many times that I didn't have to think twice about it.

Two cups dropped from the dispenser. One contained water, the other two little blue pills. I took the pills and went straight to my bedroom. Though it was the middle of the afternoon, I needed a nap. I collapsed on the bed without turning my ears back on.

⸱🚀

"Arina!"

The voice jarred me from my sleep, and I bolted upright. Flynn jumped back to avoid a collision. Holding a hand over my racing heart, I took a deep breath. "You scared me!"

Flynn's my older brother and all-around pain in the neck. At fourteen, he stands more than a head taller than me. He also seems to think he knows everything. "You scared me first," he said in a stern voice, his arms crossed in front of his chest. "You were supposed to wait for me to pick you up from class."

"You were late."

He sighed. "You knew I was going to be a little late. I had to finish my exam."

I crossed my arms in front of my chest, too, but I did it defiantly. "Other kids in my class don't have to wait to be picked up. Why should I have to?"

"It's different for you."

I narrowed my eyes. "Why doesn't anyone think I can do something as simple as walk home by myself?"

Flynn sat on the edge of the bed. "That isn't the problem. Mom's just worried because so many people give you a hard time. She doesn't want someone to hurt you."

"I can take care of myself. You and Mom don't need to do everything for me," I muttered. I paused and remembered my silent walk home, as well as the fact that I'd gone to sleep blissfully unaware of the sounds around me. Anger simmered in my gut as I realized Flynn must have turned my ears back on while I slept. My hand flew back to cover the silver switch. "Hey! I had my ears off for a reason!"

"I'm sorry, but I was having trouble waking you up!"

I raised an eyebrow. "I needed the sleep. I had a headache."

Flynn's brown eyes were suddenly sympathetic. "Where did you go?"

I didn't answer. I didn't need to. He'd found me in that food court plenty of times before. Each time had earned me a mixture of irritation and pity. This was worse than the headaches.

"Why do you go there?" he asked. "You know the noise bothers you."

It always had, and I feared it always would. I was born deaf, and the implants that made it possible for me to hear were sensitive. Too sensitive. I went from being unable to hear anything to being able to hear *everything*. It overwhelmed me easily. Doctors hoped the headaches would improve over time, but they hadn't yet. "It's nice to feel normal," I whispered as I stared at my shoes. If Mom were there, she'd lecture me for not taking them off before going to bed.

Flynn didn't say anything right away. When he finally did speak, his voice was quiet. "I understand that, but I don't like watching you hurt yourself. Is it really worth the pain?"

Flynn couldn't truly understand what it was like, but I didn't say that. I also didn't answer his question. "I have some homework to do. Maybe you should go."

He hesitated for a moment before pushing himself off the bed. "Okay. We can talk more about this later."

After he'd gone, I lay back down with my hands behind my head. I didn't doubt Flynn would be bringing this up again, but I didn't want to discuss it. What was the point? What was so wrong with wanting to be normal for a little while?

Thanks to my midafternoon nap, I was wide awake well past my bedtime. At least my headache was gone. I listened to the faint sounds of the station's oxygen recyclers and the less faint sound of Flynn snoring in the next room, hoping that they would help lull me into sleep.

It was past midnight when an unfamiliar sound started. *Tap tap tap. Clink. Tap tap. Clink clink.*

I pushed myself up onto my elbows and listened. This was nothing like the rhythmic, predictable sounds I typically heard in the dark. This wasn't machinery running like clockwork. What could it be?

Clink clink clink clink. Tap tap. Clink. Tap tap tap.

If any of my classmates heard something like this, they'd probably make a monster story out of it. That's what Flynn and his friends liked to do.

Believing in monsters was difficult on a space station. Aliens of various colors and shapes passed through all the time. Many of them looked entirely different than the humans onboard, and they stood beneath the bright lights where everyone could see them. They weren't hiding in the shadows, so they didn't seem that scary.

This didn't stop kids from telling monster stories. They told them for fun. They told them to scare their friends. Sitting in dark rooms, they could almost convince each other that monsters were real.

I remembered a story that left Flynn sleepless for days, though he'd never admit it. Flynn's friend Connor had been sleeping over, and though I was in my own room, my sensitive ears picked up the tale through the wall.

"Did you ever wonder why Sanctuary Station was abandoned?" Connor asked.

"Not really," Flynn replied. "I assumed it got old."

Connor chuckled. "Nope. Age had nothing to do with it. They shut it down because people were vanishing, and no one knew where they were going. It started with only a few the first day, but within a week, more than fifty people were gone. A monster lived on that space station, you see. The monster stayed in the dark, hidden from sight." Connor's tone had turned menacing. "No one could see it, but that wasn't what made it so dangerous. This monster moved so quietly that no one could ever hear it coming. People were snatched in their sleep, or taken when they got up in the middle of the night to go to the bathroom. Imagine it. You're lying down, just about to drift off, and all of the sudden, a clawed hand digs into your shoulder and rips you from your bed."

"That's not real," Flynn had said, though his voice trembled slightly.

"How do you know? People go missing all the time, and we don't always find out why."

"If a monster can't be seen or heard, how do you know that's what happened?" Flynn demanded.

"How do you know it's not?" Connor asked gleefully. "Every once in a while, someone escapes and tells the story. One guy managed to get away, and though people thought he might be crazy when he told them what happened, the decision was made to close Sanctuary Station and abandon it. Too many people were falling victim to take the risk."

Though I had no reason to believe in the monster from Connor's story, I understood how some people could be frightened by it. Most people feared anything that could catch them off guard. The story simply didn't frighten me the way it did others. That surely meant a few unexplained sounds in the middle of the night shouldn't scare me. Right?

"It's not a monster," I whispered to the dark. "It can't be a monster. Monsters don't exist."

I considered turning my ears off but decided against it. I wanted to be able to hear the sound in case anything changed. That didn't mean I was scared, though.

The racket continued for a good while longer. When it finally subsided, I caught a little bit of sleep.

I went to breakfast the following morning, my mind abuzz

with the possibilities. What had I heard? I needed to share my experience with someone. Maybe I should have been prepared for the reaction I received when I told my mother. I'd dismissed my fair share of creepy stories over the years, but it still stung when my mom did it to me.

"I'm sorry, honey, but that sounds a bit crazy."

I glared up at her over my cereal. "How is it crazy?"

I watched as my mom sat across from me at the kitchen table and folded her hands together. "Sweetheart, you're telling me that you heard a monster while you were sleeping last night."

"No. I said I heard something that sounded the way a monster might sound while I was *trying* to sleep last night. There's a difference."

"So, you're saying it sounded like a monster, but it isn't a monster." Her face twisted with disbelief. "What do you think it was?"

I shrugged. "I don't know. If I did, I would have told you."

Mom sighed. "Arina, what do you expect me to do?"

"Those sounds weren't normal. I know that. I think we should tell someone, because something has to be wrong."

Potential problems need to be addressed on a space station. Too many lives depend on everything running smoothly. That didn't change the fact that my mother wasn't taking my concerns seriously. "Honey, there are a lot of people working to make sure that everything functions the way it's supposed to. If there are any major problems, someone's likely trying to fix it right now. There's no sense in worrying about it."

"What if no one knows?" I asked.

"Pryvale Station has sensors and diagnostic systems to keep us safe. If something is wrong, we'll find out quickly. You just need to get ready for school."

As the head of communications, Mom worked with a lot of the station's senior staff. She could inquire about almost anything that affected the station, including safety issues.

Though I felt hesitant to ask, I still had to try. "Could you ask if anything strange has been going on?"

Mom looked hesitant too, but she nodded. "Fine. I will."

Flynn walked me to school. I tried to keep as much distance between us as I could, but Flynn would only let me get away with so much. Most of the journey passed in silence, though he kept glancing over at me and biting his lower lip. He wanted to say something.

The station's school resided about as far from our quarters as possible. The corridors there had dull blue carpet and the walls were painted white. Students bumped shoulders as they passed each other. I cringed when a couple of the students bumped into me more roughly than they did others. Flynn shot each of them a glare in return.

This crowded hallway also happened to be where my brother finally found the words he'd been dying to say this whole time. "I heard what you were telling Mom."

I shook my head. I didn't want to talk about this where other kids might overhear us. "I know you did. You were hiding just around the corner. I heard your breathing."

He didn't look surprised. "You know monsters aren't real, right?"

It's funny how people can hear something without really listening. "I never said there were monsters." I looked around, searching for signs that anyone might have overheard.

"No, but you're imagining that there's something dangerous happening when it's not, and that isn't so different. We all get scared sometimes. We let our imaginations get the best of us. Part of growing up is learning to deal with that." Flynn spoke as if he weren't only two years older than me.

If not for the possibility a teacher might see us, I probably would have slugged him in the arm. I couldn't stop the acid that crept into my voice. "Learning to stand up for yourself is also part of growing up. I don't need you trying to convince me this is all in my head."

Relief washed over me when we reached my classroom. This was where we went our separate ways. Flynn caught me by the arm before I could duck inside. "Hey, I'm only watching out for you. That's what big brothers do. Please don't be mad at me for that."

I sighed. "I get that, and I'm not mad that you want to help me. I only wish you'd take me seriously." Then I shook off his hand and went to take my seat.

Any hopes I might've had that Mom would discover something were dashed that night when she came home after her shift. "I asked around, Arina. Everything's normal. There aren't any odd malfunctions, and according to bio scans, there's nothing strange to report."

Maybe I should have accepted that and moved on, but I couldn't. I spent the rest of the evening trying, and failing, to think of other reasons why the scans didn't come up with anything. I went to bed more frustrated than ever, but still hopeful.

My covers formed a cocoon around me as I stared at my bedroom ceiling, my ears on high alert. I didn't think I'd get much rest despite my exhaustion. The comments from Flynn and my mother kept playing through my mind.

"I'm not imagining things," I told myself for what was probably the hundredth time that day. "I know what I heard was real."

I waited. For the first hour, I was almost certain it was only a matter of time before the mysterious noises started up again. The distant and measured sounds of machinery were all that met my ears.

During the second hour, I felt slightly less confident, but I kept listening nonetheless. The steady rhythm of the air recyclers threatened to lull me into sleep, but I resisted. I had to stay awake.

I'll hear the sounds soon, and when I do, I'll know for sure that this is real. This was what I told myself, though I honestly didn't know what I'd do after that.

Sometime after the fourth hour, I fell asleep without having heard anything out of the ordinary.

When I woke the following morning, I spent ten long minutes in bed straining to hear anything unusual. All I got were the telltale sounds of Mom making breakfast and Flynn shuffling to the bathroom with a groan.

I swung my legs over the edge of the bed and buried my face in my hands. "That doesn't mean it wasn't real," I told myself, though I doubted my words.

The next couple of days were uneventful. I kept my ears on all the time, which led to more headaches. I wasn't the best of company, but I was on a mission. No matter where I went, I paid attention to everything going on around me. Among disagreements between friends, parents reprimanding children, and the hurried footsteps of people running late, I found no sign of what I'd heard that night.

What if everyone else was right? What if my imagination had gotten the better of me?

I'd nearly lost all hope of figuring it out when, while on my way to buy a new pair of shoes with my mom, I accidentally overheard a conversation outside one of the station's restaurants.

"What do you mean? How could an animal have gotten into the pantry?"

This question snagged my attention, and I quickly spotted the man who asked it. The dull gray color of his uniform identified him as a security guard.

The second man was tall, slender, and bald. Almost like a Q-tip. He gestured wildly with his hands as he spoke. "I don't know, but it had to be an animal of some kind. The mess I found . . . bags and boxes were torn open. Shredded. A person wouldn't have done that."

The security guard shrugged. "Sometimes kids will go out of their way to destroy things for the fun of it. Maybe that's what happened."

"No. I don't think so." The bald man sighed. "Whoever or whatever it was, I need you to find out. I lost a lot of money because of this. I can't afford to lose anything else."

Then my mother and I had traveled too far, and the remaining conversation was swallowed by the buzz of the lunch crowd. While Mom chatted about things she wanted to buy, my thoughts remained with what happened at the restaurant.

An animal? What kind of animal could be lurking at night on a space station? How did it get here? Where did it come from? Why hadn't anyone seen it yet?

Though I didn't have an answer yet to any of these questions, I felt certain about one thing. I wasn't crazy. I *had* heard something that night, and I felt more determined than ever to find out what it was.

The next day, I barely paid attention to what my teacher was saying. She was talking about the first Martian settlers and the hardships they'd faced during their first year. I recall that much, but anything beyond that was lost on me. My eyes wandered the room, my fingers drumming quietly against the desktop as my thoughts roamed free.

The classroom had the same white walls and blue carpet the corridor did. Motivational posters about trying your best and the benefits of learning adorned the space. Normally I wouldn't pay much attention to them, but one captured my attention. It showed a little girl with dark skin and big brown eyes wearing a lab coat and standing in front of a microscope. At the top of the poster, bold green text proclaimed, "Don't wait! Investigate!"

Investigate. That's what I needed to do. If I found enough evidence, someone would believe me.

After Mom and Flynn fell asleep, I slipped out of bed and began to prepare. I wasn't entirely sure what I'd need, though. I'd never planned a voyage like this before. How often does one get the chance to pursue a mysterious creature through a sleeping space station? It wasn't as if I could ask anyone for advice, either. This mission had to remain secret, otherwise someone would stop me.

Thanks to knowledge gained from books and movies, I dressed in the darkest clothes I owned. Then I pinned my long brown hair to my head and covered it with a black fedora. Yes, situations like these usually had people wearing black stocking hats, but I didn't have one of those. Having lived on a space station my whole life, I'd never had to deal with the winter weather they were typically used for.

I snagged a flashlight from my desk drawer. It was small, purple, and strapped to my wrist. Finally, I slipped my flat, rectangular holo imager into my pocket. If I did manage to find something, I wanted to get a picture of it.

Hoping I wouldn't need anything else, I tiptoed through our darkened quarters and out the door.

The station had a different feel to it at night. The common areas, typically crowded with people, were empty. There were plenty of background noises, but they stayed at a comfortable level. My ears weren't on the verge of overwhelming me. If I didn't have a curfew, I might have made a habit of taking midnight walks.

I roamed the corridors on tiptoes, ready to duck into the

shadows if a security guard happened upon me. I'd been out for more than an hour when I finally heard it.

Tap tap. Clink. Rattle rattle. Thump.

The sounds originated from my left side. Maintenance crawlspaces and tunnels snaked throughout the entire station. One of those had to run behind that wall. I needed to find a point of entry. That proved to be tricky since we were near a cluster of restaurants and shops. Any doors leading to these tunnels were bound to be well hidden.

I eventually found what I was looking for concealed behind a large fake fern surrounded by benches. The door was narrow but tall enough to easily admit most human adults.

Clink. Tap. Clink clink. Thump. Rattle rattle. Bang.

The flashlight beam wavered as I reached for the door, the metal cool against my fingertips. I started to pull it open.

"What are you doing, *Ear*-ina?"

I froze in place, silently scolding myself for not paying enough attention to my surroundings. I should have heard him coming, but I'd been too focused on everything else to notice.

Clink clink. Rattle. Tap tap tap.

Annoyed by the interruption, I spun around and pressed a finger to my lips. My unwelcome visitor stood with his hand resting on the back of the nearest bench. "Shhh! I'm busy. You need to go away."

Raffee's jaw dropped. Of course he was shocked. I'd never yelled at him before. "What? You can't tell me what to do!"

I ground my teeth in frustration. "I know you enjoy trying to make my life miserable, but could you please let it go this one time? I have something important to do."

He snorted. "What could you possibly have to do at this time of night? You shouldn't be out here."

I rolled my eyes. "Neither should you. If you give me a hard time, I'll turn you in for violating curfew."

"If you do that, everyone will know you violated curfew, too," Raffee said.

Hmm. *I should have thought about that before I spoke. Now I look stupid. Good job, Arina.* "Getting in trouble might be worth it to get you to go away." Though he was still watching me, I knew I had to get moving. I didn't have a lot of time before I'd lose track of the sounds. They were steadily receding.

"Seriously, what are you doing?" The nasty edge had dropped from his tone. Now he only sounded curious.

"There's something in there, Raffee. I can hear it. I want to find out what it is."

He started to open his mouth, and I guessed he was about to say something mean again.

I held my hand up and cut him off. "I don't want to listen to whatever it is you have to say. You're only wasting my time, and none of your friends are around to laugh along with you anyway." Before he had a chance to respond to what I'd said, I stepped into the tunnel.

The flashlight beam bounced off the dingy walls. Beyond that I couldn't see much, though the noises were a bit louder now, echoing slightly in the enclosed space.

Rattle rattle rattle. Scrape. Bang bang. Rattle.

"Hey! Wait up!" Raffee called out in a hushed tone as he hurried to catch up to me.

"Why should I?" I asked without stopping or looking back at him.

"Maybe I can help? What do you think we're looking for?"

Curiosity is a powerful force. He'd never want to team up with me under normal circumstances, but away from watchful eyes and in the presence of a mystery, he'd changed his mind.

I sighed. I didn't feel like arguing with him, and I certainly wasn't turning back and going home. "An animal of some kind, I think." I quickly explained everything that led to me lurking around the station in the middle of the night. He listened with great interest, and by the time I'd finished, his face glowed with excitement.

That look disappeared when I asked him what brought him out past curfew.

"My parents were fighting," Raffee said, his voice barely above a whisper. "I couldn't sleep, so I went for a walk."

Those words hit me hard. I didn't know what to say. Though I was tempted to ask if this happened often, I didn't. Instead I said, "I bet you didn't expect to end up on an adventure like this, did you?"

That made him grin a little. "No, I didn't."

The louder the sounds became, the quieter Raffee and I tried to be. We didn't want to let whatever it was know that we were closing in on its position.

Rattle rattle. Bang. Scrape scrape scrape. Rattle. Bang. BANG.

I jumped a little. We were close. My heart began to race, and my palms were sweating. I wiped my hands on my pants and pulled my holo imager out of my pocket. I wasn't going to miss my opportunity if I could help it.

Raffee laid a hand on my shoulder. "Look," he whispered, pointing to the side.

A vent opened into the right wall of the tunnel. The grate, which normally would have covered the opening, had been knocked to the side. A trail of crumbs littered the ground right in front of it. My shoes crunched over them as I walked. "It's been bringing food in here," I said. "I wonder where it sleeps. Or *if* it sleeps."

"What do you mean?" Raffee asked.

I shrugged. "We could be dealing with anything. What if it's something no one has ever seen before? Isn't this exciting?"

BANG! RATTLE RATTLE! THUMP! SCRAPE! BANG BANG!

I was a little bit nervous, but I wasn't about to tell Raffee that, even though he was shivering despite the warm temperature of the passageway.

Given how near we were getting to the sounds, I shouldn't have been surprised when we saw it. The maintenance tunnel intersected with another tunnel, and the trail of crumbs snaked around the corner. We followed and almost smacked right into it. I halted in my tracks, and Raffee bumped into me, nearly sending me sprawling. I barely kept hold of my holo imager.

I counted seven large eyes that glowed red, though countless smaller things that also looked like eyes surrounded them. I squinted and saw that those eyes were set atop a flat head. The creature had a pudgy gray body and six legs. Its mouth opened, revealing rows of flat teeth.

SQUEEEEEEEEEEEEKKKKKKK!

Normally I would have switched my ears off when assailed by such a loud noise. Pain bloomed inside my skull, but instead of trying to stop it, I held out my holo imager and snapped a picture.

A second later, the creature turned and bolted, its legs carrying it away from us far faster than I would have guessed they could. Before I thought to take off after it, it disappeared into the shadows.

Raffee, whose jaw had dropped open in shock, looked over at me. "Did you get the picture?"

I took a deep breath and let it out slowly. "I don't know. Let's see." I pressed the display button.

A moment later, an image hovered in the air. It wasn't perfect. A large portion of the body was cast in shadow. The eyes, however, showed clearly, as did most of the head. It might be enough to convince someone I wasn't imagining things.

"It's the best we can do," I said. "Let's get out of here so I can show this to someone."

Raffee cast me an anxious glance, but he didn't say anything during our walk back. It wasn't until we stepped out of the tunnel that he spoke again.

"My parents would be really mad if they knew I was here." Raffee's voice was pleading.

"Okay. You go back. I won't tell anyone you were a part of this." I didn't need to cover for him, but oddly enough, I wanted to.

His shoulders sagged with relief. "Thanks, Arina." Then he turned and ran.

The security guard I flagged down didn't look pleased to see me, and it took a long minute to convince him to look at my holo imager. When he finally saw the proof, though, he immediately got his boss out of bed to see it.

It took a team of security guards and one of the station's resident biologists to capture the creature. They managed to bring it in without harming it. Now they were studying it. No one had ever seen anything like it before, which explained why normal bio scans missed it. According to Mom, the station's scientists were giddy over the discovery. She tried to tell me everything she could about their findings.

"It's nocturnal. That's why no one saw it before. Bright lights hurt its eyes," she told me one day.

"It's cold-blooded, so heat scans couldn't find it," she told me the next day. "That's probably why it was able to stow away on whatever ship brought it here."

I think she shared this information because she felt bad for not believing me.

That doesn't mean I didn't get a lecture about sneaking out at night, of course. I listened to the list of bad things my mom feared could have happened to me, but she didn't seem as worried as she had in the past. Maybe I'd managed to prove myself to her, at least a little bit.

This conclusion seemed even more likely when Captain

Ovid stopped by our quarters to see me. Captain Ovid oversaw the station. He had dark skin and dark eyes, and he was the exact same height as me. When my mom offered him a seat he shook his head. "I can't stay long. I just wanted to have a quick talk with your daughter."

I stood there, shaking from nerves as I waited for him to say what he came to say. I didn't want to get in trouble, and I knew I still could.

Captain Ovid smiled. "Arina, we're all grateful. You technically shouldn't have been out past curfew, but you might have saved the station from countless problems. The creature could have done untold damage if it ever got into any vital systems."

I shrugged, though the grin on my face was anything but casual. "I'm glad I could help."

"Listen, if you ever hear anything else, just let me know. I'll take your concerns seriously."

That comment had me smiling for the rest of the day.

Raffee also stopped making fun of me, and interestingly enough, so did his friends. That isn't to say that Raffee and I became best friends after that. We didn't. We do catch each other's eye occasionally, though, and I know we're both thinking about the adventure we shared. There are some things you never forget.

Juliet Silver and the Forge of Dreams
by Wendy Nikel

Wendy Nikel is a speculative fiction author with a degree in elementary education, a fondness for road trips, and a terrible habit of forgetting where she's left her cup of tea. Her short fiction has been published in *Fantastic Stories of the Imagination, Daily Science Fiction, Nature/Futures*, and elsewhere. Her time travel novella, "The Continuum," is forthcoming from World Weaver Press in spring 2018.

The *Realm of Impossibility* shuddered across the sky, whipped about by hurricane-force gales. Captain Juliet Silver, standing at the ship's helm, gritted her teeth and braced herself against the force as she shouted orders to her crew. They hadn't experienced a storm like this in ages, not since the previous captain was at the helm.

Despite her relative lack of experience, Juliet held her own against the storm for a good, long time—far longer than most seasoned captains would have—based on sheer stubbornness alone. She'd held her own against monsters and magic alike; no mere storm was going to defeat her.

"Captain Silver!" Her first mate Geofferies grabbed her arm. "There's a puncture in the main bladder. We need to take her down."

Juliet scowled. They were over open seas, which meant that unless they found an island, they'd have to evacuate to the inflatable lifeboats while they repaired the bobbing airship. And they were already behind on their shipments because they'd spent the last three days trying to out-maneuver the storm. The thing had followed them like a lost mutt, always lurking darkly just to the south. If she didn't know any better, she'd say it seemed sentient.

But if the *Realm* needed to be patched, the *Realm* needed to be patched, and there was nothing to do but pull the levers that lowered the ship from the clouds into the sea below.

Just as the monstrous waves lapped at the side of the ship and Juliet tasted the salty spray in the air, she spotted something dark on the horizon.

"Hold steady, crew!" she shouted through the tubular contraption that sent her voice out to the rest of the ship. "There's land! About fourteen knots, straight ahead!"

Juliet cranked the handles, steadying the *Realm* and pressing on toward the unknown island, where at least they might be able to wait out the storm.

Juliet Silver felt their eyes upon her the moment she stepped off her ship. Despite the wind and rain and the tug of the sea behind her as each wave threatened to pull her ship into its depths, Juliet felt it.

She raised her hand, halting the crew members disembarking behind her, and drew her sword from her side.

Someone was watching.

Juliet shielded her eyes and peered into the shadows of the bare, rocky island on which they'd landed. Oddly shaped forms teased her mind, refusing to resolve into discernable shapes. Deep within the shadows of moss-coated stone, something stirred.

"You there. I see you," she shouted, hoping they couldn't sense her bluff. "Come forward and tell us: are you friend or foe?"

For a moment, nothing happened. Then, slowly, a figure in a dark cloak emerged from behind a black rock. The wind whipped the stranger's garments but did not tear the hood from his face. An unbidden shiver crept up Juliet's stiffened spine.

"I might ask you the same." The voice came crisp and clear over the howl of the wind, with the twinge of an accent unfamiliar to Juliet, despite her extensive travels. "After all, it is you who are trespassing on our island."

Juliet sheathed her sword and displayed her palms. "We were caught in the storm, and our airship is damaged. We only wish to make our repairs. We will be on our way as soon as the skies clear. That is, if you allow us to remain."

From behind her shoulder, the crew's tinkerer, Sofia, leaned in to whisper over the wind. "We must be careful, Captain. There are many strange beings that dwell upon isolated rocks."

"Do you know this kind?" Juliet nodded to the distant figure. Sofia was from an oceanic race far older than land-bound humans; if any of the crew would know, she would. But the tinkerer shook her head.

"You may remain here while the storm passes," the hooded figure said, "but as soon as the skies clear, you must be gone."

"Agreed." Juliet turned to issue orders, quickly dividing up the work into rotating shifts so all would get a chance to rest before setting out again. To Sofia, she said, "We'll give these island-dwellers the benefit of the doubt, but stay alert for any sign of trouble. We're far from any on whom we might rely for assistance."

Juliet's crew pitched their makeshift tents upon the shoreline, where the *Realm of Impossibility*'s bulk could block the worst of the raging storm. When it was time for Juliet's sleeping shift, she slipped off her jacket and her precious chain-mail armor before collapsing onto her cot. Nearly instantly, she fell into a hazy, restless sleep.

Her dreams, though vivid, were unusual—full of places she'd never been, people she'd never met, and yet she felt them not just with her senses but with her emotions, as well. She dreamt of a mangy yellow dog with a limp who followed her around. With large, calloused hands that she knew weren't her own, she stroked the creature's coarse fur, her heart feeling as though it would burst with love for this thin and battered-looking canine.

The dog disappeared, replaced by the image of a woman with gray hair and crooked teeth. She smelled of cardamom and cinnamon, and when she laughed, she stared at Juliet with such familiarity and warmth that it made her gasp in her sleep. The woman reached over and squeezed her hand—a child's hand, small and soft and sticky with sweat.

But the warm and wrinkled hand warped and changed, growing cold and hard and sending terror through her. The skin had turned to a glimmering silver metal, and when she looked up, the face that loomed over her was scarred and sneering. The face drew closer. Metallic cogs on his arm clicked like the pincers of some enormous bug. His breath was hot and putrid, and the reek of decay spread out over her skin.

A shrill noise pierced her consciousness. She jolted up, suddenly awake, covered in sweat, and staring at two blindingly white lights. Something was wrong. Very wrong.

"What is that? What's going on?"

"Sorry, Captain." With a *click*, the lights dimmed, and by their softened glow, Juliet could see Sofia standing over her, holding what appeared to be a mechanical rooster whose eyes illuminated the tent.

"What is that?" Juliet rubbed her eyes.

"It's a device I've been working on. A clock, designed to wake one from their sleep at an appointed time. In my home in Prosperia, each day began with a blast of trumpets. The noise caused the phosphorescent creatures of our underwater grotto to awaken abruptly, flooding the city with light. Here on land, however, I've heard that people wake with the sound of roosters, so I thought to make this for myself. When I heard you crying out in your sleep but was unable to wake you myself, I thought my little rooster might rouse you."

"It certainly did." Juliet pressed her hand against her head.

"Yes. I believe the volume is broken." Sofia turned the clockwork creature over in her hands and then, shrugging, tucked it away in her satchel. "I'll have more time to work on it when we're on our way again."

Juliet struggled to her feet. Though the intense feeling of terror had abated, she was unable to shake the feeling that something was wrong. She was never one to believe in premonitions or signs, but she was not normally a heavy sleeper, and those were not her usual dreams. In fact, they'd felt nothing like her dreams at all. Hers were often tense and full of fears and sorrows, but they were at least familiar fears and sorrows. They were *hers*. This, though... this was as though she'd stepped inside someone else's mind, someone else's dreams, and it left her feeling strange and cold. There was something not right about this island, and the sooner they took to the skies, the better.

Juliet reached for her sword and armor in the dim light of Sofia's glowing-eyed rooster. The sword was exactly where she'd left it beside her cot, but the place beside it was empty.

"My armor!" Juliet's voice was pitched high with tension and fear, a tone she hadn't heard from herself in quite some time. After all, she was the captain of an airship now and a captain—particularly one whose dealings weren't always within the boundaries of accepted law—must maintain her composure. Yet she couldn't still the shaking of her hands as she tore apart her tent, her fingers starved for the familiar feel of the intricate metal rings, perfectly designed to slide and shift to the form of her body, to provide the greatest protection with least bulk.

What's more, it was a precious gift from the one person to whom she owed everything.

She tried to breathe deeply, to blink back the hot tears of frustration burning at the corners of her eyes. "Sofia, did you see anyone else near my tent?"

"No, Captain." Sofia, who had been standing, silent and wide-eyed at the tent flap, shook her head. "I was standing guard near the airship and heard you scream. There's a terrible fog outside. I had the hardest time even finding your tent. At one point, I tripped and fell and—"

She reached down to touch her waist and let out a cry of surprise. "My toolbelt! It's missing. I... I must have dropped it when I fell outside."

The tinkerer turned to leave the tent, but Juliet grabbed her shoulder. "We'll go together. It will be safer if we're not alone."

⋅⟩⟨⋅

Neither Juliet's armor nor Sofia's belt was found in the thick fog, nor among the others' tents. In fact, with each crew member they asked, they discovered yet another object—always something personal, something highly valued—missing from among their possessions. What's more, Juliet also discovered that the others had experienced strange dreams as well: faces and places unfamiliar to them, paired with oddly intense emotions.

"It's obvious, isn't it?" First mate Geofferies stood beside her, voicing the words she hadn't wanted to say aloud. His hand kept returning to the chain clipped to his jacket, now hanging empty without the watch he normally kept there. "It's the island-dwellers. They've crept in with fog and stolen from us while we were otherwise occupied. You know as well as I do none of our crew would have done this."

"What should we do?" Sofia asked, but Juliet remained silent. It would do no good for the crew to gather their weapons and mount an assault on an unknown people in an unfamiliar landscape, particularly with the eerie fog that had followed the storm. It unsettled her, nearly as much as the missing items, nearly as much as her growing suspicion that this entire thing had somehow been a trap. A trap that she, their captain, had led them directly into.

"Sofia and I will go in search of the island dwellers," Juliet ordered. "The rest of you must remain here and continue work on the airship repairs. If we're not back before the fog lifts, you're to leave without us. And don't allow anyone to sleep. I don't trust these dreams."

Juliet crept through the fog, feeling small and helpless without her armor. Her sword she kept sheathed; she hoped to recover the stolen objects without a fight, at least until she was wrapped in her chain-link protection again. Sofia followed, her tools—strapped to a bit of leather at her waist—clinking ever so softly with each step.

They made their way slowly through the fog, feeling along the sides of condensation-slicked rocks until, finally, a path became distinguishable. It wove through the formations, farther and farther into the island's stony heart. The women walked silently, as if afraid to wake the slumbering dream-world around them, until finally they reached a stone arch and a set of steps leading downward into the earth.

"Do you have your portable light?" Juliet whispered.

Sofia held out the bulb and cranked its handle until the filaments illuminated the path. When it was fully charged, the island descended once more into silence.

Juliet led the way, her shadow stumbling down the steps before her, until finally they reached the bottom. They turned a corner, and Juliet's breath caught.

Before them lay a vast cavern, glowing red with the heat and smoke of dozens of open pits teeming with bright-hot molten rock. Islanders stood around these, each working on his own task in this great forge. Their hammers rang against anvils. Their poles stirred the steaming pools of melted stone. And throughout the enclosed space, luminous wisps of white smoke rose from their work stations—yet upon closer look, the particles took shape, forming people... places... things that Juliet didn't know, yet instantly she knew what they were.

"Dreams," she whispered. "They look like the images from my dreams."

She didn't see the gray-haired woman or the man with the mechanical arm, but the feeling was the same, the sense of strangeness and intensity of emotions, so strong and yet not her own.

"Captain," Sofia whispered. Half a dozen canvas bags hung from hooks mounted to the adjacent cavern wall, sagging heavily with the weight of their contents. Juliet's chain-mail armor glimmered from a hook beside them.

As they watched, one of the hooded islanders opened a bag and extracted something round and glimmering. Geofferies' compass.

The islander shuffled over to an opening in the floor where the molten rock pooled up like a giant vat of fiery liquid. He held the compass aloft and then, intoning a chant in some language unfamiliar to Juliet, he dropped the object into the pit. Juliet jerked forward impulsively, but Sofia held her back.

"It's too late."

It was. The compass had melted away the instant it touched the surface. From that pool rose wisps of brilliant white smoke, forming figures that played out like a flickering zoetrope. A man hovered in midair, a man who looked very much like Geofferies, though he wore spectacles and his face was shaven. He held an item out before him, as if offering it to someone, and Juliet was filled with an inexplicable pride and admiration and a fear of letting him down. She shook her head to clear away the stolen emotions, though still they lingered deep in her subconscious.

"I know what this is," Sofia said softly. "This is a dream forge."

"A dream forge?" The term was unfamiliar to Juliet.

"Yes. My people have stories about them, very old stories. Those wisps of white—they aren't really smoke but dreams, which dissipate and spread out across the world, permeating the minds of all who sleep and weaving themselves into the dreamers' consciousness."

"So the items they've stolen from us... they're turning them into dreams?"

"The smiths of the dream forges collect items that hold strong emotions—love or anger or fear or pride. These emotions, when melted down, form the dreams. Though," Sofia said, frowning, "in the stories I've heard, they've never stolen anything. They were finders of lost things, recoverers of forgotten treasures... scavengers, if you will, not thieves."

"Did any of the stories involve people landing on their island?"

"No. Their forges are said to be unchartable, and that if one were to find them..." She hesitated.

"What?"

"The dreams here are too strong, too potent. Anyone who lingers on their islands would be absorbed into the dreams, becoming nothing more than a dream themselves. Captain, we must leave immediately."

Juliet unsheathed her sword, her eyes fixed on the glimmering links of chain upon the hook. "Not without my armor."

Slowly, not watching to see if Sofia followed, Juliet placed one foot and then the next carefully on the cavern floor, making her way slowly, ever so slowly along the wall and toward the hooks where the items were hung. The steam was hot and uncomfortable on her skin, and with each breath, it filled her head with the strangest sensations.

One breath left her desperate and underwater in a sea of green-blue brine, gasping for breath and clinging desperately to a golden locket. The next found her cold and lonely, the chill of a hard stone floor on her shoulder and tears running down her dirty cheeks. She tried to hold her breath, to keep the visions from obscuring the physical world around her, but eventually her lungs expanded again. This time, she was in a smoky tavern, her heart shattering into a million pieces as she watched two lovers embrace. She choked out a sob.

Logically, she knew these memories, these emotions, these dreams weren't her own, but with each inhalation of the fumes—so potent here at their source—they enveloped her. The glowing rock fissures and the smiths faded, and she was there, in the memories released from the treasures.

Dream and reality bent and warped around her. Which was which? Were the hooded figures truly turning to look at her, to close in around her, or was that merely a projection of her dream-addled mind? The only thing that she could see clearly was the outline of her armor before her.

She fixed her eyes on it as she urged her feet forward, focusing her mind on it, on the emotions that tied her to it: the surprise and appreciation for being accepted by the captain and crew of the airship when she'd never felt as though she'd truly belonged anywhere before; the overwhelming sense of responsibility when she'd first donned that armor; the pride she felt in wearing it each day; and the sharp pain—still crippling, even now—when the man who'd given it to her—the man who'd loved her—had disappeared.

Still, the warring emotions disoriented her, surrounded her like a thick shroud. It was suffocating her, overwhelming her, drowning her in emotion. Her knees gave out beneath her, and she stumbled and caught herself on the wall. The armor shone brightly, just out of her reach. If only she could clear her head, make the nightmares that were swirling about her dissipate. Though maybe... maybe there was.

"Sofia!" Juliet pivoted on her heel, even as she reached for the armor. "The rooster!"

Through the swirling darkness, beyond the sea serpents and skeletons, the gentle mothers and streaks of pain, Sofia's startled face brightened with understanding. She reached into her satchel and pulled out the rooster. Just as she was disappearing from Juliet's vision, being swallowed whole by the churning smoke-monsters, the rooster's crowing broke through the nightmares, scattering the visions like shards of crumpled glass.

Juliet could breathe. She could see. She could see the armor, directly before her, and the canvas bags on the wall beside it. Quickly, before the dream-creatures could re-form themselves, before the hooded islanders—now slowly setting down their tools and turning her in direction—could reach her, she snatched up the armor and bags, spun on her heel, and stumbled toward the steps, leaping over the fissures in the rock.

The women ran up the stairs, moving more quickly and surely the farther they fled from the cavern.

"The *Realm* had better be ready to go," Juliet said, panting, as they wove along the path back to the shore.

Sure enough, there before them, slowly coming into sight through the fog, was the *Realm of Impossibility*, its bladders refilled, gently ascending into the hazy skies. It was no use waiting out the storm; this island was a perpetual tempest. Instead, Juliet called out orders to launch as she ran up the gangplank. By the time the hooded islanders emerged from the fog, forming a line of gray figures on the beach, the airship was already high in the sky, the island growing smaller and more distant beneath them.

As Juliet piloted the ship into clearer skies, Sofia distributed the contents of the bags. Geofferies' compass, of course, was lost to the world, for which Juliet pulled him aside and apologized quietly. Geofferies shook his head and requested some time to himself, and Juliet arranged for the others to take over his duties for the time being. If she'd lost her armor, she'd have felt the same: unmoored, disoriented, grieving.

When the bag was empty, and the crew had returned to

their duties, Sofia approached Juliet at the helm, holding something in her hands.

"No one has claimed this one," she said, holding it out for Juliet to see. The object was a polished stone, its surface as smooth as glass. Within it, shadows shifted strangely, as if there were something sentient within it.

"Have you ever seen anything like it before?" Juliet asked.

"Never."

"And we're certain it doesn't belong to any of the crew?"

"Positive. None of them knew what to make of it."

Juliet turned the stone over in her hands, studying it, trying to discern its purpose. It was obviously valuable, at least to someone, or it wouldn't have been gathered with the other treasures. Yet it wasn't as though they could return it, even if they wanted to.

"Perhaps we ought to drop it into the sea," Sofia suggested.

"For now," Juliet said slowly, "we keep it. We keep it locked somewhere safe until we determine what it is, whether it's safe to simply dispose of. We must be careful not to tell anyone outside the crew. Agreed?"

"I'll construct a safe for it." Sofia patted her toolbelt.

Juliet turned her attention back to the skies—now crisp and clear and blue—and tried to dispel the unease in her heart. The smiths were not the only scavengers of the sea, and if the stone was something valuable, something magical, something powerful, there might be others who'd desire it as well. It was her responsibility now to keep it safe, and for her, the safest place she knew was right there, high above the clouds in the *Realm of Impossibility*.

The Altitude Adjustment
by Wendy Lambert

Wendy Lambert grew up watching classic science fiction shows with her dad. Disappointed that her rocket scientist dad never built a starship to take her to distant alien worlds, she imagines them instead. Her stories have appeared in the anthologies *In the Shimmering* and the 2015 and 2016 *Young Explorer's Adventure Guides*. Wendy lives in Utah with her family, where she cofounded North Star Academy, a top-ranked school that inspires students to reach for their dreams.

The Martian girl was technically human, but everything about her appearance looked alien. Her head looked too big atop her rail-thin body. Even with the gleaming metal braces encasing them, her twiggy legs looked like they'd snap in half if she took a single step. It was the effect of growing up on Mars under a third less gravity than Earth.

"Kara, did you hear me?" Miss Bird, my sixth-grade teacher, asked. "Briel's hoverchair can't go up these steep stairs."

I realized I'd been staring at her and shifted my gaze away from Briel only to feel the weighty eyes of my class-mates, the tour guide, and Miss Bird as they awaited a response.

"Go with Briel to the elevator?" I asked.

Miss Bird nodded.

The rest of the class clomped noisily up the stairs. The strong smell of rusted metal from the old building tickled my nose, and I sneezed.

"Bless you," Briel said. She regarded me with her huge eyes made bigger through her sparkly blue cat-eye glasses that matched the streak of bright blue in her hair. "That is what you say, right?"

"Yes." I pointed to a long hallway. "The tour guide said the elevator was somewhere back here?"

"Yep." Briel pressed the controls, turning her chair back around.

I hesitated. Should I walk ahead of her and lead the way? Or behind? The hallway was wide here, and I decided to walk beside her.

"You're staring again. Do I have something on my face?"

I looked away from her and up at the odd, scalloped-shaped lights running along the ceiling. Our class had come to tour the North Star Space Facility during its annual Take Flight Fundraising Festival. The decaying structure of steel was now a museum, displaying a variety of experimental space balloons, rockets, and ships. In its day it had been a cutting-edge lab and space tourist facility.

After seeing Briel and what living on Mars or in space did to you, I wasn't sure I ever wanted to go up. Earth gravity didn't care whether you were an Earthling or a Martian, it pulled all of us down. My body was used to the gravity. Briel's wasn't. Her frail bones and weak muscles made life difficult and different for her. She was stuck in that hoverchair, for one thing. It hummed along, inches from the ground. The chair's back bumper was bedazzled in tiny rhinestones save for a sticker that read *Mars Rocks*.

"I don't bite," Briel said in a completely flat voice.

"I, I don't—" I knew she didn't bite.

"At least not too hard." She grinned. "I wish I'd brought a mirror to show you your face."

"My face?" I touched my cheek, feeling the warmth of the blush.

She laughed; her whole body shook beneath the straps holding her upright in the chair. "I just meant that you seem a little, well, afraid of me."

"I'm not." I wasn't afraid. Just shy. Especially around people I didn't know. And especially around a Martian who might break in half if I touched her.

"Even though I'm a Martian and stuck in this chair, I *can* still talk. We do both speak English—at least I think you do." She paused expectantly while I struggled for something to say in return.

"Which way was the elevator?" I focused on our task.

"I think the tour guide said it's on the right."

A rope cordoned off the hallway with a posted sign reading *Authorized Personnel Only.*

Briel raised the rope and moved her chair under it. "Are you sure this is the right way?" I asked.

"Nope, but I think it is. That looks like an elevator." Briel gestured to the double set of metal doors at the end of the hallway.

I raced ahead to press the elevator call button. I could actually be helpful. The doors opened into a large elevator with a second set of doors at its back.

Briel moved her hoverchair forward then swiveled around. "Are you coming? Remember, I don't bite hard."

Why does she keep saying that? I forced a smile. "I don't think you bite," I said and stepped into the elevator. *I'm just shy.* I didn't know how to tell her this. I didn't know how to tell her I wasn't good with anybody, especially a Martian.

I pushed the second level button. The doors closed, and the elevator moved upward. I exhaled in relief. We'd be back with our class in a couple of minutes, and the awkwardness would end. The elevator slowed to a stop. The back doors opened into a short hallway.

Briel maneuvered her chair into the hallway. "This is weird," she called. Bright block lettering on the walls read *Odyssey Thirteen*. The hall emptied into a small, dark room with large round windows all around and above. Seats ringed its entirety, facing the windows, save for a door marked as a restroom and some sort of food stand. Briel moved straight to a large console in the center.

"Where's the class?" I said.

"I'm so speedy in my chair, they haven't caught up yet."

The door behind us whooshed closed. The lights from the hall flickered and died, plunging us into near darkness except for the faint glow coming from the bottom of Briel's chair. I bit my lip, refusing to let out my squealed surprise. I ran my hand up and down along the sides of the closed door feeling for the open button.

"Oops," Briel said. "That may have been me." She jerked her hand away from the console.

"What button did you push?"

"A lot of them," Briel said. "I'm not sure which one closed the—"

"Quiet," I said. "Hear that?" A faint hiss sounded overhead. It was pitch black above the windowed ceiling, making it impossible to see what made the noise. I ran my hands over the buttons. The door didn't open, but something I'd pushed turned on a dark screen.

"What is this place?" I asked.

"Don't know."

"Maybe we shouldn't push any more buttons," I said.

"Wait. I have my phone with me." Briel rummaged inside a bag on the side of her chair. She held it up. "No signal." She maneuvered her hoverchair around the room, holding her phone up.

"Well, Miss Bird has got to realize we got lost or something. She'll come looking for us, don't you think?" I offered.

She nodded.

The low hissing sound grew louder and louder. Briel clutched the arms of her chair, and her big eyes widened. She was scared, just like me.

"The building is really old, it's no wonder the door's stuck," I said.

The floor rocked back and forth. We floated up a few feet and bounced to a stop. I scrambled back to the door and pounded on it.

Briel pushed buttons on the console again. The hissing stopped. "That's good, right?" Briel said.

We looked at each other. One button blinked green.

"I don't think—" I said.

Briel pushed the button. The room shook as a metallic scraping sound rumbled overhead. Bright daylight flooded overhead revealing what we hadn't seen before—a massive silvery balloon attached to what I now knew was no room at all, but a pod. The balloon floated slowly and silently out of the hangar into the sky.

"There's this lever with the words *balloon detachment*," I said.

Briel gave a snort of disagreement. "Sure, pull it if you want the balloon to keep floating up and us to fall to our deaths. We're too high already."

"Your phone," I said.

We looked at her phone and it had a signal. She called her mom. It went straight to voicemail. "So Mom, I'm in trouble. We accidentally took off in a balloon. We need help." Briel hung up. "She didn't answer."

"This definitely counts as an emergency, call 911," I urged.

She dialed. And each second seemed like forever as the balloon rose steadily into the sky.

"911, what's your emergency?"

Below us the world shrank. Our yellow school bus was a tiny rectangle of orange-yellow surrounded by asphalt and glints of sunlight off rearview mirrors and the chrome trim of parked cars. In the fields surrounding the gray building, scattered booths for the festival were tiny pops of color. Another hiss of helium fed the balloon, carrying us higher and higher away from the open roof of the facility.

It'd taken a ridiculously long time for emergency personnel to find the right person to help us. The voice was faint and crackled back. "This is Captain Stevens. Everything's going to be okay. We're going to bring you home safely. How's that sound?"

"Fantastic!" Briel shouted.

And it was fantastic, except for the part about having to wait until we were nearly into space before we could begin our descent. Captain Stevens explained how to turn on the space balloon's communication system. I put on the headset and learned that while the balloon and pod were very old, they were flightworthy, having been readied for a flight that was supposed to happen tomorrow as part of the festival.

I guess they'd decided the easiest way to get us back on the ground was to let the space balloon take its normal preprogrammed flight all the way up to space and then gently float back to Earth on a parasail. All we had to do was wait and pull a lever to detach the balloon on the given signal. It was a lot of waiting. Floating up one hundred miles seemed to take forever.

"You think we'll make it back?" I asked, nervous despite Captain Stevens' assurances.

"Of course. We should just relax and enjoy the ride," Briel said.

"Easy for you to say. I bet you're used to flying."

"Not like this."

I flopped into one of the chairs. We'd risen very high in the sky. I pressed my face against the cold window, the warmth of my breath fogging it up. We were floating towards space. Cold, dark, airless space.

"What's your favorite color?" Briel asked cheerfully. She'd moved beside me.

"What? What kind of question is that?"

"Look, there's nothing we can do but sit here, enjoy the ride and view. I might as well find out if you're worth knowing."

I opened and closed my mouth in stunned silence. *Worth knowing?* Who even says that? Was she joking? I couldn't ever tell with her. But she was right about one thing. There was nothing more we could do. "Blue," I said.

"Mine, too," Briel said.

I snorted. "I thought it'd be red."

Briel winced. "Yeah, I get that a lot . . . Mars being the red planet and all." She studied me long and hard. "What do you like to do for fun?"

"I play soccer and—"

"Me, too!" Briel cut me off. "Don't look so shocked. Of course I don't play it anymore—at least on Earth. But I used to play forward in the top club team. I even played a year up."

"I have a hard time picturing soccer on Mars." I imagined an enormous field, with players wearing bright orange space-suits kicking the ball to the opposing team in bright green spacesuits. One kick would send the ball halfway around Mars.

"It's pretty much the same except for more protective gear, a softer ball, and indoor fields."

"I just play rec soccer," I confessed. I couldn't let her think we were even close to the same league. "I like to swim, too. My parents put in a pool last summer. I pretty much got out only to sleep."

"Really? That's my favorite thing to do now. Except I don't get out to sleep."

"You sleep in the water?"

"In a special water bed. It's the only time I don't feel like Earth is trying to crush me."

"Oh." I felt my face grow warm.

"It's okay," Briel said, sensing my embarrassment.

We sat in silence for a while, watching the Earth and clouds. A gust of wind rocketed the pod back and forth. Instinctively, I grabbed onto the edge of my seat and didn't let go. My heart pounded so loud I was sure Briel could hear it, exposing my fear and awkward shyness. I took in a deep breath and then exhaled. "Why'd you leave Mars?"

With her big eyes, Briel gaped at me like she didn't understand my question.

"I mean," I stuttered, "why would you leave Mars and come to Earth? It's got to be so hard to be in that chair."

"My parents were born on Earth and remembered it from when they were little, before their families moved to Mars. It's a tough life on Mars."

"But..." *But how could they do this to you? Life on Earth is hard for you,* I wanted to say, but I didn't. Her parents would have known of Earth's crushing gravity and that she'd be stuck in braces and a hoverchair, perhaps for the rest of her life.

Briel watched the clouds. "They told me about the braces and the chair and all the therapies. I agreed. I wanted to see Earth." Her voice was sullen. Her eyes brimmed with tears. "It's harder than I thought."

"I'm sorry." I wanted to say more. To tell her that I wanted to be her friend. That I loved the blue streak in her hair. That her big blue eyes were beautiful. That despite the chair and braces and leaving school early every day for therapy, she always had a courageous smile on her face. That I loved that she could talk to anyone—an adult or a shy girl like me. But all I could get out was, "I'm so sorry."

"Don't be. I'm not. Hard things are worth doing." She winked at me and brushed away the tears. "Besides, I'd have missed this whole space balloon adventure if I'd stayed on Mars."

We both giggled.

⟨🚀⟩

"I spy something grayish white," Briel said.

"Could it be a cloud? Again?"

Briel grinned mischievously. "But which cloud?"

"Enough with the clouds!" I said in mock exasperation. There were only so many times one could spy the Pacific Ocean, clouds, and blue sky. "Maybe we should do something different."

"Like what?"

I shrugged my shoulders. She'd already told me all about life on Mars including stories about her annoying little brother. I told her all about my annoying little brother, too. Together we dreamed up a colony on Pluto where sisters could send their brothers. It was more talking than I could ever remember doing before. She liked math. I didn't. She liked to read. I did, too.

We both leaned our heads against the cold window, peering down at the Earth, a swirl of bright blues, white and gray clouds, and patches of browns. Our balloon floated high enough that we could see the curve of the Earth with the distant moon gleaming enormous.

"It reminds me of when our ship approached. It was amazing," Briel said. "It's beautiful."

I agreed.

Briel struggled to sit back. She pulled her head away from the window, only to lean it back against the glass.

"You okay? Need some help?"

"Yes," she whispered. "I'm tired. I've never been in this chair for so long. I'm usually in the water by now."

I hesitated to touch her. I knew her bones were fragile. I gently lifted her head and shoulders and pressed them back into the straps holding her up. "Is that better?"

"Yes."

The radio squelched and crackled.

"I think it's almost time," I said. I rushed over to the console and held the headset up to my ear and mouth. The Captain had been checking in with us every half hour to make sure we were okay. All we had to do was pull a lever and disengage the balloon when an indicator light flashed green.

"The light will..." His voice cut out. He'd warned that the com might cut out at the height we were at. "... signal ... don't—"

"Don't what?" I said into the headset. "Captain Stevens, I can't hear you. Captain Stevens?" The com crackled.

Briel and I regarded each other for a moment. The light blinked green.

"Captain Stevens, do I pull the lever now? It's blinking."

Static roared over the com. I bit my lip and glanced at Briel.

"Pull it, Kara."

I gripped the lever, closed my eyes, took a deep breath, and pulled.

The massive balloon sailed towards space while our pod dropped free. Long thin drogue chutes shot up from the top of the pod to slow our descent so that the parasail could be deployed. I clung to my seat, looking in turn at the console, then at Briel and up at the drogue chutes flapping in the wind.

Strands of Briel's hair floated up, then whole clumps of her hair. I touched my black hair and knew it floated up, too. I lowered my arm; the movement tipped my body to the left.

Briel beamed. She slipped free of her shoulder and chest straps and pushed off her chair, sailing up. She kicked off the ceiling, curling her body up into a tight ball, doing somersault after somersault, laughing all the while.

I copied her movement, kicking off my chair. I thumped against the ceiling and pushed off it, curling into a ball like she had. The first couple of spins were clumsy but exhilarating. It was just like floating in a pool but without the water.

I couldn't stop spinning. I pawed uselessly at the ceiling. My stomach reeled, protesting the spin. I was going to be sick. I choked back vomit. Briel grabbed my waist, wrapped her arms around my belly, and matched my spin. She tapped her legs against the ceiling, slowing my spin.

"You, okay?" she asked, guiding me to one of the handles spaced evenly along the ceiling, where she wrapped my fingers around it.

I cupped my free hand over my mouth, hoping my stomach would settle, and I wouldn't need one of those barf bags tucked in the pockets on the side of each seat.

"We'll only be weightless for another few seconds," Briel said with regret in her voice.

All sorts of buttons flared red across the console, and an alarm started beeping. I glanced up a split second before a black boomerang-shaped aircraft soared overhead, narrowly missing our pod but catching on the drogue chutes. The pod pitched hard to the right as the chutes tangled in the aircraft, pulling us along with it. As I held on for dear life, Briel dropped to the floor and slid across, crashing into the far wall.

"Briel," I screamed. She lay in a crumpled heap. I worked my way across the pod, gripping each handhold, afraid at any moment the pod would plummet and I'd become weightless again.

"Briel? Briel?"

She stirred. I exhaled in relief.

"I'm okay," she said. "I don't think anything's broken." She sat up and extended her arms and legs, studying each limb in turn. "I'm probably going to have some nasty bruises, but these braces did the trick." She ran her hand from her wrist to her shoulder over the gleaming braces embedded in her skintight suit. "Help me back into my chair?"

I helped her back into her chair and gently tightened the straps holding her in. Now that she was safely back into her chair, we assessed our situation. The drogue chutes were still caught on what appeared to be an unmanned internet plane.

The weight of our pod had shifted the plane's angle downward. If we stayed tangled with the plane, we'd crash.

"What are the chances of that happening?" Briel pointed at the plane.

"One in a million?" I guessed.

"Sure. Why not? One in a million. We just happen to be so lucky."

I studied the console lit up with flashing red lights. This was not supposed to have happened. I now understood the garbled message from Captain Stevens. They'd probably seen the plane on the radar and had wanted us to wait to pull the lever. That understanding came too late now.

"Captain Stevens? Can you hear me?"

The com was silent. "Captain Stevens?"

A voice emerged through the static. "Kara, thank heavens. Are you two all right?"

"Yes." Relief flooded through me.

"Let's bring you home."

"Sounds great!"

"All you need to do is pull the lever again to release the drogue chutes and at my signal, press the button to the right of the lever. That'll deploy the parasail. Did you copy that?"

Briel gave me a thumbs-up.

"Copy that." I pulled the lever. The pod's ceiling groaned and the cables released. The plane and tangled drogue chutes kept heading westward while we dropped away.

"Very good, Kara. Wait a few more seconds."

Each second seemed like an hour. The pod rocked back and forth, buffeted by the wind.

"Press the button now," Captain Stevens said.

I pressed it and watched above me as the parasail shot out from the pod's roof.

I gripped the edge of my seat at the momentary jolt as the

rainbow-colored parasail caught on the wind.

"Well done, ladies. Buckle up for the landing. The computer will take care of the rest," Captain Stevens said.

Briel sighed. "I guess it's almost over."

"You sound disappointed. Did you honestly enjoy this?"

"Of course. Didn't you?"

"Aside from the weightlessness, almost barfing, and, oh, facing near-certain death, I had a blast!"

Briel laughed. "That was almost my favorite part, not you getting sick, but the weightlessness."

"Almost?"

"Yes. My favorite part was talking to you."

I grinned. "Mine, too."

The parasail carried us gently back towards Earth. The blue of the Pacific slowly winked out of sight as the green and brown land between patches of clouds grew bigger and bigger. We gripped each other's hands and smiled.

My Mother the Ocean
by Dianna Sanchez

Dianna Sanchez is the not-so-secret identity of Jenise Aminoff, also known to her children as the Queen of Sarcasm. She has worked as a technical writer, electrical engineer, programmer, farmer, and preschool cooking teacher, among many other things. Her middle-grade fantasy novel, *A Witch's Kitchen*, debuted from Dreaming Robot Press in September 2016, and she is hard at work on the sequel, *A Pixie's Promise*. A Latina geek originally from New Mexico, she now lives in the Boston area with her husband and two daughters.

Itao stared out at the wrong, wrong, horrible ocean. Deep blue-green instead of purple, its waves rose impossibly high. It smelled of salt and garbage and decay. It smelled *warm*. Worst of all, it was silent except for the crash of waves on the beach at his feet. No Mother Ocean. He was still alone.

"Wrong," Itao muttered, clutching his head. "All wrong. Wrong!"

Turning, he darted away from the humans surrounding him, found a suitable sand dune, and dug in.

Ambassador Michaelson followed him. "What are you doing? What's wrong? Hey!"

Itao pelted him with sand, burrowing furiously. He quickly scuttled into his hole and curled up, miserable. Even the sand smelled wrong.

"Itao?" Michaelson asked. "What's wrong, buddy? I thought you really wanted to go for a swim."

He moaned and curled tighter, ignoring the human. Itao knew he was being rude. It still gave him an odd shiver, this new freedom to choose whether or not to obey. He knew he should stay with the ambassador, help him, teach him, but Itao couldn't help himself. Everything was just too strange.

Encounter, the ship that brought him to Earth, had been strange but in an exciting way, full of newness and ideas. The crew had been kind and helpful: Chen, the pilot, who taught him chess and showed him how machines work. Tuttle, the leader, who made certain things ran smoothly and who studied Itao and samples from Mother Ocean. Patel, the linguist, who taught Itao human speech and instructed him on human behavior. Still, he had missed being in water more and more as the weeks passed. He wanted to swim so badly his bones ached. But not in that, that weird not-Ocean. He wanted to vomit.

Patel crouched down and peered into the hole. "Itao? Are you okay?" she asked.

He peered at her through the webbing of his left hand. Patel was nice. On the ship, she had saved the fish rations for him, and she sang to him at night when he had trouble sleeping. When they arrived on Earth, Chen and Tuttle had gone home to their families, but Patel had stayed with Itao.

"No, Patel," he moaned. "Nothing is okay. Everything is terrible and wrong."

"Good grief," Michaelson muttered. "He's having a melt-down. Why on earth did they send us a child?"

"You've never been on an alien planet, Ambassador," Patel told him. "Believe me, it can be very, um, disorienting."

"Can you get him out of there?" Michaelson asked.

"I think we should give him some time to acclimate."

"We have a schedule to keep. He's supposed to be at the press conference in an hour."

Patel chuckled, that strange human sound like stones clicking together in surf. "Do you want the press to meet him in this state?"

"Hrm. What if I buy him a balloon or an ice cream or something?"

"They'd all be strange to him, too."

Footsteps. Another shadow fell across the entrance of Itao's burrow. "Is there a problem, sir?" Ortega, one of the guardians who watched over Itao. He liked Ortega, too, who was quiet and did not ask him questions. The guardian stood and watched and occasionally nodded at him, just as a guardian should.

"Temper tantrum," Michaelson said.

Patel replied, "More like culture shock."

"Should we dig him out?" asked Michaelson. Itao huddled deeper in his burrow.

"We may hurt him doing that," Ortega pointed out.

"Well then, what do you suggest?" Michaelson asked.

Ortega was silent for a moment, then he said, "Let me make a phone call, Mr. Ambassador. I have an idea. In the meanwhile, let's do as Dr. Patel recommends and leave him be."

"Oh, wonderful. There goes our whole day." Michaelson stomped off.

Patel peered in the burrow again. "Itao? Is there anything I can do?"

"Take me home," Itao whispered. "I want to go home."

"Oh, honey," Patel said. "I wish I could. Would you like me to sing to you?"

"No. Leave me alone. I want to be alone."

"Okay, but I'll be right nearby if you need anything." Her footsteps grew faint, awkward on the sand. How could they be any other way without webbing to grip and keep the sand stable under her?

Itao lay quiet, listening to the pounding of the surf, like a slow, insistent drum with no pattern, no meaning. All hollow and empty, just the way he felt inside, so alone and far away.

Light footsteps broke the droning of the surf. Someone new approached him. A face blocked the light at the burrow entrance, small and round, framed with fur. Dark eyes, almost as dark as his own, looked in at him, wide with wonder.

"Hellooooo? Are you the alien?"

Her voice was high, so she was probably female. And small, so small. Shorter than Patel, who was the smallest human he had met, only a head taller than Itao himself. A child! Itao suddenly realized. He had not met any human children yet. Despite himself, he pulled his hand from his face to look at her more fully.

She breathed in sharply and pulled back a little, then leaned back in, interested, her mouth open slightly, ready to be fed information like any child.

"Yes," he said then added politely, as he had been taught, "I am Itao. Who are you?"

"I'm Teresa Ortega."

"Like Guardian Ortega? Are you kin?"

She made a gurgling sound. "He's my dad. He said you were feeling lonely and might like some company. Can I come in?"

Itao shifted, intrigued. "I did not know humans burrowed."

Teresa lifted her shoulders. "Grownups don't. Kids do. Is there room in there?"

"I think so. You may enter."

Teresa slid down into the burrow. "Wow," she told him. "You did a good job. All nice and firm. This would be a great hideout."

"We burrow like this in the warm times to keep cool," Itao told her. "Your world is very warm. Why doesn't everyone burrow like this?"

The human girl laughed, and her laughter was like the tinkling of a waterfall, bright and crisp. "Your skin is such a pretty shade of purple. Like lilacs."

"It is a normal shade, boring," Itao told her. "Not like your brown skin. Brown is an unusual color on my world. Your skin is like wusuo, a strong plant that grows on the ocean floor and makes homes for many fish. We use it to make jewelry, like this." Itao showed Teresa his necklace of wusuo beads. He uncurled a little, stretching out his feet.

"Wow! Your feet are like flippers!" Teresa exclaimed. "You must swim really well."

Itao felt proud. "Yes. At home, I swim in Mother Ocean every day for many hours, hunting fish. I am one of the best hunters in my clan." He paused. "My sister, Suho, is better, but she is older than me."

"I swim every day, too. There's a pool at my apartment complex."

"A pool? Fresh water? Does it have fish?" That would not be so bad. There had been a pool on Itao's island. He had swum there occasionally. Perhaps that would not be so different.

"No fish," Teresa told him. "It's treated with all kinds of chemicals so it doesn't make you sick. They would kill the fish. Hmm, they might hurt you, too. Oh, but there's a lake nearby. No chemicals. I swim there sometimes, too. And it has fish! Sunfish and catfish and other fish, I can't remember their names."

"Could we go there?" Itao asked.

"I'll go ask my dad."

Teresa scrambled out of the burrow and ran off, returning moments later. "The ambassador guy says that if you'll go to his press thingy, we can go to the lake after."

"Will you come, too?"

"Sure, if my dad says it's okay."

The press conference place reminded Itao of the ship, though it was many, many times larger: enclosed and metallic, full of sharp corners and edges, and smelling of humans. The temperature never changed, remaining just barely cool enough though he wore only his wrap. The humans who filled the room wore layers of clothing. He had no idea how they could stand it. Many of them flashed bright lights at him, so he closed his inner eyelids, and then they flashed even more. A human woman spoke, saying his name and Patel's, introducing Ambassador Michaelson. The ambassador stood, giving him welcome, explaining how he had been chosen to come to Earth and meet its people.

Then Michaelson waved at him, and Patel nudged Itao. "Go and stand next to him," she said.

Itao looked for Teresa and found her in the back of the room with another guardian. She bared her teeth at him, which Itao knew meant she was happy. He felt better; if Teresa felt safe, surely he was safe, too. He stood and walked to the podium with Michaelson.

"Itao, can you answer some questions?"

Itao carefully bobbed his head up and down, as humans did to agree with each other. "That is part of why I am here. To tell you about me and my Mother the Ocean."

Many humans raised their hands in the air, and Michaelson pointed to one.

"Only part of why you are here? What are your other reasons for coming?"

Itao blinked. "To learn about you. To learn new things. To bring these new things back to my people and my Mother the Ocean. And, if you wish, to bring my Mother the Ocean to you."

Michaelson pointed at another human. "Why were you chosen? And why did you agree to come?"

"I was chosen because I like learn. Like to learn, sorry. Your language is slow in my mouth." The humans laughed like thunder. "I am curious, always looking at things and trying to understand them. Mother Ocean thought I would like to look at things here."

"Were you excited to be chosen?"

"No," Itao said.

The human took a quick breath, which meant she was shocked. "You didn't want to come here?"

Itao rolled his shoulders back, then remembered humans did not understand that this meant no. "I was frightened. I did not want to leave my home. I did not want to leave my Mother the Ocean. I am lonely without her."

The humans were all looking at each other and shuffling their feet.

"Then why did you come?"

"Because Mother Ocean told me to." Itao had answered this many times already, but he was patient. "She wanted to send a child because I am not so scary as an adult. And because a child learns fast, not like an adult. And because adults are needed to hunt and care for babies and elders."

Michaelson made a face and pointed at a different human, who asked, "How old are you, Itao?"

"I am twenty of my years. That is like twelve of your years. My Mother the Ocean dances very fast around our sun."

"When will you be grown up?"

Itao stood taller. "I am nearly grown up now, but it will be a few more years before I begin a family."

"What do you like about Earth so far, Itao?"

"There is so much land!" he burst out. "I have never seen so much land. We have only little bits of land, you call them islands, but we just call them lands. There are many lands, but they are all small, not like your lands. And you have many more plants and animals on your lands than we have. Big animals! My people are the biggest land animals on my world. I like horses and elephants and giraffes. I want to go to a... what is it? A preserve. I want to see the big animals for myself."

Michaelson bared his teeth. "I'm sure we can arrange that." He pointed to another human.

"Can you tell us about Mother Ocean? Is she your god?"

Itao took a deep breath. He had explained this many times, but none of the humans had understood. He tried again. "My Mother the Ocean is the mother of all my people. Mother Ocean holds us and watches over us. She provides food for us and keeps our world in balance. She is inside all of us, and we are all part of her.

"She is curious about your world, your Earth. That is a good name, Earth, because you have so much land. My Mother the Ocean sent me here to see if Earth is like her. And if it is not like her, then I can give you a Mother Ocean.

Michaelson chuckled. "I think we have enough religions on Earth already."

The humans laughed and nodded, but they still did not understand. He was not sure how to explain it. He needed to know more about humans, about what they wanted. He knew already that their ocean was not like Mother Ocean, but he did not think it was polite to say this. Would they feel bad, knowing they had no Mother Ocean?

They had lunch after, a variety of different fish in many colors, not just white as all the fish on the ship had been. Best of all, the fish was not cooked! It was laid raw on a cooked grain called rice that was familiar to Itao from the ship, though this rice tasted much better. This type of food was called sushi, and while Itao did not like the spicy green paste or the salty brown liquid, he liked everything else.

Teresa refused to eat the fish, saying it was gross. She ate cooked shellfish called shrimp on her rice and strange wrinkled pods called dumplings. She tried to show Itao how to use chopsticks.

"Hold them like this," she told him, showing him her hand. "Oh, you can't do that. Your webbing gets in the way." Teresa put down her chopsticks. "That's okay, we can eat with our hands, like when I was little." She picked up a du *My Mother the Ocean* mpling and popped it into her mouth.

Itao followed her example, placing a bundle of pink fish and seaweed and rice in his mouth. He hummed in satisfaction. He had not eaten so well since he had left home. He carefully stored a sample of the salmon to share with Mother Ocean when he returned. As an afterthought, he stored some seaweed as well. He did not like it as much, but Mother Ocean might like it.

"So we can go to the lake now?" he asked when they were done eating.

Ortega nodded. "Security has cleared the area. We can go."

"It is as big as Laughing Rock Home, my land. My island, I mean."

Teresa stared. "Really? Your whole island is only as big as this lake?" She was dressed in a small suit that covered only her torso. It looked comfortable, good for swimming.

Patel nodded. "It's true. Their islands are tiny. Lots of them, but very small."

Itao drank in the sight of it. It was so much more like Mother Ocean, though it was still blue instead of purple. The waves were very small, driven by wind instead of tide. The water did not smell so salty or strange. It smelled full of life. He felt himself trembling.

"May I?" he asked Patel. "May I swim?"

She laughed. "That's why we're here, Itao."

It was all he needed to hear. In two great leaps, he plunged into the water, the glorious water. It wrapped around him, caressed him. He opened his gills and fully tasted it, the sweetness and richness of it, the tang of life. Silent life, but good life, healthy life.

Itao heard a splash beside him, and he came to the surface. Teresa and Ortega had joined him. They swam slowly but surprisingly well without webbing.

"Do you like it?" Teresa called to him.

"It's wonderful!" he cried. "It is like home! Thank you, thank you for bringing me!"

And then he could wait no longer. Itao dove. He swam right to the bottom, tasting and touching, turning over rocks, storing information. He ate two fish and stored bits of them, too. He felt in the silt at the bottom of the lake, studied the stones and the sand. And he thought, just for a moment, that he heard a whisper. Like Mother Ocean, but not. It was so faint. I am hearing things, he thought. I am missing Mother Ocean, and this is so like her, I think I hear her. But he wondered.

He found human things in the lake, cans and bottles. He came across a round black thing that was wrong, making the water taste bad. I will help the lake, as I would help Mother Ocean, he thought. And he pulled the round thing out and brought it to the surface.

"Itao!"

He looked around and found Ortega and Patel nearby in a metal boat. He had seen pictures of metal boats in the ship's computer.

"Is that a boat?" he asked.

"It's a canoe, yes," Patel said.

Ortega said, "We were worried, Itao. You were down there a long time."

Itao felt ashamed. "I am sorry. I forgot you do not breathe water. I will stay closer to you. Also, I found a bad thing in the water." He pulled up the round thing.

"That's a tire. You're right, it's not a good thing to have in here," Ortega told him. "This lake is protected. People aren't supposed to throw stuff like that in. Give it here."

Itao swam to the canoe and handed it up to Ortega, who

grunted pulling it up into the canoe. "You're strong, Itao. I don't think I could have brought that tire up."

"I am a hunter," Itao told him. "I have hunted and brought back fish as big as me."

Ortega glanced at Patel, and she nodded. "I've seen him do it."

"We must be strong," Itao said. "We must protect our kin against the flyers."

"Flyers?" Ortega asked.

"Think pterodactyls," Patel said, "though they're more amphibious than reptilian."

Ortega whistled. "Don't tell Teresa about that, she'll have nightmares."

"Is it true that you have giant flying frog-birds on your world?" Teresa asked.

They were under a tent made of blankets in Teresa's room, having a sleepover, which was when a child slept in another child's home. There were guardians outside the door, just in case. Teresa was in a sleeping bag, which kept her warm. Itao lay on top of his sleeping bag, a little uncomfortably warm but happy to be with a friend.

Itao blinked. "Your father-guardian said not to talk about the flyers. He said you would have nightmares."

Teresa laughed. "I read all about you and your Mother Ocean when the *Encounter* came back. I could hardly wait until you got out of quarantine. It took FOREVER. Look."

She pulled out her little flat computer, orange and decorated with interesting designs on the back. Teresa showed many pictures of him, and of the Argo shuttle landing. Pictures of him in quarantine with Chen and Tuttle and Patel, being tested for harmful organisms. As though he would let anything harmful out. Pictures of his home that made him ache.

Teresa saw this and quietly put the computer away. "You miss home, don't you?"

Itao nodded at her. "I am missing it a lot. I have never been away before."

"I was homesick once," Teresa told him. "I went to visit my grandparents in Guatemala. It was so different there! Everyone spoke Spanish, and I had only learned a little in school. I couldn't understand them because they talked so fast. The buildings were all different, and the trees and plants and everything. I liked the food, though." She looked at him. "This must be harder for you, though, because I had my parents and my grandparents, and you're all alone."

Itao swallowed hard. "Yes, I am very alone. I have never been away from family before. I have never been away from my Mother the Ocean. It is so quiet here. So lonely."

Teresa put her head to one side, which is what Patel did when she did not understand something. "Why isn't Mother Ocean here? My mother says that God is everywhere."

"Mother Ocean is not like God. Mother Ocean is my world. How can my world be here?"

"But you can still speak to her, can't you?" Teresa asked. "We call that praying."

"How can she hear me? She is so far away." Itao was silent for a moment, then asked. "Does God speak to you when you pray?"

"Well, no," Teresa said. "Some people say they hear God, but I never have. But Mom says when you pray, God hears you."

"Mother Ocean is not like that. She speaks, and I hear her. I speak, and she answers me."

Teresa's eyes got big. "Really? She speaks back to you?"

"She is loudest when I am in her."

"In her? You mean, in the ocean?"

"Yes, in Mother Ocean. When I am in the water, I hear her loud."

Teresa was blinking rapidly. "You mean," she said slowly, "you mean your ocean really talks to you? Like a person?"

Itao nearly went limp with relief. Finally, someone who understood. "Yes. Like a person, but talking inside me, not mouth-talking."

"Like talking in your head? Like you have headphones on?"

"Like my whole body is a headphone."

Teresa stared at him. "What does she say? Your Ocean, I mean."

"My Mother the Ocean tells us many things. When the fish are coming, when there will be a storm, when the cold season will begin. When we are hungry, she can send fish to us. She helps us when we are sick. We thought she knew everything until the ship came. That surprised her. Mother Ocean is never surprised."

"What did she think about us? About humans?"

Itao lay back, looking up at the blanket, with its pattern of small animals. "Many, many things. I don't understand them all. She was curious, but also worried. She is our guardian, but she doesn't know how to guard against ships that fall from the sky. She learned many new things from Patel and Tuttle and Chen, and from the taste of the ship when it landed in her, but she wanted to know much more. That is why she made me come to you."

Teresa thought about this. "That's creepy. A whole ocean talking to you, telling you what to do. I don't think I'd like that. It's bad enough that my parents always tell me what to do."

Itao considered this. It had been strange and lonely, having no Mother Ocean to tell him what he should do. He'd had to make many decisions by himself. He was not sure he would choose well here. But Mother Ocean had been very specific.

I am giving you a seed of me, she had told him. *If you put it in their ocean, it will make a Mother Ocean there, but slowly, perhaps a hundred years. If their world already has a Mother Ocean, do not use it. If it does not, you must ask the people of that world. If they want one, if they say yes, then you may use the seed.*

"Do you think there are other humans who would like to have a Mother Ocean?" Itao asked Teresa.

She made her mouth small and tight, then said, "Maybe. I guess someone might want a Mother Ocean like yours. But I think most people would not." Teresa pulled back from him. "I'm tired. Let's go to sleep now."

Itao swallowed what he wanted to ask. Who can I talk to? Who will understand? Teresa had crawled into her sleeping bag and turned her back to him. Alone again.

Three days later, they went to the animal preserve, and Itao saw his first elephant.

"Huge!" he gasped.

He saw hippos and giraffes and zebras and rhinoceroses and lions and hyenas and so many other animals, he could not count. He wanted to taste them all, but this was not allowed.

"With so much land, you can have so many animals," Itao babbled. "Amazing! Such variety! It is like the ocean."

"Our ocean has far more variety than our land," Vincent the tour guide told Itao. "You should visit an aquarium."

They went to the aquarium. They saw many fish from all over the world, and turtles, squid, lobsters, penguins, and boneless jellyfish just like the floaterfish in Mother Ocean. Some of the sharks reminded him of knifefish, which were dangerous to hunt but delicious. The aquarium did not have whales, but they did have three dolphins, and after a great deal of negotiation with the aquarium staff, Itao was allowed to enter their pool for a short while.

They surrounded him, curious. Their water speech washed

over him, so different from his people's but interesting and beautiful. He touched them, tasted them, surfaced with them when they needed air, and they touched and tasted him, too.

He tried to ask them, Do you speak to the ocean? Does the ocean speak to you?

They squeaked and clicked back to him, but it was in no language he could understand. Itao gave up and climbed out.

"Did you talk to them?" asked the dolphin scientists. "Could you understand them?"

"No," Itao told her. "They are very loud and they chatter all the time, but I didn't understand them. They did not like me. I think it would take me many weeks to learn their language. It is as different from my water speech as your English is from my land speech."

The scientists were disappointed, and so was Itao. He had hoped to ask them if they had a Mother Ocean he could not hear, if they had ever had one. If they would like to have one.

Teresa had to go back to school, and Itao missed her. He moved to a special house they had set aside for him, called an embassy. He spent his days talking to scientists and press people and Ambassador Michaelson. He read a great deal and watched many videos on the little computer they gave him, like Teresa's but purple, like Mother Ocean. He went to the lake as often as they let him.

One weekend, he had a picnic at the lake with Teresa and her family, spreading a blanket on the land and eating there. Itao nibbled politely. He had already eaten many lake fish, but he liked the fruit, too, especially the watermelon. He leaned back, placing his webbed hand on the grass.

And that was when he heard it: the whisper. It was much louder, here on the land. This surprised him! How could there be a Mother Ocean here with no water? But it was a voice, nonetheless.

He stood up.

"What is it, Itao?"

"Do trees talk?" he asked Teresa.

"I don't think so. Mom?"

Teresa's mother, Gloria, said, "Well, not talking out loud, but I remember reading that they do communicate with each other." She picked up Teresa's computer and said aloud, "Search. Tree communication."

Teresa looked at it. "Mushrooms? They talk through mushrooms?"

"It's more complicated than that," said Gloria.

Itao took the little computer. There was a diagram there, showing a fine network of tendrils called mycelia between the roots of trees, connecting them, exchanging nutrients between them, caring for them. This network could be enormous, extending for miles in some places. Could this be what he had heard?

"I would like to walk in the trees," Itao said. "May I do that?"

Ortega rose. "Sure, I'll come with you."

"Me, too," said Teresa.

They walked along a path among the trees, and through his feet, Itao heard the whispers. He touched trees with his hands and heard it there, too. They came to a tree with branches that stooped down toward the ground.

"I love climbing this tree. Want to climb with me, Itao?"

The idea made him dizzy. "I do not think I am good at climbing. I will watch you climb."

"Dad?"

Ortega glanced at Itao, then said, "Sure. Not too high, though."

"Okay."

Teresa began to climb, one branch at a time, higher and

higher. "How can she do that? Be up so high? She could fall! She would die!" Itao cried.

Ortega chuckled. "She does this all the time. We evolved from tree-climbing animals. We're good at this the way you're good at swimming."

Itao covered his eyes and sat down. "I can't watch."

"Teresa! Come on down, now."

"No," Itao said suddenly. "Let her climb if it makes her happy. I will just rest a little." He could hear the voice loudly now, at the base of the tree with his eyes closed. He concentrated.

It was old, this voice, very old like Mother Ocean. It spoke, and he began to understand. It was a land voice, but like the ocean, it was vast. It saw many places. It connected the trees and the plants. It watched the animals and the people. It was old and sad and angry and frustrated. It could only talk to the plants, not the animals. Not the humans. It could not tell them to stop damaging the land. It could not help them heal the land.

Itao listened, and then he spoke back to the voice. He told the voice about Mother Ocean. He told it how she balanced the life of his world, how she brought his people fish, and how she prevented them from taking more than they needed. How she breathed the rain to them and protected them from storms. He told the voice, and it listened. I would do that, the voice said, if I could.

Then Itao told the voice about the seed of Mother Ocean and how he could release it to grow into a new Mother Ocean. Then you can work together, Itao said. You can teach the humans. And you won't be alone anymore.

I would like that, said the voice. Give her to me, and I will place her in the ocean.

Itao sighed with relief. From his skin, he released the seed of Mother Ocean into the soil. The mycelia took it and carried it away. A hundred years, he thought. My children's children can come in a hundred years and speak to the new Mother Ocean. He was glad.

Teresa landed with a thump on the ground beside him. "Wake up, sleepyhead!" she shouted.

Itao opened his eyes. "I am awake. I am ready to go home."

After the End

by Bruce Golden

Bruce Golden's short stories have been published in more than thirty anthologies and across a score of countries. *Asimov's Science Fiction* described his novel, *Evergreen*, "If you can imagine Ursula Le Guin channeling H. Rider Haggard, you'll have the barest conception of this stirring book, which centers around a mysterious artifact and the people in its thrall." More recently, his book *Tales of My Ancestors* combines the historical with the fantastic, and has been characterized as *The Twilight Zone* meets Ancestry.com. Golden's upcoming novel, *Monster Town*, is a satirical take on the world of the hard-boiled detective, one populated by the monsters of old black and white horror movies. http://goldentales.tripod.com

I don't know why I started remembering things long forgotten. Maybe because I was truly alone for the first time in my life. Maybe it was the quiet desolation of the landscape—nothing but remnants of the past from horizon to horizon. Of course things weren't as bad as they were immediately after the comet set the world ablaze. In the years since, much of the plant life had regenerated, the way it does after any major fire. But barren, scorched areas where nothing flourished but a few hardy weeds still blemished the earth. In a sense, I was like those weeds.

My progress was slow. Navigating the Durango around countless derelict vehicles dotting the highway was always time-consuming, especially with the trailer I was pulling.

Sometimes I was forced to detour off the highway completely to make my way around. I had to proceed slowly each time. I had no mechanical knowledge, so if the Durango were damaged—if it ceased to function—my precious cargo and I would be stranded.

I didn't know where I was going—not specifically. I just knew I was headed north. Why north? Because, before he died, my dad suggested that if weather patterns held true, the rich forestlands of the north would grow back first. It was there he thought I'd best be able to live off the land while avoiding the plague that had decimated erstwhile cities.

Dad was much on my mind as I drove. My memories of his death were as clear as they were frayed and sorrowful. But I tried not to think of how he was after he fell ill. Instead I did my best to remember what he was like before, at the beginning... at the beginning of the end.

Those memories were not so clear. They came to me piecemeal and in dark dreams. I was only seven, and none of it made much sense to me at the time, even though Dad had tried to explain it. I hadn't really understood what was happening.

Two days before its arrival, Smith-Kim had become the brightest "star" in the sky. Of course it wasn't a star. I remember looking up at it as Dad packed our brand new white Dodge Durango with food, water, books—everything he could think of.

"Is it going to hit us?" I asked.

"It might, so we're going somewhere safe just in case."

"Is it going to hit Mommy?"

"No, she'll be okay."

He didn't tell me then that he'd read all the scientific reports and knew it wasn't the collision but the aftermath that would cause the most destruction. Incredible heat incinerating anything on the surface, dust thrown into the atmosphere blocking the sun for months, acid rain, nuclear fallout from damaged power plants, and weapons set off by the heat. I don't think, at the time, he really expected us to survive. But that didn't stop him from trying.

Fully packed, we drove off to the place he'd found. I remember, on the way, I saw thousands of people out on the streets, on rooftops, waiting for the comet's arrival. I don't know if they thought it was going to bypass Earth and give them a show, or if they were just resigned to their fate.

Dad drove us to an underground parking garage, going as far down inside it as he could. A few other people had the same idea, but I was too young to grasp why we were sitting down there, waiting, listening to the one radio station we could still get beneath several levels of concrete. At the time, I felt like I was missing out—that I wouldn't get to see what everyone else was waiting for.

I recall the radio went static minutes before the chilly air of the garage grew so hot I burned myself when I touched the door handle.

When the heat got so intense I didn't think I could stand it, another family decided to drive out. Dad warned them not to go yet, but they left anyway. We never saw them again.

We waited in the stifling heat for longer than I could keep track. I remember crying at one point, and asking about Mom. Dad told me she was far away on a business trip, but that he'd warned her and told her to find a safe place like we did. He didn't tell me she believed less in what her own husband was telling her and more in the assuaging news reports and adulterated government websites designed to lessen panic.

I drifted off to sleep in the heat and woke with Dad putting a wet towel over my head. I fell back asleep, and when I woke again it was much cooler, but the garage had gone dark—except for some emergency exit lights.

When we finally drove up, it was as if we'd been transported to another world. We drove out onto this harsh, alien landscape—a hellish vista I still see in my dreams. Fires were everywhere. Everything was burnt or burning—cars, buildings, bodies. There was no sky—only layers of smoke and ground fog. The smell filled the Durango, and ash cascaded around us like black snow. It was so dark I didn't know if it was day or night.

I remember being scared—so scared I turned away from the window and looked at my dad. He was silent, but tears rolled down his cheeks. He looked at me, saw the fear on my face, and forced a smile.

"It's going to be okay, Adam," he said, wiping away his tears. "We're going to be okay."

That's when I had my first seizure. I didn't know what was happening to me, and neither did my dad.

I remember crying out—whether in pain or confusion I don't know. I remember my head hurting, dizziness, and feeling like I was going to vomit. At some point, I blacked out. When I finally woke, I was soaked in urine, still lightheaded, and very scared. It didn't help that Dad looked scared, too.

Having never seen such a reaction before, he naturally assumed the seizure was in some way related to the comet. It wasn't until after many more such seizures and years later, when he began to scour library books and talk with other survivors, that we realized I'd been struck by epilepsy.

Looking back, I always felt sorry for my dad. Not only had the world as he knew it come to an end, but he discovered his son was defective. At least that's how I used to think of myself. Now it's just one more thing I have to be wary of in a world full of hazards.

The way ahead began to narrow. I hit the brakes, put it in park, and turned off the engine. I got out and climbed onto the hood for a better look. I had to shield my eyes from the glaring sun, but the clear air gave me a good range of visibility.

The highway ahead was so clustered with derelicts, I knew I'd never be able to maneuver through. It had happened before,

but I'd always been able to go off the road, around the obstacles. This time that wouldn't be possible. I was approaching
a stretch of highway cut out of a mountain, with no room to
either the left or the right. I'd have to backtrack, take a smaller
road I'd passed earlier, and hope to find a way around.

This wasn't anything new. I'd grown up among the vestiges
of civilization. Some burnt-out hulk of a building or rusted,
corroded machine always stood somewhere nearby. I know my
dad found such sights depressing, but to me that's just the way
the world was.

As I grew up, I forgot the old world—for the most part. A
seven-year-old doesn't know much anyway, but eventually I forgot all about video games, watching TV, and playing baseball.
Those things didn't exist anymore. Such recollections faded
with time. Yet some memories lingered—like how I used to
laugh when Mom and Dad would put on their favorite music
and dance.

That was the old world—their world. This was my world,
the one I'd spent most of my life in, the one I had to live in. I
didn't have a choice. But then I guess no one did.

The first few months after Smith-Kim hit were a struggle to
survive. I remember it was a long time before we saw the sun
again. There was only dust and ash, tornados and hurricanes,
earthquakes and ants. Ants were chief among the many insect
species surviving the inferno. They not only survived, they
flourished. It was a perfect world for scavengers. That's what
we'd become—we humans. We were scavengers, like the ants.

After the food Dad had packed was gone, we'd had to
scrounge for everything. Most of it had been destroyed in the
fiery aftermath, though we found canned and bottled food here
and there. There came a time when we nearly starved, and all we
had to eat were mushrooms and various bits of meat Dad always
told me was chicken. I realized later it must have been rat meat,
or whatever kind of animal he could catch and kill.

Like the ants, the surviving rats flourished. For the first few years it seemed as if they might overrun the planet. But when the pickings grew slim, so did their numbers. It seems rats were somewhat dependent on the leavings of mankind. A certain symbiosis existed between the two species. Of course they didn't disappear entirely. When I was older, I became very good at hunting rats... even better at cooking them.

There were other human survivors as well. Not many—Dad once estimated less than one in ten thousand. Whether they'd been as smart as my dad or just lucky, I never knew till later. Some were friendly—as friendly as one could be in such circumstances—and some weren't. Mostly Dad tried to avoid others at first. He'd packed a gun with our supplies and had to brandish it a couple of times to warn off some particularly nasty people. But the only time he ever fired it was to scare away a pack of hungry dogs that had caught our scent.

In time, we met up with people we liked. Soon we had group of seven, then thirteen, then twenty. Before long we had small community, eventually growing our own food, creating our own little patchwork society. Looking back, those seem like halcyon days now.

For years, we lived together on what had been the grounds of San Diego State University. Thousands of books had survived in its underground library, so we had a wealth of knowledge to work with. My dad had a thing about books, so it was the perfect spot. We used the books as references for farming, first aid, water purification, sanitation—everything we needed to survive. They were also important for our sanity. There was little entertainment other than reading. Eventually, Dad introduced me to such storytellers as Twain and Heinlein, Poe and Howard, King and Brin. He once told me fiction was as important as fact when it came to telling the story of mankind.

I didn't think any of it was very important at first, though he made me learn to read. The older I got, the less significant it seemed, until one day something finally clicked. It was a revelation of sorts. I came to understand all of mankind's accumulated knowledge, thousands of years of science and art, was still there in books, still available to the survivors so they wouldn't have to start all over again. I thought about the cache of gold coins we'd found one day, and how Dad told me they once represented great wealth, but now gold was just another useful metal—if you had the knowledge to use it. He was right. Real wealth was knowledge, and that made books the most valuable things in the world.

I remember walking with Dad one day to the hills overlooking an immense valley. I'd just finished reading *The Postman*, and we were talking about whether such a scenario might come true someday. It was near sunset, and the clouds in the westward sky were adorned in reds and pinks and yellows. Down the middle of the valley, traveling in both directions as far was the eye could see, was a multi-lane highway. Dad called it a "freeway." North of this vast roadway was a concrete stadium that had survived the fires, though an earthquake had collapsed one section.

He told me how he'd been in that stadium with his own father when the local baseball team had won its first championship. He said the noise of fifty thousand fans was so loud it hurt his ears. I believed him, but it was hard for me to imagine that many people, when my world consisted of fewer than fifty. At least until the plague came.

The detour I was forced to take led me up a coastal road with very few derelicts. It was a much more pleasant drive, seeing the ocean glistening off to my left instead of the scattered ruins of a past civilization. We'd gone to the beach many times when I was younger, but I hadn't seen the ocean since the end of everything. The waves churning onto the sand, the retreating tide, and the chill wind blowing off the water gave it a sense of life compared to where I'd come from.

Only once, late in the day, was I forced to slow and ease my way around an overturned truck. As I drove by, I looked down. The driver had tried to crawl out of the wreck. He didn't make it far. I knew by the state of the corpse that it wasn't the trauma of the accident that had killed him. It was the plague. I was familiar with those symptoms, and I knew he hadn't been dead long.

Once the disease had hit our community, it spread quickly. Within ten days most everyone was dead. My dad lived for twelve.

As soon as people started getting sick, we searched every medical journal and scientific text we could find to determine what it was and whether there was a cure. Those last four days Dad was too sick to help, but I kept at it... for all the good it did.

We were never able to determine whether the disease was something mankind had dealt with before or a genetically engineered biological agent unleashed from some laboratory by the cataclysm. We had no doctors or real scientists in our community and not enough understanding of cellular biology or virology.

Why a few others and I didn't contract the disease we never figured out. There seemed to be no reason why we were immune and so many weren't. We were certainly in constant contact with those who were sick, but some dynamic of biology or whim of fate protected us. I considered that maybe my epilepsy somehow made me resistant, but it was just another useless theory.

In those last few hours of Dad's life, I didn't want to be protected. I didn't want to be left alone. I railed against providence, cursed the universe, and tried to put my fist through a door. In the end, none of it mattered. All I could do was sit by his side and watch him fade away.

I remember him saying, "There's so much I wanted to teach you—tell you." He stretched his arm out, so weak I didn't think he could hold it up, and put his hand on the small stack of books by his bedside. "Don't let it all die, Adam. This is humanity's legacy. Don't let the words die."

He took his last breath less than an hour later.

Anger overwhelmed me. I was angry that those same books he praised were no help in saving his life. I was angry at myself for not being smart enough to save him. I was angry that, for some reason unknown to me, I was still alive and healthy.

When my anger cooled and reasoned returned, I hitched the small trailer I'd found to the Durango and packed them both with all the food and books I could fit inside. I attached my Honda scooter to the carrier on the vehicle's rear, said goodbye to the few others who'd survived the plague, and left, heading north as Dad suggested.

As the day grew long, I stopped to eat and watch the sun setting over the ocean. The colors streaming across the horizon, bouncing off the clouds and sinking into the sea were breathtaking. It was more beautiful than anything I remembered. But then I'd grown up in an ugly world.

At first Dad tried his best to hide the ugliness from me. But there were only so many ways he could turn, so many things he could do to protect me from the sight of seared bodies or the brutality of scavengers... animal, insect, human.

I didn't like to travel at night. Even with headlights it was hard to see all the obstacles in the road. I didn't want to take a chance on damaging the Durango, so I decided to stay there for the night and to see if I could find a way down to the beach.

First I drank a lot of water. I was careful, because dehydration could cause a seizure, along with stress, poor nutrition, lack of sleep, and a dozen other things. Some I could control, others I couldn't.

Getting down to the beach wasn't hard, and once on the beach I took off my shoes to feel the sand between my toes.

The texture of the fine granules and the smell of the sea air brought back memories of being at the beach with Mom and Dad, and how I used to dig a big hole in the sand, climb in, and wait for the tide to roll in and create my own little pool.

The sand on this stretch was near-white, but it wasn't a pristine beach. Rocky outcroppings protruded here and there—dwindling fortresses of stone battered by centuries of surf.

I rolled up my pants and walked across the damp sand. The water was cold—too cold to think about going in any farther. I strolled through the shallow surf, lost in thought but careful to avoid the sporadic mounds of seaweed. When I looked up, I saw something small move behind one of the rock formations. I was certain it was an animal of some sort, but the glimpse I had was too quick to be sure exactly what it was.

It didn't matter. Drawn by the sight of another living creature, I walked quickly as I dared, not wanting to scare whatever it was. I looked behind the rock. There was nothing there. So I stepped up onto it and looked around. There, down the beach a short way, was a cat.

It was a striking animal with a snow-white face, a golden sheath around one ear, black around the other. Its lower torso was all white, but its back was a patchwork of gold and black running down to the tip of its tail. It seemed so out of place, so unreal, that I considered, for just a moment, that I was imagining it—seeing things.

I began walking towards it, slowly, saying, "Here, kitty, kitty."

It was unimpressed with my cat call and sat there on its haunches for a moment. As I drew closer, it walked away—not like it was scared, but nonchalantly, like it had better things to do.

I quit calling it but kept moving forward. After a moment, it sat back down and waited.

When I was close enough, I squatted and reached out to pet

it. I was afraid it would run off again, but it stood its ground and wallowed in my touch. It even began to purr.

"Where did you come from? Are you by yourself out here?"

It accepted my attention for a bit, then sauntered off.

"Wait," I said, getting to my feet. "Where you going?"

It wasn't running, but it was moving steadily down the beach. I followed it quite a way, sure it was leading me somewhere and not just out for a stroll. The farther we walked, the higher the shoreline cliffs rose, and the rockier they got. It wasn't long before I spotted more cats up ahead. When I got closer, I saw a large opening in the cliffs—the mouth of a cave. The cliffs were dotted with smaller such crevices, and I didn't think anything of it until I saw the chair. It was right there, just inside the opening. A large wicker affair with a red cushion. I had only seconds to contemplate the misplaced furniture when a man rounded the section of cliffs jutting seaward. All around him, following him, were cats. A half-dozen at least.

At this point, the feline that had led me here pranced over and began rubbing against my legs as though we were old friends. I bent down to scratch its head. That's when the other fellow saw me.

"Go away!" he shouted, walking towards me and waving his arms. "Shove off! Get! Go away!"

I stood.

"I don't mean any harm. I saw this cat and followed it down the beach."

He looked at the cat, still rubbing against me, and slowed his walk. He stopped waving his arms but continued to draw near. His cats still trailed him, though haphazardly. A couple of small kittens paused to play. Another larger one took a moment to scratch and lick itself.

I saw as he approached he was an old fellow for sure. Both his hair and beard were gray—in sharp contrast to his sun-dark-

ened skin—and he walked with a slight limp. I was no judge
of age, but he had to be least 60—probably older. His feet were
bare, and he wore one of those rolled-up woolen head covers.
His clothes were as tattered as I imagined Robinson Crusoe's
must have been. That's the image which came to mind anyway.

"My name's Adam," I said, hoping to break the tension.

He didn't respond at first. He looked me over with a suspicious eye. I didn't particularly like the way he was sizing me up.
A part of me wanted to turn around and go back the way I came.
Another part was just plain curious, even though I expected him
to start screaming at me again. Instead he said rather mildly,
"Well, I guess Kimber likes you." He half-gestured at the cat between my legs. "Come on up if you want."

With that he turned and headed for the cave.

Up close he looked even older. The backs of his withered
hands were a maze of wrinkles, veins, and bony ridges, crisscrossed by long, thin scars. Judging by his companions, I guessed
the scars were cat scratches. But there was something not quite
right about his eyes—something askew—as if there were times he
was somewhere else, seeing something no one else could see.

He had an eclectic array of old furniture inside the cave,
including a small bed that rested under a mottled wooden sign
that read "Home is wherever I drop anchor." A large cast-iron
pot hung over a fire pit, and something was cooking. It smelled
good, but I didn't ask what it was.

"Do you live here?" I inquired, gesturing at the cave.

"Course I do."

"All alone?"

"Do I look alone?"

His sarcasm was justified. With all the cats, he was hardly alone.

Cats were everywhere. The longer we sat, the more that
appeared. Black cats, white cats, gray cats, orange and gold cats,

tabbies, calicos, Siamese, and combinations thereof.

"I've never seen so many cats. I thought most of them died in the cataclysm."

"Cat-what?"

"You know, when the comet Smith-Kim hit."

He didn't respond, and his blank look made it seem he didn't know what I was talking about. I guessed it was a memory he didn't want dredged up.

The same two playful kittens diverted my attention, taking center stage when one pounced on the other. The resulting ball of fur rolled over and over, their high-spirited battle compounded by tiny snarls and hisses. They separated and faced off, each with a paw poised to strike the other, their tails whipping back and forth like crazed pendulums. One of them growled menacingly then pounced again.

While this was going on, another cat with a thick, fluffy patchwork of gray and gold fur jumped onto the old man's lap. It spoke to him in a half cry, half purr, punctuating and accenting its sounds as though forming the words of some ancient feline language.

"I catch your drift, Banshee. I was thinking the same thing."

The cat settled on his lap and I asked, "Do all your cats have names?"

"Course they do," he snapped. "Cats are people, too."

I ignored the inanity of that. "How many cats do you have?"

"Too many," he said with a short, wheezy laugh. "More than a shark's got teeth."

Paying no heed to the cat on his lap, he stood. The cat landed easily and walked away as though the affront were nothing new. He walked to the side of the cave entrance and lit a lantern.

I hadn't noticed how dark it had become—maybe because a full moon was already shinning down on us.

"How do you remember all their names?"

"Each one's an individual," he said with authority. "Each has got his own mind, his own disposition, his own voice. Hell's bells, they even walk different." He sat back down. "If you give a cat a unique name, it'll be a unique cat—that's just common sense."

"How do you feed them all? How do feed yourself?"

"The sea is bountiful."

"You mean fish?"

"Fish, kelp, crabs, sea spinach, sea beets...whatever it brings me. You go ashore a ways, there's licorice fern, crowberries, cotton grass, mushrooms. There's cures, too. Irish moss is good for fevers, you know... and laver prevents scurvy."

I'd read about edible plants, but most of those he mentioned I was ignorant of.

"Is that why you live here?"

"I like the sea. Used to be a seaman, a navigator, long before you were born. There ain't no crowds out in the deep, no long lines to wait in, no noisy highways and byways and gizmos. Just quiet. I sailed the seas in more than dozen different ships. Freighters, tankers, tuna trawlers... you know what I'm talking about?"

"I've seen pictures in books."

"Psssss, pictures in books," he said with contempt. "You have to see a ship up close, smell the rust of its gunwales, hear the groan of its engine as it turns into the wind, feel its deck roll under your feet. You can't see that in a book. Hell's bells, you could even navigate by the stars if you knew what you was doing—and I did."

I felt chastised by my lack of experience in such matters. My only real experience was post-apocalyptic. The only things I knew about the world before *came* from books. So, somewhat defensively, I said, "Did you know the light from the stars you navigate from is billions of years old? It takes so long for the light to get here, that some of the stars we see might not even be there anymore. I read that in a book."

"That so," he said, apparently unimpressed by my factoid. But he turned and looked up at the night sky as if contemplating the essence of it. Or maybe he was just remembering another time, another place.

It occurred to me I was likely the first person he'd talked to in years. I wondered how he went on, day after day, this ancient mariner, this cat man. How he faced each day alone. Of course he wasn't alone—not to his way of thinking. But if all he had to talk to were cats....

Then I realized the real question wasn't about him. It was the one I'd been asking myself. Not out loud, but deep in the recesses of my thoughts.

What's the point? Why go on? For what reason? To end up like this wretched fellow?

I didn't have an answer. I didn't know if I ever would... or even if my dad did.

I remember asking him once, when I was older, why he didn't just let us die—how he kept going in those first, dark, desperate years. He told me he didn't believe in giving up—whether you were playing cards, baseball, or board games—you did your best until it was over, no matter how badly you were losing. You competed until the end. He said the human race needed to compete now more than ever. Winning was surviving.

An ebony tomcat with yellow eyes and a torn ear stalked in from the darkness. Adults and kittens alike moved aside, leaving no question as to his dominant status. He sauntered close to Kimber, the she-cat that had taken a liking to me, paused and snarled at her. She responded with a warning of her own, but the male ignored her and casually settled next to the old man.

He chuckled. "That was just a shot across the bow. Reefer here doesn't get along with Kimber—never has. She usually gives him a wide berth. Like some people—oil and water—they never mix."

A mewing sounded from deeper in the cave. He looked back, concerned, and I followed him when he went to investigate. There, on an old blanket, lay an exhausted mother and four newborn kittens. Fatigued as she must have been, she raised up and began cleaning one of the babies.

The old fellow turned to me and said, "Nature keeps marching on, doesn't she?"

That's when I was hit by that feeling of *déjà vu*. It was a familiar feeling, one almost always accompanied by dizziness and the smell of burnt toast. They were the first signs of an oncoming seizure. I tried to sit, but I was blinded by flashing lights, and my muscles wouldn't respond.

I woke covered with a blanket. I was confused, thirsty, and my head hurt. But I wasn't so confused that I didn't know what had happened. I'd experienced too many seizures not to know. I waited while the nausea and fuzziness went away. When I finally sat up, I saw the old man sitting close by.

"Those were some rough seas you sailing on there," he said. "You all right?"

"Yeah, I'm okay."

"Happen often?"

I shrugged. "Once in a while."

"What's wrong with you?"

"It's epilepsy."

"I've heard of that," he said, "but don't rightly know what it is."

"A seizure's kind of a disruption of the communication between neurons." I could see by his expression he had no idea what I was talking about. "It's kind of an electrical storm in the brain."

He nodded. "Seemed like you were riding out quite a squall. You okay now?"

"Yeah, I'll be fine."

He walked back out into the open and looked up at the moon. I was about to break the silence when he said, "It's almost time."

"Time for what?"

"You can come, if you're feeling up to it," he said, ignoring my question.

"Come where?"

He didn't respond. It was like he was somewhere else again. He started down the beach. Slowly, but eventually en masse, the cats followed him. What I thought was maybe a score of felines became dozens. Some came down from the cliffs, others out of the darkness. It was startling to see them all moving as one, avoiding the murky fingers of the tide.

I followed, not asking any more questions, and when he reached a stretch of beach that met with his approval, he turned and walked straight into the surf. I was afraid he'd be swept out to sea, but he stood there, knee-deep in water, holding his ground against the surge, waiting. Waiting for what I didn't know. But all the cats, and there must have been half a hundred, kept vigil at the tide's edge.

The sound of the waves was gradually infiltrated by a growing number of deep-throated cries—a scattered chorus coming from the waiting felines.

"What's happening?" I finally called out.

The waves crashed, the tide rushed forward, then retreated, and suddenly, magically, the lifeless wet sand was swarming with activity. Hundreds of tiny fish, glistening silver in the moonlight, squirmed and wriggled in the sand. The cats silenced as abruptly as the fish appeared, but a grunting sound emanated from the sea creatures.

It was an astonishing sight, spellbinding, surreal—except it *was* real. Just as amazing were the cats. Each and every one held its ground, watching, waiting, as many of the fish struggled to burrow into the sand.

The old man returned to shore, walking among the fish.

"What are they doing?"

"Propagating," he responded as he knelt and grabbed hold of one fish. "Life goes on." He tossed the single fish towards his waiting friends. It was a signal. As it dropped the cats raced down into the mud and shallow water and began to feast.

I woke near the mouth of the beach cave with Kimber curled up next to me. I didn't see the old man anywhere, so I started down the beach in the direction of the Durango, followed by my feline friend. Doubt crept into my head. I worried about the car. Not only was it my transportation, but it contained all my supplies and worldly possessions, as meager as they were. I didn't usually sleep so far away from it. I wanted to check on it and get back on the road.

As I walked, I glanced seaward and saw something odd. Far out, almost at the horizon, was a mountain of blue-white ice, floating with the current. I thought of what I'd read about ice, about the expression "tip of the iceberg," and considered how large it must be under the surface. I wondered, too, how enormous it must have been before it began its voyage to this warmer clime—wherever it came from.

Before I reached the lower cliffs where I'd descended the previous day, I came across the old man—with a small contingent of cats. I figured he never went anywhere alone.

"I wanted to thank you for letting me spend the night... and for the soup." He responded with a slight nod. "I'm going to have to be on my way now. My car's up the hill."

"Time and tide," he said, shrugging. "Well, if you gotta weigh anchor, I'll walk with you."

It was more of a climb than a walk, and I was worried the

grizzled fellow might not make it. But he did, with more grace than I managed.

Kimber and the other cats followed us up. She hadn't left my side since I'd first happened on her—except for the fish feast. I don't know why, but the thought sparked a memory of my mother, who, when I was little, followed me everywhere when she took me to the park or the playground. She was afraid to lose sight of me even for an instant.

At some point, after the world went to hell, I asked my dad, "Is Mommy dead?"

He'd looked at me with a forlorn expression and said, "I don't know." For a moment, I thought he might cry, but he contained his emotions and added, "I know she'll never be dead as long as we remember her."

I know, from then on, I tried hard to remember my mom. But over the years those memories dissipated like wisps of smoke until all I could picture was her dark, wavy hair. It saddened me I couldn't see her face anymore.

Kimber followed me all the way to the Durango, even though the old man and the rest of his tiny entourage paused at the cliff's edge.

"Go on," I said to her with a shooing gesture, "go on, go back with the others."

"I think she wants to go with you."

I picked her up and scratched her head as I carried her over and set her down with the others. But when I walked away, she followed me again.

"She likes you—no getting around it. She's always been kind of a loner, fighting with Reefer all the time. I think she's decided you should take her."

"I can't do that—she's yours."

"She's not mine. You don't own a cat."

"But how will I... how will I take care of her?"

"Cats pretty much take care of themselves. And they pretty much go where they want."

I didn't know what to do. All I knew was I didn't want the responsibility, not for another life, not when I'd seen so many lives extinguished while I stood by helplessly. Not even a cat's life.

"They say cats have nine lives," he said as if privy to my thoughts. "They're healers, too. She'll take care of you as much as you will her. Help you keep an even keel."

"I don't know..."

"You don't always get the post you want," he admonished me. "You can tread water for a long time, but eventually it's sink or swim. Life's funny that way."

I wasn't sure what he meant, but I gave in. "Okay. I guess she can come with me." I wouldn't have admitted it then, but deep down I was lonely. Part of me liked the idea of a companion—even a feline one.

I unlocked the door, picked up Kimber, and made space for her on the passenger seat. The old fellow turned to leave. "Wait a minute," I said. "There's something I want to give you."

It took me a minute to search through the books stacked on the floorboard, but I found the one I was looking for.

"Here, you take this. I've got as many books as you have cats. Call it a trade."

He walked over—almost cautiously—and took the book from me.

"I'm not sure I need a book," he said. "Haven't read one in a whale's age."

"Books can be good companions—like cats," I said, not knowing if he'd take offense. "I once read that books are lighthouses erected in the great sea of time." I thought he might appreciate the metaphor.

He looked at the cover and slowly read the title as if rediscovering each word, "*The Old Man and the Sea*." There was a glint of silver in his smile.

As quickly as it was born, the grin faded, and his countenance grew thoughtful.

"We had saying when we were at sea and things got bad—storms and such. We'd say we're closer to what's ahead than what's behind. You'd do good to remember that."

With that he turned and headed for the cliff's edge, followed by his feline honor guard. He stopped short of the drop-off, looked at me, and raised his hand to his forehead. I couldn't tell if he was saluting or just shading his eyes from the sun.

"You keep her trim and true and you'll be fine."

I didn't know exactly what he meant, but I had an inexplicable feeling he was right.

Abduction Assumption
by Stephen Blake

Stephen Blake lives close to the sea in a small Cornish town in the UK. He's never really grown up and still reads comics about superheroes and books about trips to magical lands.

When he's not reading, he's watching films and cartoons and thinking up new stories to tell the world. He also practices T'ai Chi and Kung Fu. He needs it, as he fights for space in his house, which he shares with eight cats and a dog called Frodo.

Sneaking out at night to meet up with your friends for a midnight snack is always difficult. Doors always seem to creak extra loud when it's late. That one squeaky floorboard you miss at any other time of the day gets caught right in the sweet spot and practically yells out. I try to move silently, and for once, being in a wheelchair helps. The creaking door can't be avoided, but my wheels roll over the squeaking floorboard quickly enough that it sounds like an extra-large rat instead of a girl escaping for a bit of fun.

There are a few of us staying at the camp. It's basically a farm. I think they want us city kids to see exactly where our food comes from and learn to appreciate it. I've been here a week, long enough to think seriously about becoming a vegetarian.

I roll down the outer ramp and head off to the nearby barn.

The gravel beneath my wheels sounds really loud, but I'm positive it's not louder than our chaperone's snoring.

The bright moonlight makes everything crystal clear. Dark shadows seem to stretch out all around, and the sound of an owl hooting in the distance causes me to pause for a moment. The air is cool but not really cold.

A hand is placed on my shoulder. "Hey, Dani, need a push?"

It's Jack. He's a little younger than me, about eleven or twelve. "You idiot," I say. "I nearly elbowed you in the groin. Do you have to sneak around like that?"

He grins at me, like he always does. "Uh, yeah, I do have to sneak. That's what we're all doing—sneaking."

A flashing torch from the barn distracts us. We head over and find Jenny, along with about ten others.

"I thought this was just the three of us," I say to Jenny, trying not to raise my voice.

She flicks her long blonde hair back and lifts her chin up. "Well, what can I say? I'm popular. Besides," she looks at Jack, "I was hoping it would be two."

The sound of a cow outside the barn distracts us. It seems to be crying out in distress. All the kids in the barn stand frozen, more concerned about being caught out of their dorms than seeing if the cow is all right.

I tut loudly and then roll out the doors to see what is going on. As I turn the corner of the barn I shield my eyes. A bright blue light blazes down onto the ground, as if a giant were shining a torch at the floor.

My eyes adjust just enough to see the cow levitate up through the light, and to my amazement, straight into the opening of a flying saucer.

I sit there for a moment and then realise my mouth is hanging open. I can't believe it. All those people I had thought were lying or just plain crazy must have been telling the truth.

I'm still staring upwards open-mouthed when I realise the light is creeping towards me. The saucer hovers silently, not even moving, but it seems the light is being redirected towards me.

I snap out of my trance and put my hands on my wheels. I push and pull, but I seem to have got myself wedged in a rut. This isn't the first time this has happened to me. I rock the chair backwards and forwards, trying to build a bit of momentum. All the while the blue light gets closer and closer.

"Come on," I cry to my chair, like it might listen to me.

"Yes," I say as I get the chair free. Only, it's not me that's got the chair free—it's them.

The blue light makes my skin tingle. If I weren't panicking so much I'd go as far as say it sort of tickles.

Desperate not to be taken, I decide to throw myself from the chair. Unfortunately I find that I cannot move a muscle. Pinned into the seat, I slowly rise.

A jolt from below and I descend a little. I look over the edge to see Jack hanging onto my wheels.

"I've got you," he cries.

The dip downwards was nothing more than that. I start to rise again.

"Let go," I call down to Jack. "This thing lifts the weight of cattle, so you're not going to be able to do anything."

"I'm here to rescue you, though," he says in a small voice.

The opening above us edges closer. It seems completely black. We are right underneath the ship now, and I can hear a hum. As we enter the dark void, the humming stops. A door is sliding beneath us, shutting out the farm below. Jack lifts his feet up to avoid getting them caught as the last view of the outside world is closed off. I feel my chair touch down on the ground gently, and I sense Jack is standing next to me. I can't be absolutely sure as it is pitch black. I cannot see anything at all.

I try desperately not to panic, despite my senses feeling like they've been shut off. Somehow sound seems to be blocked.

Unable to even hear my own breathing, I become frantic. I reach out with my hands and scream. My scream is silent, which is just as well as I quickly realise the clammy hand I'm holding is Jack's.

Relieved that I still at least have my sense of touch, I squeeze his hand for all I'm worth. I can feel him doing the same to me. It hurts, but it's a good, reassuring hurt.

Without warning, another of my senses starts working. I can smell. It's something sweet. It smells like incense, kind of warm like smoke but smelling quite nice. I inhale without realising it, and my eyelids start to droop. I fight it, trying hard to stay alert. My head nods forward. The realisation that I've been sedated hits me just before the effects do. My whole body gives in to the power of whatever has been pumped around us. I feel Jack's hand slip from mine. I stretch for him before I slump forward unconscious.

I wake up to an orchestra of sound. Animal calls ring out all around. There are cows, pigs, cats, and dogs. Lions roar, snakes hiss, and then there are the creatures I don't even think are from our planet. Strange looking beasts with giant eyes on stalks blink at me; another looks like a human-sized frog with a grin that would suit a whale. All of them, me included, don't at first appear to be in cages. The same blue light that lifted me into the spaceship now provides thin, glowing walls to keep each of us separated.

I reach out to touch the barrier, expecting some sort of shock. Surprisingly, it is soft and warm like your favourite pillow might be.

It's only now that I realise my wheelchair has gone. I'm seated in some sort of a hologram. The blue light has been used again; this time it mimics my chair. I try to wheel forward, and whilst it does not have wheels that go around, I find that I glide around my pen as if I were a feather in the wind.

As I spin around I suddenly notice that behind me in another pen is Jack.

"Hey, Jack. Are you okay?"

He's lying on his side and rolls over. "Just five more minutes," he mumbles, obviously half asleep.

I try again. "Jack. Do you want to wake up and deal with our alien abduction?"

He jumps to his feet, "What? But, that was just a dream!"

He stops and stares past me. I glance over my shoulder and realise he's looking at the grinning frog-like creature.

He starts shaking and gulps air like a goldfish. "Calm down," I tell him. Perhaps I shouldn't have woken him up that way. I'm not very good at sugarcoating things. I think of the best thing to say. "Um, everything will be all right." I say it slowly and deliberately, talking to him like he is a complete idiot. It works.

He snaps his mouth shut and holds his arms close to his body. I'm guessing he's trying to stop the shaking. "I'm good," he says, totally unconvincingly.

The blue light that makes up our pens creeps out beneath us. It's like watching a bowl fill with water as the light trickles across the floor until it has filled the space. I look around and see the same is happening in every pen. Slowly, each containment area rises a little, and we start to slide along as if we are on a conveyer belt.

The movement is so gentle that none of the animals appears distressed. Well, no one but Jack.

"We're doomed!" Jack cries.

"Will you pull yourself together?" I snap. "I'm sure we'll be..." I don't finish my sentence. Up ahead I can see tables, lights, tools. It looks like a hospital.

Jack loses it. "I knew it! They're going to cut us up and experiment on us! We've got to escape." He starts bouncing off the blue walls like he's in a pinball machine, frantically trying to get out.

I try to get him to calm down but realise it is hopeless. I leave him to get it all out of his system, and I turn to look up ahead.

I see that the weird alien creatures seem to be moving away from the tables, whilst my pen and those in front are moving toward them. I try and see what is in front of me. They are all animals I recognise, such as pigs, cats, dogs and, I think, the cow who had cried out.

As I look more closely, they all seem to be carrying an injury. I wonder if they've already been experimented on but choose to keep those thoughts to myself. Jack is having a hard enough time as it is.

As we glide up to the tables, I can at last see a few of our hosts. I gasp as the reality that we really have been taken by aliens hits me. I guess I shouldn't be surprised, what with the lifting beam of light, the flying saucer and the strange animals, but standing in front of me are actual aliens. Now it is really real.

They are short, maybe the same height as a seven-year-old. They have two legs and two arms like us, but it's the heads that are different. Their heads are like large U's, almost magnet-shaped. At the top of each side is a single eye. At the bottom of the bend, above the neck, they have a mouth and a couple of holes just above it, which must be their noses.

They tap away on little holographic screens, and lasers seem to sweep across the animals, who cry out in distress.

I see the cow that arrived with us drop down on to the table. I can clearly tell that she has a broken leg. It's twisted horribly. I immediately feel anger towards these aliens. Their cruelty must be terrible. Surely there are other ways to learn about our planet.

Jack interrupts my anger. "Do you think this is the first part of an invasion?"

I look at him, taking a moment to consider his words. "Maybe, that might explain the injuries. Perhaps they are seeing what hurts us or..." I leave the sentence hanging unintentionally.

Jack finishes it. "Or what kills us."

The cow in front of us lifts away toward our captors. She's on her side, unable to stand because of her injury. She thrashes about in obvious distress. Again the blue light sweeps across her. Two of the aliens look at a screen and seem to discuss the poor animal.

They move, blocking our view of the cow. The cow screams and then falls silent. I feel a tear slip out. She didn't need to die.

The aliens part, and I see the cow lying prone on the table. Again she is lifted up, and her pen slots opposite us. As it travels nearer I look away, not wanting to see her body.

"Look!" shouts Jack.

I turn and follow his pointing arm. The cow is back on her feet. All four feet that is. They are all perfect. Her eyelashes bat at me, and she lets out the most satisfied *moo* I think I've ever heard.

I'm really confused now. Are they helping, testing, or something else?

"Dani, help me!" Jack shouts.

Behind me Jack is levitated away. The blue light seems to wrap him up as if he were in a sleeping bag. They scan him and fall into another discussion. If they had shoulders, I think the movement they make would be the same as when we shrug. I'm sure that's what one of them did.

They waste no more time with Jack and move his pen behind the cow. He is slowly moving away back down the line. He stands up, patting his body, seemingly checking that he's in one piece.

He calls to me, "Hey Dani, if I turn around, can you tell me if there are any holes in my clothes?" He turns.

"You look fine," I call.

"You sure? I don't wanna find out I've had any probes put anywhere."

The look on his face is so serious I almost burst out laughing. I might do if it weren't for the fact that I'm moving onto the table now.

If Jack looked like he was in a sleeping bag, then that is exactly how I feel. The blue light makes a cocoon for me, and it is soft and warm. The scanning ray sweeps over me. One of the aliens calls over to his colleagues. They look at their screen and then look at me.

In the distance I can see another group looking over my wheelchair. A flash of light and the ray goes across me again. It hovers on my back and legs.

The lead alien speaks to me, but I have no idea what he is saying. He seems to chirp like a mother bird. He might be a she for all I know. He points at my legs and then to the screen. I think he shakes his U-shaped head at me. Then all at once, I understand.

"It's okay," I say. "You don't have to fix me, I'm not really broken. This is who I am."

I've no idea if he/she understands me. There are five of them now. A discussion takes place amongst them, or at least that's what I think is happening.

It seems like an age before the group finally parts, and I am moved back to my pen. The holographic chair awaits me, and I am gently dropped into it.

"Are you okay?" asks Jack.

"Yeah, I think they wanted to make me better," I say, sounding a little dazed.

"They seemed to spend ages on you. I thought they were gonna cut you up or something." Jack looks genuinely concerned.

"I'm fine. I think they are helping, or at least trying to help." I look past Jack at the cow.

"What are they doing? Do you think we are going to go back to their world?" Jack asks, his eyes darting everywhere.

I ponder his question for a while before saying, "You know, I think this is like a hospital or veterinary clinic. I think the cow hurt herself before they lifted her up. I think that is why they lifted her up."

"But what about us then?" asks Jack.

"I guess they thought I needed help, too, and well, Jack, you brought yourself along by hanging onto me," I say. "Why did you do that?"

Jack looks embarrassed. "I, uh, well, um, you're my friend, and I didn't want anything to happen to you."

There's an awkward moment between us. I don't know what to say. "I..."

My words are cut off as we are plunged into darkness. It's the same as when we were first taken. Silence has engulfed us. I call out, but cannot hear my own voice. I'm calmer this time. I know what is going on. Well, I sort of know, and that makes it a little easier to deal with. I reach out with my hands, wondering if I'll be able to hold onto Jack again. There is only emptiness.

It's a strange thing to be in absolute darkness. You think your eyes will adjust, but if there is not a hint of light anywhere. There is nothing to adjust to. It really puts you on edge. I feel like I'm waiting for something to jump out and grab me. I start thinking about the grinning, frog-like creatures with the mouths so big I wonder if they could swallow me whole.

My calmness is slipping. I don't want to panic. Then it hits me. The smell is back. That sweet, smoky smell that means I am going to be knocked out. This time I'm grateful. I feel like I need to escape my own imagination.

I breathe deeply and slump unconscious.

I open my eyes to see a pair of eyes staring back at me. I'm startled and pull back thinking it's those things with eyes on stalks. I blink fast and focus. The haziness leaves my vision, and I realise it's the farm cat sitting on my chest and looking at me.

"Get off, Whiskers," I say as I push him off me.

I sit up and realise I'm in my bed on the farm. I lift the covers and see that I'm in my nightdress. Beside my bed is my wheelchair, waiting for me.

"Was it all just a dream?" I ask out loud.

There's a tap at my door. "Who is it?" I call, slightly flustered.

"It's me, Jack. Just checking that you are where you're meant to be." He sounds relieved.

"Uh, yeah, I'll be out in a minute. I've just got to get dressed." I want to call him in. I want to talk to him but decide I need to take a moment to gather myself.

I dress quickly, skip cleaning my teeth, and wheel myself out of the room. I find Jack outside, his face screwed up like he is deep in thought.

"Hey Jack, sleep well?" I ask.

"Not really. I had this weird dream that we were abducted by aliens, who turned out to be nice aliens. Sort of vet aliens." Jack rubs the back of his neck.

"I had the same dream, Jack. Exactly the same, but it couldn't have been real. Could it?"

Jack shakes his head. "Nah, there's no way. I think one of the sweets we had last night made us hallucinate."

Before we can say any more, Jenny jogs up to us. "Where did you two get to last night? Well, never mind. Did you hear about the cow?"

"What cow?" I ask.

"The one that had a broken leg yesterday and the vet came to put to sleep today. Well, the leg is fine today. The vet is really angry. The farmhand reckons he's been tricked. It's the most exciting thing that's happened on this boring trip." Jenny stifles a yawn.

Jack and I look at one another. Is it our cow?

"Where is the cow?" I ask Jenny.

She grins. "It's this way. Come on, I'll show you both."

We follow her away from the main buildings. Beyond the paddock we can see cattle grazing at the top of the hill. I get why she was grinning now. I can't get there in my chair.

Jack turns to me and says, "I'll go and see if I can tell if it is our cow."

Jenny threads her arm though his. "I'll show you, Jack." She winks at me.

They race off up the hill. I doubt very much if Jack will be able to tell if it is our cow or not. I look down at my legs. I don't need to do anything to know they are the same as yesterday.

I wheel my chair to the far side of the paddock. I wonder what happened to us. Did we simply just get dropped back home? Have we got nothing to show for it?

I reach down to my wheels to manoeuvre myself into a better position when I notice something is different about my chair. There is a small panel on the side. I run my finger across it, and I see a flash of light. It's a flash of blue light.

The blue light pours out from the panel, trickling along the frame, immersing my wheels until the whole chair glows.

I look to the top of the hill, and then I look back at my chair. I give my wheels a little push and then, *whoosh*, I'm off.

I'm like a streak of blue lightning as I zoom to the top of the hill.

I sit there panting and grinning as I watch Jenny and Jack come over the crest of the hill to join me.

"How did you...?" Jenny looks dumbfounded.

"My chair got an upgrade," I smile. "Shall we go see our cow?" I ask Jack. "Or are you happy with this one?"

Jenny spins on her heels and makes her way back down the hill.

The cow trots over to us, seemingly recognising us as fellow space travellers. She licks my face. Her pretty eyes seem to give off a smile, if that's possible.

"This is nice," says Jack.

"It is," I say. "I think it's just the beginning, too."

"How come?" asks Jack.

"This chair doesn't just go fast. It does other stuff. And it has a message."

"What's it say?"

"When I activated the chair, it sort of put an instruction manual for it in my head. Along with details of how to call the aliens if we want to join the crew, if we want to head off into space."

Jack is quiet for a moment then says, "Do you want to be a space vet?"

"Eventually, I might," I reply.

What I don't tell him is that I definitely will. Just as soon as I explore all that Earth has to offer. I'm going to go to college, and then I'm going to take a break and go travelling. Everyone else can do Europe or Asia; I'm going to check out the universe.

The Smell of Home

by anne m. gibson

anne m. gibson is an information architect and general troublemaker just close enough to Valley Forge, Pennsylvania to think a wander through a revolutionary battlefield is not noteworthy. In addition to designing websites, she writes about websites (or much weirder things), plays competitive pinball, and watches the terriers destroy things.

I knelt on the porch, the bare pads of my toes cooling on the cement. The late summer sun hadn't made it around to this side of the house yet, and the roof kept the porch a good ten degrees cooler than the grass, except where the shadow of the cable bisected the field.

Caroline said our house needed guarding because of the cable. It was slate grey, wider than an oak, and it soared through our roof into the sky and out of sight. Caroline said thousands of lives depended on it.

Caroline had never suggested, or even implied, that my stay here was dependent upon my guardianship. I was pretty confident that she was as devoted to me as I was to her. But we both knew it was in my nature to guard, and this house and its cable needed guarding, so she didn't discourage it. Over time, others had joined me—Maggie and Rocks and Jess—but I was the leader.

Inside the house, Caroline was talking to someone on the vid
screen about the refugees of the Asteroid War. Despite the insu-
lated, blast-proofed walls, I could still make out the occasional
name or exclamation. I tried to tune it out; politics was boring,
and it really was none of my business, but my ear flicked in the
direction of the reinforced window frame anyway.

The "Terrier/Tutis" tags on my collar jangled when I turned
my head. They indicated the government program that funded
my placement here with Caroline. Caroline was Army, and I
was Terrier, and we were both proud of it.

I squinted out at the trees for too long, and the effort of
trying to make sense of the occasionally-shifting patterns of
brown on brown gave me a headache. I snorted at myself for
my foolishness.

I let my eyes unfocus and "listened" to the smells the light
breeze carried across my nose. The headache disappeared.

Down low at the grass roots, the smells were all earthworms
and rotting vegetation with the occasional whiff of clay. Above
the thick essence of the root system, a spectacular landscape
of odors shimmered over the lush brown grass. The peppery
scents of squirrels, birds, and rodents who had been feasting on
the berries of a nearby bush crisscrossed the yard.

The bitterness of raccoon spray still lingered from the over-
night hours near Caroline's compost heap, which carried its
own warm perfume into the air. I smiled a little, remembering
Jessie's excitement when she told us all about the masked invad-
er she had chased off. Caroline had been annoyed; Jessie was
supposed to use her blaster on anything she didn't recognize.
But Jessie was less than three years old and still full of spunk.

The screen door banged open. I turned to watch Caroline
step out onto the porch. She was beautiful. Her freshly oiled
leather boots and crisp brown uniform smelled like home. The
gun-oil on the pulse rifle slung over her shoulder mingled with
the flowery scent of her soap as a breeze drifted over her shoul-

der and down to me. Her short-cut yellow fur was tucked under a flat-brimmed hat that didn't succeed at hiding the sadness in her eyes. I tilted my head at her, questioning.

"Morning, Old Grey. Everything in order?"

I thunked my tail in assent, ignoring the pain that the knocks against the cold porch were causing in my tailbones.

"Ready for patrol?" She smiled sadly, looked around the yard, then stepped down off the porch. I followed at her side but letting her lead. She smiled and kneeled down. "You're, what? Fifteen? Sixteen? Getting up there, even for a Terrier," she said, scratching the space between my ears. I wagged my tail approvingly then watched the shadow of a bird cross diagonally from the treeline toward the house. The fur on my neck bristled, and Caroline pulled her hand away to raise a pair of binoculars around her neck to her eyes. "Looks like just a redtail hawk, but we'd better not risk it."

With a well-practiced flip of my muzzle, I raised my blaster's firing trigger up off my collar and gripped it gently between my teeth. I watched the hawk carefully. It was circling over an area of the grass where I had caught more than one field mouse in my younger days. The bird gave me no mind, though—at thirteen pounds—I was more than he probably wanted to take on. I waited, lined up my shot, and bit down hard on the trigger.

The pulse of energy that left my harness pushed me backwards, but I was used to the recoil and never left my feet. I'll admit it wasn't what my hips needed right then, and I uttered a low bark of annoyance. To Caroline it probably sounded like contentment, as the bird disintegrated into tufts of feathers that fell to the ground.

The binoculars still at her eyes, Caroline grunted her approval. "Nice shot, Old Grey." She slipped a piece of stinky cheese out of her pocket, and I gulped it down with zeal. Caroline put down her binoculars and rolled the rifle off her shoulder. "Let's go check it out."

We walked slowly across the yard. I led the way, though
it wasn't easy with the blades of grass tickling my belly and
blocking my path. Still, this was the first clear shot I'd had in a
couple of weeks, and it was exciting. I loped through the grass
until I was close then followed the scent to the various pieces
of the hawk. Too stiff to lift my leg, I arched over one to mark
it as my kill, but a sharp "Hey!" from Caroline prevented me
from completing the job. I huffed impatience at her.

Caroline watched me find the pieces and gave me a piece of
cheese for each one I recovered. She gathered them into a bag
"so the lab can tell us if he was armed." I never understood
why she needed my help at this. The stench of burnt hawk was
the smelliest thing in the whole field—so powerful that Maggie
and Rocks trotted over from the side field to smell what it was.

Maggie nuzzled me. "You got cheese!" she said.

"I blasted a hawk!" I replied proudly, making sure to flip my
blaster back down to its safety position. Maggie was nursing a
litter of pups so young they had only just been chipped, and I
wasn't about to let an accidental shot bring her to harm.

"I didn't know you still had it in you, sir," Rocks said with
gleeful respect.

"I told you, once a hero always a hero." Maggie leaned into
me and made a face at Rocks.

Caroline shooed the others away. "You have patrols to do,
now git!" They bayed at her but jogged off immediately.

Once we could no longer make them out in the grass except
as shimmers of movement, Caroline sighed. "You're a good
boy, Old Grey. But you're getting old, and I need to tell you
something important. Something about what's at the other end
of the cable."

I listened, but Caroline's chatter bored me. I looked back at
the house, its clapboard walls, wraparound porch, and stone
chimney belying the technology of the structure. Still, it was
hard to miss the cable that snaked up into the sky.

I wasn't interested in what was at the other end of the cable. My job was to protect this end. Slowly, I made my way back across the field. Caroline followed, talking.

"Your hips are starting to fail, and I think your hearing might be, too."

I snorted. My hearing was fine.

"Soon you're going to have a day where you can't get up any more, and we can't control the pain, and when that happens, we're going to have to make a hard choice, you and I." Her voice caught, and I looked back at her. She smelled of stress and fear. "Oh boy, I don't want you to go."

Honestly, I don't think I'd heard anything more nonsensical since Rocks tried to convince me that the teeth that fell out while he was chewing on a stone were diamonds. I wagged my tail comfortingly and waited for her to catch up. She continued to talk while I scanned the area for potential threats.

"When that day comes, I want you to promise me you won't panic. There are people on the other side who are going to take care of you—"

I cut her off with a low growl. There, in the treeline, a flash of movement and a smell.

Caroline raised the binoculars to her face again. "I don't see anything," she said. "Now listen," she started again, but I growled again.

Explosives. I was sure of it. I called to the rest of the pack with a short bay and ran forward so I could get a better smell, and a better view, of what I was searching for.

I stopped suddenly and turned. There, the acrid scent of explosives mixed with the greasy stink of human sweat reached me again, just a whiff. And just at the same time, the slightest movement. I flipped up my trigger and let my nose do the aiming. A rush of movement, and something big and black flew out of the trees low to the ground, aimed right at our house!

I didn't hesitate. I bit the trigger hard. The bright pulse hit the device dead-on, and it exploded in a fire of bright browns. The blast blew me off my toes, and I landed a dozen feet away, almost to the porch.

I was dimly aware of Caroline blasting into the trees with her pulse rifle and of the sound of the pack coming to her aid. I panted heavily and tried to get up to help, but I ached all over and decided maybe I would rest here just a minute before I joined the others. I closed my eyes.

I heard voices—lots of voices, like Caroline's, not like the pack's. They were muffled and garbled and deep. My body ached, but more than that, it felt wrong. My bones felt heavy. Lying on my back, I felt like my entire spine was twisted. I couldn't feel my tail. My skin itched from the air passing over it as if all my fur had been shaved off. The pads of my toes were too far apart. I could barely smell anything at all.

I opened my eyes. The walls of the room were an old and scuffed white. A brass "Terrier/Tutis" logo like the one on my collar collected dust on the wall. My bed had fresh, clean sheets of the brightest blue I'd ever seen. Around me, people tapped on consoles that resembled holiday lights, blinking and flashing in amazing colors. Everything seemed deeper and more discernible. I could see the difference between a lamp on a nearby table and the wall behind it, and it *wasn't even moving.*

Someone had restrained my head and limbs. I couldn't lift my head to see my chest or limbs, and for some reason my nose was misshapen. Was I injured in the blast? I cried out, but the sound was all wrong. I started to panic.

A man towered over me with a funny white thing over his face. And his hair... It was a shade of brown that almost glowed. I tensed to challenge him. The man pressed something cold against my leg, and I felt air hiss against it. Without intending to, I relaxed.

I tried to growl but couldn't find my voice. There shouldn't be a man at my house.

"Shhhh... Grey, it's going to be okay," a woman's voice responded. It was perfectly clear, almost as if it were inside my head. I turned my head to see a brown-faced woman with beautiful brown eyes staring back. She reminded me of Maggie.

"I'll take that as a compliment. And the bright-brown color is called red, although on Doctor Ninian it's closer to orange." The woman stroked the top of my head, and I realized my ears were in the wrong place. This vexed me almost as much as the man.

"My name is Eleanor. Caroline told us what happened. She said you weren't told about our side of the connection. I'm here to help you, Greyson. There are some things I need to tell you, now that you're old enough to understand, okay?" She stroked my head.

I was vaguely aware of the other people in the room doing things to my half-numb, half-aching body, but the woman kept me distracted with her voice.

"You are not a dog," the woman said.

I snorted. Of course I'm not a dog, I thought. I'm a Terrier. A dog is a brainless mongrel that, if it comes near the house, I shoot with my blaster.

"You are a Terrier, yes, but you're something else, too," the woman said as if she could understand me. Caroline could never understand me, though I understood all the words she said.

"I'm listening to your thoughts through the chip in your head," Eleanor explained. She slid her hand to the base of my neck, and I could feel her fingertips outline a foreign lump underneath. Like everything else, it was hot and sore. "It lets me listen to your thoughts just like the dog-Terrier-down on the planet."

I tilted my head at her.

Eleanor sighed. "Your cable, the one that you guard at the house? It's one of the anchors for the space elevator that connects to a space station high above the sky. Space stations are like giant space houses for many people and—"

Space houses? I huffed with annoyance. I know what a space station is, and even what the elevator system is. Caroline watched videos and talked to people on the vid screen about it all the time.

"You... You understand about the station?" the woman asked. Somewhere in my mind I felt a tickle, as if someone else were remembering my memories. I pushed against it, annoyed. Of course I "understood" the space station, and the war, and the cable. I understood the Republic, the Mars colonies, and the socio-political opportunities that asteroid mining had provided the historically poor Appalachian miners who'd owned our house before we did, too. I just didn't care. They didn't affect me. My job was to protect the house, guard the cable, and keep Caroline and my pack safe.

"I'm sorry, Greyson, I didn't realize just how smart you are," Eleanor said softly. I could feel her emotions, like a far-away echo of a memory. She was surprised, confused, sad, and a little bit proud.

I growled softly. My voice startled me.

"What do you know about the Tutis, Greyson?" she asked.

My brows furrowed, and my ears tried to twist downward. The war between the separatists and the Republic had been going on a long time, and it was mostly a stalemate now, so I didn't bother listening to the news every day. Tutis was a government program to help refugees when the war began, wasn't it? But something had gone wrong, and there were protests. Some of the separatist groups were using the program to justify their attacks on the asteroid colonies. Somehow the elevators were involved. It was never important enough that Caroline briefed us on it.

Eleanor ran her hands over the top of her tightly braided fur and paused a long time, as if she didn't know where to start. I waited.

"The first people who moved to space—outside the astro-
nautical program—were asteroid miners. They were poor. The
companies that funded them were cheap. Radiation shielding
was substandard. Whole families were living in ships with
barely the protections needed for a single person. There were
mutations, and...

"Well, the children that were born of those early settlers
weren't very much like their parents, and they came to be
called Tutis. They were severely physically disabled compared
to Earthborn children or the children on the settlement colonies. I, I don't mean they're incapable. In fact, in some ways
they're superior to Earth-normal humans. They've got neural
olfactory processing and auditory processing capabilities that
someone like me could only dream of.

"The Republic decided that the best thing for the children
was to confiscate them from their parents and move them here
to the moon where they would at least have the opportunity to
grow to adulthood. But we wanted them to live fulfilling lives
doing something worthwhile. Their sacrifices have meant so
much to us, our society..."

I huffed. I didn't like the way this story was going, and I
was tired of listening. Listening to Eleanor was like watching
a pigeon fake a broken wing to distract me from her nest. My
heart thunked heavily in my chest.

"You're right, I should cut to the chase," the woman said.
"And you've guessed correctly. You are a Tutis. You were born
to impoverished asteroid miners, taken from them, and raised
here. The day that you were turned over, we implanted that chip
and connected you to a device that allows you to control a dog's
body instead of your own. This body that you feel now *is* your
real body, that of a color-seeing, mostly deaf fifteen-year-old
young man who's lived in a pod since the day he was born."

I heard the words. I understood them, but they meant nothing to me. She may as well have told me that I was a giraffe on

the Serengeti from the nature shows I watch with Caroline.

"You're also a hero," she continued. "You saved the lives of three million people today by foiling that terrorist plot. The insurgents had a stockpile of explosives hidden in that treeline, with the intent of killing you and your pack and your Caroline and destroying your cable."

Caroline was okay! My pack was okay! Relief washed over me in waves of chills. I just needed to get home, and everything would be okay again.

The woman's tone became abruptly professional. I didn't trust it. "Grey, you've served your time. You've earned a life free from danger and hard work. Today is the day you get to retire. You are now a resident of space. We've prepared you an apartment. I will be your guide and will help you transition to your new life. You can travel the solar system, get a full education. You will meet other Tutis. You can teach us what you know."

I growled and pulled against the bindings that held me to the table. This was ridiculous. I didn't want to meet other Tutis, or become a "resident of space." I certainly didn't want to live on the moon! I didn't want to do any of these things! I wanted to go home to my Caroline!

"You need to understand you *are* home, Grey."

No. No! I have a cable to protect!

I pushed back against the woman's voice in my head, trying to drive her out. No! I wanted my sense of smell back! I wanted my hearing back! I wanted to run in the yard and practice firing my blaster at mice and lie on Caroline's lap while we watched nature shows about capybaras on the vid screen! I had a pack to protect! No! No! No!

My barking did me little good. The force of my mind couldn't drive out whatever put the woman's voice in my head, and my body was too sedated and too restrained to help. Still, I couldn't stay here. I pushed and pushed, mentally nipping at the connection between us. My head hurt. It hurt a lot. But I had been in pain since I arrived, and I was angry.

Something in the connection suddenly changed. Eleanor jerked her head back, a grimace on her face.

My eyes narrowed. I had pushed so hard on the connection that it had back-fed. At least, that's how Eleanor would have explained it, I knew. I knew everything that Eleanor knew.

I flipped through memories of Eleanor's childhood in my mind. She'd grown up on the moon, visited Earth and Mars on childhood vacations, and had a passion for studying psychology. Scholarships earned her degrees on Earth and strong field work landed her a job with the Republic just out of college. Eleanor had been part of the Tutis program since the beginning.

I was the beginning of the Tutis program. I was the first of the abducted children to be implanted with the neuro-transmission chip. Some adult humans had tried, but they couldn't rewire their senses fast enough. The others had gone unstable and had died here at the research compound before their dog bodies had reached three years old. My successful implantation saved the program, saved Eleanor's job, and saved years of research.

I was also the first to die on the planet and survive in space. A few other Terriers across the globe had been killed in attacks, and each time the trauma had killed the Tutis host. The team had been preparing for my Terrier body to die of old age, and their plans for a new "extraction technique" were the only reason I was alive now.

In the eyes of the bureaucrats, the program was a troubling and secret success. On one hand, the children who had been "saved" by their government were now model citizens repaying their families' debts to the Republic. On the other, the kidnapping had caused mass outrage and had sparked the Asteroid War. Eleanor didn't even know whether the public knew about the Terrier program. She doubted it would be well-received.

No one at the facility knew quite what to do with me. There were no protocols and no policies. Would I become a poster child for some politician's definition of success, paraded across the Republic to repair their reputation? Would I even be able to adjust to their way of life? They were heartbroken for me, and they were afraid for their program.

Send me back, I demanded.

"You know we can't do that, Greyson. It wouldn't be the same. You can't run, you can't hear, you can't smell. You'd be miserable."

Make me a Terrier again. Send me home.

"There's a very good chance you'll die if we try to implant you in another dog," Eleanor said, her hand rubbing her aching temple.

I knew. Somewhere deep inside the thought scared me a little, but not nearly as much as being in this terrifying place. These sights were overwhelming, the sounds were all garbled, and the lack of smell was stifling. I was wearing an ill-fitting human suit that grew more uncomfortable by the second.

I'm a Terrier. I blew myself up protecting my house! I'm a good dog!

I growled low in my throat.

"Stay," Eleanor growled back. She empathized with me, but she didn't like that I knew what she knew. It was a *complication*. She had been watching me—listening to me—for years. She'd had no idea how developed I had become, and now all the ethical concerns she'd ignored when she thought I had the intelligence of a dog were rushing to the forefront of a career she'd fought hard to protect.

Send me back! I have the right to choose my fate!

She doubted they could do what I had asked for. She thought I was throwing my life away.

I growled again, determined to stand my ground. This was *my* life.

Eleanor reached up and disconnected a cable from the back of her head. I watched her talk to the doctor with the red hair. They pulled in two more doctors and a woman in a suit. I couldn't hear the conversation or smell their emotions.

Eleanor approached my side, but I didn't look at her. I had no reason to challenge her. She knew what I wanted. I turned my attention to a picture on the wall. It was a brown rabbit in what I now understood was a green meadow. The contrast was amazing, and I suddenly understood why Caroline was so much better at spotting threats in the trees. I wondered if my fuzzy ball was green, too.

I stared at the painting, angry and anxious and sad. My legs twitched with the desire to race across the meadow. Anguish welled up in my chest. I wanted to run. I wanted to run just as fast as I could away from all this nonsense. I wanted to go home!

Eleanor shouted something to her companions about my vital signs. My heart raced. My head throbbed with pressure, and my toes tingled. I was hyperventilating, panting with exhaustion, and I knew from the knowledge Eleanor had pushed to me that I was in real danger. My Tutis body had taken serious strain when my Terrier body had died, and I was rejecting its sensory input. If they didn't do something soon...

"What choice do we have?" Eleanor shouted across the room to the angry orange-haired doctor. "We'll be shut down permanently!"

I felt the hiss of another spray, and I slept.

I awoke to a new voice. "Grey, it's me, Caroline."

Caroline! I tried to lift my head, but it was so very heavy. My eyes could barely open, and when they did it was just a fuzzy sea of yellow and brown and blue. I tried to stand, but my paws went out in all directions. But oh, I could smell. And I smelled Caroline!

"Okay, okay, slow down, little one," she said as she stroked the top of my head. Her hands were huge, but they were as soft as I remembered, and they smelled like home. I felt myself lifted up into the air. Caroline nuzzled me, her tears wetting my fur. "They sent you back to me, little Grey. You're a puppy again—one of Maggie's. You'll have to learn to walk and eat and house-train all over again."

I wagged my tail and howled just as well as I could, a high squeak Caroline probably couldn't even hear.

She laughed anyway, even as the tears coursed down her cheeks. "You're home, Little Grey Hero, you're home!"

Blaise of Luna

by Blake Jessop

Blake Jessop is a Canadian writer, lecturer, and bouncer.

1. July 12, 2060

Dear diary,

My name is Blaise Tasker Malisse VII. I am a girl, I'm about to turn eleven, and I don't see either of my dads as much as I want. As of last week, I live on the moon.

I've decided to start writing a diary because it looks like the next few weeks will be very busy. Also, Miss Charlottine said I could use it for extra credit so I won't be too far behind my friends when I get back to San Francisco. Writing also helps distract me from wanting to throw up all the time from living in microgravity, which is what it's called when you live somewhere where gravity is not as strong as it normally is on Earth. I learned that today at school, which I attend every morning on my tablet. Papa Terry says that you learn something new every day, so I'll be writing those things down, too.

Did you know that your eyes change when there isn't enough gravity? I didn't, but mine are already getting tired writing this. I'm going to stop for now except to say that I thought changing schools every year when my dad's job at the United Nations made us move was hard when we only changed cities. Changing planets is *a lot* harder. I'm going to go to bed; I have to sort of strap myself into it to try and get to sleep.

2. July 16, 2060

My dad has a really important job. Just to clear things up, when I say "my dad" I usually mean Blaise Tasker Malisse VI, not Papa Terry, who usually just gets "Papa." I'm not sure why I settled into that, but I did. It just seemed right, and it's been that way since I was little. I don't have any brothers or sisters, partly because there are so many people living on Earth already, and partly because I suspect that my fathers have enough trouble just dealing with me. I am not a troublesome person, but I do sometimes get into trouble. Those are different things.

Anyways, my dad has a very, very important job. We all learned about the Ansible Array in school and that talking to aliens is now a normal thing for humans, even if their home planets are really far away. Ms. Charlottine said it caused "a stir" when it worked for the first time, by which she usually means "a disaster." Ms. Charlottine is *exceedingly* polite. So when the United Nations, which used to just deal with nations on Earth, realized that there were totally other nations in space, they started dreaming up jobs for people so that we could talk to aliens without sounding dumb. That's what my dad does. We've been moving around, once a year mostly, for as long as I can remember, but this is the first time we've moved to outer space.

I'm not sure I like outer space. I still feel sick a lot of the time and brushing my teeth is weird. There's barely enough gravity to keep water flowing, so you brush your teeth the normal way, but you have to swallow the toothpaste, which is supposed to taste good but doesn't. There are a lot of bathroom activities that used to be easy and now cause all kinds of problems. Today's lesson is *don't take gravity for granted*. You'll miss it when you have to drink your evening glass of water out of a soft plastic balloon.

I will say that the view is very nice. We live under a dome, but there are thick plastic windows you can use to look outside. This past Saturday, Papa woke me up so we could watch the Earth rise together. Dad was at work. The view was amazing, and watching my home planet appear like a beautiful marble floating in ink made me feel both very big and very small. I think I'm changing today's lesson to that—you can feel both those things at the same time.

3. July 19, 2060

I have had a birthday in space. I'm now eleven, or more like twelve and a half if I had been born here, because it takes the moon only twenty-seven days to orbit the Earth. It was not a great birthday because Six and I got into a huge fight. I don't really want to mention what it was about except that sometimes I can't believe that half of my DNA comes from my dad. That's who I mean by "Six," by the way. Dad calls me "Blaise Tasker Malisse the Seventh" when he's angry, and lately it's just been "Seven," so I decided that I would do the same. I wonder if he calls my Grandma Blaise "Five"?

What I learned today was that cake somehow tastes worse when you've had a fight with your parents. Even when it's your Grandma Blaise's chocolate cake, even if it's almost impossible to bake it properly in microgravity, and your Papa figured out how to do it anyways. Seeing Amina and Harjit and Carter was nice, but it was just on screen, and that isn't the same as having a party in real life, either. They had lots of questions about living on the moon and meeting aliens, but I didn't feel much like answering. I haven't met any aliens yet.

I think ~~my dad~~ Six is worried about work. Not many humans get to meet aliens, and he's one of them. He'd never admit he's nervous, but I think he is. There are a lot of different kinds of aliens; we learn about them in school. Cygnians, who are a bit like huge birds with beautiful feathers, and Centauris, who are very tough and war-like. Humans are the new kids on the block, so more and more aliens are coming to meet us now that we can talk to them. It's like a huge version of my life, and I guess Six is feeling the same kind of pressure I do when I meet my fellow Lunars. Lunarians. I've learned that no one has agreed on a name for people who live on the moon. I like "Moonies," but my classmates up here all think it's silly. They do laugh when I say it, though, so that's a win!

4. July 22, 2060

Having a bad birthday party apparently hurts your feelings for longer than I thought it would, but I'm trying to get over it. I think my dad is getting sick. That's a thing that happens to people no matter where they live, and it is not much fun on the moon. It's harder to sleep in space, even with the hum of the air machines and the occasional rumble of a ship taking off or landing rattling your sleeping couch the way a streetcar would back in San Francisco.

There are all sorts of interesting ways to get sick on the moon. Most of them make you throw up, which is why I have taken to always carrying a barf bag around with me. I am getting used to how to walk up here—you don't really walk, you skip. I have always been great at that (and many other sports, thank you), so I've been getting better fast.

Anyways, my dad's big week is coming up—a whole bunch of important meetings with aliens to negotiate treaties and cultural exchanges and hopefully convince the Centauris not to blow us up and other ceremonies. If he doesn't get some good sleep, he won't be able to do his job, and where will we all be then?

5. July 25, 2060

I have always dreamed of being a pilot. I like the idea of flying in the air, not being an astronaut, which is a shame, because I would have basically already won my life if that had been my dream. Papa Terry is a poet, and he thinks I could be good at that if I tried harder instead of spending all my time on flight sims and reading and surfing the mesh for news about my favorite musicians.

I bring this up because something has gone seriously wrong, and all my plans have been ruined. I am apparently not going to be Blaise Tasker Malisse the test pilot, but Blaise Tasker Malisse the ACCIDENTAL INTERSTELLAR DIPLOMAT.

Dad is really sick. Like, so sick that they're thinking about sending him back to Earth. This is a problem because he's supposed to meet Mara-Téa, the Cygnian ambassador, for an informal dinner tonight before they have a serious meeting with cameras and news crews and such tomorrow. I already knew that, because the ambassador is bringing her son, and so Dad has to bring me. I got a long lecture about how not to say anything and look *demure.*

Now Dad can't do it. Like, absolutely no way.

You'd think there'd be some other diplomats available to do his job, right? Sure there are! But none of them are named Blaise Tasker Malisse. I learned in school back on Earth not to expect alien cultures to be the same as mine. I already knew that Cygnians take ceremonies very seriously and hate to have their plans changed, especially if it involves meeting new people. It's probably something to do with how they evolved back on Kepler-186f, which is what we call their home planet. I did not know that being unable to present them with someone named Blaise Tasker Malisse would cause a serious diplomatic incident.

While I was crying at Dad's bedside at the Lunar hospital, listening to him yell at his aides about all this, I had an idea.

"My name is Blaise Tasker Malisse," I said. "Why don't you let me host the Cygnian ambassador?"

Everyone just looked at me. Dad tried to yell, but all he could do was sort of croak. Everyone was *really* quiet.

"It is just an informal dinner," one of Dad's aides said to him, "and you might be better by tomorrow."

They called the UN back on Earth to see if anyone had a better idea, but no one did. So now I am having an alien and her family over to dinner. I will write again when it's over, and my fingers aren't shaking trying to tap the screen.

5. July 25, 2060, part 2!

I was supposed to watch a little video about Cygnian customs last week, but I may have skipped some of it because I was too busy researching lady heroes of classical music and playing Wing Commander 12 on the mesh with my friends back in San Francisco. (I don't always love living on the moon, but all the satellites do mean we have a super-fast connection!)

Anyways, I really, really should have watched the part about how they eat.

The dinner was going pretty well. The UN had a chef who was cooking food that both humans and Cygnians could eat, and even though things were a bit strained at first, I found Mara-Téa very easy to talk to. It helped that her son was an adorable little ball of feathers who chirped happily through most of the meal.

Everything was fine until the little Cygnian started getting hungry. I asked Mara-Téa if anything was wrong, but she said no, and did I mind if she fed him at the dinner table?

I'm no prude and told her that was quite fine. It was even a chance for me to explain that feeding babies is something humans consider totally normal and that it was okay to do it wherever.

What I didn't expect Mara-Téa to do was start regurgitating her food straight into her baby's mouth. Did you know that "regurgitate" basically means "throw up into someone else's mouth?"

I didn't, but I do now.

As Mara-Téa was throwing up little spurts of half-digested tofu and salad down her son's throat, I struggled not to barf. The smell was terrible. I felt my own dinner rising up my throat, unhindered by the moon's scanty gravity.

I threw up. Not all over the table. I grabbed an empty salad bowl and barfed into that. The UN chef looked totally horrified. Mara-Téa glanced over at me with a look of surprise creasing her feathers. Her bright, intelligent eyes fixed on me. *I am the first human to have dinner with a Cygnian*, I thought, *and I have totally blown it.* I expected Mara-Téa to get angry and storm out.

Instead she said, "That is wonderful, thank you so much."

She picked up the salad bowl with a delicate claw and presented it to her son, who cheerily stretched his neck out and started lapping up my barf with his little beak. I felt the urge to vomit again, and I put a hand to my stomach.

"That's fine, thanks," Mara-Téa said. "He has quite enough."

The rest of the dinner is a blur. I remember gulping down cool water from a fancy plastic bulb to try to keep everything down. I don't recall what we talked about after that, but pretty soon Mara-Téa left, saying that she'd see me at the formal meeting tomorrow.

I had barely settled my nerves when my tablet rang. My dad was calling. I prepared for a scolding of epic proportions.

What he actually said was, "Well done, Blaise. The Secretary General has had a message from Mara-Téa, and she said you were great. She told him that she had no idea humans were so sensitive and kind. I'm not sure how you did it, but well done."

So, not only am I now a diplomat, I'm fantastic at it.

6. July 27, 2060

Most kids on Earth do not get jobs until they are twenty, so I am a little young to have one of the most important jobs on the planet (or maybe I should say *off the planet*). There is an old phrase that my dad uses quite a lot: "There is no rest for the wicked." It comes from an old book, though I can't remember which one.

Anyways, I now know what he means. I barely had time to come home from the big meeting with Mara-Téa before the UN told me about the next one. The meeting with Mara-Téa went very well, by the way. She was happy to see me, and we had a quick chat about how well our two races would get along in front of a bunch of tiny drone cameras. It was strange, but because I felt like I knew her, I wasn't nearly as nervous as I had been the night before. Having dinner with someone, just eating and talking, is a really great way to forget that you're different.

My dad is still sick. His aides and assistants were hoping he'd get better in time to meet with the Centauris tomorrow, but he hasn't. Happily for me, the Centauris don't care nearly as much about ceremonies as the Cygnians, so it would be no problem for another diplomat to take Dad's place.

Unhappily for me, the Centauris were so impressed with how well the Cygnian meeting went that they absolutely demanded to meet with me and no one else. I'm off to a very important meeting right now to talk about how I'm going to manage this.

Things are so serious that the Secretary General of the UN, who is a very tall Norwegian man, has taken an emergency rocket to join us on the moon. I suppose he wants to make sure that my dad's illness isn't going to doom the entire human race. It's like he has no confidence in me at all!

7. July 28, 2060

It's over. The first epic battle between humans and an alien species. The war was fought among the stars. There were hundreds of explosions. Space ships turned into tiny stars as their fusion drives blew up after being hit by rail guns and laser beams. Most amazing of all... the humans won!

Before you get nervous, dear reader, it was not a real war—
Earth doesn't have nearly enough space ships for that, and the
Centauris would certainly win. After all, they've been flying
between the stars for hundreds of years!

My meeting with the Centauris started out okay. Their
ambassador, Krolik the Thrice-Honored Atmosphere Venter
of the Six Systems, kept asking me about all the wars humans
had gotten into with each other. I tried to tell him that we had
fought each other a lot, yes, but that things were much more
peaceful now, especially after we found out that there are other
species out here, like my most honorable guest.

That turned out to be the wrong way to talk to a Centauri.
Krolik laughed at me and said that all of humanity must be very
weak if we had abandoned fighting and were as tiny as I was.

That wasn't really fair; I am not short for an Earth girl, and
my hair is really frizzy in low gravity and makes me look even
taller. It's not my fault I wasn't born with horns or a tough
outer skin like a rhinoceros.

I was worried that I had made a major mistake, because Krolik started yelling about how easy it would be for his infinite
fleet to fly to Earth and blow up the moon, just to prove that
they could. Not good—I *live* on the moon.

I didn't know what to do, exactly, but my dad has taught me
a lot about dealing with bullies. "Stand up to them," he always
says. When the yelling stopped (which took a while), I said, "Is
that a challenge?"

All the blood drained out of the Secretary General's face.
He's pretty pale to start with, but now he looked like a ghost.

Krolik looked surprised for a second. I think it was surprise.
His horns were quavering a bit.

"Because on Earth we have a tradition," I said. "If you challenge me to a duel, I get to choose the weapons."

Krolik laughed.

"Very well!" he roared. "Explain how we will fight!"

How on Earth (or the moon) could I beat him? Centauris are *huge*. They have a much bigger fleet of space ships than we do. I probably couldn't even beat him at chess or a Centauri kid's game. Suddenly, I had an idea.

"Wing Commander 12," I said quietly.

Everyone gasped. The Secretary General fainted.

Over the next few hours I showed Krolik and his retinue how to play the game. I woke up my friends in San Francisco. After a short period of extreme surprise, they gathered our gaming guild from all over the mesh. Soon, our digital fleets were ready, and the battle began.

It was an epic conflict. The best I've ever played in. Even though they were new to the game, the Centauris flew brilliantly. I could see that their reputation for toughness and ferocity was well earned. In the end, it all came down to Krolik and me, champion against champion. Krolik was a fierce competitor, but I've been playing Wing Commander for a long time. The look of surprise on his big face when my final torpedo smashed his fighter to bits was almost comical.

With the battle over, all the tension of the meeting drained away. Krolik demanded food and drink (another Centauri tradition that the UN was mercifully ready for) and insisted that I give a speech (a tradition I was *not ready for at all*).

My first idea was to rub it in the alien's face, so that humans would look strong, but Krolik seemed hurt, so I talked about what a fantastic pilot he was and how amazingly well the Centauris did for players who had just tried the game for the first time. He puffed up visibly (like, with an actual gland in his neck), and his speech was all about how honorable Humans are, and how happy the Centauris would be to use their mighty fleet to show us around their star systems.

On my way home after another exhausting day, I thought about the advice I'd used to survive my meeting with the Centauris. I know I'm pretty hard on my dad sometimes, but he was right. There's a second part to his bully strategy: "Stand up to them, and you might make a friend." I'll have to tell him it worked.

Anyways, today's lesson is not for me, but for the aliens: *If you want to beat up on humans, do not challenge them at video games.* We are incredibly good at them, even by intergalactic standards.

8. July 30, 2060

What a week! It's finally over!

Today I executed my final duty as Earth's ambassador. The UN totally could have made someone else do this, but I guess they liked how I was doing the job. Short story—I had to give *even more speeches.*

As public events go, this one should have been easy. After a week of meeting aliens, the UN Navy was preparing to show off Earth's three newest and best space ships. They are the first ones to be built with the help of our new friends, and will be the first to make return visits to meet the aliens on their planets.

All I had to do was host yet another ceremony, this one to announce the names of the three ships. Of course I had to give the speech, but at least it was a chance to go outside.

Living under the dome, you can almost forget you're on the moon. Sure, you have to skip everywhere and wash yourself with moist towelettes, but once you stop feeling space-sick (finally!), it's not all that different from home.

When I put on a space suit and went outside to the platform where all the humans and aliens would watch the naming ceremony, I was reminded that I really was on another planetesimal. It was totally beautiful. Through the visor of my space suit I could see the pearly belt of stars that make up our galaxy, and the Earth was just about to rise between the huge space ships.

Then the Secretary General of the United Nations ruined everything by telling me over the suit radio that it was time for my speech.

What I was supposed to do is reveal the names George Washington, Zhou Enlai, and Steve Jobs. There's nothing wrong with any of that, but who has honestly ever heard of those guys? Okay, probably everyone, but none of the aliens, right? The names were supposed to be a big surprise, and no one but the Secretary General and my dad and his helpers at the UN knew what they were. I was supposed to name the ships, and say a bit about who the old guys were. It was all tragically boring.

Well, they made me the ambassador, right? And it has been a very, very difficult and trying week, right? So I may, possibly, just maybe have had what Ms. Charlottine would call a "fit of pique." That means, "got super annoyed and did something crazy."

We all stood in our space suits with the beautiful lunar dome behind us, staring at the three magnificent space ships. These three vessels would carry the human way of life to the stars, and show the universe how amazing humans can be. They were shaped like normal space rockets, but a lot bigger, and giant LED panels stood blank on their hulls, waiting for someone to type in the names and upload them for everyone to see.

So I typed and said, "Ladies, gentlemen, and all sentient creatures here assembled, I give you... the Earth Ship Beyoncé Knowles! The Earth Ship Yolandi Visser! The Earth Ship Angela Gossow!"

The names popped up in hundred-foot-tall glowing letters; *ES Knowles, ES Visser, ES Gossow*. All the aliens applauded by flapping or waving their tentacles or grunting. I'm pretty sure they were impressed. The Secretary General of the United Nations didn't say anything, but I could see his face through the visor of his suit. He was very, very red. Serves him right for turning me into a diplomat when I wanted to be a pilot.

I gave a little speech about each of my lady heroes of classical music. About how they inspired me as a young girl, and how they reminded me of my home planet. I spoke about how each of them changed music in her own special way—one by being the best, one by being the most original, and one by being the loudest. I said that I hoped that humans would carry their spirits into the stars.

When I got home, my dad didn't even get mad. I think he's getting used to how I do his job; loud, original, and the best. Papa Terry was so happy with my speech that he couldn't stop laughing and tousling my hair.

We fly back down to Earth in a few days. I'll see my school friends in San Francisco again. This trip has been long, difficult, and pretty amazing. Everything is going back to normal, but I think I'll keep the diary. After all, who knows what I'll do next?

No Place Like

by William B. Wolfe

In his career as a sometimes-serious journalist, William Wolfe loved writing the occasional weird story that was tossed his way. Robots, ghosts, Bigfoot, space aliens—nothing was too strange. Now he writes middle-grade fiction, which generally wanders into weirdness, too, with stories of psychic pets, haunted libraries, and modernistic fairies. William grew up near Monkey's Eyebrow, Kentucky, (weird) and now lives in Louisville, Kentucky, with his weird-but-lovable family and weird ninja attack cat, Miyabi. He is an award-winning member of the Society of Children's Book Writers and Illustrators, loves science fiction, fantasy, and superheroes, and has a little blue car named Pepe. Learn more about him at www.facebook.com/wolfetales.

Dottie poked her head out of her brother's room, scanning the darkened hallway for any sign of Mom and Dad. They had an uncanny ability to be "just wandering by" whenever Dottie was about to do anything the least little bit naughty.

And what she had planned that evening wasn't the least bit little.

Dottie stepped back, tugging the door closed.

"All clear," she announced.

"Are you sure, Dot?" asked her brother Arthur, who sat on his narrow bed in the center of his small, tidy room. "If we get caught, we'll both be in big trouble."

Arthur was home now for his spring visit—one of only four times a year Dottie got to see her favorite brother—though to tell the truth, the competition for favorite wasn't all that keen.

At 15, Arthur was just three years older than Dottie. They shared the same unruly red hair and striking green eyes, as well as a stubborn streak that frequently landed them in trouble with their parents and three older brothers.

More importantly, Arthur was the only one who treated her like an equal. He was the only person, besides her dad, whom Dottie allowed to call her Dot—which to her was the same as labeling her an insignificant spec.

"Relax. I was careful," Dottie said. "Besides, if anyone comes in, we have our story ready. Do you remember?"

Arthur spoke in a learned-by-rote monotone: "Dottie is just leafing through the book, looking at the pictures, while I tell the stories."

"You've got to lie like you mean it," Dottie chided.

A single candle lit Arthur's room, but that was enough to show his frown. "If they ever find out that I taught you to read—"

"They won't," Dottie declared. "Now gimme."

Arthur reached under his pillow, pulled out an ancient-looking book, and held it out to Dottie. She treated it gently, as if its pages were butterfly wings that might crumble into dust—which could indeed happen to some of the volumes he had brought home from the Branch.

The front cover of this book showed a spectacle-wearing, red-maned lion, tail between his legs. Above him, in red and green letters, were the words "The Wonderful Wizard of Oz." The back cover portrayed three characters: a strawman, like the one her father sometimes placed in the fields to ward off crows; a girl with loosely tied pigtails not unlike Dottie's; and—it couldn't be—a bot. The most dangerous of all the Old Tech devices.

Bots, like all the Old Tech devices, were outlawed. Learning about bots was forbidden. Even talking about them was risky, except in warnings to children. "Behave and do your chores, or the bots will come to get you."

Part of Dottie wanted to hurl the book out the window. But the thrill of holding something so forbidden—so dangerous— was impossible to resist.

"Where did you get this?" she asked in a whisper. "How did you get this? *Why* did you get this?"

Arthur smiled. "I know what you're thinking. But that's not a bot on the cover—just a human who replaced all of his parts with ones made from tin."

Dottie scrunched up her nose. "I don't see how that could work, even with Old Tech."

"It's not about technology, just magic and make-believe. That's why it's not forbidden. We're all encouraged to read it at the Branch as a cautionary tale—a warning, in other words."

"What's this non-forbidden book about?" Dottie asked.

Arthur paused.

"It's about a girl who leaves home and enters a new world of strange people, different ways of living, and danger. At the Branch, they say the moral of the story is that we should follow all the customs, obey all the rules. And that there's nothing better in the whole world than what we have at home."

Something in her brother's voice hinted that he wasn't telling Dottie everything.

"What do *you* think this book is about?" she asked.

Arthur's eyes shifted left to right, as if he expected that someone might be hiding in the shadows of his room.

"I would never dispute the teachings of the Branch," he said in a voice louder than necessary. "But I believe each person finds his or her own meaning in every book. Read it and decide for yourself."

"But—"

"It's late," Arthur said flopping back on his bed and rolling over, his face away from his sister. "Blow out the candle when you're done."

Sleep for Dottie came much later, after the little girl from Kansas had tapped the heels of her magic shoes together three times and returned to her dull, dirt-farming home in Kansas.

Even in her dreams, Oz and its characters remained with her, filling Dottie's mind with visions of a dark forest, misshapen winged monkeys, and a wart-nosed, witch who was angry that Dottie carried a book.

"Prohibited," the witch screeched, pointing a crooked finger in Dottie's face. "Illegal! You and your book shall *burn!*"

With a wave of her gnarled hand, the witch conjured a blistering ball of red and yellow fire and sent it hurtling.

Dottie dove to the ground, expecting to be consumed by flame. Instead, the witch only called her name.

"Dottie, get up."

"No! You'll kill me!"

"Stop this nonsense, Dottie Ray, and get up."

Dottie rubbed open her sleepy eyes and found not the wicked witch but her mom—not wicked, but also not happy.

"You should have been up an hour ago. These floors are not going to sweep themselves, and you can't wish the dishes clean. You'll have a house of your own to keep before long, so you'd better get used to cleaning and cooking and tending to babies," her mother said.

"I don't want babies. I want adventures," Dottie said, sitting up in her bed.

"You've been listening to Arthur's foolish stories," her mother said. "There's plenty of adventure to be had right here in Proper."

Proper was Dottie's hometown—if it could even be called a town. It included the local farms and the township, with its general store, ironsmith, grain mill, livery and post office. But not, of course, any places where people could drink sweetmix or dance. Those things just wouldn't be Proper, her parents said, and especially not for a Proper young lady. But Dottie didn't think an occasional dance would be so bad, or a sip of sweetmix—not that her parents had ever let *her* try either one.

"There are plenty of girls who want dozens of children. I don't even want to think about things like that!"

"You need to think about them," her mother said. "In two months, you'll turn 13. That means betrothal. Then 14. That brings marriage. Then 15 and, hopefully, your first blessing!"

"A blessing that cries all the time, burps up milk, and poops its diaper," Dottie said, frowning. "That's not the life I want."

"You've been saying than since you were ten. But this *is* your life," her mom said. "And mine. Like it was for my mother, and her mother before that. Some things don't change."

"I'm going to make things change," Dottie said, her arms crossed and her face set like stone.

"Good," her mother said. "You can start by changing the sheets on all the beds. Then you grab a broom and change the floors from dirty to clean."

Dottie helped Arthur pack for his return to the Branch the next day. As he tucked in the last item—the Oz book—she slipped over to his door, clicked it shut, and turned pleading eyes to her brother.

"Let me go with you!" she said.

Arthur's face fell. "We've talked about this before."

"And you always say the same thing. 'Only boys can go to the Branch.' So, I'll dress like a boy."

"That only works in books," Arthur said. "There's not a lot of privacy there with bathrooms and such. No way a girl could pass herself off for even a day. You're better off here with the family."

Misery filled Dottie's face and her voice. "If you really believe that, why did you even teach me to read?"

"I don't know. Maybe because of your nonstop begging and wheedling," Arthur said with a half-smile. "Maybe because I thought it would be a respite from the drudgery that is Proper. But I wonder now whether I just made your life harder. Maybe you should forget all about reading—forget even how to read."

Dottie grabbed her brother's arm and squeezed until he winced. "Never—even if I could! Without books, I wouldn't know that there's more to life than this drab little story that's been written for me. I want to float down the Mississippi River like Huckleberry Finn or find a Wonderland like Alice. I'm suffocating here. I've got to go where I can breathe!"

Arthur bit his lip, then turned his eyes to his shoes, as if they had suddenly become the most interesting objects in the room.

"Arthur Ray, that's your guilty look," Dottie said. "What are you hiding?"

"Nothing," Arthur said. But his sister knew better. She grasped his face between two hands and pulled it close, forcing him to make eye contact.

"What are you not saying?"

Arthur whispered. "I don't recommend it, but—"

"But what?" Dottie said, the words catching in her throat.

"There may be a way out. Only if there's a *real* emergency."

Dottie suppressed a squeal. "Tell me!"

"There's a story about a safe place. Some say it's just a legend, but I've known people who swear they've been there. The journey is long and hard, and going there means leaving your home and your family forever."

"Just *tell* me," Dottie insisted. "What is it? How do I get there?"

Arthur frowned. "It's called the Main, a place of freedom 'north of north, south of the Ville, guarded by giants, even now still.'"

"What does that mean?" Dottie asked.

"Head north and look for giants, I guess," Arthur said, shaking his head. "I've never been farther than the Branch."

"Big help, brother."

"When did I say it would be easy?" Arthur said. "It might be better if you just stay here and try to be normal."

"I don't want to be normal," Dottie said. "I want to be me."

"In this world," Arthur said, "that will always be dangerous."

Weeks passed in endless repetition for Dottie: Sweeping and mopping. Scrubbing pots and pans. Sewing ripped clothing and knitting winter wear. Nothing in her boring life seemed to constitute an emergency. Until it did.

One morning Mom called Dottie to the kitchen, where her father was already seated at the table, a cup of NewCof in his hand. He smiled broadly.

"My little Dot, I've got good news for you!"

Dottie looked at her mother. She was smiling, too. This couldn't be good.

"Sweetie, we know that you're not happy here on the farm," Dad said.

Guilt stabbed at Dottie, and she opened her mouth to apologize. Before she could speak, her mother shushed her with a touch to her lips.

"Country life is not for everyone," Mom said. "That's why we've been trying to find something different for you. Something better."

Dottie's heart leapt, and she spoke without thinking. "You're sending me to the Branch?"

Mom's face went ashen. Dad frowned.

"Don't be ridiculous," he said. "That's only for boys not strong enough to do real work. I told you this would be good news, and it is. You know Zeb Hugson, don't you?"

"The farrier?" Dottie said. "I don't know anything about him, other than that he shoes horses and always seems to smell a lot like a horse himself."

"He's a fine Proper man," Mom said. "He makes a *very* good living, and he lives in town in a nice house. He's perfect!"

"Perfect for what?" Dottie asked, genuinely puzzled.

"Why, perfect for *you*!" Dad said with a grin. "It's all arranged. You'll be officially betrothed the day of your 13th birthday. Zeb has even agreed to cut short the engagement period. Six months after your birthday will come your wedding day!"

"This can't be," Dottie said, clutching her hands against her stomach and feeling as if something terrible was inside her, trying to gnaw its way out.

"You'll have hired help for the cooking and cleaning, and you can get started on your first blessing right away," Dad said. "You won't have to stop at five like your mom and me. You can have ten or twelve children—maybe even more!"

"But I don't want to get married—not to Zeb or anyone else!" Dottie wailed.

"Hush, child," Mom said. "You don't want to wind up like Muckrake Molly."

Dottie shivered. Every girl knew about the tale of the muckraker, who rebelled against her betrothal and disappeared into the wilderness that surrounded the township. When she returned years later, thin and ragged and begging for forgiveness, she was accepted back into Proper—but only as a muckraker, the person who sweeps manure from the barns.

Dottie had seen Molly at Zeb Hugson's. The strange woman never spoke, but whenever her eyes met Dottie's, they fixed on her with an intensity that Dottie found alarming. Dottie didn't want to be a muckraker, but she didn't want to marry Zeb Hugson, either.

"I can't do what you ask. I won't!" Dottie wailed. "I refuse!"

Her father's eyes flared. "That is not Proper," he said, aiming at Dottie with a finger which, at that moment, looked a lot like the one on the wicked witch of her nightmare. "It has been arranged. You *will* marry Zeb Hugson."

"I'd rather die," Dottie said. She turned and ran from the kitchen to her room, latching her door behind her.

Dottie knew that Mom and Dad could have forced their way in, but they didn't, and for that, she was grateful. But she wouldn't open the door even when her father told her in a kind voice that evening that he wanted only what was best for her.

"When you come to your senses, come out. We'll fix you a nice dinner and forget this little disagreement ever happened," he said. "But until then, your meals must wait."

Dottie never considered accepting Dad's offer. She did, however, think a lot about what Arthur had said: "There may be a way out. Only if there's a *real* emergency."

"If this isn't an emergency," Dottie said to herself, "I'll never see one." She had no choice. Tonight, she would escape!

She packed a shoulder-slung bag with a change of clothes and a blanket, then waited until the house was still, when even the crickets that should be serenading outside her open window seemed oddly quiet. Dottie slipped one leg through her window then hesitated. This wasn't an adventure from a book. This was real. This was final. This was goodbye forever.

She could put away her escape kit, apologize to her parents in the morning and... lose herself forever. A fierceness she had never known possessed Dottie, and she practically hurled herself from the window's opening, landing lightly on her feet a few feet down.

The milky light of a quarter moon was just bright enough

for Dottie to see her way through the yard and to the dirt path that led away from her house. Glancing back where her parents and three of her brothers lay sleeping, she choked down a sob.

"Goodbye, Mom. Goodbye, Dad," she whispered, curling her hand in a wave. "I'm sorry."

Just then, Dottie thought she saw a flash of movement beside the house. Her heart skipped a beat, and her legs felt weak. Was her journey over before it even began? She waited for what seemed an eternity, but there was no further sign of activity.

Dottie breathed a sigh of relief. Probably just an owl or raccoon. It was time to go.

After a two-mile walk down a series of paths, Dottie reached North Highway 61. She didn't know why people called it a highway, since it was no higher than the surrounding ground. But it was still the easiest, fastest way to travel.

The highway had once stretched smooth and unbroken for hundreds of miles, Dottie had been told. But that was long ago, before the War. Now the road was cracked and smothered with weeds.

Dottie traveled for hours, walking what seemed to her feet to have been at least a hundred miles. Her mind argued that she could not have walked more than ten miles, but her feet were unconvinced.

She stepped off the highway, set down her bag, leaned against a tall oak tree, and let her heavy eyelids fall shut, for just...a...little....

"Excuse me!"

Dottie's head snapped up, and her pulse raced. Where was her bed? Where was her house? Where was she?!

"Are you OK?"

Dottie jumped to her feet, almost fell, and grabbed the tree to steady herself. Then she remembered. She was running away, and she had foolishly let herself be spotted.

At the edge of the highway stood a figure—a man, certainly,

since no Proper woman would be out alone at night. Dottie couldn't see his face, which was hidden by a dark cowl, but she imagined a look of concern, because that was clearly in his voice.

"I—I'm fine," Dottie said. "I was just resting my eyes."

"Indeed. And maybe some other parts, too," the man said, and Dottie didn't like the note of amusement she heard. Worse, he sounded more like a boy than a grown man—more tenor than bass.

"Do you make a habit of rousing sleeping strangers?"

"I was just worried about you. What are you doing out here in the middle of the night and the middle of nowhere?"

"I should ask you the same thing, young man," Dottie said.

The hooded figure shrugged. "Just passing through."

"Well, me too. Just passing through," Dottie said.

"Great. Maybe we can pass through together."

"I don't need your help," Dottie said.

"Obviously," the stranger said. "But we could talk and keep each other company. Besides, I was just preparing to have a snack. Would you join me?"

Without waiting for a reply, he reached into the bag tied at his waist, bringing out a wedge of yellow cheese and a curved knife. He sliced off a section for himself and slipped it into his mouth.

Dottie's stomach grumbled. Well, perhaps it wouldn't be so bad to travel a few miles with this stranger. She picked up her bag and stepped toward the boy. He lowered his head, keeping his face hidden beneath the cowl.

Very odd. But maybe he had a disfigurement he wanted to keep hidden. And that was fine. Dottie wasn't looking for a husband or even a friend. All she wanted was a slice of that cheese.

"What should I call you?" the stranger asked, cutting off a generous portion of the wedge and handing it over.

"Darlene," she said, using a fake name she had already picked out. "What's yours?

"You can call me Poe," he said.

"That's an odd name," Dottie said.

"I had another name once. This is the one I use now," Poe said.

Dottie tried to take dainty bites of her cheese, but gobbled up most of her portion in less than a minute. A noise escaped Poe's hood that sounded a lot like a chuckle.

"Sorry," she said. "My last meal was a long time ago."

"Don't apologize, Darlene," Poe said. "I've been there myself. Now let's see what there is in here to drink. Aha!" He pulled a slender bottle from his bag and tucked on its cork, which relinquished its hold on the bottle with a satisfying pop.

Dottie reached for the bottle, then drew back.

"What's in there?" she asked, her eyes narrowing.

"Nothing dangerous," Poe said. He tilted the bottle upward to his lips, and after an audible *glug* and swallow, held the container out again.

This time, Dottie didn't hesitate. She lifted the bottle to her mouth, turned it up, and let the drink inside flow onto her tongue. And it was *amazing!* Sweet like molasses, but with a sharp, refreshing edge. She took another gulp, and would have taken a third if Poe hadn't pulled the container away.

"Easy there," he said. "That's the only bottle we've got. You act like you've never tasted sweetmix before."

"I haven't," Dottie admitted. "It's prohibited in Proper."

"Well, we're not in Proper anymore," Poe said. "But if we want to put some more miles behind us tonight, we should get moving. Are you ready?"

Surprisingly, Dottie found that she *was* ready—ready to walk a thousand miles, if that's what it took to find freedom.

For the next few days Dottie and Poe traveled in the dark and slept shielded among the trees that lined the road during the light. The few times they saw approaching lanterns at night, they hid until the strangers passed. Poe proved skilled at living off the land, finding edible berries and wild fruit trees. He never asked Dottie why she was running away, and she never questioned him. Nor did she look at his face, which he always kept buried in the shadows of the cowl. Whatever his secrets, they were his to share or not share, she decided.

After their fourth night of travel, Dottie got ready for bed. "Good day," she told Poe—their joking ritual, since their bedtime began at dawn, not night.

Poe, already half asleep, stirred slightly and murmured, "Good day, Dottie."

Dottie froze. She had claimed her named was Darlene, and that was the name Poe had used—until now. Had she slipped up somewhere and given away her true name? No! She was certain. Then what kind of a game was Poe playing? Was he leading her into a trap, so she could be captured and returned home? If he was, in fact, hideously disfigured and unable to find a wife, maybe he hoped to keep her for himself. But none of that explained how Poe knew of her disappearance only hours after she had left Proper.

Whatever his plan, Dottie would have no part of it. She waited until Poe's breathing had settled into the slow rhythm of slumber, then she rose and crept away. She wanted to take his satchel for whatever food might remain, but it was still tied to the mystery man's waist. She would have to do without.

Dottie trudged up the highway through the day. "Step, step, step, step," she repeated, losing herself in the rhythm of the words.

Maybe she began sleepwalking, or maybe she fell into a trance, but Dottie was suddenly jolted into consciousness by the whinny of a horse and a jumble of voices.

Her eyes rose to find a family of travelers riding in a horse-drawn wagon yards ahead. The man kept a long beard and was dressed all in black, including a wide-brimmed hat. The mother wore a long blue dress, not unlike one Dottie's mother had at home, with her hair pinned up under a simple white bonnet. The five children looked like miniature versions of their father and mother—minus the beard.

They were Amish—the only people whose lives had remained unchanged by the War

The father stared at Dottie through suspicious eyes. "Why be thee out alone, child?"

"Oh, my parents are near," Dottie lied. "I think I hear them calling now." With that, she turned and bounded from the road, out into the surrounding knobby hills. The family called after her but made no effort to pursue, and Dottie hid until she heard wagon pulling away, and the clip-clop of their horse faded in the distance.

It wasn't until then that she realized how very, very thirsty she was. Dottie's mouth felt as dry as straw, her tongue like dried jerky. Poe had always just seemed to know where to find a clean stream to drink from, but Dottie had only a vague idea where to even look.

She needed to make her way down to lower ground, she figured, and maybe scout for animal tracks or listen for flowing water. But there were no animal tracks—only bramble briars and bugs. Soon she was covered with scratches and bug bites, but with nothing to show for it. Plus, she was so very tired, the sun was straight overhead, and her thirst was turning from uncomfortable to desperate.

Dottie finally came to a long, rocky slope, strewn with precariously perched boulders. Below, she saw a glimmer of light in a wooded area. That must be the sun reflecting on water! She could almost taste it, cool and sweet, from a pure, gurgling stream.

Abandoning caution, Dottie sprinted down the hills until, almost safe at the bottom, she stumbled, falling like a tree at a lumberjack's axe. She rolled all the way down over painful, pointy rocks.

Finally coming to a stop at the edge of a thicket, Dottie took in a shuddering breath and did a quick self-inventory. She could move her arms and legs, so that was good. Her right ankle throbbed, but not intolerably.

Then she noticed the bushes growing around her. They were thick with large purple berries—huckleberries, just like the ones her mom made pies with.

"Food," Dottie thought, crawling forward and grabbing handfuls of the berries and stuffing them into her mouth. Tart but still tasty, they filled her stomach, and their juice quenched her thirst. But her feast came to an abrupt halt when she pulled back a dense growth of vines to discover a steel boot. Attached to a steel leg. Which led to a metallic torso and head.

Cold, glass eyes stared down at her. The eyes of a bot!

Too scared even to scream, Dottie sprang up—then collapsed at the pain. Her ankle was worse than she had thought.

The bot made no reaction.

It's dead. Or at least deactivated, Dottie thought, feeling a little silly for her reaction. The bot had to be ancient, and it didn't look like the weaponized monster she had always imagined. In fact, it looked very human, except where its paint had weathered away, leaving bare metal. That, she realized, was what had reflected the light she had seen. Probably just an abandoned, dilapidated servant bot.

Still, Dottie had a terrible problem. If she couldn't walk, she couldn't get to the Main. She was going to sit out here until she someone found her and dragged her home—or until she died of exposure. She wasn't sure which fate would be worse.

Dottie spoke to the bot as if he could hear. "I could use a friend, like the tin woodman, but I don't dare activate you."

Dottie would never know if it was the word "activate" or just the sound of a human voice, but the eyes of the bot suddenly flashed with light, and a metal hand shot forward and gripped her arm.

This time, Dottie did scream—long and loud. The bot turned its eyes to her.

"Identity," it demanded.

"Dottie," she said, trembling. "Dottie Ray."

"Unrecognized," the bot replied. "Pass code."

Pass code? What could that be? "The War is over," she said.

"Incorrect," the bot said. "Please provide the correct pass code."

"Um...Victory to the bots?"

"Incorrect. You have one more chance to provide the correct pass code before termination."

Termination? That ruled out the friendly helper bot idea. But maybe she could get through this the way she got through so much of life—with guts and bluster

"I am Commander Dottie Ray. Robot, your memory is damaged. Cancel termination and release me," she ordered.

Maybe the bot really had been damaged, because it seemed to relax its grip for a moment—and that was all the time Dottie needed. She yanked free and scrambled backwards, ignoring the pain from her injured ankle as she struggled up the hill on hands and knees.

The bot lurched into action and took slow, lumbering steps forward. Metal screeched against metal, and Dottie noticed that the robot was dragging one leg. Fair enough, she figured. Maybe they could compete together in the one-legged sack race at the county fair.

Halfway up the hill, Dottie had gained a fifteen-yard lead, but she was afraid that wouldn't last. While the bot felt no pain, each time she put weight on her right foot, it felt as though someone was smashing it with a hammer. Soon she would collapse with fatigue, and the bot would be on her. Unless...

Dottie neared one of the boulders she had passed on the way down the hill. Dragging herself behind it, she waved at the bot and, using skills honed from years of practice against her brothers, hurled insults at her pursuer.

"You're pathetic. I'm just a little girl, and I can crawl faster than you can run," she shouted. "Better run away, Mr. Scary Bot, or I'll beat you into pots and pans for my mom."

The bot fixed Dottie with a steady gaze. And it could have been her imagination, but the machine seemed to gain a little speed and intensity with her taunts—and that was good. Dottie wanted him to be going full blast.

Seating herself squarely behind the boulder, Dottie waited as the bot moved closer and closer. Finally, when she saw the glow of its mechanical eyes, she raised her legs, placed her feet against the huge rock and *pushed.*

Nothing happened. The bot took a step closer. Dottie pushed again. The bolder quivered. Dottie gave one final, agonizing push, and the boulder began tumbling. The bot tried to change direction but was unable to halt its momentum. The rock struck it with the force of a herd of rampaging bulls, rolled onward into the mulberries, leaving a flattened junk heap behind.

Dottie sighed heavily and fell onto her back—just in time to see a face, darkened by a hood, peering down. Poe! He had caught up with her after all. Her flight and her fight had all been for nothing.

"Nice job, girl," Poe said. Even in the hood, Dottie could see white teeth grinning broadly.

"Guess you've got me," Dottie said, making no effort to hide the bitterness in her voice. "What are you going to do to me?"

"I'm not going to do anything *to* you," Poe said. "I'm here to do something *for* you."

With that, the hood came down, and Dottie found herself staring not at a callow boy, but a grown woman, her face glowing and her eyes shining with intelligence. It was the muckraker!

"Molly?" Dottie said, unable to trust her eyes. "What do you have to do with any of this? Why would you want to help me?"

Poe/Molly laughed. "Your brother Arthur spoke to me on his way back to the Branch. He thought you might try to leave Proper, and he asked me to watch out for you. When I heard Zeb brag about the arranged marriage, I knew you would make your move soon. I wanted to help you reach the Main."

"How do you know about the Main?" Dottie asked.

Molly smiled. "I know because I've been there. I was once as you are now—a girl willing to risk everything for a better life. Someone else helped me, and I wanted to return that favor to another."

Poe/Molly looked down at her feet. "But I messed up. I called you by your real name and nearly wrecked everything. Thank goodness, I met those Amish travelers. They told me where to look for you."

Dottie's jaw dropped. She felt like she was caught in a cyclone, and her whole world was spinning.

"I'm sorry I couldn't tell you sooner, but I had to hide my identity," Poe/Molly continued. "I wasn't sure you wouldn't change your mind, return to Proper, and expose me. I may have to return there someday to help another girl."

"I messed up, too," Dottie said. "I would never have made it this far without you. Guess the men are right: I'm just an insignificant little dot."

Poe/Molly's eyes widened. "Are you serious? You were amazing! The way you escaped me? The way you battled and beat a bot? You were so smart and brave. And you showed great heart."

Dottie smiled. Poe continued.

"No one should ever call you a dot again! In fact, you'll get a new name at the Main. You can pick one from any of the greatest writers in history! That reminds me, I'll have to introduce you to the real Poe—well, to his books, anyway."

"How far away are we?" Dottie asked.

"Just another day's walk. Maybe two, with the way you're hobbled up."

With the help of a walking stick that Poe fashioned from an oak branch, Dottie left the next morning, walking at almost normal speed. They came to a spot where Highway 61 North disappeared—turned to rubble in the war, Poe said. Ahead lay only unmarked dirt paths.

"North of North," Dottie mumbled. "Why don't you just tell me these things?"

"I enjoy watching your eyes light up when you understand," Poe said.

They came to a sign. "LOUISVILLE 5 miles."

"That's it! The Ville! But where is the Main?"

"Patience," was all that Poe would say.

They approached the remains of what must once have been a great city. Little remained in the distance except the steel skeletons of buildings. Forest had reclaimed what had been suburbs. Poe held up a hand.

"I don't see anything," Dottie said.

"Exactly," Poe said.

The two walked to a sheer cliff, covered with vines. Poe stuck two fingers in her mouth and blew out a shrill whistle. Instantly, from somewhere inside vines, two burly men emerged, both holding at the ready long guns like the one used by the Proper sheriff.

They relaxed when they saw Poe. One ran to her and swept her up in a fierce hug. "It's been too long," he said. "Edgar's books are getting dusty."

"They can wait, Faulkner," Poe said. "I have a new Reader to add to the community."

Dottie, too stunned to speak, followed Poe through the vines to find a cave-like opening. "These are the Louisville Caverns," Poe told her. "Miles of tunnels dug out by miners in the old days. Now they serve a much more important purpose."

As they entered the main tunnel, Dottie's eyes widened. Before her were thousands and thousands of books, stacked on tall shelves carved into the tunnel wall.

"Louisville once had great storehouses of books, called 'libraries.' Before they were destroyed, people who loved to read carried every book to these caverns where they have been preserved ever since."

"And the giants?" Dottie asked.

"Are the people you see around you, devoting their lives to saving this repository of knowledge."

Poe gestured at a metal plaque overhead. "Louisville Free Public Library – Main."

Dottie started to cry.

"Are you disappointed? Do you want to go home?" Poe teased.

"This is home, now and forever," Dottie whispered. "And you know what they say."

"What's that, Dottie?"

Clicking the heels of her shoes together three times, Dottie looked at Poe with misty eyes. "There's no place," she said, "like home."

Until We Have Faces

by J.P. Linnartz

J.P. Linnartz grew up wild in the Appalachians before migrating to Durham, North Carolina, where she's a writer, scholar, and designer of empowering clothes for girls. She and her husband live happily with their lazy cat and wild daughter.

The sirens screamed all night, but the men with guns never came.

It's been one day, and I've finally stepped out of the city's dark places. I'm in the middle of a Lowtown sidewalk, gawking at a flickering sign that reads, "Face the World!" while strangers—normal people—walk by, unable or unwilling to face me.

My heart hammers, and I can hardly breathe. Black bars encage the window, but behind them I see faces so large that they're impossible to take in. Faces glowing with warmth, faces with distinct eyelashes, faces with full lips that surely serve pleasant voices.

Above the faces, the sign shimmers in the brightest colors: electric pink, red, green, and blue, as if I've never seen true colors until now.

"Beautiful," I say so loudly that someone could've heard me, but no one stops to share my awe.

I've finally found it, after searching day and night: a store of faces.

It's all I've wanted since I learned I don't have one. A face. To be seen without making other people's faces turn ugly. "Revulsion" is what Ava called it. "Revulsion, or apathy."

I want to grab passersby just to see if they notice—if they can look at me—but I don't. Amidam said not to get noticed. Keep my hood up, he said. Men with guns can appear in seconds.

I inch closer to "Face the World!" and fall into its shadow. Instead of entering, I turn my back on the giant faces to rub my palms on the coat that Amidam gave me. I never knew it could be so cold outside, and my hands are so pale and gray, far from invisible even in the shadows. Someone might still spot me and report me to the exterminators. I stand out—that's what Amidam said before he told me to run—and I won't be safe until I have a face of my own.

I can see down Wall Street to the Whitewalled City looming over Lowtown. Now that I'm here, I'm wondering if Amidam is wrong. Would I be safer in the dark places, where men with guns and exterminators don't seem to find me? Getting a face is dangerous: it means getting seen. I'd have to speak to a stranger. I've never spoken to anyone besides Amidam and Ava.

Darkly outlined eyes watch over Lowtown from the horizon of the white Wall. It's a sign that says, "Eyes show the soul. What's *your* soul like?" On schedule, the eyes wink and the words change. "Visit Face-O-Rama today for your soul-lift."

The wind blows, and I pull the hood tighter. Anonymous trash skitters on the sidewalk and rises in eddies beside the doorway as if possessed by secret magic, and the storefront whispers promises of sharing just a little of that magic with me.

With one last look to the Wall, I know I have to risk it. Maybe the people in the shop are like Amidam.

From across the street, a bent man no taller than me lifts a stick into the air and cries, "Behold! A lamb for the slaughter!" He's looking right at me, but no one else notices.

I act at once. Flinging the door open, I rush into a lobby

and halt so hard that my shoes squeak on the tiles.

Behind a high counter sits a fleshy woman with smooth skin and bright hair. She shouts, "Just a minute!"

An adult. How silly to hope for young people. Amidam and Ava are not fully grown, but maybe adults can be nice, too? Better, maybe this one is old enough to know about me. "A relic" is what Ava called me, "from before," but she didn't know much because she and Amidam were imported from a country where things like me never existed. Where everyone always had faces.

I look over my shoulder as if hoping to see Amidam cheering from the Wall. He said the exterminators didn't care about him and Ava and the others who live and work in the Wall itself, where he found me in "eye-ber-nation."

"Well, isn't that a lovely coat! What fur! Is it real?"

I snap my head around to see the woman looking right me— at least, right at the coat that swallows my body.

"Yes," I say. "Of course it's real." I pat it and wonder what an unreal coat would be like. "It's very real!" A year ago I couldn't even talk, not until Amidam opened my mouth, but I've known lots of words for a long time.

"Well, how lovely! I had myself a real pelt like that as a girl, I did, though maybe mine fit better. Now, what's your order?" She looks for my face under my hood, but her eyes rove back and forth. She squints. "Here for the Christmas package, eh?"

I don't know what that means, so I say, "A face, please."

"Oh, sweetheart!" She laughs as she slides off her stool and pulls open a gate that's built into the counter. "You are too much. Come on back."

She's much taller than me, about Ava's height, and she takes my hand before I realize what's happening. "Come along," she says, guiding me beyond the counter just like Amidam used to do in the Wall's narrow passages.

"Oh, my!" she exclaims as we enter the space beyond the

counter. But she's not gaping at the two shining, mechanical arms that hang over two misshapen cots. She's staring at my hand. "Your skin! It's so..."

I try to pull my hand free, but she doesn't let go. I take a deep breath and prepare to run.

But she gives my hand a squeeze and leads me to one of the funny cots. "Youths these days, I swear, you all dye yourselves in such strange ways! Up you go. Tell me just what kind of face you want. A new nose? Chin? Cheekbones? Orbits?"

I exhale and wiggle onto the cot-like chair. So far, so good. I survey the mechanical arm and the contraptions that stick out alongside my seat. My stomach clenches. "So you'll really help me? Get a face?"

The woman chuckles. "A full Christmas package, then, is it? Have you picked out your components? Do you want 'em at once, or piecemeal?"

"A full face. Fast."

"Well, pull off that coat and let's see what we've got..."

I don't want to take it off even though I'm beginning to sweat.

The woman pushes back my hood. "Oh—you've shaved off your hair! If that just doesn't do it."

I don't tell her that I've been awake for a year and have yet to grow hair.

"Do I hear a customer?" someone shouts, making me jump. A second person doubles the danger.

"Get in here, Rika! Kids are just so silly these days, aren't they? This one has gone and dyed herself gray and shaved herself bare even though it's winter!"

I glance back to see a woman with hair stacked up high, braided and coiled and multicolored. Like a snake.

Rika's eyes bulge. "Jeepers and shivers! What the heck is that?"

I squirm back into my seat and don't say anything.

"Oh, you're awful! Kids are always experimenting—be nice!"

"Seriously, Gin, where's her *face?*"

Gin leans forward, getting that look that some of the Wall workers get when trying to see me: narrow eyelids, slack jaws, pupils darting as if their gaze keeps slipping to either side. That's one of three reactions I get from the workers. The second kind ignores me altogether, and the third hates me right away. I've got Types 1 and 3 here.

"Shut up, will you, and get me the microscopal viewer?" Gin sits back on a stool and rubs her eyes. "I'm having a hard time seeing...like my eyes have gone all wonky."

"Fine, Miss Wonky Eyes."

Rika wheels something up beside me just as the mechanical arm lowers, and Gin connects the two. "Now, stay still, hon, so I can analyze your face." Gin presses her forehead against what I can only guess is the "viewer" and aims a cylinder at the place my face should be. "You haven't told us yet what you want—be *specific*, now. AZ500 has been popular with girls your age. You eleven? Thirteen? But that's not a good reason to get the AZ series, 'cause this is your chance to be unique!"

I can't tell her my age because I don't know it. I think she wants me to give her a code to get a face. "AY500?"

"Don't get fresh—"

"Sorry, could I just have your face? And three-colored hair like yours?"

Gin pulls back from her viewing device and laughs. "Three color? You mean my *two* colors and the roots that're showing? Girl, you are *too much*, I swear, I'll have to call the authorities just to rein you in!"

"Please, don't!" *Authorities* means men with guns!

This makes Gin laugh all the more, but in a reflection, I see Rika cross her arms. "Maybe we *should*," Rika says. "See? She's actually worried—"

"Jeepers, Rika, take your pills, would you, 'cause you're being a real pit-suck." Gin plants her hands on her hips. "Just see if you can't make this out. The viewer might need calibrating."

Rika is much skinnier than Gin, as if kindness is a function of size.

"Sweetie, Rika's gonna take a look 'cause, honestly, I'm having trouble finding your face. Never had nothing like this happen. But let's go ahead and program your destination, 'kay?" Gin stands on my other side and touches her face as she speaks. "This here's a Christmas nose, and this is a Christmas chin. That was maybe five years ago—"

This is too confusing. I interrupt. "What's a Christmas nose?"

Gin shakes her head. "A nose you get with your Christmas monies, silly! That's what you're here for, isn't it—to use your Christmas monies? Everyone knows...at least everyone from, well...I thought you were from the City proper with a coat like that, but you're from Lowtown, aren't you? No matter. I live here, too, and it's not all that bad. I was just saying that my nose and chin are discontinued, but I can pull up their series, if you're serious. But you won't want to look *exactly* like me. Gotta be a little different, right?"

My head is spinning, and I feel like I might cry. Ava said I shouldn't cry because it upsets people. "I just want a face, one that people can see and be happy with. You can decide the particulars?"

"Gin, you're right..." Rika mumbles as she plays with dials and knobs. "Something's wrong—maybe if I just—no—let's try—nope—what the heck—looks like, looks like something's in the way...there we go, maybe if we skim this fuzzy stuff... Here, Gin, you take over."

With Gin back in command, the mechanical arm jerks forward and rotates a hand with laser-tipped fingers, drawing so near to where my face should be that I feel burning. I squeeze my eyes shut and clutch the cot's rails.

"You know, Gin, I'm wondering..."

"Hang on, I'm just taking off this layer—"

"...I think I remember something about this from school. Not at Cosmegenic Academy, but when we studied history, you remember?"

"No one remembers history! Don't study that after First School, when we were, what? Ten? No bigger than sweetheart here. But this is incredible...maybe historical..."

"You don't remember? What was it...something to do with the Union and test tubes that got shut down with the Reforms, one of the crimes against humanity back when those existed? They used *facelessness* for something or another. Remember?"

I want Rika to keep talking but am scared of moving. If I could get a face *and* learn where I come from...

Gin addresses me as if ignoring Rika. "I think you've a beautiful face just waiting somewhere, sweetie, but I just can't find it. I didn't think this was possible..."

"You know, on the news this morning...lots of laborers have been shipped in, you know, for the Wall, and the renovators found all these old hidden places and one of them was, like, yesterday. What was it—a cyber-nation-something lab, used for organs, or cells..."

"Ugh! Rika, please—"

"Gin, stop!" Rika throws a hand on Gin's shoulder and whispers. "They say crime has spiked where they're working, lots of theft, of things like *pelts*—"

I hold my breath as Gin spins on Rika. "Jeepers, show some compassion! It's Christmas, after all!"

"And we could lose our business! I'm calling the authorities!"

I sit forward and shove the mechanical arm aside. I need to know how to get out of here. Fast.

"Oh, don't be like that!" Gin has followed Rika to the backroom, but I hear everything.

"She stole that coat and got into that hidden lab place, I'll bet anything!"

"She's a paying customer, and—"

"Did you run her account?"

"Don't be ridiculous." Gin raises her voice. "Sweetie, you can pay, right?"

I slip out of the chair, fingering the place my face should be. It feels smooth and indistinct. As usual.

No face.

I sniffle, unable to control it anymore.

"See? Told you. I'm calling it in."

Gin looks my way. "Oh, sweetheart... Rika, stop, it didn't cost much so far, she can just do some cleaning. She probably just got a botched job from some seedy vender, no need to call—"

"Don't let her leave. Why do you insist on being a doormat?"

"Why do you insist on being a real suck? She's no different from us at that age—"

"She's a monster, Gin, you're blind—yes, I'd like to request authority presence—"

"You're such a bigot! You think she's imported! So what if she is?"

I know it's over, but it takes my feet an extra second to react. I sprint through the counter's gate and throw myself against the door.

"Sweetie, don't!" Gin shouts as I stumble onto the sidewalk. Glancing back, I see her rounding the counter and reaching toward me. "The street's no place for a girl! Not tonight! Rika, stop, look what you're making her do! Come back, we'll use the night-door!"

The sun has set and the street is so busy that, before I find my footing, I'm knocked down amid a horde of adults with perfect faces and big coats. They're roaring and singing and shouting and waving lights that leave red and green contrails.

I land on all fours. A boot catches me in the ribs.

I cry out, terrified by the countless feet whirring past.

As I coil into a tight ball with my hands on my head, some-one falls on me.

"Oof!" The faller snatches my wrist. "Watch it, will you!" He's a young man with skin that wants to be touched like Amidam's, but he's lanky and has gold hair. Seeing me, his blue eyes grow wide, and he laughs. "It's a street rat, boys!" Someone hoots.

"No!" I crawl toward Face-the-World, but his grip is strong. He's so close that I can smell his breath—he reeks like the Wall workers who stumble around at night. Amidam always kept them away. "I'm not a street rat!"

"Oh, come on!" he pleads, sweeping me to my feet so that I've no choice but to shuffle along with him. "A street *mouse*, then? My Christmas mouse, boys!"

I squirm, but he tightens his grip.

"It's okay, Christmas Mouse! Not much to look at, but who am I to turn down a Christmas gift, eh?" He's looking more at his mates than at me, but his long arm locks me to his side. "Here, have something in return, make you happy? A gift exchange?" He shoves a heavy coin into my palm. "Ha ha! See that? I gave her a whole pig!" Someone laughs.

Hot tears warm my unseeable cheeks. No one had noticed me until now. What's happening? The bodies pressing all around threaten to suffocate me. We turn the corner, along the cross street that leads back to the Wall. I ball my hands into fists. "Please!" I cry. "Let me go!"

No one answers. Instead, they're belting out a song that they don't seem to know well. "The snow! The snow! The snow so white! Everything I ever want, oh, jeepers, what a pretty sight! Let's have it now, have it out, that's what Ex-mas Eve's about!"

This is not what Amidam freed me for. This is not why I left him, left home.

I stop writhing for one heartbeat and bolt, wrenching free and shoving toward the road.

"Hey!"

Fingers grab at me.

I emerge from the mob and dart across the street, bright lights spinning all around in the otherwise dark world. My shoe catches in a groove, sending me hard to the pavement.

As I push myself up, I'm blinded by the headlamps of an auto-car.

"Watch out, Street Mouse!"

Something tugs my arm. The first auto-car zooms by.

I can see in the light from the long line of auto-cars that my rescuer is a man leaning heavily on a stick. He has white stubble and skin with lots of folds. That means he's old.

He pats my back and says, "Best come along, Street Mouse. This is no time for rodents."

I stare. It's the man from before, the one who called me a lamb. Now he's calling me a mouse. I don't like it.

"Don't hurt me," I say, stepping back but wary of getting too close to the road again.

He wags his head. "No, no. You want a safe place, a moment's peace, so you best follow an old rat who's got just that. Unless you want to go back to your friends." He nods at the raucous rabble across the road, who continue to skip and jog and shuffle and shout. "Yes, that's what I thought, and I always think right. Now just follow along and you can scamper off if you get scared, but you won't, Little Mouse, because little mice have to get brave fast."

He hobbles into a dark space among the bricks, and I hesitate. He's old. He's old and seems to know things. I follow.

Once in the dark, we go down stairs and enter a den with a mini-table and blankets and hot-eyes for cooking. And lights— thousands of tiny lights, some of which work.

"Come, sit. Old Rat was having Ex-mas Eve stew when he heard the peeps of Little Mouse."

He lowers himself to the table and scoots a bowl toward me.

"I'm no mouse. Or rat."

"Sure! But that's what we are to them up there, and they're the ones who decide. There're many kinds of rodents. Little mice, big rats, imported ones, native ones that weren't always rodents—rodents under the streets, rodents in the Walls. The thing about rodents is that people'll let you be if you don't get too noticed. But if you force yourself on them, well, then you're not invisible anymore. That's when they kick and shoot. And you know the other thing about rodents?"

I shake my head.

"They all need to eat."

My mouth waters. I haven't eaten since the Wall. I haven't slept, either. All at once, I realize how very tired and hungry I am, and how much my feet hurt. This man is like an old Amidam. An old Amidam who talks crazy.

I can't resist the food, or the chance to collapse on the soft blanket. Ex-mas Eve stew tastes better than Wall food but not as good as the stuff Amidam smuggled in. Thinking about Amidam hurts. I will never have a face. I will never see him again.

"Don't cry, Little Mouse. It's Christmastime. Time for miracles. Even for vermin."

I wipe my nose with a wrist that stings from the young man's hold. "Really?" I've never heard this before, and I'm too old to believe just anything.

"Yes, that's the truth. Old rats know old truths, forgotten things. Things about docks and clocks, and little lights and long nights and high Walls before they were high and low girls before they were low. People don't see me if I stay out of the way, but I see so very much. Sharp rat mind, sharp rat eyes. Long in tooth, long in memory."

I don't know what he's saying. "You know things because you're old? Why don't I see other old people outside?" I haven't been impressed with adults, but maybe that's because none of them are properly old.

"We're few, it's true! Most old folks get new faces, but not me—I care none for delusions. Others get shut away, but not me—I work, earn monies, do what old rats do to build nests and store treasures."

I examine his face. The stubble is patchy and sparse. His chin has a dimple, and his cheeks grow innumerable lines when he grins. Creases radiate from little eyes, beneath long eyebrows. Like me, he has no hair on his scalp. I do not think many would say this face is "beautiful." Ava certainly wouldn't. But maybe they're wrong.

"Why are you being nice?" I ask between bites. "Aren't you scared?"

He licks his spoon. "Why should I be? I know all about little mice. Even little mice without faces."

I fumble the bowl. "You know about me?"

"Long memory, remember? Walls and dolls, I know it all! And I'll tell you if you do something for me, Little Mouse."

Despite my fatigue, I leap to my feet. "Anything."

"Come," he says, beckoning for me to help him stand. "Like so many rats, I am a street cleaner, cleaner of the streets that get filthy not with vermin but with the gilded refuse of those wretched uplanders. I clean these blocks, and tonight will be a real humdinger. But only if I can get it all, because otherwise they'll replace me with another rat. Lots of rats want my turf, see, but I just need a little more money, and a little more time, Little Mouse."

He grabs a broom. "You take the mop."

As he leads me back up the stairs, he says, "We'll start on Peace Street. They abandon that one first."

Peace Street was easy, but Love was much harder. I was almost done rinsing off the confetti and vomit when I fainted, catching myself with my mop.

It's beginning to snow, and I hear the horde singing many blocks away, close to the Wall. It almost sounds nice. I imagine brother and sister standing on tiptoe to see out their tiny Wall window, marveling at the lights and music. I'm not there to help them with their tasks tonight, but I hope they're having a Christmas miracle.

Farther down Love, dark figures flit in and out of view. Old Rat says they're other street cleaners, but not to get close. They won't hesitate to stab trespassing rats during cleaning.

"Little Mouse tired already?" Old Rat limps over, pushing his cart of trash, which we'll take to a trash deposit to get paid.

"I'm sorry. I'll try harder." I lower my head so that I won't feel so dizzy as I steer the slush toward a drain.

"We can slow down."

"I need to finish. I need to know what I am. How I can get a face. Otherwise they'll exterminate me. I'll never see Amidam again."

Old Rat leans on the cart and looks around. No one is in sight, save for Face-O-Rama's eyes. "Amidam, is it?" He spits. "Sounds imported."

I never knew how bad it is to be imported. "Amidam is my *friend.*"

"Don't misunderstand an old rat. Do you know that just as rats come *in* on ships, they go *out* on ships? To better places? The docks are just over there." Old Rat points away from the Wall. "Little mice can hide on ships, especially if they know docks and clocks like old rats do. Like, say, in seven days' time, a ship goes to a new country in a new year, where the faceless rats swam to long ago?"

I stop mopping. I think I'm beginning to understand Old Rat. "You mean I can leave, go somewhere, where other faceless rats went?"

Old Rat looks around again. "Rumors, rumors! But if I tell you, then it's so."

"Will you tell me? Help me get to this place?" It might be too much to ask of someone who only makes half-sense, but I can't help but hope.

"Of course!"

"Can I get a face there?" My pulse pounds in my ears.

Old Rat resumes pushing his cart. "A story is the thing for you. Long ago, before I was an old rat, I was a young man. Cleaned laboratories. High-end stuff, before the Reforms. Back then, people grew surrogate bodies for their parts. But we *are* our bodies and vice versa, mind you, Little Mouse. And deep down they knew it, but didn't want to *see* it. No face, no guilt. Surrogates had semi-faces, true, but undeveloped and hard to perceive. Misdirection, it was. Easier to cut something up if it doesn't look like you."

I'm walking beside Old Rat in the fresh snow, feet dragging and mind racing.

"A few medical advances and political shifts later, it's an easy charge to heap on an outgoing regime. Corporations burn the evidence. At least...most of it." Old Rat glances at me. "They weren't meant to go past infancy. Those freed by radicals fled from the secret burnings. Rumors said to Turkoma. Rumors said they grow faces, truer faces. Others said their faces are mirrors. More said they're just myth."

Old Rat stops. "Now, Little Mouse, which rumor do you believe?"

"Truer faces?" Any face would be better than none.

"My dear Little Mouse, don't you see?" He pokes my shoulder. "*You* are a Christmas miracle! You have the gift of *seeing*. How others react to you shows you who they are. Not everyone has that gift. I have it a little. You have it a lot."

"But I can have a face? Be seen, for who I am?"

"Come. We have one more street."

"Yes, but, please—"

"You *are* seen, Little Mouse."

I'm growing impatient with Old Rat's riddles. "By you? Amidam? Rika? It's not the same." I follow his gaze. "You mean Face-O-Rama?"

Old Rat laughs. "One day we'll know what we look like, when we have faces. True faces. Only then will we see and know what we're seeing."

I shake my head and help push the cart. "I don't know what that means."

"You will."

I need to focus. "So...I just need to get on the right ship at the right time, and go to...Turkoma? Get a face there? Then come back?"

Old Rat snorts. "Come back? Why?"

"My friend and his sister. Why don't you go?"

He stares off. "Old Rats don't travel to new places. Besides, I've a daughter, with a pup of her own, in Darro. I'm saving to move there. Almost have enough. Storing treasure for years. Now just a few more weeks."

"Oh. But why can't I go and come back?" Things outside the Wall are complicated.

"Too hard, Little Mouse. Not all things are symmetrical. Easier outbound than inbound. And it has to be in six days, leave on the seventh, for the seventh is holy."

I consider it. Old Rat is wrong. I'm not the miracle. He is. He's offering a chance to find others like me, to escape exterminators for good, to fulfill all that Amidam hoped for me. Just for washing Peace and Love.

"Then I know what I have to do."

"Do you? Little mice learn fast."

"I'm going back to the Wall. Amidam and Ava—they're imported. I'll bring them here, and take them on the ship on the seventh day." I'm certain they'd prefer Turkoma over the Wall.

"The Wall? No. That'll be too hard, even for little mice."

I can't bear the thought of leaving them somewhere that hates them, too, even it means missing the ship and never having a face. "I've escaped it before. No one sees rats if they don't get too noticed."

"What if you grow a face? What if you get noticed?"

My mind is set. "I don't want to be the kind of person who'd leave them behind."

"Your Amidam is very special, then. And Ava is lucky."

"Yes."

Old Rat nods.

"But first we've got to finish Wall Street. So you can get to your daughter."

Old Rat studies me as if I have a face. "Really? You're not off to the Wall?"

"Oh! Can you use this?" I hand the coin to Old Rat, who takes it in shaking fingers and lifts it into the red and green light.

He opens and closes his mouth. His eyes are on the coin. "Yes," he says in a whisper, as if seeing colors for the first time. "Do you know what this is?"

"It's a Whole Pig."

"It's a whole lot, Little Mouse. More than everything I've saved. You sure?"

Old Rat is full of silly questions. "You've given me more. Once I get Amidam and Ava, you'll get us on the ship?"

"Yes, Little Mouse." I see a glint in Old Rat's eyes.

I don't mind the snow, the wind, or the exhaustion because I have a plan. I will clean, sleep, and make it to the Wall and back in time to catch our ship. Our salvation. I will save Amidam. It's better than a Christmas package.

But I don't know why Old Rat is crying. I put my hand on his shoulder. "You okay?"

He's looking at me with a look I've never seen before. "More than okay, Little Mouse." He smiles. "I'm beginning to see who you are."

Anjali
by Rati Mehrotra

Rati Mehrotra lives and writes in lovely Toronto. Her short stories have appeared in *AE – The Canadian Science Fiction Review*, *Apex Magazine*, *Urban Fantasy*, *Podcastle*, *Cast of Wonders*, and many more. Her debut novel, *Markswoman*, will be published in January 2018. Find out more about her work at http://ratiwrites.com or follow her on Twitter: @Rati_Mehrotra

The man from Genex Corporation came by again. He skimmed over the cesspool our street had become, his nose wrinkled like it wanted to be elsewhere. I leaned over the balcony of our third-floor kholi and watched him, wishing his scooter's antigrav would fail and throw him into the floating trash.

The man looked up and caught sight of me staring at him. I ducked behind the sheets I'd been hanging out to dry, but it was too late. Ma would kill me if she knew. She always forked her fingers when she saw him. Every time he came, some kid from our street disappeared.

When I raised my head from behind the sheets, the man was gone. Too bad he hadn't fallen into the muck. I finished hanging up the rest of the clothes. It wasn't raining today, for a change. But I'd have to take them down tonight, or they'd

be soaked by tomorrow. The monsoon in Mumbai and the
drought in Punjab—both got worse every year, Ma said.

The sun came out, and sweat trickled down my forehead.
I caught sight of the government school float and ran inside,
stopping to grab my bag and my sister before heading downstairs.
Ma had already left for the garment workshop, my little brother
Anshuman slung on her back.

"Quit pulling me, I'm coming!" Bela yanked herself out of
my grasp and trotted to the raised platform outside the building. Water lapped at the edges. Old Uncle waved goodbye from
his window. The other kids were already waiting, clustered near
the edge.

"Did you do your homework?" I said. "Did you study? You
have a chem test today."

Bela rolled her eyes. "Don't get all 'big sister' on me, Anjali.
I'll be first again, just you see."

The school float neared the platform, and everybody
jumped in. Seven in the morning and it was already almost
full. One more street and eight more kids to pick up, and then
we'd start lessons. As we pushed away from the building, I
caught sight of the man from Genex again. He hovered behind
the float, watching. I forked my fingers like I'd seen Ma do.

That night, Ma made Bombil fry. We could hardly believe
our luck. It wasn't a wedding or a birthday or anything special.
We stuffed ourselves with the spicy deep-fried fish, licking our
fingers when it was gone.

Ma put Anshuman to sleep in the main room while we
cleaned up the kitchen. When we were done, Ma came to the
door and said, "I've lost my job."

We stared at her, shocked.

"So why the celebration?" said Bela, her voice brittle.

Ma ignored her. Her face had gone all hard and closed, like
the day our father left, taking our savings with him. "They

gave us notice a month ago," she continued. "I've been trying to look for something else, but there's nothing. All the workshops are closing. No one wants hand-made clothes any more. Why should they, when the printed stuff is so much cheaper and better?"

Bela and I exchanged a glance. Ma had worked twelve-hour days in that workshop for three years, ever since our father walked out on us. Without that income, what would we eat? How would we pay the bills?

"Maybe we can take a loan?" said Bela. "Perhaps Old Uncle..."

"He doesn't have a rupee to spare," interrupted Ma. "You know that. His pension is barely enough to survive on. No one here can afford to help us. And I already did take a loan."

"From whom?" said Bela.

"A moneylender," said Ma. "Last year when I fell sick and couldn't work for six weeks. I've been paying the interest out of my wage ever since."

So that's why we hadn't been able to afford new clothes this year. Usually when school started, Ma made us new clothes out of bits she'd scavenged from the workshop. This year, she must have sold everything she could lay her hands on.

"What are we going to do?" I said. I didn't want to leave school. Two more years and I could get my high school certificate, perhaps find a better job than Ma's.

Ma looked at me. Still that hardness on her face, as if she had removed herself from us, gone elsewhere. "He picked you because you're thirteen, just the right age."

I looked at her, confused. Bela began to cry.

"You'll be able to study," said Ma. "You'll get good food, new clothes. You'll stay in one of those places where rich people live, all dry and nice. He promised me that."

"Who? What are you talking about, Ma?" I couldn't stop the panic creeping into my voice.

Ma finally looked down at her hands. Worn, lined hands that had held me, soothed me, slapped me, fed me. "The Genex man. He'll come for you tomorrow."

A roaring filled my ears. She continued to talk, but I didn't hear anything else she said. I wrapped my arms around myself, feeling cold. After a while I realized that Bela had run out to the balcony, into the rain. Ma stood still as a statue, her eyes empty.

I got up and walked past her, my limbs feeling stiff and unnatural, like they weren't mine. I pushed open the door and went down the stairs. Women stood at the doorways, laughing and gossiping, babies on their hips. Bits of plaster flaked off the damp ceiling, and I brushed them off my face.

This was my home. This was where I was born, where I grew up. I wondered how much Ma had sold me for, what I was worth to her.

By the time I walked out on the platform, the rain had slowed to a drizzle. I remembered, too late, the clothes I had left hanging to dry on the balcony.

The man from Genex arrived at dawn, before anyone else was up. He didn't come in, just beeped Ma on her cell. I dressed in the only salwar kurta I had that wasn't falling apart. Ma tried to embrace me, but I pushed her away. Bela had vanished. She must have been scared the man would pick her instead. She looked as old as me, even though she was a year younger.

Ma and I went downstairs, not speaking. The man was waiting outside on the platform. Up close, he wasn't frightening at all. Just a small, slight man with a thin mustache, dressed in a white shirt and dhoti.

At the last moment Ma hung on to me, clutching my arm so that I almost felt sorry for her. She slipped something small and hard into my palm. I sneaked a quick glance at it. It was just the black stone idol of Mumba Devi, the patron Goddess of Mumbai that adorned the temple in our kitchen. I slipped it into the jute bag in which I had packed my few things: notebook, pencils, underclothes. Then I disengaged myself from her and walked toward the man, waiting with his scooter at the water's edge.

"Take care, Anjali," said Ma, her voice thin and uncertain. I didn't trust myself to look at her or respond. I looked at the man instead.

"Namaste," I said, pleased that my voice came out all strong and confident even though I was shivering inside. "Ma said I'm to go with you."

The man smiled, showing a row of perfect teeth. "Good. You can call me Uncle Sunil."

He stepped onto his scooter, and I climbed up behind him. He jabbed a green switch, and the scooter revved up and sped down the street. I clutched the handrail and tried to slow my galloping pulse.

I could feel the eyes watching us; I could imagine the forked fingers, the whispered conversations. Ma would never live this down. Other families had sold children to the Corporations, but never in our chawl.

Down another street, and then another. We climbed and the water receded. Overhead the SkyTrain roared on its way from Colaba in the south to Borivali in the north.

"How much did you pay my mother?" I blurted out at last.

"Enough," he said. "She can return her loan and pay the rent for the next three years—if the chawl doesn't collapse before that, of course. I don't know why you people refuse to move."

Because it was close to the beach. Because we could play cricket on the platform in dry weather. Because, apart from the occasional Environment Ministry official, we were left alone. Because, even though there were over three hundred people squeezed into forty kholis, we knew each other by name.

But none of this would have made any sense to him, so I kept quiet.

The traffic thinned. We passed the first corporation dome, a huge white structure that blotted out half the hazy sky. It began to rain again, sheets that pelted the scooter's transparent hood. I didn't realize we'd arrived at our destination until the scooter flew into a broad, light-filled tunnel.

It was eerie, so much empty space. All three hundred people from my chawl could easily have fit in there and played cricket.

At the end of the tunnel was a platform, a row of scooters docked to one side. An elegant woman clad in a sari stood on the platform, waiting. As we glided to a stop beside her, she folded her palms and bowed.

"Welcome back, sir." She glanced at me. "And this must be...?"

"Arya 14," said Uncle Sunil, getting off the scooter. "She's here for the procedure." He turned to me. "This is my assistant, Revati. She'll help you get settled."

He walked toward the wall and pressed his palm on it. A section of it slid open, and I caught a glimpse of gleaming corridors. He turned and gave me a small wave before disappearing inside. I made to follow him, but Revati stopped me.

"Not there. That's the lab. You'll go to the shower first. We have to get you clean."

She walked to another section of the wall and pressed her palm on it like Uncle Sunil had. A door opened into an elevator. She turned around. "What are you waiting for? Come on."

I followed her in. "What procedure was he talking about?" I said as the door closed and the elevator vibrated.

"Sunil Sir will explain it to you," said Revati.

The door opened and we walked out into the biggest room I'd ever seen, all white walls and marble floors. A woman sat at a curving wooden desk to our left.

"Decontam?" she called, looking up from her screen.

"The usual," replied Revati. She pointed to a row of doors.

"Second stall from the right. Drop your clothes into the bin. That bag, too."

I remembered the statue of Mumba Devi and clutched my bag. "Please, can I keep it?"

"No," said Revati. "Leave the bag in the bin. If you need something from it, I'll give it to you later."

I was sure I wouldn't see it again. I stepped into the stall and removed my clothes. I took the idol out before dropping my bag in the bin. Next thing I knew, I was pelted with spray on all sides. I closed my eyes and tried to breathe.

After several minutes, the spray stopped. Revati pushed open the door and thrust a hospital gown at me. "Can't I wear normal clothes?" I asked, but she shook her head.

I stepped out, trying to keep the flap of the gown closed with one hand and holding my Mumba Devi in the other.

"This way." Revati led me down a corridor and propped open a door. I entered a bright room with a big bed and a table with a tray of food on it: a cheese and chutney sandwich surrounded by ripe yellow slices of mango. My stomach rumbled; I hadn't eaten since the night before.

"Enjoy." The door shut behind me with a click. I perched on the bed and wolfed the food down. Perhaps they mixed something in the chutney, because my head grew all heavy and stupid. I barely had time to slip the idol under my pillow before oblivion hit.

I woke to voices and people bending over me. Something sharp pricked my arm, and I yelped.

Someone made a shushing noise. I looked up to see Uncle Sunil sitting by my bed. A couple of women I hadn't seen before bustled about. I tried to move, but my limbs wouldn't listen to me.

"Time for the procedure," said Uncle Sunil. "Aren't you excited?"

I didn't speak; I couldn't.

"So many problems." He waved his hands, encompassing the city, the country, the whole planet. "War, disease, hunger. Some think it's Kaliyuga, the dark age that will bring an end to humanity." He paused. "I think that's superstition. Science can solve every problem our planet faces. You, Number 14, will be proof of that." He got up. "Good luck."

Number 14? What happened to the first thirteen? I tried to swallow, but something stuck in my throat. My last thought before I went under was that whatever he'd given Ma, it wasn't enough.

Darkness and pain. My throat raw from screaming. My body on fire. Scorpions bite my flesh. My mother stands in one corner, watching me writhe, a cold expression on her face. *Help me*, I cry, but she turns away, and the flames engulf me.

When I woke up I thought I'd died and gone to hell. I was in a dark, warm room. Shapes and shadows danced on the wall.

One of the shadows detached itself from the wall and came toward me. "Ah, you are awake. Took you three days to recover. How do you feel?"

The voice was familiar. From somewhere, I dredged up a name: Uncle Sunil.

"Shall I put her back under?" said a female voice.

"No. Take the tubes out and leave us."

Lights blinked on. The bed moved up, and my head was raised. I found a cup at my lips and drank, grateful.

After a while the cup was removed. I sank back, exhausted with the effort. I could remember being in pain, so much pain that I wanted to die.

"What did you do to me?" My voice sounded weak and distant.

He smiled, cat-like. "I have modified you. No, I have *trans-*

formed you. You, Arya 14, are the world's first posthuman reservoir."

I must have looked bewildered, because a look of impatience crossed Uncle Sunil's face. "You can go days without food or sleep. Repair yourself if you get hurt. You're strong, self-healing *and* self-replicating."

"Self-replicating?"

"The injections we used take months to create and billions of rupees to produce. Once you've recovered from the effects of the injection, the viruses will finish replicating inside of you. After that, we won't need the injections any more. We'll just need your blood. Don't worry—the process will not hurt you. *Nothing* can hurt you, super Arya. You are an unmitigated success. You can fully expect to live at least twelve years."

Twelve years? Some of the horror I felt must have shown on my face because Uncle Sunil frowned. "My first subject lived only for ten days. Do you not realize how privileged you are? You will never fall sick, feel hungry or grow old. Death, when it comes, will be quick and painless. What more could someone from a chawl ask for?"

I struggled up on the bed. My hands were locked into metal handcuffs on either side. "Let me go."

Uncle Sunil leaned toward me, his face aglow with passion. "Think of what we can accomplish. Imagine a factory worker who never needs a break. Imagine a soldier on the front line who can heal his own wounds. Imagine every poor child in Mumbai growing up healthy and productive!"

"And dead at twenty-five?" I spat at him.

Uncle Sunil spread his hands. "That figure might change as my research progresses. But what do you want—an uncertain, poverty-ridden life, or twelve glorious years free of sickness, pain, and hunger?"

"I want to go home," I said.

"What home? Your father abandoned you, and your mother sold you. You mean nothing to them."

The truth of his words ate through me like acid. Tears stung my eyes.

"Don't cry, Arya," said Uncle Sunil. "You may not mean anything to them, but you mean a lot to me. Everything that I have worked for, hoped for, has borne fruit in you." He patted me on the head and got up. "Time to rest. Tomorrow, when you're stronger, we'll move you to our secure facility in Madh Island. We don't want the media to get a whiff of this, or some petty politician with an eye on chawl votes will find a way to shut us down."

I didn't say anything and he left. I sank back on the pillow, tightness in my chest. I didn't want to go anywhere with him. I didn't want him to use me to do this to other kids.

But what choice did I have? He was right—I had no home, not any more. I cried then, for Ma and Bela and Anshuman, for the school certificate I'd never get, for the years I wouldn't live.

When I was all cried out and empty, something else came to take the place of the hurt: something hard and dark and angry. I strained against the handcuffs, and the metal bit into my skin, but I didn't stop, not even when I felt my flesh tear and blood trickle down my wrist. The metal snapped, and my ravaged hands were free. I kept them down, out of sight. If they were watching me, they would come in now.

No one came. Perhaps they wanted to lull me, see what I would do next. I sat up and looked around. Dim, recessed light, enough to show me that I was alone in a dorm-like space with empty beds on either side. Narrow tables with glass tubing, shelves stuffed with books and instruments, most of which I'd never seen before. A lab of some sort, rather better equipped than the one in our school float.

I spied an open door at one end. An escape route? I got up and hobbled toward it, pretending to be in much more pain that I actually was. Slow and weak, my face contorted, just in case someone was looking at me.

But the door just led to a bathroom. I leaned against the door and tried to think. I had to escape. But how? I caught sight of my hands, and my heart jumped. The blood was dry, the skin sealed. He hadn't lied. I looked back at the rows of shelves, the glass equipment, and a small ray of hope cut through the despair I felt.

I entered the bathroom and closed the door, like I needed to use it. Tiles and porcelain gleamed in the blue light. I peered into the cupboard below the sink. Cleaners, scrubs, rinses—normal stuff you find in most bathrooms. I read the labels and picked the one that was closest to what I wanted. I slipped it in a flap of my robe and pushed open the door.

Back in bed, I hid the bottle under the blanket. I waited at least half an hour before making my second trip to the bathroom. On the way back, between the rows of tables, I stumbled like I was too weak to go on, one hand clutching a table top and sweeping several things off it. I groaned and crouched on the floor, grabbing the item I needed. Shards of glass slashed my newly-healed hands, but I didn't care. I staggered back to bed, hiding my hands in my gown.

It was quite a crowd that came for me in the morning. Uncle Sunil, Revati carrying a glass of orange juice, a robot cleaner to sweep up the mess I'd made the previous night, and four uniformed men, dart guns strapped to their chests. I kept my hands out where they could be seen. Uncle Sunil glanced at them and grinned.

"See how strong you are?" he said, while I gulped the juice down. "Really, the best result we could have hoped for. Ready to go?"

I put the glass back on Revati's tray. "Sure. Can I take my statue of Mumba Devi with me? It's under my pillow."

"Of course," said Uncle Sunil. "We left it there especially for you. Something to remember your old home by, when you go to your *new* home."

Perhaps it was the word 'home' and the prospect that such a place might yet exist for me, or perhaps it was the way he smiled at me so proudly, but I almost couldn't go through with it. Then I remembered what he wanted to use me for, and movement returned to my limbs.

I slipped my hand under the pillow and grabbed the pipette gun. I whirled around and sprayed them with the drain cleaner I'd found in the bathroom. Revati screamed and stumbled back. Uncle Sunil sprang toward me and got a full blast on his face.

I leaped out of bed and ran for the open door through which they'd come. One of the uniformed men grabbed hold of me from behind, but I elbowed his face hard and he let go, grunting. A dart whizzed past my ear and another buried itself in my neck, but I was out the door by then, ducking the darts with a speed I wouldn't have believed possible. I threw the empty glass pipette at one of the men before I slammed the door in his face, bolting it from outside.

I turned and found myself in a long, empty corridor. My head swam. I reached behind my neck and pulled the dart out. I lurched forward, willing myself to stay conscious, clutching the stone idol I'd tied to my gown. *Stay awake. Get out of here first.*

An alarm began to sound, a wailing scream that cut through the fog in my head. I ran down the corridor to the fire exit. Stairs. Up or down? I raced up, guessing that we were underground. Adrenaline pumped through my body.

When I reached the exit door at the next level up, I hesitated. They'd be waiting for me. Perhaps they knew where I was. Maybe the entire facility was rigged with cameras. But I hadn't seen any in the stairwell.

I just kept going, up and up. They would expect me to come out in or near the platform in the tunnel, and that's what I wasn't going to do.

By the time I reached the last flight up, my legs felt like rubber. But I still hadn't seen any of my pursuers. I thought that was strange, until I pushed open the door and walked out on the roof of that dome, into the warm drizzle of a Mumbai monsoon.

There was nothing. No helipad, no convenient scooters, no elevator. Just the vast, curving glass and metal roof, edges blurred in the rain. Uncle Sunil must be laughing—if the acid hadn't eaten his face, of course.

I walked as far to the edge as I could without slipping and peered down.

My stomach lurched. It was at least five or six stories. No way I could survive a jump that high, modified posthuman or not. No wonder they hadn't bothered searching the upper floors. They knew I had to come down to escape.

But what if I *slid* down? The sides of the dome were convex—not enough to come down safely, but better than a vertical drop.

The door clattered open, and I didn't stop to think. I launched myself off the edge, the glass slick underneath my legs. Rain stung my face, and my heart nearly leaped out of my mouth. I screamed—as much from fear as exhilaration.

I fell feet first on wet grass. The pain was so intense I blacked out. It must have been only for a few moments, because when I came to, they still hadn't caught up with me. I struggled to my feet and bit back a cry. I'd broken something. Perhaps several somethings.

I hobbled away as fast as I could, though every step was agony. My only hope was to get on the road, into the traffic. They wouldn't chase me in broad daylight, not with media helicopters always on the prowl, looking for a story.

But then I heard scooters, revving up on the other side of the dome. They were coming to get me. *No. Not now. Not after everything.*

I turned to face my pursuers. When they appeared around the sides of the dome, I held my hands up in the air, smiled and prayed they wouldn't shoot any more of those darts.

They didn't. They just hovered, waiting.

Then I realized who they were waiting for. The rain had stopped and I saw his half-burned face through the transparent hood of the scooter. One eye was bandaged, the other glazed with pain.

He stepped out of the scooter, followed by a couple of guards.

"I'm really sorry, Uncle Sunil," I said. "I didn't mean to hurt you."

He didn't move what was left of his mouth, but I had no trouble hearing the words which came from the vocoder strapped to his forehead: "Arya, I hand you the world on a platter and this is how you repay me?"

I had expected him to shout, to abuse me, but he just sounded sad. I swallowed and said, "My name's Anjali."

"Is it?" He stepped closer, shaking his head. "Such an ordinary name for such a special girl. Arya means great, a noble and valuable person. That is how I think of you. Unlike the mother, who grudged you two meals a day and a pallet to sleep on. Which name do you prefer, chawl-girl?"

I felt like I'd been punched in the stomach. My torment must have shown on my face, because Uncle Sunil gave a small smile, one side of his ruined mouth moving up. *I know you,* that smile said; *I know what you will choose.* And in that moment, I chose.

Uncle Sunil's shoulders relaxed, and he turned to the man behind him. That was when I leaped. I punched him on the side of his head, sending him sprawling against the nearest guard. The others raised their guns, but I was too close, too fast. I jumped into the scooter and jabbed the green switch like I'd seen Uncle Sunil do. The scooter revved up. I kicked one guard off the side before I shot through the air, my heart racing faster than a hummingbird's wings.

Darts bounced off the hood. They mustn't want to kill me, or I'd already be dead. I risked a glance back. I was being followed, but if I could just get away from the dome, I had a chance to make it.

A helicopter whirred in the sky overhead like the answer to my prayers. I looked up and relief flooded me. *Thank you, Goddess.* I never thought I'd be so happy to see the logo of the *Marathi Times*.

The scooters behind me fell back one by one. They'd hunt for me later, but meanwhile I would put as many miles as I could between myself and that dome.

I pulled on a raincoat I found in the storage compartment just below the controls. Then I headed southwest, leaving the corporation domes way behind, letting the scooter weave through the traffic on autopilot.

I abandoned the scooter in one of the artificial market beaches of Bandra and stole the clothes of a firang woman in a bikini who was arguing with a boy about the price of coconut water. She didn't notice me sneaking off with the pile of clothes behind her deck chair.

I changed in a filthy public toilet at one end of the beach. The clothes were a little too big for me, but there was no help for it. I hitched up the skirt and walked away from there fast, head down. I threw the hospital gown and raincoat into a beach trash can, and then I was free.

Free. I tasted the word. It had a bittersweet flavour. What next? There was no going back home. I couldn't face Ma, and I was no longer the Anjali everyone knew. Who was I?

I tried out various names in my head. Mumbai Girl? No,

too plain. Miss India? Sounded like a beauty queen, which I definitely wasn't. Super Anjali? Too silly. Arya? No, *that* one I had rejected already.

Perhaps I'd just stick with plain old Anjali. Anjali, which meant "divine offering." My mother named me, and then she sold me, so I should have hated her. But I didn't, not any more. In giving me the statue of Mumba Devi, Ma had told me what she couldn't say in words: she was offering me up to the Goddess, into her protection.

But the Goddess helps those who help themselves. I would have to be brave and cunning to stay alive in the city and out of Uncle Sunil's grasp. I had twelve years left in the slowly ticking time bomb of my life. It would have to be enough. Enough to destroy Uncle Sunil, Genex, and everything their polluted ideology stood for.

My fingers closed over the idol I had slipped into the pocket of my skirt, and I smiled.

Eyes Wide Open

by Deborah Walker

Deborah Walker lives in London with her partner, Chris, and her two teenage children. Her stories have appeared in *Nature's Futures*, *Lady Churchill's Rosebud Wristlet*, and The *Young Explorers Adventure Guides* 2015, 2016, and 2017. She's recently published *As Good As Bad Can Get*, her debut novel, a space opera set in the Dark Expanse Universe. Find Deborah in the British Museum trawling the past for future inspiration.

For the first week, Maia concentrated on keeping her head down and not getting eaten.

Her duties weren't taxing. All she had to do was take care of the small crop field and the animal pens. Her owner was the only other orbital inhabitant. The Serpente must have been very wealthy to rent a ball around Farther's World. Orbitals don't come cheap.

Maia was given a bedroom to herself; it even had a proper bed. But there were no entertainments and no video link to her hut on Trash Ball Station. She couldn't get used to sleeping on the bed and spent her nights on the floor under a blanket, thinking about her hut brothers and sisters.

After a week, she so was lonely she plucked up her courage and sought out the Serpente.

Maia found her owner coiled in the room with many

wall cabinets. All of them were locked; Maia had found that out in her first week. With a little spare time, she could've opened them all. A lock hadn't been invented that could hinder Maia Wells.

"What do you want with me?" asked the Serpente.

"I wondered if you would let me vid-link my hut mates, if it pleases you, Madam Owner."

"No. I will tolerate no additional communication to the Human world."

"Then I wondered if I could have access to the entertainments, please. Thank you very much. Please."

"No."

"Madam Owner Serpente, the entertainments are free to all Farther's family. It won't cost you anything."

"No. I will not have lies here."

"Lies?" asked Maia. "You mean the stories in the entertainment shows?"

"My people do not tolerate lies and stories."

"Stories aren't lies."

"Are they the truth?"

"They're a kind of truth," said Maia. "Ancient John told me so."

"I will not tolerate them. The Serpente never lie."

That seemed hard to believe. "You never tell a lie? Not even a little white lie? And you never tell a story to your little 'uns? After a hard day's grind in the trash pits, we like to tell each other stories. I don't see anything wrong in that."

"No lies, no stories."

She had not granted Maia's requests, but neither had she eaten Maia—which was a bonus. So the next evening Maia sought out the Serpente again. Politely and persistently she asked for permission to contact her hut mates.

Too persistently, it seemed, because eventually the Serpente reared her body and hissed and flicked her long, forked tongue. "No and no and no. Maia Wells, you are improper, disrespectful, overly insistent. Like all your kind, you are reprehensible."

"*What?* Don't you like Humans?"

"I despise all Humans."

"Oh. Even me?"

"All Humans are riddled with lies. When Farther's ambassador came to my home world he spoke of trade and mutual respect."

Maia said nothing. The Serpente must be very gullible if they believed that Farther—the Collector of Worlds—only wanted trade and respect. "At least I'm a good worker," said Maia. "Ancient John says *Labor omnia vincit.* That means *Hard work conquers all* in dead talk. You're getting your money's worth with me, Madam Owner."

"You'll do as little work as you can get away with."

That stung. "There's hardly any work for me to do." But Maia realised that the conversation had veered off topic. She tried another approach. "Without my hut mates and without the entertainments, I'm very lonely. And if I'm lonely I might get sad, and then I won't be able to work hard for you. Sometimes Ancient John gets sad. He calls it the Black Dog, and he can't even go out scavenging. I think he'd die if I didn't take him food. You don't want that to happen to me."

"I don't think it will happen to you."

"It might. *The mind can be a dark labyrinth.*"

"Is that another one of Ancient John's sayings?"

"It is."

"Can you write, Maia Wells?"

Maia nodded. "Ancient John taught me when he was laid up with the judders."

The Serpente slithered to one of the cabinets and opened

it to reveal a fabricator. She tapped in a code (Maia couldn't quite see the password), and the machine produced a paper notebook and an eternal pencil. "You must write your own stories or keep a diary to entertain yourself," said the Serpente. "If you want lies, then you must make them for yourself."

"But I don't know what to write. I'm not clerical class."

"Write a record of your experiences. I will not read it."

"But what about vidding my hut mates? They'll be awful worried about me."

"You can write them a letter. I will see that it is sent to them."

The Serpente was peculiar and no mistake. Maia wondered why she'd been hired. There wasn't enough work for her to do. She wasn't a bit tired at the end of the day, not like after a proper day's work in the trash. That night Maia tried to write in the notebook, but she couldn't think of anything to pen. Except complaints about how bored she was.

She stared out the window, gazing at Farther's World. Unfortunately, Trash Ball's orbital was 90 degrees clockwise, so she couldn't see it. She decided it was stupid to write things down. Maia wasn't cleric class. She was trash class, a waste-picker ever since her soldier mother and father bit the bullet.

Two days later, Maia asked the Serpente what she should write.

"Whatever you want."

"But I don't know. I can't think. This is like the worst torture ever. Mental torture. And you're not supposed to mistreat me—unless you pay the supplement."

"Well then, record the events that have occurred to bring you to this state."

That seemed like a good idea to Maia.

So, when Marther said one of us kids would be hired out to an alien orbital for six months, you can imagine the clamour. Any chance to get off the trash ball, yeh? But then Precious Goggins, who is the smartest of us all, asked "What alien?"

When Marther said "Serpente," we all went quiet. We hear things on Trash Ball. And none of us fancied being hired out to the newest of Farther's family, because they were snakes. Might be nice snakes for all we knew, or might not.

"So, who wants to go?" asked Marther. The thought was turning in all our heads that snakes might be worse than the trash pile. "Youngest then," said Marther pointing to Jewel.

Then I steps up and volunteers. "I'll go," I said. Because Jewel was too young, and hadn't got used to being a trash orphan. She cried a lot.

"Why not Jewel?" asked Marther with a sly smile on her face.

"I'm oldest, and my skills are the most valuable. If anything happens to me on the Serpente's orbital, then Farther will get the best price to compensate him. It's my duty to go."

"Can't argue with that, girl," said Marther.

And that was that. Soon after I was fastported to the Serpente's orbital that rotated around Farther's World with all the others.

I should say something about the Serpente. It has been ten days, but she still hasn't told me her name, so I call her Madam Owner.

Madam Owner is legless and lean. I guess she is seven meters long. Her body is thick, a meter across until it tapers to a tail. She is covered with overlapping golden scales that are ridged in the middle. They are not slimy. She looks powerful. If all her people are like her, I imagine they put up a good fight against Farther's soldiers.

She moves by slithering. She can raise her body up, slowly, oh so slowly, so she can look me in the face. She does have arms—tiny, thin arms that can be retracted into side slits in her body. She takes them out of her body like slipping her hands out of a pocket.

Madam Owner sleeps a lot. One peculiar thing is that she sleeps with her eyes open. Sort of. I thought she did. But she said no indeed, her eyelids are permanently closed, but they are transparent, like Ancient John's spectacles. It just looks like she's always watching. Most of the time she sleeps with her face buried in the coils of her body.

She has a flickering tongue that is constantly in motion.

She does not have any external ears, but she can hear good.

Sometimes, she does not mind me asking questions. Like today, when I asked her about her eyes being always open. "We evolved from burrowing lizards," she told me. Which is why she has no eyelids or proper ears and why her arms slip into her body pockets.

Today I asked her name. The person who is looking after me is called Lozz Yezzan Anell.

Every day Maia wrote a letter to the hut, telling them that they didn't have to worry about her, telling them that she landed on her feet and no mistake, telling them that she'd do her six months easy, and she'd be back quick as a blink. As the weeks passed, her letters and her diary entries got longer as Maia found it easier and easier to commit her thoughts to paper. What seemed so torturous at first became easy as using a magnet to peel the metallic skin from a robotic skink.

"Do you like me yet?" Maia asked Lozz. "I'm a hard worker, aren't I?"

The Serpente made no answer.

"I like you, Madam Owner."

"Do you, indeed?"

"I think you're just the nicest of Farther's alien children I've ever met, and I've met quite a few."

"How many alien races *have* you met, Maia Wells?"

"Eleven."

"That *is* quite a few," admitted Lozz. "Far more aliens than any of my subjects or I have met."

It's hard to be cold to someone who is being nice to you. Maia's compliment was opening the door of conversation that night. Maia pushed it farther open and asked about Lozz's homeland.

"It was during winter, the time of brumation, a time of inactivity in our great hibernaculas. I had drawn the lot to remain active to care for the palace eggs, warming them with my shivers. Farther's soldiers slaughtered everyone in the palace hibernacula. All my family were killed, including my five daughters. The soldiers smashed all the eggs I was caring for. They beat me with clubs, knocked me unconscious. They left me for dead."

"That is very sad," said Maia. "Before I came to this orbital, one of my hut mates was killed."

"I am very sad and shocked for your loss," said Lozz.

"It happens. Trash kids die all the time on the rubbish slags. At least Trigger died quick when the trash slide crushed him. That's the best way, or being run over by a truck. Fires are bad. Or a sickness picked up from the biological waste pits, or from staying too long in the fermenting quarries."

"Death and pain are your companions, Maia Wells."

"It's not all doom and gloom! We have laughs as well. We are all trash orphans, so any time we have is pure jam. If it wasn't for the trash, no one would feed us. In my hut, we're all grateful for the time that Trigger had with us. He was a good worker, and he was very good at riddles. You should focus on the good, Madam Owner. You must know females who didn't have any children, so you should be grateful for the time you had with your daughters."

"Grateful that Farther killed them?"

"No, of course not! But in a war people get killed. You should have sat back and let Farther take what he wanted— hardly anyone gets killed when that happens."

"And how many peoples just sit back and let him take what he wants?"

"Not so many, I reckon. But if they were smart they would. Madam Owner, you said the palace hiber-thingy, and earlier you said your subjects. Are you a queen?"

"A queen protects her subjects. I am no queen, Maia Wells."

"But—"

"That is enough conversation for tonight," said Lozz, and she would say no more.

Maia could hardly wait to write all the conversation in her diary, which was admittedly becoming more interesting than she could possibly have imagined.

The next night, Maia wanted to talk about Lozz being a queen, but the Serpente would not discuss it. Maia was fairly certain that her owner was royal, because she had that kind of high-handed but fair way about her, which was typical of royalty, in all the entertainments, at least (unless they were evil royalty, and that didn't seem Lozz's style).

As Lozz wouldn't talk about being a queen, Maia decided to set the record straight about Farther. She felt her owner had got the wrong idea about Farther. "You see, Farther is building something. It is like a web. It started out very small, but every time he sends his soldiers out, it grows a bit."

"Farther is the spider in the web?"

"There's nothing wrong with spiders. They eat flies, and the flies can get something terrible in the trash pile. But perhaps that is not the best comparison for Farther. I can't say everything I want to, nicey-nice, like a cleric or a manager. I just wanted to say that Farther's family is growing bigger, and he is at the centre. He won't stop taking new worlds because he has responsibilities. But once you're part of his family, he looks out for you."

"And how does Farther look out for the trash children?"

"We do the trashing, the soldiers do the fighting, and the managers look after the businesses. And there are a hundred different jobs with everyone knowing their place in Farther's family."

"But you can't change your place."

"Sometimes you can. Ancient John is artist class, and he shouldn't really be on Trash Ball, but the marthers like him. He can be very lovey-dovey to them when he's in the mood. And we trash kids were all set to be something different before we was orphaned. That's how I know so much about everything. We are mostly children of soldiers because they get killed a lot, but there are also cooks' or weavers' or scientists' kids. Any kid who doesn't have a family gets to be a trash worker."

"Thrown to the rubbish heaps?"

Maia knew what Lozz was implying. "We work with rubbish, but we're not rubbish. We have a job to do. We eat most days. We have a marther to look after us. We make the best of what we've got."

"Thank you for sharing the truth of your life, Maia Wells," said Lozz.

"Why did you hire me and bring me to this orbital, Madam Owner? To be honest, as you like honesty, there's not much work for me to do."

"We do not lie," she said. "But that does not mean that we answer every question."

Lozz would speak no more. And Maia realised that her owner was a clever conversationalist, as it was Maia who had done most of the talking that night.

Maia got a letter, at last, from the hut. It was nice to get something that she could hold in her hand, but she couldn't see their faces as she would in a vid, so it was six of one and half a dozen of the other. They were all doing well and filling the quotas without her. Precious Goggins was keeping everyone in order, and he wrote about some funny happenings that made Maia laugh out loud and then cry a little bit for some reason she didn't understand. She read and re-read the letter, wishing that they would write more often but knowing that they would be busy making the quotas, especially with one less in the hut. You gotta eat.

꒰ꑄ

I have seen Madam Owner dancing, and it was wonderful.

Today I went looking for her, expecting to find her in the middle level, sleeping with her eyes wide open as usual. But she was not there. I searched all over until I finally found her in the outmost orbital level, which is one long empty room. I often wondered what it was for. Now I know it is a dancehall. I hid in the shadows and watched her dances with many patterns. In waves, alternately flexing from left to right. On smooth portions of the floor she side-winds, a rolling, slow motion. She moves like an elegant inchworm, squeezing her body together and then rippling forwards, and that was the slowest movement of all. She coils and raises her upper body; she weaves through the air. She switches through moves as quick and slick as an eel through the fermenting pools.

Oh, I can't describe it, but it was dancing all right. There was music, but none that I could hear.

When her motions slowed down, I tried to slip away, but she caught me. I had forgotten that she could see in the dark. She smelled my warmth in the grooves of her snout. She said that some things were private and that I should not have spied on her.

I said that I was sorry but that her dancing was very lovely, and that I wished Jewel could have seen it, because she told me once that her mother had loved to dance with her. But I have never seen Jewel dance on Trash Ball. It might even have made her smile.

"Jewel? She is the youngest in your hut, isn't she?"

"Nothing but five years old," I said. "And a good little worker but awful sad. It would be a nice thing if I could tell her about your dancing, Madam Owner. She'd like that."

Madam Owner told me that there was a time when her people danced across miles and miles of open land. These long and complicated dances would last for weeks. Now Farther has built factories all over their land, and the people work in them and no one dances anymore.

I reminded her that the people were working for the family. And that it was a good thing and all jam. Then, because we were getting on so nicely, I asked her point-blank why she'd hired me.

She was silent for a long time, but I gave her answer some time to breathe, and she finally said, "I wanted to get to know an innocent."

"And where will you find an innocent?"

The trouble with Madam Owner is that she has no sense of humour. By the time I'd explained it, the joke was dead. I was the innocent, yeah, yeah, I got it. But I also pointed out that though I was just a kid, I knew a lot of things, and maybe she should have taken one of the managers' children, as they are very innocent. Sometimes we have a giggle at how soft they are.

But she rightly pointed out that the managers' children never get hired out, so she is stuck with me.

Serpente said a lot of things that night. She said that every child should have a right to innocence and a right to education, too.

How are we supposed to work if we don't have jobs, I asked her? And she said that children should be free from work. All children? I asked her. Not just the ones in the upper caste? And she said yes. And I don't think that she was lying because it would have been an affront to her beliefs.

And she said previous to the Farther's Empire, a lot of kids had to go to school. On Old Earth in some countries it was the law. And her own daughters apparently had spent lots of time lounging around at school, not earning a penny.

I said that I didn't see the point of it, because even if I had an education, what good would it do me? I knew enough to be a good trash worker. I could recognise valuables in the trash. I was good at winkling them out. What else is there to know?

And she said that it pained her that my life chances were so limited. For a change it was me who had nothing left to say, so I went back to feed the animals.

I've written another letter to the hut. But I didn't put all my thoughts down because I don't think it would go well for Madam Owner if Marther found it and passed it on to security. I think it will also not be a good idea to bring this diary home. I never thought that thoughts could be dangerous, but it seems to me like they can be. Perhaps Farther is right not to encourage education, because it would encourage people to think too much, and thinking only leads to dissatisfaction.

It was the last month, and Maia was very worried about her owner. "Why are your eyes all cloudy? And your skin looks terribly dull. Are you sick? I know a tonic that will perk you up. It is an all-purpose miracle cure, made of commonly scrounged materials. I'm pretty sure it will work on you too, Madam Owner."

"Thank you for your concern, Maia Wells, but it is only ecdysis."

"Ecdysis. I am *so* sorry. Is it contagious to Humans, do you think, if you don't mind me asking?"

"No indeed. It is the shedding of my scales. A natural process. I shall retreat to my private quarters for seven days. Traditionally, this is a time for reflection. But it is private. I do not want you spying on me. Afterwards, I will have a proposal to put to you."

And no matter how much Maia begged, Lozz wouldn't give her a hint about this mysterious proposal, but Maia suspected it was something to look forward to.

Before she left, Maia asked, "Madam Owner, do you like me now?"

And Lozz replied very solemnly, "Yes, I like you, Maia Wells."

So for a whole week Maia Wells was left to her own devices. She stayed away from Lozz's private quarters, but she was free to roam the orbital, the outer dancehall, the inner pens and fields, and the middle rooms of locked cabinets. But as Ancient John often said, *Idle hands are the devil's playthings.* And there never was a lock that Maia couldn't get into, given enough time.

⋖🚀⋗

So then this is the last of my diary entries. Afterward, I will burn this notebook. But there is something about writing that sets my thoughts in order. There is a slowness to it that helps me think.

Afterward the words might burn, but the thoughts will remain.

A week on my own was too long for me to abide without getting into mischief. For nearly six months I'd been wondering what was behind those locked cabinets. It was easy to break into the locks but hard in the sense that I was breaking her trust. Whatever was in there, she didn't want me to know. And she was right not to let me know.

Afterwards, I did what I needed to do. And then I waited for her.

After the seven days, Madam Owner emerged from her room, her scales shining like new gold, her eyes clean and clear.

"I found something while you were gone," I said, laying the drone and the air particle distributor onto the table. "I couldn't take the risk of it, so I incinerated the vials. I guess they were full of venom. Was it your venom?"

"Yes. It was mine. Royal venom, so potent it could have killed every animal and person on Farther's World. There you have my secret, Maia. I came here to destroy Farther and his family."

"They would have stopped it before it got close, you know. There are all sorts of security. You aren't the first to try and kill us. And then they would have killed you."

"I know. I would have died in the attempt. And it would have been better than the utter hollowness that I felt when every tomorrow seemed to promise the dreadful, unchanged emptiness. You don't know what that feels like, Maia Wells. I hired you because I wanted to know an innocent, a Human child, before I made my final decision."

"You wouldn't have done it anyway," I said. "You are a good person. Even though you are cold sometimes. Cold in your blood and cold towards me sometimes. I like you very much. You never lie to me, and you make me feel safe. You have cared for me better than any of the marthers on Trash Ball. I have wanted to be a good worker for you and to make you love me. I don't know why."

"I have found love for you, Maia Wells. That is why I would like to bring you to my home world, so that my people can learn that all Humans are not like Farther or his soldiers. But there are no girls and boys on my world. Perhaps you would be lonely."

"Not lonely," I said, "but I must return to Trash Ball. I have responsibilities; they count on me to return."

"Of course."

"And you have given me something," I said, "with all the talks we have had. Your truths have filled a hole in me. You have changed me, Lozz Yezzan Anell."

She bowed her head to me. "As you have changed me, Maia Wells."

"Madam Owner, you have made me think about truth. And while I can't say I won't lie ever again, I want to go back to Trash Ball and make it my job to tell others about truth. And maybe it will spread all over Trash Ball and the other orbitals and to Farther's World. The truth will spread from worker to worker, to the supervisors, and spreading out, even to Farther's court and to Farther himself, because I wonder, with all his privilege and wealth and power and everything in the world that he has, I wonder if he has truth. And if he don't, then I don't see that he can be happy. For isn't he just a man, after all? That is the truth of it. And the truth is bigger than any man."

As you can see with that speechifying, my thoughts are bigger than anything you can imagine. This truth is expanding, growing bigger than the highest trash heap, bigger even than the sun, or the galaxy, or the universe—beyond the edges of what is known is the truth.

All because I started talking to an alien snake queen and thinking about things and writing it down.

The words will burn, but the truth will rise from the ashes.

I had my things packed and was ready to go, and the last thing I said to Madam Owner was this, "You are a people with your eyes open. I think that maybe we could be, too. If we talk and think, I will open their eyes and do as I always do and make the best of things."

Solemnly Madam Owner nodded, and said, "And I will try to teach my people to make jam."

And that made me laugh all the way back to Trash Ball.

Clockwork Carabao

by Marilag Angway

Marilag Angway likes writing about girls who have big dreams; big enough to take them to the skies. She is, however, not opposed to a good romp on terra firma, so long as mechanical shenanigans are involved. She's a writer of science fiction and fantasy and occasionally dabbles in horror and humor (though success at the latter remains to be seen). Her stories can be found in various anthologies, including those published by Bards and Sages Publishing, Hadley Rille Books, Deepwood Publishing, Ticonderoga Publications, Rosarium Publishing, and Dreaming Robot Press. When she's not writing, she's filling middle schoolers' heads with the wonders of mathematics and the marvels of science. For her random book and overall nerdish musings, check out her blog at storyandsomnomancy. wordpress.com. Don't forget to grab a cookie and a cup of tea on your way out!

The mechanical carabao was the strangest contraption Hati had ever seen.

By that point in time, she'd already seen much more than a normal young girl with regards to mechanical animals. She'd even *made* a few of them herself and had been proud of the prize she'd won at the Junior Mechanicking Competition back at floating Rizal. The prize invention, a mechanical kitten that was also used as a pill dispenser, which her father and mother found quite charming, sat at home—a strange, metallic center-piece on their large dining table.

And yet this carabao was something new.

She would have missed it had she not walked down her porch steps and turned the corner to her neighbor's house. In fact, she would have missed it altogether had she decided to go to her regular haunts on the other side of the neighborhood. For some reason, though, there was just something pulling her in the other direction, and she quietly thanked the skies that she had followed her instincts.

The junkyard she wound up in had almost nothing of note, save for the massive structure standing right next to a cart of brass pots and pans. Her breath gave way to wonder and awe. In front of her stood a great bull sculpture, one much larger than Hati's gawky frame. From a distance, its entire body seemed cloaked in darkness, an object formed from black mica and baked until its sheen glowed in the sun. Upon closer inspection, Hati realized it was much more than that.

Much, *much* more, in fact.

For one, it was made out of metal. The metallic black had been a good trick to the eye, and had Hati not moved in for a closer look, she would have thought the carabao was nothing but a sculpture. In all respects, it might still be just that, except she eventually found the wires that were cleverly concealed behind the bull's horns.

Hati pressed a hand upon the carabao's snout, feeling the smooth metal beneath her fingers.

It moved.

Hati jumped, scrambled back. For a brief moment, she'd been scared of what the clockwork carabao would do, but her fear turned quickly to fascination, and by the time the carabao had stopped moving—a matter of a few seconds, really—she'd already started moving forward again.

The carabao had been a passing interest, but now it was

slowly becoming an obsession. It invited more in-depth scrutiny, and all she needed were her tools.

She would have to go back to her house and leave the carabao's mystery for now. Hati did not like this fact, but for the good of science, she was going to do it.

With a quick pat on the carabao's nose, Hati bounded back toward her house, whistling happily to herself and thinking of the possible ways she could open up the carabao and see what mechanisms were inside.

Cebu City smelled of engines and smoke and hot gas. It was hard to breathe when walking the street sometimes. If this was the only thing that kept Hati from loving her new home, she would have gotten over her disappointment by now. But...

There was the fact that she couldn't bring most of her pets with her. Not *pets* pets. Animals were much harder to maintain on a general basis, and the most her parents were willing to do in terms of keeping animals was to catch several glowing jellyfish and put them inside a protective tank with glass walls almost ten centimeters thick. It was all well and good for her parents, who bragged about their jellyfish, because that's what everybody did in the high-class circles, but Hati *hated* the blasted things. They wriggled their plentiful arms, and there was no telling where their brains were. Did jellyfish even think?

Not to mention the fact that the jellyfish were venomous. She'd almost fallen in the tank once, and that would have been the end of it, had her nanny not dragged her out of the way of their tendrils.

No, not actual pets. Hati was not allowed such a thing. The pets she kept were alive, but they were strictly mechanical. And aside from the pill-dispensing cat, none of them actually moved.

Back in Rizal, Hati had loved tinkering with the small clockwork birds she'd been given as toys. Her nanny always found it a strange pastime for an eight-year-old at the time, but at eleven, it had become an acceptable hobby. By the end of the summer, Hati had already amassed a collection of unfinished and finished oddities: typewriter-winged birds, spiders with clock-hand legs, fish with fan-tails. Her favorites had always been the big, four-legged creatures, because those were much harder to find parts for, and that meant asking to be taken to the closest junkyard to salvage said parts.

"Salvaging?" her mother raised an eyebrow, "Shouldn't you be doing something better with your time, my utok?" Whenever her mother referred to her as "my brain," it always made Hati blush.

"It's a phase," her father said, giving Hati a quick glance. "You know how it is with girls her age, Reggie, she's curious. And she likes to get dirty."

"Well, I suppose. Though curiosity and cleanliness are not mutually exclusive." Her mother sniffed, looked at Hati again. Hati knew the best way to get a nod from her pristinely clean mother was to stare at her unblinkingly. Really, staring always made the grownups uneasy. And it got Hati what she wanted.

So off to the junkyard she went, reluctant nanny in tow.

At least, that's how it had been before they'd moved to Cebu City. If there was one thing Hati loved about the city, it was most certainly the fact that the junkyard was not very far from her house. That had been her mother's first complaint upon arrival, that their new home had a horrible view of discarded machines. Hati's father had called the miniature city "charming" and "interesting" and all sorts of words that tried to ease her mother's worries, but it only half-worked.

Her mother whined anyway. "The house in Rizal was *much* bigger. I don't even know where to put my papers. The office upstairs is only a fraction of my old workroom."

Hati also missed her mother's old workroom. Before her parents finally decided she was big enough to have an office of her own, she'd shared a space with her mother, whose work-room was about the size of a sitting room. Most of the space had been filled with mountains of paperwork and boards. Boards with etchings that showed her mother's latest calcula-tions. Hati had always been awed by the numbers that quickly left her mother's fingers, and she'd been fascinated at how often they changed every day.

She never knew what her mother did with the numbers she found at the end of the long scribbles of letters, symbols, and other numbers, but she knew that her mother was paid well for such answers.

"This is temporary," her father said. "Before you know it, we'll be back in Rizal and in your old workroom. And Hati will have her little space, as well."

Her mother had stopped whining then, only sighing some-what at the change. She'd retired to the office soon after, and her father murmured something about another one of his business meetings. That left Hati alone to explore the neigh-borhood on most days. Nobody had invited her nanny down to Cebu City with them, which was a shame. Hati had liked her nanny, though she supposed being eleven meant she was now too old to have one.

She walked back into the house, removed her shoes, and put on the slippers she'd left to the side. She climbed the stairs to the second floor and knocked on the door of her mother's office. She heard the muffled "Hati?" and opened the door a crack.

"Something the matter, my utok?"

"Can I grab my tools, Nanay? I found a carabao in the junk-yard I'm wanting to open up."

The fact that her mother didn't say anything about there being a carabao in the junkyard meant she was doubly focused on her math problem. Instead, she licked her teeth and nod-ded. Hati made sure to dash in without disturbing her moth-er's other thoughts—which were largely on a dark green board half-filled with her most recent calculations—and dash back out. She murmured a quick thank-you to her mother then left the house, her backpack filled with the tools she would need to open up the mechanical carabao.

But by the time she made it back to the junkyard, the carabao was no longer there.

◄🚀►

The first thing Hati did was search the junkyard. When that produced nothing, she huffed with frustration. It was the largest mechanical bull she'd ever seen; it couldn't have moved away from the junkyard so quickly, could it?

"That's the problem, isn't it?" Hati murmured. "And just when I thought things couldn't get any better."

The junkyard was by no means grand. It was large and filled with knick-knacks, and if someone looked closely, she'd find ways to put the pipes and gears and discarded parts together. Hati had become quite an expert at looking at piecing things together to look like metal animals, and she had plenty of material to work with right there. Her only problem was the fact that she couldn't make any of her animals move. Not in the way automatons moved in Rizal. Not in the way the metal horses moved to pull carts and jitneys. So she couldn't understand how a carabao—as large and as complicated as it was—could move away from the junkyard without much effort.

In Rizal, she had a friend who could have helped her, but Hati was far away from Ysa and from the floating city of whirring gears and chiming clocktowers.

What would Ysa think about her discovery of the moving metal carabao?

None of that helped Hati now, though. What she needed to do was look for the darn carabao. If it were no longer in the junkyard, then by the skies, it must have moved somewhere nearby. She'd been gone under an hour, and even a metallic carabao—for all its movement—could go only so far.

When she left the yard, she saw it. Clunky movement beside a cottage. No, not a cottage. Even cottages were a little more complicated than this house. Hati vaguely remembered the pictures in a book she'd been given when she was smaller, of snow-capped homes and other wintry objects. She remembered reading the book over and over, the images of winter ingrained in her head. Snow was nonexistent in Rizal and even more impossible in Cebu City, where the sprinkle of ash-snow meant danger and death.

But if igloos existed in tropical climes, this house of metal would definitely be an igloo, with its rounded dome shape made of an assortment of junkyard sheets. There was one massive door leading into the igloo, though it didn't look like anyone was coming out.

The carabao stood there, motionless once more.

Hati waited a while from her vantage point to see if anyone would emerge from the igloo-that-was-not-an-igloo. When it began to grow dark, Hati decided that whoever lived there must have been away and would not be coming any time soon. So she descended the hill, down, down, down toward the carabao, which still had not moved.

She made it to the bottom, and a little out of breath, she began to examine the carabao's wires. The moment Hati touched its metal snout, however, it moved again, rearing its head up to a point where Hati had to stretch her arm. Its horns caught the last rays of the sun before it fully set, and Hati could not help but think how utterly magnificent the creature was.

"Who made you?" Hati murmured, knowing full well the carabao would not answer.

Unsurprisingly, it made no attempts to answer her question. Instead, it swished its tail—insomuch as it could "swish," the tail being made out of long, metallic strips strapped together at the long ends. Then, as though it had waited for Hati to finally reach it, the carabao moved its head and pointed its horns toward the door.

Hati raised an eyebrow. That was interesting. "You want me to go in?"

It remained immobile once more, its head bowed, horns pointed straight toward the igloo's door. With a sigh, she pressed her ear toward the door, listening for any sound whatsoever. Nothing. So she knocked. And knocked. *And* knocked.

Satisfied that no one was there, she jingled the door, noting that it was not locked. She glared at the carabao. "I'm going to be in big trouble if somebody catches me breaking and entering into their house."

And yet the carabao remained where it stood. Eventually Hati opened the door.

What she saw inside would have made her whistle, except she didn't know how. Instead, she gasped and said, "Ohhhh, skies above."

Hati felt the cold point of the carabao's horns against her back, and she realized it was trying to push her farther inside. When she finally moved, the carabao walked toward a large open gazebo with wires rolled up on the sides. Once it reached the gazebo, it knelt down and put its head down, as though to rest. Only, mechanical animals don't *need* rest. Whatever this mechanical carabao was doing had been wired in somehow.

Leaving the carabao in its "nest," Hati examined the igloo. It was a workshop of some kind. Hati had seen workshops of the like in the clocktowers on floating Rizal, and like the ones she'd seen in the city above, this igloo workshop contained tools all across the walls. There were hanging wrenches and screwdrivers of varying sizes and shapes. There were nuts and bolts in labeled boxes, an assortment of hammers and nails right next to each other. There were levers and buttons on some sort of mainframe near the center of the room. There were wires that snaked their way up the poles that held the gazebo together.

Unlike the workshops she'd seen in Rizal, this particular igloo had not been disturbed for a long time. Dust covered the books on the tables, and cobwebs spread all over the upper walls, dripping down onto the open boxes.

The most prominent feature of the igloo's interior, however, was not its organized, untouched tools. No, what had caught Hati's attention had been the pictures and diagrams on the walls, of real and metallic carabao standing next to each other, of detailed sketches and notes about what part went where. Scribbles of calculations made and crossed out. Numbers that capped at 40. Then, on the farthest section of the wall, Hati saw pictures of people standing atop carts, their demeanors filled with concentration, their hands holding onto tethers that were connected to carabao. *Actual* carabao.

It looked like a race, from what Hati saw, and she shook her head. She had no idea that carabao could even run that fast. But then again, she shouldn't have been surprised. *This* mechanical carabao certainly knew how to disappear quickly enough.

It was a lot to take in, and slowly, Hati explored the room, opening drawers and examining sketches. On one of the drawers, she'd found a small journal, and upon flipping it, realized it was a manual for working the carabao. Hati's eyes widened. This was *exactly* the type of thing she was looking for. She looked up at the carabao, who still remained "sleeping" in the center of the gazebo.

She bit her lip. Hati had been told at a very young age that taking what didn't belong to her was considered stealing. Her parents were staunch followers of the law, and she was sure that if they knew her thoughts at that instant, Hati would never be allowed to leave the house ever again.

Yet the decision had been made, and Hati decided she wouldn't tell her parents what she'd done. Besides, she'd only be *borrowing* it. She'd bring it right back on the morrow.

Hati put the journal inside her pocket and quietly slipped out of the igloo. She gave one final glance toward the carabao, and satisfied that it wasn't moving anytime soon, she walked out, hurrying home as though she were being chased by a herd of stampeding water buffalo.

⋖❯❯❯

That night, Hati could not sleep. Not because she felt guilty about taking something that wasn't hers (though she felt plenty bad about that), but because she couldn't put the journal down. Whoever had written the thing made sure to put as much detail and instruction as possible on the building of the mechanical race carabao.

By the time she'd finished reading, her father had already woken up to get ready for work. Hati switched her lights off before her father passed her room. She didn't want him to inquire about yesterday's activities, and she was sure that if he found out, her mother would be dragged into the conversation, and they would *never* get anywhere.

Hati lay still, her mind swimming with what she'd learned about building and operating a mechanical race carabao. She thought about the one in the igloo, and how it seemed to lead her toward the workshop, as if it *wanted* her there. Mechanical creatures didn't think, did they?

Perhaps it was in its wiring. The journal had mentioned that each mechanized carabao would be expected to last for several years until it needed maintenance. The carabao must have been dormant a long time, judging from how dusty the igloo had been. Perhaps it only chose to move around now because it had to be maintained. Perhaps Hati had been there at just the right time.

She wondered briefly whether she could make the clockwork carabao run faster than the number on the journal. She wondered about the challenge that would bring her, and she wondered all this with excitement. And as she thought about the journal and the carabao, her eyelids fluttered closed, and in no time flat, she fell asleep.

⋖❯❯❯

The first day back into the igloo, Hati almost set the gazebo on fire.

On the second day she was late getting to the igloo because her mother insisted that she go to school-taught by her ever studious mother. Then she almost was electrocuted by a loose wire.

By the third, Hati was exhausted. So exhausted that she'd almost dropped the entire box of nuts and bolts onto her feet, which would have caused a *lot* of pain.

Yet each and every time she did something potentially dangerous, the carabao did not move. It was frustrating to the extreme, and she wondered if this was how her mother felt whenever she struggled with the same problem for days on end. It must have been.

By the end of the fourth day, her parents noticed the exhaustion.

"My utok, I worry for you," her mother said. "You barely eat, you don't really sleep, and I see you each day gazing out the window instead of trying to solve the math problem I just gave you."

"What do you *do* when you're outside, anyway?" her father said. "You're always covered in grime and grease. Are you tinkering again?"

"There's a problem I'm trying to solve," was Hati's mumbled reply. "And the answer isn't there for me to see. I can't..." her lip trembled. "I can't fix this."

Her mother, who almost always had the answers, pursed her lips. "You've always known how to fix things, Hati. Sometimes when you're not thinking so hard on it, the solution presents itself. And then you get your *Eureka!*"

"Eureka?"

Her mother smiled. "A moment of clarity, my utok. A moment of clarity."

On the fifth to tenth day, she decided not to go into the igloo. Instead, she walked around Cebu City, taking in the sights—or what few there were. She took the time to rest when her mother suggested, and by the eleventh day, she began thinking about the *inside* of the carabao. She began to remember finer details. The fraying wires. The rusted metals. The ungreased cogs and gears.

The clockwork carabao didn't just *need* to be recharged. It needed actual, skies-honest *maintenance*. And all this time, Hati hadn't realized because she just wanted to take the next step.

"Eureka," she said, pleased at how the word rolled off her tongue in the midst of her inspiration.

She found her breakthrough on the twelfth day, though she wasn't sure how that happened.

It was somewhat an accident, you see.

Hati had walked into the igloo, expecting to spend the entire day assessing the wear-and-tear the carabao was sustaining. Sure enough, she'd made correct note of the wires, which needed replacing, and the inside surface, which needed polishing. There were a few loose gears that needed to be screwed back in and a couple of bolts that needed tightening.

She wrote everything down on her clipboard, then headed toward the desk. At this point, she knew where everything was. Whoever had lived in this makeshift igloo behind the junkyard was precise and open to sharing secrets. She wondered if the person had expected someone like her to go in and help maintain the carabao. She wondered—only briefly—if the person would ever come back.

"First, the wires," Hati murmured, rummaging through the box of fuses. She pulled a few yellow wires out and inspected the ends. Confident that they would work, she headed toward the gazebo with wires and pliers in hand, ready to make the changes.

She continued to work until all she had left to do was return all the tools to their regular places. She bounded toward the workshop desk but didn't quite make it. Hati had built too much momentum with her speedy start and walked straight into one of the gazebo's columns. The collision caused her to fall flat onto the floor, her free hand smacking into the pillar, dislodging one of the long wires that had been tangled around it. The wire turned out to be a long tube that spewed out gas. Gas that was most definitely *not* oxygen.

Hati coughed, scrambled up. She covered her nose, the fumes getting absolutely everywhere. She almost panicked, then remembered this was an igloo, and if she didn't open the workshop hatch above, she'd suffocate from the fumes.

The door, she thought. She had to open the door first.

She ran to the door and pushed it open. When fresh air came in, she gasped with relief, though for only a short time. There was still the matter of the gas and the hatch above. She covered her nose again and looked up. Sure enough, there was a circular roof hatch that opened from above. Hati followed the sliver of rope that coiled around the hatch opening to one of the igloo's walls. When she found where the rope ended, she went toward it and pulled. In no time flat, the hatch released.

Whoosh!

Most of the gas moved upward, and already it was becoming easier to breathe inside the igloo. Now all Hati had to do was put a stopper in the gas tube.

Unless...

There was a reason the tube released gas. Perhaps there was a reason the gas was needed.

"Of course there is!" For the second time that week, Hati had her Eureka moment. "Silly Hati, it's what powers the carabao!"

It was what powered airships in the East. It was—until recently—what used to power the mechanical horses in Rizal. Nowadays, people used stone-fuel, but this particular carabao ran on volcanic gas.

So Hati poked and prodded the carabao until she saw that the buffalo's snout had an indentation in the middle. She pressed the snout in, and sure enough, an opening became visible, large enough to fit a single, familiar gas tube. Hati pulled the writhing tube from the floor and plugged it into the carabao's snout.

She waited a few minutes then released the gas tube again and re-wound it on the pillar. She found the button she'd accidentally pressed—which had released the gas in the first place—and turned it off, and then she checked the carabao.

It began to move.

At first, it was a slow movement, as though the clockwork mechanism inside wanted to test its working state. The carabao took a small, tentative step, then another, and then another. And finally, it reared its head and whirred.

"It worked!" Hati cried, clapping her hands together with joy. "The gas worked!"

The carabao knelt down, as though allowing Hati the chance to ride it. Hati hesitated, not knowing what to do in this situation. Was she *supposed* to ride the mechanical carabao? Was she supposed to refuse?

Before she could do anything, though, the carabao opened its mouth. From the slot within, a piece of paper emerged. Hati pulled it out and unfolded it and found that the handwriting was the same as that in the journal.

If you are reading this, congratulations! You are now the proud owner of one very quick and very sturdy clockwork carabao. I had hoped someone would find my little pet after I'd gone, and if you managed to get him working again, then I am sure he is in good hands.

Sadly, I could not take him where I went; I do not think floating cities would find any value in a racing carabao of this peculiar nature. However, I can tell you this about my creation: once you've refilled it with the fuel that it's lost, it can take you anywhere on the surface. It can go even farther away from Cebu City, should you find that the city is too stifling. I urge you to test its mettle; you will not find it wanting. Details of choosing direction and entering coordinates

*are found in my journal, which I assume you've also found. The map
is beneath the carabao's feet, just in the gazebo.*

Sure enough, when Hati looked, she found that the gazebo's
floor was indeed a map. She saw Cebu City, then the other
places that the carabao could possibly travel.

*Feel free to use my workshop for as long as you have need of it. I assure
you that I will not be coming back, and I can equally assure you that only
the truly mad and the truly inspired would wade through the back of a
junkyard just to reach this lovely place. You and my carabao are safe here.*

*Many thanks for your maintenance, and all the best in your ad-
ventures with my clockwork creation!*

- Z

Hati had to read the letter more than once. She had been
sure that the entire thing was just a trick of the light, and
maybe too much of what she'd wished for. Upon the third and
fourth time, however, she was beginning to think the whole
thing had been true—she was now the owner of a clockwork
racing carabao.

And she could go wherever she wanted on the surface.

This demanded a lot of thought. She wasn't even sure where
to go first. The northern part, where the isles were broken and
ravaged by volcanoes? Refugee Hills, where most of the farm-folk
lived under the protection of Cebu City's government? Or even
the south, where a skybridge would take her to northern Borneo?

The possibilities were endless. Hati's head swam.

Again, the carabao knelt, and this time the message was clear.

Hati climbed on and found that there were footholds and
handholds for her to keep herself from falling off the mechanical creature. Then, with a deep breath, she looked at the map
and found the place she wanted to see. She remembered the
notes in the back of the journal, that coordinates worked by
looking at latitude and longitude on the map, and she put the
numbers into the carabao's back. She held on tight.

The carabao ran.

Safe in the Dome

by Anne E. Johnson

Anne E. Johnson lives in Brooklyn and writes whatever her imagination conjures up. She studied music for a long time, so many of her stories and books include music in their plots. Strong female heroines, especially young girls, often drive her stories. As for why she loves making up stories for young readers? Well, maybe she never grew up. Learn more about Anne on her website, AnneEJohnson.com.

Through the top of the dome, the clouds always looked like they blended together. Ossri closed her single eye and tried to imagine each cloud individually. Somebody could see clouds that way. She was sure of it. Somebody outside the dome.

She didn't dare say that thought out loud. One time she had mentioned the Outworld—land, air, life beyond their sustaining shelter. Her father became so stressed, the webbing under his arms turned gray and cracked.

"Never, never," Mother had said, "never even *think* of what's out there."

"Up there," Ossri had answered, waving her webbed fingers at the dome's highest panes of tempered glass. "I want to know what is above us."

Her mother, her father, her teacher, her priest—all had gathered around her, chanting, "Thoughts low and inside.

Flourish in the maternal dome. All we need, all we want is inside the dome."

It was a prayer Ossri's people, the Sirol, said every day, morning and night. The Sirol species had been chanting these words since Ossri's grandparents were babies, ever since the poison darkness rolled over the eastern hemisphere of the planet Nurissa.

Those few who did not die built a huge dome to sustain and protect the Sirol for the coming generations. "And we live facing forward," the preacher loved to say when she noticed Ossri's eye gazing curiously at the dome's panels. Or when she was exploring her own webbing, wondering what it might be for. "We do not think of the Before Days."

And then there was the bony hook at the end of each finger and toe. Those seemed important, strong enough and shaped right to tear open the side of a building. But dome laws made it illegal to use the hooks for anything at all. Custom said they should be sanded down, or everyone said you looked sloppy.

Most mysterious of all were the urges Ossri felt when she looked up. Her muscles twitched in her arms and legs, as if they longed to squirm free from her body. And the ends of her fingers, the base of her claws ached and tingled. When she felt this discomfort, Ossri hurried to be by herself, not an easy thing in the overcrowded dome. And when she was sure nobody could see her, she did the unthinkable: Ossri climbed.

This was one of those rare opportunities. When her mother's back was turned, she had slipped from her cube-shaped house of dark red glass. Ossri had to hurry. There wasn't much time before her mother would send a group of neighbors to find her. Or maybe someone in the Seventh Zone would see her try to climb the dome wall. Red glass houses afforded only a little privacy, whether looking in or looking out. Still, it was worth the risk—she had been caught only twice, although she had climbed a dozen times.

Confident and excited, Ossri hooked the middle claws of each hand onto the ridge at the top of the lowest dome panel. Only those two finger hooks and two toe claws did she dare to keep a bit longer than folks thought was polite. While she climbed, the longer, thicker hooks kept her from falling. She could only imagine how quickly and surely she could move with all twenty-four hooks in their natural state.

As she pulled herself from one panel to the next, Ossri pressed her flat face against the slightly curved glass. The dome wall was clear, but the panels so thick they made everything outside look like dark blobs and swirls. Ossri's eye swept slowly left and right, never blinking. For just a moment, something blackish appeared and moved; a few blurry dots broke through the usual fog of nothingness. And then the dots were gone.

Ossri rested her forehead against the panel while she tried to get a better grip on its frame. She was three body lengths above the dome floor, the same distance she'd always climbed in the past. This time, her disappointment turned to frustration. With a determined growl of "higher!" she lifted her head and reached for the frame of the panel above. Her longest right claw slid in and out of the groove between panes.

Since she hadn't climbed to that level before, Ossri could only assume that frame was built the same as the lower ones. She just couldn't get a grip. The claw found a shallow notch. Not well enough to hold Ossri's weight and pull her up. But she couldn't figure out how to climb down, either.

One arm up, one down, feet splayed far apart on a lower frame, Ossri pondered: was it better to fall while going up or going down? Downward might hurt less, as it was closer to the floor. On the other hand, going up would be better for her spirit, she reasoned, since at least she would have tried to keep going. So, with a snort of effort, she released her left hand and right foot, trusting in her blind instincts to find grooves to hang onto. With a satisfying click, her claw found a perch. She'd made it!

That same moment, she heard her father's voice below her. "We already looked on Second Ring Street. She can't have vanished into thin air." Ossri's muscles tensed. Both hands popped loose from the frame. She scrabbled madly at the glass, but there was no way to hang on. Screaming, arms flailing, she fell backward.

She did not plunge straight down. Air caught the webbing under her arms and between her fingers. Ossri floated. As her father and some Peacekeepers rounded the corner, she skated to a bumpy stop on the synthetic street pavement.

"Ossri! There she is! Darling, are you all right?" Her father scurried to her side, gathering her up in his arms. "Are you hurt?"

With her eye still glued to the top of the dome, she said, "I'm fine," and let the Peacekeepers help her to her feet.

"Please tell me what happened," said her father.

She stretched out her fingers, now understanding the purpose of the skin stretched between them. "I fell," she said. But she did not add the more important part of her answer: "I almost flew."

It wasn't actually a prison cell, but it might as well have been. From the room where she'd been grounded, Ossri could not see the sky. Her own bedroom was at the top of the family's house, and on her name dedication day when she was little, her aunt had replaced one of the red panels with clear glass. "Wanna see up," little Ossri always used to say, or so her parents claimed.

No wonder, then, that they used distance from the sky to punish her. It was her big brother's room. Layer upon layer of red building glass above her left Ossri in the dark.

Her mother swept her hand across the sensor panel, raising the artificial light. "There, that's better," Mother said from the doorway. "Your father and I want you to stay down here and think about how dangerous climbing is. Can you tell me why climbing is a bad idea?"

Ossri studied the webbing under her right arm as she mumbled an answer. "I could fall. Hurt myself. Hurt someone else. Break the dome wall. Break somebody's house." She was absolutely sure she couldn't possibly do those last two things, but her mother expected them to be on the list.

"Yes, and what else, Ossri?"

It was painful to force the words out. "It makes me look like an irresponsible citizen."

"It certainly does."

When Ossri curled up on her brother's bed, back to the door, her mother's voice softened. "I know you don't believe me right now, sweetheart, but the way we behave in the dome really matters. It's how the Sirol species will keep going. Sometimes fitting in is the only way to survive."

Ossri dug a claw into the mattress of silicon beads. "Yeah. Okay. Whatever." Glancing up, she compared her mother's blunted, smoothed finger hooks to her own rough, overgrown ones. She thought words she did not say: "We are not surviving. We're pretending to be some other species. What's the point?"

Her parents had grounded her for seven days. When that was over, they followed her everywhere—her parents, neighbors, not to mention the Peacekeepers. She had to behave perfectly all the time and never even glance at the dome ceiling.

One day, when her father watched her from down the block, she struck up a conversation with a neighbor. This was not just any neighbor, but an Old One, one of the handful still alive who had breathed air outside the dome. Selless sat in front of his building every day, staring forward. He had always been kind to Ossri, although these days he didn't say much to anyone.

"Why don't they want me to climb?" she whispered to Selless, first making sure her father was still beyond hearing. "We have hooks and webbing to help us climb. The Sirols are supposed to be climbers, right? You must remember from the

Before Days." A shudder of shame chilled Ossri's skin when she broached the forbidden topic.

But her gamble paid off. Selless moved his eye steadily to her face. "I remember the Before Days." He spoke so softly, she could barely hear him. "I call them Real Life Days." He waved his hand around, fingers splayed so their webbing stretched out. "This. This is not my life. My real life is in the past."

Ossri's curiosity burned. She didn't care who heard her now. "The webbing, it—"

"Keeps us from falling when we climb."

"Climb! I knew it! Where did we used to climb?"

"Everywhere." The Old One opened his gnarled arms. The curtain of underarm webbing was ragged and torn, as if it had been used for its true purpose for many years. "We had tall buildings with hand-holds on the outside."

"Wow! How high could you climb?"

"Me? Well, it was a matter of pride, wasn't it? Seven stories. See?" Selless angled his wide, flat face so he could squint straight up. "I was one of the best. That's why they asked me to work on the ceiling."

"You made the dome ceiling?!" Ossri could hardly breathe. "How can I get up there?"

The most mysterious gleam shown from Selless' eye. "Climb and climb and climb some more. And when you get up there, look around carefully. I've left you a hidden gift."

"For me?"

"Well, for your generation. It's a gift for the future to find when you and the world are ready. Whoops, they're coming." Suddenly his eye lost focus and his jaw went to slack.

Before Ossri could ask if he was all right, her father spoke behind her. "Are you two done chatting? We have shopping to do, Ossri."

She studied his face and manner—he had not overheard her

unthinkable conversation. "I'm ready, Father." She turned to Selless and tried to make her innocent words hold a message: "I enjoyed talking to you, sir."

That scheming glint flashed across his face again for just a moment.

If Ossri had been fascinated by the sky before, now she was completely obsessed. Every thought was about how she could reach the dome's top to find the mysterious gift Selless had hidden there. She invented a hundred plans to climb the outer wall, or climb buildings and then jump to the wall. She even thought of convincing the Mayor to raise a new building that reached all the way to the top. But even ambitious Ossri had to admit her plans were only dreams.

She was one little Sirol girl who had only climbed to a height of three panels. No way she'd ever make it up twenty panels—she'd counted many times—to the top. At least, not without help. And she knew just who to ask.

"Mother?" Ossri shuffled through the red-lit rooms of her family's living unit. "Mother?"

"I'm here, Ossri." Mother sat in her office, surrounded by hologram plans of the dome's sewage system. "I'm in the middle of a project for work, sweetheart. What's up?"

"May I go visit Selless, please? He was so nice to me when we talked a few days ago. Maybe I could keep him company." She thought fast. "I could clean his living unit. Heat up his meal portion this afternoon. Would that be all right? You look upset, Mother. Aren't you glad I want to spend time with an Old One?"

Her mother pulled away from the hologram projector and stretched out her arms. Light from the 3-D images glowed through her webbing. "Selless died yesterday, Ossri."

"What?" Ossri's skin tingled.

"He lived longer than most. Did you know that he helped to build our dome?"

Ossri did know that. But she wished she'd also known Selless was so near the end. How many questions she would have asked! Without looking at her mother, she ran from the building.

"Don't get in trouble, Ossri!" her mother called.

In minutes, she was at Selless' door, arguing with a Peacekeeper. "He told me I could look through his stuff," she said. "He said he left something for me, but he never got a chance to give it to me." She was hoping to rummage around, maybe find clues about the secret in the ceiling.

The Peacekeeper angled her eye suspiciously. "What did he leave you?"

"I... I don't know. Can I just look for it? I'll know it when I see it."

Barring the door with her body, the officer replied, "I've never seen so much stuff as this Old One had. His piles of Before Days belongings have no place in the dome's future. You know that. It all must be destroyed. Now, go home."

Furious and frustrated, Ossri stormed off. She headed straight for her favorite climbing spot in the Seventh Zone. And if someone saw her and she got in trouble? It didn't matter today. Climbing was all she could think of. "I'll go up and up, and they won't be able to reach me." The thought prodded her to pick up her pace.

Soon, she was charging through the alleyway that led to the wall. But it wasn't deserted as usual. Dozens of citizens and Peacekeepers crowded the area. By pushing to the front of the group, Ossri found many of them had their faces pressed to the wall's lowest panels.

"The glass is too thick to see anything," a Peacekeeper said.

"I can kind of see shadows moving," said a citizen, his fingers pressing against the pane. "Someone is definitely out there."

"Or some*thing*," a young guy said. "There's a reason we're not supposed to communicate with the Outworld. It's dangerous."

"They told us in school that everyone out there was dead," somebody said. "That nothing could live."

"Then what kind of monsters are these, lurking around our safe dome?"

Ossri could not keep silent. "There's someone out there? What if they're not monsters? Maybe they're just people who need help!" The group turned to stare at her. "We have to at least find out if they're okay."

"You." One of the Peacekeepers who had found her when she fell now grabbed her shoulder.

"I didn't do anything, officer, I was just saying—"

"You know about the dome wall."

"Well, sort of."

"How do we open it?"

"You can't," someone shouted. "Why ask some little girl? I'm an engineer, and I'm telling you that nothing can get in or out of the dome. Not without destroying it."

Many folks gasped. Someone shouted, "Leave them outside, whoever they are. Let us stay safe."

Blobs of darkness moved outside the glass. One seemed to grow before landing with a dull *thud* against the outside of the panel.

"We have to help them." Ossri tried to say it as her mother would, clear and strong. "And I think I know how." She craned her neck to look at the top of the dome, and pointed. "There's an answer up there."

Once she had convinced the Peacekeepers to try to reach the ceiling, the project had to be organized. "We'll need cable. And a net." Essorg, the dome's Mayor, shot Ossri a desperate look. "What else will we need for... for *climbing*?" His face wrinkled when he said that word.

"Nothing. We just climb." Ossri then corrected herself.

"Hooks. Your own hooks. Whoever has the longest finger and toe claws will probably climb best."

Someone called out, "It's a crazy plan." Several others murmured agreement.

Another *thump* against the dome wall prompted the mayor to say, "There may be living beings outside. We climb." Once again, he addressed Ossri with a worried tone. "Exactly what did the Old One tell you?"

"Selless said there was a gift, a surprise for the future. And I would find it if I climbed all the way up."

Her father, who would not let go of her hand, asked, "How did the Old Ones build the dome anyway? How did they get up so high?"

"Like this. Watch." With a reassuring smile, Ossri pulled from his grip and ran to her favorite climbing spot. She took a deep breath, focused her mind, spread her webbing, and slid her finger hooks into the top of the first panel. She pulled her legs up. Her arms reached for the second panel. Her legs followed. Third panel. This time she caught the groove securely. The fourth panel was a bigger challenge—her muscles complained a little.

She paused before trying the fifth panel. "Don't look down," she told herself. Of course, her eye immediately sought the ground. The view from above did not make her frightened or dizzy. It felt natural. She grabbed the top of the sixth panel. Her legs shook, but she found a place to hook her claws. Almost a third of the way up now! That thought helped her climb the seventh panel.

Now her limbs were heavy as glass. She didn't have the strength to climb any higher.

"Come on, Ossri, you're doing great."

"You can do it, Ossri!"

The voices flooding from below stirred her heart but weren't enough to charge up her muscles.

"Leslo!" Her father shouted her mother's name. "Leslo, what are you doing?" When Ossri dared to glance down, her surprise nearly made her let go. Her mother's fear-widened eye stared up at her from the second panel.

"No, mother! Go back down. I can do it."

Mother kicked up her leg, trying to hook her foot into the same groove where her hands had a weak grip.

"You'll flip upside down, Mother. I've got this. Just wait there." With no more thought for how tired she was, Ossri climbed. In her mind blazed a clear image of sky and clouds. Some source of energy deep inside her drove her upward. She felt like she weighed nothing, like the air was lifting her.

And she realized it was true. A stretching sensation tickled her underarm webbing. Somehow the air currents in the upper half of the dome were holding her, pushing her toward her goal. "Woo hoo!" she hollered, thrilled right down to her center. "Look at me. I am a Sirol, and I'm climbing."

Glancing down, Ossri got quite a shock. Everyone looked tiny. Her view of the red glass buildings showed their roof panels. The streets might have been painted by a child's finger. Without knowing it, Ossri had reached the dome's apex.

And she wasn't scared. It felt like the right place to be. Her first instinct was to press her face against the highest pane, to find out if she could see the sky. Really see it. Fear bubbled up, but Ossri ignored it and reached one arm out at an angle. The air supported her webbing, and she easily touched the frame of the topmost panel. On its edge was a latch. A *latch*. Latches opened things.

Gasping, Ossri pulled back. Her whole life, she'd been taught that the dome must stay sealed forever. All she had to do now was release the latch and push that window up. Her fingers trembled as they wrapped around the handle. "This is some gift, Selless," she said out loud, hoping the Old One's spirit could hear. "I'll either kill everyone inside, or I'll set us all free. How am I supposed to decide if I should open it?"

Ossri closed her eye and listened—for what, she wasn't sure. The rush of air was all she heard at first. Then her memory played back Selless' words: "It's a gift for the future to find when you and the world are ready."

Her eye popped open. "I found it. That means we are ready." Taking a huge breath for courage, Ossri pull down the metal tongue holding the latch closed. Robotic hinges on the other side of the panel caused the glass to rise automatically. Screams ringing upward from the ground told Ossri that everyone was paying attention. She did not look down. Instead she climbed up. Up and out.

She easily fit through the large opening. The air was cold. She had never felt cold air. The air smelled sweet, and bitter, and metallic, and like plants. So many scents all at once! In every direction, the land was red and gray. Small, scrubby bushes like the ones planted along streets in the dome grew in unorganized clumps. There was wreckage of buildings, a roadway of water running through a field of mud, and a place where the land was piled high like a solid dome. There were just too many things for her greedy eye to take in.

But best of all was the sight on the ground near the dome. A group of ten or so Sirols waved and shouted. Alive in the Outworld. "Come and join us," called one of them. "It's perfectly safe."

And that, Ossri knew, was the Old One's real gift.

Far From Home

by Dawn Vogel

Dawn Vogel has written and edited both fiction and nonfiction. Her academic background is in history, so it's not surprising that much of her fiction is set in earlier times. By day, she edits reports for historians and archaeologists. In her alleged spare time, she runs a craft business, helps edit *Mad Scientist Journal*, and tries to find time for writing. Her first novel, *Brass and Glass: The Cask of Cranglimmering*, was published by Razorgirl Press in 2017. She lives in Seattle with her awesome husband (and fellow author), Jeremy Zimmerman, and their herd of cats. Visit her at http://historythatneverwas.com.

There's somebody dragging something down the hallway outside of our apartment. I hear it all the time. Mom says it's old Mrs. Pears from down the hall, taking her laundry to the lift.

"Why would someone put their laundry in the lift?" I ask, my nose wrinkling. We do our laundry in our apartment. The clotheslines draped with sheets make a maze that Michi and I can play in.

"Mrs. Pears is old," Mom says.

"Older than Gran-Gran?" Gran-Gran is Mom's great-great-aunt. She lives with us at Zenith Arcology because we have a big apartment with three bedrooms, and she doesn't have any children to take care of her. When Mom is as old as Gran-Gran, my children and grandchildren and I will all take care of

her, because I'm going to have a big, fancy house and people to
wash my laundry and dry it and fold it, too.

"Not quite as old as Gran-Gran," Mom replies, "but she
does things the way people did when she was young."

Michi's family lives in an apartment smaller than ours. I
sometimes think that's why she spends so much time visiting
me. She has to share a room with two sisters. I have a bunk bed
in my room only because it's built into the unit. Michi always
takes the top bunk when she stays over. She says she sleeps on
the top bunk at home, but at home, she has to share it with
one of her sisters. Sometimes she tells me she can't sleep unless
I sleep on the top bunk, too. Mostly, though, she tells me to
stay in my own bed.

We're in my room, playing with dolls, when we hear the
dragging sound.

"What is that?" Michi asks, her eyes wide.

"Mrs. Pears is taking her laundry to the lift."

Michi narrows her eyes. "That doesn't sound like someone
dragging laundry down the hall."

"Mom says that's what it is."

"I don't believe it. I dare you to go look."

"I double dare you to come with me," I retort. It's easier to
double dare than to admit I'm afraid Michi might be right.
It does sound strange today. And Mrs. Pears doesn't normally
take her laundry to the lift during the week.

"Fine," Michi says, flipping her perfect curls over her
shoulder.

We tiptoe out of my room and past Gran-Gran, who is
watching her "stories." When Michi doesn't come over after
school, sometimes I watch them with Gran-Gran. But it's mostly about people fighting and then making up and sometimes
faking their death. She likes the ones with only human actors
the best, but sometimes we watch one with alien actors, too.

I don't understand why she thinks they're interesting, but I know we shouldn't bother her while they're on.

By the time we get into the hallway, the lift doors are already closing. It's definitely not Mrs. Pears—or at least it's not her standing in the lift. But there's something on the floor, at the feet of whoever it is, that looks an awful lot like what I imagine Mrs. Pears would look like if she had fallen down.

Michi makes a strangled sound behind me, and I turn around before I get a good look at the standing person. "What is it?"

"I let the door close! I'm sorry, Ayano."

I shrug. "It's okay. Gran-Gran can let us back in." I knock on the door to the apartment.

We wait for at least a minute, but Gran-Gran doesn't answer. I knock again, but there's still no response. We could go downstairs and outside and buzz the apartment from there, but Mom doesn't like for me to go outside without my mask. The air is bad outside, all gray and thick.

The lift at the end of the hall dings, and we both turn, eyes wide.

No one is there.

I grab Michi's hand and move toward the lift.

"What are you doing?" Michi wails.

"We should go see who took Mrs. Pears!"

"No, we don't even know if that was Mrs. Pears. We should go back inside."

I turn and glare at her. "I double dared you. Are you going to wimp out?"

When I put it that way, she has no choice. She has to follow me.

We hurry into the lift.

"What floor?" she asks, her fingers hovering over the buttons.

That's when I freeze. I have no idea where the person went. But I make myself think. I poke my head out of the lift. The down arrow is lit. "They must have pressed both buttons. So we go down first, and count how long it takes us to go down and back up. Then we should be able to figure out how many floors they went up."

Michi narrows her eyes at me, but she pushes the "L" button anyway. "You're too smart sometimes, Ayano."

"It's just logic," I mumble, as I count the seconds in the back of my mind. "Fifteen."

"Fifteen what? Fifteenth floor?"

Now I have to remember how long it took before the elevator came back. Maybe a minute? Maybe two? The fifteenth floor seems possible. "Sure, let's start there."

"I thought you would know," Michi says, jabbing at the button.

I shrug. "Do you know about the vents?"

Michi shakes her head.

"I'll show you."

The lift slides up to the fifteenth floor, and we step out. I strain my hearing, listening for any sign of someone still dragging something in the halls. But it's quiet, except for the faint noises that come from behind the doors of the other apartments. Children are home from school, and some parents are home from work, and it's nearing time for dinner. My stomach growls, and I poke at it to hush it.

I lead Michi down the corridor to a spot where there's a grated metal cover on the wall. In some parts of the building, they've still got the screws that hold them in place. But after a lot of the screws disappeared, they reattached most of the covers with little clips. I fumble along the side of the cover until I find the place where it's clipped in, and I release it. My other hand shoots out to catch the grate before it clatters to the floor.

It's dark inside the vent, and Michi's eyes go wide. "Where does that go?"

"Anywhere," I whisper. I put my finger over my lips. "But so does the sound of our voices. You have to be quiet if you want to come with me."

"Where are we going?" she whispers.

Before I answer, there's a thumping down the hall. It's not like normal knocking. It's rhythmic, a pattern. I nudge the cover back over the vent and run down the hallway on my tiptoes. I pause at the corner, back to the wall, and then peek.

It's the person from the lift, with a big bag on the floor, and they're drumming on the door with both hands. I can't see into the bag, but I swear it moves. I clap my hand over my mouth to stifle a gasp and run back to Michi.

"1524," I whisper.

Michi chews on her lip, and I know before she says anything that she's going to try to get me to change my mind.

So I don't let her. "Double dare."

"I know, Ayano, but it... what if...? I think we should go back up to your apartment and knock until Gran-Gran lets us in, and then we can call the security force to go find out what they were dragging."

I cross my arms over my chest. "I'm going to go spy on them. You can wait here if you want to, or you could go home."

Michi hesitates, the conflict clear on her face. She doesn't want to go home. I don't know if she'd actually wait for me here or not. But it doesn't matter. "Okay, I'll come with you."

I open up the cover again and usher Michi in first. Then I climb in, pulling the grate closed behind me.

Michi whimpers when I do.

"It's easier to open from the inside," I assure her.

The ventilation system isn't meant for two little girls to move around much inside, but it's almost big enough for us to crawl comfortably. Even if it wasn't, I'm too focused on making the right turns to get us to 1524. Everything in the whole building is connected to the ventilation system. It's just a matter of being able to follow the passageways instead of the hallways.

And watching out for the drops.

"Michi, up here you're going to have to stretch out and go across a hole. Don't look down."

I show her what needs to be done. It's easy for me. I've done it a million times before. But when I turn back to look at her, her face has faded to the palest brown I've ever seen it.

She shakes her head. "What if I fall?"

"You won't fall. Come over here and take my hand."

"Ayano, I don't want to," Michi says. Tears threaten to spill from her eyes. "You go find out what's happening. I'll wait here."

"You'll get scared if you wait here by yourself, Michi. The system will turn on, and it will get windy right here." I hesitate for a moment. I don't want to scare her too much, but what I'm about to tell her is true. I drop my voice to a loud whisper. "There are things in the system that move when it turns on."

She scoots away from the hole, shaking her head. "I'm going home."

Below, there's a rumble. The system is turning on. "You can't, Michi. Come on!" A thought occurs to me. "If you come with me, I'll tell everyone at school that you're braver than me."

I don't feel bad about manipulating Michi. She does it all the time to me.

And it works. She inches closer to the edge of the drop and lays flat on her belly, reaching her arms across the chasm. She hooks the tips of her fingers under the seam and pulls herself closer to me. As soon as I'm able, I grab her under her arms. Her armpits are wet and clammy, but I ignore that and help her across.

With Michi across, I continue. She's not likely to stop now. It only takes a few more turns, and we are looking through a grate into 1524.

The person we saw earlier is there, taking off his jacket. His back is to us, and when he turns around, I realize he's not a person after all.

Or, rather, he's not a human person. He's covered in red, bumpy skin with ridges on his neck that move up and down when he speaks. "Mother, I have my bag full," he says. His voice is throaty, but he speaks Creole English as well as I do.

I've seen aliens before, but never in Zenith Arcology. Mom talks about the aliens she sees at work like they all live somewhere else. Like they have their own arcologies. But Gran-Gran sometimes talks about how there are too many aliens coming here. I thought she just meant to Earth, but maybe she meant to Zenith Arcology.

I'm still processing coming this close to an alien when Michi tugs on my sleeve. "Can they see us?" she asks, her voice barely loud enough for me to hear.

"I don't think so," I reply.

At that, Michi inches closer to the grate, shouldering me to the side of the ventilation system. I bump against it, and the metal shudders, though the sound of the air rushing past us muffles the sound.

Another alien joins the first, taller and wider than he is, but with the same skin and neck ridges. This one wears a housedress like Gran-Gran's. She opens the bag the other alien was dragging. The sound that comes out of her mouth is somewhere between a cough and a sneeze. "Why does it smell so awful?" she asks.

"I don't know, Mother."

"They must have Mrs. Pears' body in that bag," Michi whispers. "We should go find the security force." She turns to crawl away and bangs her shoe against the grate.

This time, the air rushing through the system is not enough to mask the noise we make.

"What was that?" the female alien asks, her voice taking on a sharp tone like the one Mom uses when I'm in trouble.

I don't wait to find out what the one who calls her Mother says in response. I scramble backward and turn around once I've passed Michi.

Without warning, the light from 1524 blinks out. All the lights that shine through the other grates in the ventilation system follow suit. The air stops blowing past us.

"Grid off," I say, sitting back on my feet. There's no sense in crawling around in the dark. I know how to find the drop if I have to, but even if the aliens wanted to, they can't come after us in the dark.

The grate from 1524 scrapes against its frame.

I begin to sweat. Some aliens can see in the dark. I don't know what these aliens are, but they must be that kind.

"Crawl," I hiss toward Michi, or the place I saw her last. A hand lands on my ankle, and I almost scream. "Michi?"

"It's me," she whispers. "Ayano, how do we get back?"

"Grid off doesn't last long—" I trail off when the first thump against the metal of the ventilation tunnel comes.

It's behind us. It's one of the aliens. Maybe both.

"Hold on!" I don't worry about keeping quiet any more. I crawl forward, and Michi follows, her hand clenching my ankle so tightly that I worry about my foot falling off.

I'm sure I know the way back to where we came in. Take a right before the drop, then across, then two lefts and two rights.

Or is it two rights before the drop?

In my panic to get away from the alien, I can't remember. I lose track of where we've turned. I feel along the walls, hoping to find a way to go left or right, up or down.

I don't realize my mistake until the ground falls out from under me.

I fall only a foot, but it seems like more when Michi lands atop me. We are a tangled mess of limbs when the grid off ends.

Towering above us is the alien mother.

She shrieks, and there's a scraping sound behind us as the other alien emerges from the ventilation system.

"Don't kill us!" Michi cries, scrambling to her feet. She tries to pull me up with her, but all I can do is stare at the ridges on the alien mother's neck. They're fluttering. I think that means she's angry. I want to turn around and see if the other alien's neck ridges are fluttering, too, but I can't move, in spite of Michi tugging my arm.

"We will not kill you," the alien mother says, and her voice is calm. "What are you doing here?"

Michi thrusts a finger forward, glaring at the alien mother. "What are you doing with Mrs. Pears?"

The alien mother frowns. "We are doing her laundry."

Michi looks at me, mouth agape. For once in her life, she doesn't know what to say. But I have questions.

"Why are you doing her laundry?" I ask, standing up as I do. "She takes her laundry in the lift, to wash somewhere else."

The alien mother shakes her head. "She has grown too old to do that. My son saw her struggling with her bag and offered to help. So now we will do her laundry." Her eyes narrow. "What were you doing in the ventilation system?"

"We were afraid something bad had happened to Mrs. Pears, and we wanted to make sure she was okay," I say.

Beside me, Michi nods. "It didn't sound like a laundry bag from inside Ayano's apartment."

"No, I suppose not," the alien mother says. "I have another question for you. How do you make human laundry not smell bad?"

I frown. "I don't know. How do you make your laundry not smell bad?" I ask.

She draws herself up to her full height, the top of her bald head nearly touching the ceiling. "Our laundry does not stink. Human laundry smells different."

I sniff at the air and realize that their apartment smells different from ours. Sometimes our apartment smells like whatever Mom is cooking, and other times, it smells like Gran-Gran's breath. The aliens' apartment smells like nothing at all—almost like there's not air or anything. It doesn't make much sense to me, but I guess it's just one of the ways we're different from them.

"My mother uses soap. Scented soap?" I squeak.

"Scented? Ah, yes, to have a smell. Scented with what?" she asks, relaxing her stance.

I shrug. "My mother uses lavender-scented soap. I've never seen a lavender, but I guess it's purple. At least that's what color the bottle is."

The alien mother nods. "Would you acquire some of this scented soap for me? In exchange for me not telling your mother that you were in the ventilation system?"

I blush but nod.

"Good." She gestures at the door. "Come back with it right away."

I grab Michi's hand and drag her out into the hallway.

She blinks at me. "Are we helping aliens do Mrs. Pears' laundry now?"

I shrug. "Why not?"

Michi considers for a moment, but then nods. "Sure, why not?"

When we get back down to my apartment, Mom is at the door, letting herself in. She watches us leave the lift. "What are you girls doing in the lift? Not playing around again, I hope?"

"We're helping the neighbors upstairs with Mrs. Pears' laundry," I say. "She won't be dragging it to the lift anymore. But I guess someone else will be. They asked if they could borrow some detergent."

The Shepherd's Way
by Barbara Webb Sinopoli

Barbara Webb Sinopoli has had a lifelong passion for the natural world. A degree in geology prepared her for a variety of jobs, including geophysicist, gardener, florist, and finally, sheep farmer. Sinopoli imported and raised Icelandic sheep for over twenty years. Now retired from farming, Sinopoli lives in the Berkshires with her husband where she loves to cook, garden, and travel to exotic places to visit her children.

Zsenala squinted up into the clear sky and wiped a trickle of sweat out of her eyes. All three suns blazed down; yellow Sol, Ruthur the red giant, and tiny blue Blarta.

The hottest day of the year, I should be inside the cool house, not outside shearing these poor creatures, Zsenala grumbled to herself. *But when the fleece collector for the sah'Korloo says she's coming for the tithe, then you go outside and shear, even if it is AllSuns.*

Zsenala reached for Lalu, the most ill-tempered tokka on the farm, whose emerald green fleece was earmarked for the tithe. *And when your baba has slipped away to join the resistance, leaving your family without money for the shearer, then you do it yourself,* Zsenala thought with a sigh as she dragged the kicking animal onto the shearing platform.

Her baba said Lalu had the sweetest, silkiest fleece on the farm and maybe in the whole da'Zuna clan. He should know—

his family had been raising tokka since before they settled by the cliffs generations ago.

Lalu thrashed suddenly, almost escaping Zsenala's grasp. "Oh, no you don't!" she said. With a tokka's sharp horns, a smart shepherd never let go.

"Zse-zse!" Zsenala's eight-year-old brother shouted as he pelted across the dusty yard.

"Zin, can't you see I'm busy?" Zsenala said as she stood to stretch her back, still holding Lalu tightly. It was so unfair that she'd been left in charge of shearing *and* Zintan. Although tall for her age, Zsenala was still two months shy of her fourteenth birthday and the Gathering ceremony. "This had better be good."

"It is! There's someone here!"

"Who? Who's here?"

"That's what's so exciting—it's no one we know!"

"But someone from the clan, right?" Zsenala asked sharply. "They're wearing our colors?" Strangers were rare in their corner of the territory, and with both Baba and Momee away, Zsenala's heart sank with worry.

Zintan's face fell. "Well, yes, but she's got a funny gold braid on her sleeve."

"A governor!" Zsenala dropped Lalu's horns and quickly stepped away. The green tokka leapt up, swinging her horns at Zsenala, and leapt out of the shearing pen in a single bound.

"Why didn't you say so?!" Zsenala hissed as she untucked her shift from her sash. She grabbed her robe from the wall and hurried up the farm road, brushing the dust from her hands. Zintan trailed behind. "I hope you offered her a cool drink?" Zsenala asked nervously.

As they approached the front yard, Zsenala saw that the visitor's back was facing them, so she stopped and took a deep breath. She was trying to remember, *how did Momee address the governor in the marketplace that day?*

"Madame Governor—" She breathed a sigh of relief when the visitor turned with a calm smile.

"Zsenala, you're looking well."

Like Zsenala and her family, the governor had the coloring of their clan—skin like warm sandstone, rich maroon hair, and eyes the purple of the spring flowers that bloomed along the cliffs.

"Thank you, Madame Governor," Zsenala said, nervously pulling at her headscarf. She wondered how the governor knew her name.

"You're approaching your Gathering in a few months, is that right?"

"Yes, Madame, two months."

"Well, with a number of our adults away just now, it will be good to have you join us. Although, growing up on a farm, I see you already carry many adult responsibilities," she said with a nod towards Zsenala's work clothes.

Zsenala swept nervously at the dust on her robe.

"Please—" The governor held up her hand. "I know I'm interrupting. I had come to speak with your momee, Ba' Rozu, but your brother tells me she's away from home."

"Yes, she's been called to a birth across the valley. A young mother with twins, so she'll be gone for a day, or maybe two. And of course, Baba..." Zsenala trailed off. She suddenly couldn't remember what Momee had told her to say about his absence from the farm.

"Yes, of course, I heard your baba was helping at the Kala farm after the incident there..." She stopped and glanced down at Zintan. "So I realize you already carry many burdens on your shoulders."

"Yes, Madame Governor."

There was a long pause. Zsenala felt the governor was waiting for something— but what? Was there some protocol Zsenala had forgotten?

"Would you like to come in for a cool drink, Madame Governor?"

"Just 'Madame' is fine, Zsenala. And no, thank you. Your brother has already politely offered, and I have already politely declined. So we have both done our duties."

Then what are you waiting for? What do you want?

Zsenala almost missed the governor's fleeting glance to Zintan and back.

Ah.

"Zintan," Zsenala said, ruffling her brother's hair, "I left Lalu's fleece on the shearing floor, and we'll need it for the tithe. Can you go gather it up? And please feed the chikchiks while you're there."

Zintan glared at her. He knew he was being shooed away, but he also knew better than to argue.

Zsenala waited until he was out of earshot. "Madame Governor, Zintan won't give us much time alone, and it's clear you've come for a reason." Her heart pounded at speaking so frankly to a governor, but Baba always said it was honorable to speak truth on behalf of her clan.

The governor smiled. "I see you are indeed your baba's daughter. Yes, I have come for a specific reason, I—"

She stopped suddenly, turning to look toward the desert. Zsenala heard it, too, a low whining hum that could mean only one thing; a sah'Korloo sand hover was approaching.

The governor's hand shot out and tightly gripped Zsenala's arm. Her voice dropped to a hiss. "Zsenala, listen to me—"

Zsenala's heart skipped a beat at the look on the governor's face.

"The sah'Korloo are here for more than our wool," the governor said. "They've come to our planet to steal our genetics. Our suns' radiation is constantly mutating our genes, and yet we thrive. And the sah'Korloo want to know how. Their own planet is poisoned, and their people are dying, and they think we have the cure, so they're stealing our people and—"

"Wait! What are you saying?" Zsenala interrupted. She stepped back, her palms outstretched.

"No time—" the governor muttered. She leaned down and removed something from her eye. Then she straightened and looked right at Zsenala.

Zsenala gasped. Instead of their clan's friendly purple, the governor's eye now shone a brilliant yellow. The governor put her fingers to her eye again and suddenly the purple was back.

"It's a contact, Zsenala. We've discovered that these new eye colors are markers for a cluster of genes that help us thrive here, even with all the radiation."

Zsenala's heart pounded and she felt sick to her stomach. Mutations? *Radiation?* What was she *talking* about?

The governor took a step closer. "There's a bounty on those of us expressing these genes, Zsenala. Sometimes they'll take the entire family. You *must* have noticed the disappearances—"

Zsenala felt herself nod.

The governor glanced over Zsenala's shoulder at the approaching hover. "We've been saying they've joined the resistance so no one will panic."

"What?!" Zsenala blurted out. "Did the sah'Korloo take my *baba?*"

The whine of the sand hover rose as it settled down onto the dusty yard behind them.

"Tell me about Baba!" Zsenala cried again, but the governor shook her head.

"Your momee was supposed to be here. A shipment's on its way, but you'll have to handle it."

"But—"

The governor's glance flickered over Zsenala's shoulder and then back, searching her face.

"Get them to the next station, Zsenala, your momee was

supposed to—" The insistent beeping of the sand hover stopped her. The governor stepped back, a pleasant calm settling on her face, the urgency slipping away.

Zsenala was afraid to look. But she knew the sand hover had landed, so she straightened her headscarf and turned to greet the visitors.

The plexidome on the hover folded back, and a sah'Korloo female stepped out onto the sand. Tall and thin, with long pewter hair hanging straight around her pale, narrow face, she stood and glanced around with disinterest, one hand twitching at her side. Her eyes were mirrored silver. Two males climbed out of the hover and stood silently behind her.

The sah'Korloo had come early for the tithe.

Zsenala took a deep breath and bowed her head, her right hand to her lips. The governor did the same, and they waited as Zintan ran up and hastily joined them. Then they straightened together.

No one spoke.

Zsenala shot a nervous glance to the governor, but she stayed silent, a bland smile on her face.

Of course, with Momee away, I'm head of household, Zsenala thought. *It's up to me.*

"Greetings, Madame Bjurklak," Zsenala said, stepping forward. "We are honored by your visit."

Zsenala spoke the ceremonial words she had been taught as a child. The elders had decreed in the first tumultuous weeks after the invasion that the People's dealings with the sah'Korloo were to always be about honor and welcome, never occupation or theft.

The sah'Korloo technology was unimaginable to the People, their starships powerful enough to destroy entire villages, yet the People would endure.

When the sah'Korloo destroyed the schools to keep children working on the farms, the parents became teachers and taught lessons while they worked. And when the sah'Korloo broke up a child's Gathering ceremony, a governor smuggled the blood cup to her in her home, so she could rise to adulthood and join the clan.

The People were occupied, but they would not be conquered.

And so, Zsenala spoke the ceremonial words of welcome.

"Our hearth is your hearth, Madame Bjurklak, and our flock is your flock. We welcome you to our home."

Zsenala had heard these words of honor spoken her entire life. But suddenly, they felt bitter in her mouth with the governor's harsh warning still ringing in her ears.

"Yes, yes," Bjurklak said, glancing around the dusty yard with disinterest. "Enough. I know how you love your ceremony, but I'm in a hurry today. I want to get to the marketplace. There's an embroiderer there who makes those, what do you call them—?" She gestured at Zsenala's shift. Made from linen grown in the wetlands, they were traditionally embroidered with intricate clan patterns.

"Kamala, your honorable Madame."

"Yes, kamala. I will buy one today, even though her prices are ruinous. But the best ones will be picked over if I don't leave soon. I won't be planetside again for many weeks, so it was good these two offered to help with the tribute today." Her lips thinned with irritation.

She seemed to notice the governor for the first time. "Who are you?" she asked.

The governor bowed again, her face mild. "Your honorable and excellent visitor, I am a minor leader in our clan."

"Why are you here? Where are the farmers?"

"Ba'Rozu is attending a birth, Your Excellency, and Da'Rozu is working at another farm." The governor bowed again. "But be assured Zsenala is more than capable. We were just now discussing arrangements for her upcoming Gathering ceremony."

Bjurklak narrowed her silver-mirror eyes as she stared at the governor. Then she nodded, turned to Zsenala and said, "Well, girl, get moving."

Squeezing her palms together to hold in the panic, Zsenala led the way to the barn. She had never been in charge of the tithe before, but she knew she would need to count out each bag of fleece and enter those chosen into the farm ledger.

But what about these terrible things the governor was saying? And where *was* Baba?

Zsenala tried to catch the governor's eye several times, but she would only smile and look away.

The two men worked silently, opening gates and carrying bags to the sand hover. Zsenala could feel their constant gaze on her and her brother. After they stowed the last bag in the hover, they climbed in and waited silently.

Bjurklak turned to the governor. "You, come with me now. Perhaps the embroiderer will show you pieces that she would hide from me."

For a moment, the only sound was the hum of the sand hover. Then the governor nodded and turned to Zsenala. "May peace be with you and with your flock." And then she climbed into the hover.

Zsenala's heart pounded in alarm. What if they discovered the governor's mutant eye? Would they kidnap her?

Zsenala shaded her eyes against the whirling sand as the hover lifted off. She hoped for a glimpse of the governor's face, but the hover turned and sped towards town, leaving Zsenala standing alone in the settling dust. She felt a deep pang of loss, which quickly turned to anger.

Why did she come tell me this? What am I supposed to do? I'm only thirteen! Then Zsenala's thoughts quickly skittered to her father. *And where's poor Baba?*

"Zse-zse!" Zintan shouted as he ran from the barn.

"Yes, Zin, I'm here," Zsenala said, dropping her arm on his shoulder. "Come on, we have work to do. It's DarkNight tonight, and we need to bring the animals in."

Zsenala looked to the horizon, shading her eyes against the setting suns. Little Blarta was sinking below the mountains, and soon Sol and Ruthur would follow her down, sinking the valley into sudden darkness.

Their world was usually a shifting kaleidoscope of light and color as their suns danced across the sky. But once a year the People suffered through the blazing heat of AllSuns as the three tracked across the sky together. And at sunset they would lock up their animals, go light their lamps, and shutter their windows against the deep, dark hours of DarkNight.

"Come on, Zin, we'd better hurry. I'll round up the tokka, and you get the chikchiks, and don't forget to set the latch on the coop!"

Zsenala was too exhausted to sleep, and her thoughts buzzed over what the governor had told her.

Where *was* Baba? And those two men, were they looking for mutations?

I wish Momee were home, Zsenala thought as she turned again. *If this is what it's like to be an adult, I don't want to turn fourteen.*

A noise jolted her upright. *What was that?*

Zsenala threw off her covers and lit the lamp by her bed. *I've got to go check the tokka.* Should she bring the lamp? It was the darkest night of the year, with just thin starlight to guide her way. But maybe it would blind her against the dark. She left the lamp on the table.

Zsenala unbarred the door and slipped through, quickly shutting it against the light slanting across the yard. She waited, willing her eyes to adjust. She had never been outside alone on DarkNight, and the darkness pressed down on her chest, making it difficult to breathe. But Baba was counting on her to keep the tokka safe, so she took a deep, steadying breath and headed for the barn.

As she approached, the thick darkness resolved into the shadowy outlines of tokka shifting restlessly in their pen. *Whew! They must have been scared when they found themselves outside in the dark. I'll bring them in, and then I can get back to bed.*

But I was so sure I checked the gate...

Zsenala whirled at a tiny sound. A shadowy figure huddled against the tokka pen.

sah'Korloo! They've come!

Zsenala turned to run, but a hand shot out and grabbed her wrist.

"Let me go!" Zsenala shrieked, trying to pull away.

"No, please!" a voice croaked. "We call sanctuary!"

Zsenala stopped, paralyzed, torn between her fear and the honor of her People.

"Step back," she finally shouted. "I've got a weapon!" She hoped the darkness could cover her lie.

The figure stood, pushing back the hood of a dark robe. It was a girl, not much older than Zsenala. She reached down and lifted something, no, someone, from the shadows at her feet—a small boy child, barely past weaning. The girl turned him to face Zsenala and slipped off his hood. He looked at Zsenala, his eyes gleaming red in the faint starlight. Zsenala froze, her thoughts racing.

"You'd better come inside," she finally decided.

The girl followed Zsenala into the dark house, the child clinging to her neck.

"We can't wake my brother," Zsenala whispered. "He's asleep in the other room."

The girl watched as Zsenala stirred up the fire and set out water with rye cakes and cheese. Zsenala motioned her to the table. "Please, eat."

She nodded and eased into a chair, the boy in her lap. He snatched a hunk of cheese and settled back down into her arms to eat. "There you are," she crooned, "that's better then." She offered him a cup of water, which he greedily guzzled with his glittering red gaze fixed on Zsenala.

"You, too," Zsenala said softly, but the girl hesitated. "There's plenty, enough for both of you."

The girl sniffed at the tokka cheese, took a nibble, and then was suddenly gobbling big bites.

"Whoa, slow down," Zsenala said. "You're safe here, there's no need to rush."

The girl shook her head as she slurped some water. "No time. We've got to get to the next station before Blarta comes up. The Eye will be looking for us.

"I'd have gotten here sooner," she continued, "but there was trouble at the radiation pens, and then I missed the first shepherd. I couldn't wait so I headed out by myself, and then we got lost. It's been two days, and we're out of food."

"Wh-what do you mean?" Zsenala asked.

"Well, the plan was to rescue him before they put him into the pens, but it turned out they were a step ahead of us the whole time. So thankfully, we got lucky with a sleeping guard." The girl stood up and started sorting her pack. "We really have to go."

"Wait! I don't understand any of this," Zsenala said. "Who are you? What are radiation pens?"

The girl slowly set down her pack and stared at Zsenala. "Aren't you the shepherd?" she whispered.

"I'm *a* shepherd, but I don't think that's what you mean..."

Then Zsenala remembered the governor's harsh whispers. "Wait—Momee must be the shepherd," she thought out loud, "and she was supposed to be waiting for you... and now *I* have to get you to the next station." She looked at the girl, her face bleak. "But I don't know where it is! Do you?"

The girl shook her head. "We never know—we just depend on each shepherd to get us to the next station. We can't tell the sah'Korloo anything that we don't know."

Zsenala's eyes searched the girl's face. Then she nodded. "You'd better sit down and tell me everything you know. I'll make tea."

"...and most of us shepherds are children," the girl finished. "The sah'Korloo don't understand that we're given real responsibilities, so they never notice us. I've been a shepherd since I was eleven."

She fell silent.

"You have to wait until Momee gets back," Zsenala finally said.

"I can't. They're really after this baby. Both of his parents have the mutations, so he'd be a real prize for the testing pens."

Zsenala noticed the bloody bandage on his wrist. "What happened?"

"That's where I cut out the chip. They put them in for the testing data and for tracking in case someone escapes." The girl grimaced. "I'm not good with sutures..."

"Let me look at it," Zsenala said. "With those horns, I'm always patching up some fool tokka." She brought warm water, and bandages, and salve. The boy's eyes grew wide when she reached for his arm. "I'll be gentle, I promise." Zsenala said.

She patted his arm when she was done. "He'll be fine—just a little scar."

"Thank you." The girl said. The silence stretched out. "Oh—and your baba wanted me to look in on you."

"*Baba!*" Zsenala leapt up, almost knocking over her chair. "What do you know about my baba?"

"Well, I know he just liberated this poor baby from the pens, and when he heard I was taking the cliff route, he asked me to check on you. Although," she added thoughtfully, "I *was* meeting your momee, so I probably wasn't supposed to say anything to you..." She ducked her head as she offered the child more water. "And what did your baba tell you about where he was?"

"They told me he's helping out at another farm, but *I* decided he'd joined the resistance."

The girl looked up. "He did. This *is* the resistance—"

Zsenala sat down. Then she brightened, "Wait—did you say the 'cliff route?'"

"He said, 'You'll go through the Rozu farm on the way to the cliff route.'" She nodded. "That's it, exactly."

That's the mountain path we take to the tokka swaps, Zsenala said to herself. *Maybe he was preparing me for this when he brought me last year...*

"Whatever," the girl said, standing up. "We need to get moving. I'm *not* letting them get this baby. They already have his momee, and with their family history they won't let her go until, well—" she stopped, her face grim. "Anyway, I have to get him to the rescue caves. They'll make contacts for his eyes, and then they can foster him out."

Zsenala turned away to hide her sudden tears. What if this were Zintan, stolen from his family and sent to grow up amongst strangers?

"So, we need to get going," the girl prodded.

"I can't go; I've got Zintan and the tokka!"

"Then just pack me some food. I'll go by myself."

Zsenala shook her head. "No, the mountains are too dangerous, and besides, it's DarkNight!"

"Then help me figure this out," the girl hissed. "I pledged my life for this baby!"

The child whimpered at their rising voices.

"You say the sah'Korloo won't be watching for children," Zsenala said, looking away. "Well, that means they really won't be watching for poor *shepherd* children." She turned back. "I've got a plan, but it means no traveling in the dark, and we bring Zintan. And you'll have to give the baby sleeping tea. I don't want Zin to see those eyes."

She reached her hand out to the girl. "I'm Zsenala."

The girl shook her head, "No name... but I call the baby 'Lek'."

⋖⊃⦁

"Who are they again?" Zintan asked, rubbing his eyes.

The girl was wrapping cheese and dried apples, and the child was asleep in his sling.

"I told you, Zin, they came to find Momee because Lek is really sick. And this is his sister, um—" Zsenala thought quickly, "—Neelo. We're going to walk them over the cliffs to the Da'Baleen clan on the beach, to see their healer. And I thought we could bring a few rams to swap. We might find a color we don't have yet."

There, she thought. *He'll be so busy thinking about seeing the beach, he won't wonder why we're taking the tokka out right after AllSuns. It's going to be another scorcher.*

"Now, finish your mash. I've done the chores so we're just waiting for you."

They stepped out into the indigo predawn. Two rams stood browsing on the stubby grass, their traveling bells clinking softly as they moved. One was a raven-dark blue-black, and the other was a rich violet.

"Why are you bringing Surtur and Snorri, Zse-zse?" Zintan asked. "They're too skinny, no one will want them."

"They're leader rams, Zin, and they're always thin," Zsenala said, "but they're also smart, so they're easier to lead. Plus, remember how they helped Baba when he got lost last year in the sandstorm? Sometimes the leaders know the paths even better than we do."

Zsenala led, followed by the rams, Zintan, and then the girl carrying the child. The only sound was the dull *klonk, klonk* of the bells, broken occasionally by the *skree* of hawks coasting the thermals rising over the cliffs.

It took half the morning to reach the base of the mountain. The suns blazed as they headed up the stony path, zigzagging across the face of the cliffs. Just past midday, the rams ran ahead to a small plateau and dropped their heads to slurp at a tiny spring. Zsenala called time for a rest.

Zintan wiped his face and threw himself down in the shade of a boulder. "Zse-zse, I'm so tired! Are we almost there?"

"Almost, Zin, it'll be downhill soon. But close your eyes for a while; we're going to stop until it's cooler."

Exhausted, Zintan fell asleep almost immediately.

"Is that true?" the girl asked quietly. "Are we almost there? Because I swear I can feel the Eye burning a hole in my back."

"The Eye?" Zsenala whispered.

"You know, the *satellite?* It's always watching. It's probably looking at us right now." She lay down with the child pillowed on her chest and closed her eyes.

Zsenala struggled not to look for the satellite. The spot between her shoulder blades started to itch. *Well, then, we'll just have to look like shepherd children out tending our sheep,* she said to herself.

The rams drowsed in the shade, their eyes closed as they chewed their cud. The girl woke the child, fed him, and then gave him more sleeping tea. The air finally cooled as Blarta sank towards the horizon.

Zsenala woke her brother, "It's time to get moving." They ate a quick meal, filled their canteens at the spring, and continued up the mountain.

When they reached the summit, Zsenala turned to look back over the dun-colored cliffs below, still shimmering with heat. Their trail wound down to the valley behind them like a dusty river.

When Zsenala turned to head down the mountain, the girl pulled at her sleeve. "Don't look," she whispered. "Just put up your hood and keep walking—the watchers at the satellite can read lips."

Zsenala slid up her hood and said to her brother, "Zin, go on ahead and look for the turnoff. There are two red slashes on a boulder."

After he scampered ahead, Zsenala said quietly, "What's happening?"

"There's a drone following us. I think it picked us up on the plateau."

Zsenala turned around to stare. "Keep walking!" the girl hissed.

Zsenala leaned down to make a show of digging through her pack for her canteen. She took a few swigs and wet the corner of her robe to wipe her face. "How do you know?" she whispered as she put her canteen away. "About the drone, I mean?"

"You can hear it; there's a light hum."

And suddenly Zsenala *could* hear it, a tiny sound like a bee buzzing over the spring flowers.

"They must really want him," the girl continued when they started walking again, "if they're sending the drone."

"What do we do now?"

The girl's lips pressed together. "I don't know," she admitted. "I've never seen one, they just told us what it sounds like."

Zsenala watched her feet on the thin, rocky path. "Well, I guess we just keep walking our rams over the mountain while we figure it out."

Zintan ran up the path, pebbles skidding out underfoot. "Zse-zse! There's someone up ahead!"

"Shush, Zin," Zsenala whispered, trying not to look up over her shoulder. "You'll scare the rams. Now, what did you see?"

Zintan dropped his voice. "sah'Korloo soldiers on the path—three of them, with guns!"

The girl turned to Zsenala. "Is there a different way to the beach?"

"I don't know, I only came that one time!" Zsenala hissed.

"What's happening, Zse-Zse?" Zintan asked, his voice rising anxiously. "Why are they here?"

"It's okay, we're figuring it out." Zsenala scratched Surtur between the horns while she thought. *Was* there another route to the beach? She was afraid to leave the path; she'd been raised on stories of shepherds who got lost and fell to their deaths or died of thirst.

Surtur leaned in to encourage her scratching.

"Wait," Zsenala said suddenly, looking down. "That's it! The rams will show us!"

"What are you talking about?" the girl asked sharply.

Zsenala leaned down and whispered in Surtur's ear. "Find the beach, Surtur." He turned toward the path Zintan had just run up, but Zsenala gently pulled him away. "No, Surtur, the *other* way." He looked up. Then he lifted his nose to the breeze, breathed deeply, and scrambled down off the path into the brush, with Snorri following close behind. Zsenala grinned, "I knew it! Come on!"

"No way," the girl protested. "I'm not trusting some stupid tokka!"

"No, this is what they do, they're bred for it. They remember paths, sometimes for years!" She slid down the slope after them. "Come on, Zin—"

Zintan looked at the girl. Then he shrugged and slid down the slope after his sister. Zsenala called over her shoulder, "You wanted to act like a shepherd, well, this is what shepherds do—they trust their leaders!"

The girl growled, hitched up the baby's sling and followed them into the brush.

The rams trotted steadily, stopping occasionally to check the breeze. The children scrambled after them, running sometimes to keep up. The rams stopped in a tiny clearing and dropped their heads to graze.

"I told you this was stupid," the girl gasped as she caught up to the others. "They have no idea where we're going."

Zsenala looked around the clearing. It did seem to dead end at a boulder, with the cliff face on one side and a steep slope on the other. "The leaders always find their way," she said, trying to sound confident. "But this is a good place to rest. Sol and Ruthur will go down soon, so in case anyone's watching, make it look like we're settling in for the night."

They spread their cloaks out for beds and passed around food and water. The sky darkened to a dull red as Sol fell below the horizon, then true darkness fell as Ruthur followed her. Zsenala started a small fire and kept it fed with deadfall from the brush. The rams settled down against the warm boulder, and Zintan began to snore. Zsenala and the girl wrapped themselves in their cloaks.

After she was sure Zintan was sleeping, Zsenala hissed to the girl, "What would happen if they found us and saw his eyes?"

The girl turned to face Zsenala. "They would take him—and us—and put us all into the radiation pens. I thought you knew that."

Zsenala held her gaze for a moment, then rolled over into her cloak and turned her back to the fire.

She woke a few hours later and blinked into the darkness, wondering why she was awake. She realized the night was silent, and she nudged the girl, "I don't hear the drone."

The girl sat up. "You're right. Go wake your brother."

Zsenala threw more wood on the fire and banked the coals to burn through the night.

"What are you doing?" the girl asked.

"If the drone passes over, maybe they'll think we're here sleeping."

Zsenala was still convinced the rams could find the path down the mountain. "Surtur," she whispered to him, "find the beach." He got up, trotted around the boulder, and squeezed in behind it, disappearing into the gloom with his brother trailing behind.

Zsenala peered behind the boulder. There was a shadow on the cliff face, a gap, dark against the stone, shimmering silver in the starlight. The opening was just large enough to walk in. Leaning in, she could hear the hollow echo of the rams' hooves. *Well, at least they haven't fallen to their deaths,* she thought. *That's a good sign.*

She turned to the girl. "This is our chance to escape that drone." Then with her heart hammering, she grabbed her brother's hand and stepped into the darkness.

Except that it *wasn't* dark. Their hands and faces lit up in a phosphorescent glow as shining patches of green and blue and orange glimmered down from the tunnel walls.

"Whoa..." Zintan whispered, his eyes widening.

"I think they're lichens, but let's not touch them," Zsenala said stepping back from the wall.

Surtur and Snorri turned from where they were waiting and trotted ahead, the *tok, tok* of their hooves echoing off the stone. The children followed as the path twisted and turned and occasionally doubled back, but always, always sloped down into the mountain.

The girl stopped suddenly and grabbed Zsenala's arm. "I don't like this. It feels like we're following two wandering tokka who don't know where they are!" The child woke in his sling as her voice started to rise. "And we're going to be lost in here forever, and we'll starve, or die of thirst—" Her voice caught on a sob.

"It's okay," Zsenala said lifting the child's sling off the girl's shoulders. "*We're* okay. The leaders always know where they are. We'll stop for some food and water, and you'll feel better." She stroked the boy's head, and his eyes started to close.

"I want to go back."

"You can't. The drone will start searching again at daybreak, and they'll be suspicious if they see you walking alone with a child—there's no good reason to be in the mountains with a baby in this heat. We haven't caught their attention yet because we look like shepherd children, leading our rams across the mountain."

"I can't just bring him in here to die!"

"You're not. I may not be *your* shepherd, but I'm a *tokka* shepherd, and tokka shepherds survive by trusting their leaders. We'll find the way.

"And if you go back," Zsenala continued, "the drone will find you, and then they'll take you both. And I'm not letting that happen."

The girl was silent. "Why are you doing this? Why didn't you let me cross by myself?"

"I may just be the daughter of a poor tokka farmer, living out on the edge of the territory, but I know right from wrong when I see it. And letting the sah'Korloo put you or the baby into the radiation pens is *very* wrong.

"I'll do anything to prevent that, and I would hope someone would do the same for me."

The girl searched her face and then nodded. "Okay."

Zsenala turned around to see the rams disappear around a corner. She realized she couldn't hear their hooves. *Did they just fall?*

She eased around the bend and found the rams waiting at an opening with golden light shimmering on their faces. Zsenala tiptoed closer and peered in.

A large rock cavern opened up in front of her, lit by jars of glowing golden lichens. The space was filled with people, some adults standing and talking quietly, and children and adults scattered in small groups, bedded down for the night. A work bench stretched across the far wall, scattered with beakers of colored liquids.

The girl came up behind Zsenala. "I can't believe it," she breathed. "They found the caves." Her foot nudged a pebble, and a woman leaning over a crib nearby looked up at the sound. The woman grinned and called over her shoulder. "They're here!"

Cheers filled the cavern, and people came running.

The woman stood and smiled. She bowed with her hand to her lips.

"Ba'Lowan, of clan Da'Baleen, welcomes you. Be at ease, our home and our hearth are yours."

Then she reached towards Zsenala for the boy.

If you enjoyed the 2018 *Young Explorer's Adventure Guide,* please take a moment to review it where you purchased it!

We're always happy for you to come by the site, let us know what you think, and take a look at the rest of our science fiction and fantasy books.

DreamingRobotPress.com

Or email us at books@dreamingrobotpress.com

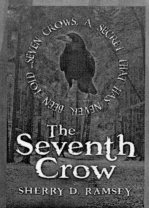
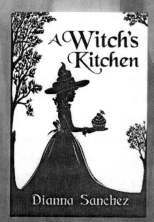

CPSIA information can be obtained
at www.ICGtesting.com
Printed in the USA
LVOW10s1612250318
571083LV00016B/815/P

Girls, Boys, Robots
Everyone is Welcome here!

What's it like to dance in an environmental pod, to
hack a space station, or to be abducted by aliens?
If you're lucky, you might discover how to be an
interstellar diplomat, a scientific detective or outwit
space pirates!
Curl up in your favorite rocket ship and set your
coordinates for adventure!

"...a must-have in science fiction collections."
~ Kirkus Review

A treasure for young readers.
~ West Coast Book Reviews

Don't miss any of the adventure!

ISBN 978-1-940924-25-0
51795

9 781940 924250